YOURS TRULY

ALSO BY ABBY JIMENEZ

Part of Your World
Life's Too Short
The Happy Ever After Playlist
The Friend Zone

CONTENT GUIDANCE

This book is close to my heart for a lot of reasons, but before you dive in, I just want to give you a heads-up about a few themes, including a main character who was cheated on in a past relationship, a flashback to a pregnancy issue, a mention of suicide, and a character who has clinical anxiety. Yet despite these heavy topics, readers will be treated to laughs and happily ever afters for all. You can find further content guidance on my Goodreads page. Thanks so much for reading, and I hope you enjoy the book.

Best,

Abby

YOURS TRULY

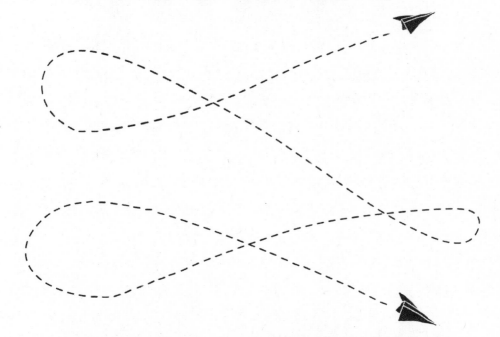

ABBY JIMENEZ

FOREVER

New York Boston

Copyright © 2023 by Abby Jimenez
Reading group guide copyright © 2023 by Abby Jimenez and Hachette Book Group, Inc.

Cover design and illustration by Sarah Congdon. Cover copyright © 2023 by Hachette Book Group, Inc.

Forever
Hachette Book Group
1290 Avenue of the Americas, New York, NY 10104

Forever is an imprint of Grand Central Publishing. The Forever name and logo are trademarks of Hachette Book Group, Inc.

The publisher is not responsible for websites (or their content) that are not owned by the publisher.

Printed in the United States of America

ISBN 978-1-63910-688-2

*To my wonderful husband, Carlos, who has nursed
me through some very tough times. Thank you for
always being harmless to me.*

CHAPTER 1

BRIANA

They're calling him Dr. Death."

Jocelyn stood, peering at me dramatically from beyond the nurses' station where I sat at my computer charting my patients.

I glanced up at her over my screen and rolled my eyes. "Give him a break," I said, typing in my notes. "The guy's been here all of eleven hours. It's his first day."

"That's the point," she whispered. "He has a hundred percent kill rate."

I scoffed but didn't look back up. "You cannot call him that. We don't need patients hearing nurses whispering about a Dr. Death."

"Can we call him Doctor D?"

"No."

"Why?"

"Because Doctor D sounds like a penis thing."

She huffed. "Okay, but seriously. Somebody should look into this. Six patients dead?"

I checked my watch. "We work in an ER, Jocelyn. It's not entirely unheard of."

"Aren't you supposed to be chief of emergency medicine? Isn't it your *job* to investigate stuff like this?"

I did a final tap into my computer and looked up at her. "Dr. Gibson hasn't retired yet and the board hasn't voted on his replacement, so no, it's not my job."

"But it will be. You're totally going to get it. Don't you think you should dress for the job you want and stop the carnage?" She stood back and crossed her arms.

I could feel the eyes of a dozen other unseen nurses peering at me from around the floor. Jocelyn was sent as an ambassador. Once the nurses latched on to something, they weren't letting go. This poor guy. He was *not* going to like it here.

I let out a long sigh. "The first patient was a ninety-six-year-old with a bad heart. The second one was an eighty-nine-year-old stroke victim who had a DNR. There was a car accident crush injury—I got a peek at the X-rays, and nobody but God could have saved that man. Patient four was a gunshot wound to the head, which I don't need to remind you is ninety percent fatal. The victim was comatose with no evidence of brain stem function upon arrival. Five was a cancer patient on hospice, and six was so septic he was practically dead when he got here." I looked her in the eye. "Not. His. Fault. Sometimes it happens."

She pressed her lips into a line. "Sometimes. But not on your first day," she pointed out.

I had to agree with that. The odds were a little low. But still.

"Just...send all the new patients to me, okay?" I said a little wearily. "He only has another hour. And no Dr. Death. Please."

She gave me a look. "He's rude, you know."

"How is he rude?" I asked.

"He told Hector to put his phone in his locker. *You* never make us put our phones away."

"Isn't Hector in some epic breakup with Jose? He's probably

checking his phone every five seconds. I probably would have made him put it away too."

The door on room eight slid open, and an auburn-haired white guy in black scrubs came out. His back was to me, so I couldn't see his face. I watched him peel off his gloves and drop them into a hazardous waste basket. He pinched the bridge of his nose, took a deep breath, then dragged himself toward the locker rooms with his head down.

Hector came out of the room behind him and looked over at us. He held up seven fingers and sucked air through his teeth.

Jocelyn gave me an I-told-you-so look, and I shook my head. "No Dr. Death. Now go. Do something productive."

She pouted for a second, but then she left.

My cell phone pinged, and I pulled it out.

Alexis: I want to come see you on the 19th.

I typed in my reply:

I'm totally fine.

I wasn't fine. But I also wasn't summoning my pregnant best friend out of the warm embrace of her honeymoon period to come hang out with me in the abandoned haunted house my life had turned into. I loved her too much to condemn her.

My phone rang in my hand.

I got up and ducked into an empty room, and swiped the Answer button. "I'm telling you, I'm okay," I said.

"Nope. I'm coming. What time are you off?"

"Alexis." I groaned. "I just want to pretend that day is like any other day."

"It's *not* like any other day. It's the day your divorce is final. It's a big deal."

"I'm not going to do anything stupid. I'm not going to drunk-dial him. I'm not going to get shit-faced and throw up in my hair—"

"I'm more worried about you throwing Molotov cocktails through his windows."

I snorted. "I guess that's a valid concern," I mumbled.

I didn't exactly have a history of being calm and rational when it came to Nick. When I finally found out he'd been cheating, I'd like to tell you that I acted with poise and grace, a vision of dignity in the face of unfathomable betrayal and heartache. What I *actually* did was lose my fucking mind. I flushed my wedding ring down the toilet and watered his houseplants with bleach. Then I called his mother to let her know what kind of a man she raised—and that was me just getting started. I'd shocked even myself with the levels of pettiness I was willing to sink to. The grand finale of the depths of my depravity was so embarrassing I forbade Alexis to bring it up to this day.

"Unless you have a date, I'm coming to see you," she said.

"Ha. Right." I sat on a gurney and put my forehead into my hand.

Since Nick, I had been through some of the worst online dating in the history of the internet. The amount of garbage I sifted through on Tinder over the last year was so bleak, Nick looked like Prince Charming by comparison.

"Still no luck?" she asked.

"Last month I went on a date with a guy who had a court-ordered Breathalyzer installed in his car because he'd had that many DUIs. He asked me to breathe into it so his car would start. There was the one who showed up to our coffee date with a swastika tattoo on his neck. The last date I went on, the guy's wife, which I didn't know he had, showed up to the Benihana and asked if this was what he was doing with the money he said he needed for the kids' school supplies. He told me he didn't have kids."

She must have blanched into the phone. "Oh, *gross.*"

"You have no idea how lucky you are that you found Daniel.

Seriously. Make a sacrifice to the dating gods for that one." I looked at my watch. "I gotta go, I'm on shift. I'll call you after work."

"Okay. But really call me, though," she said.

"I will really call you."

We hung up. I sat for a moment just staring at the wall. There was a pain-assessment chart hanging there. Little cartoon faces in various expressions over coinciding levels of pain. A green smiley face over the number zero. A red crying face over the number ten.

I fixed my eyes on the ten.

I'd managed not to think too much about the nineteenth. I was hoping if I didn't focus on the date, maybe I'd luck out and be a few days past it before I realized it had come and gone. It's not like much would change when the divorce was finalized. Nick and I had been split for a year. This was just making it paperwork official.

But still.

Maybe Alexis was right and I shouldn't be alone for it. In case it crept up and boob-punched me.

The last hour of work was uneventful. I took the only patient who came in—nobody died. But to be fair, it was just our regular, Nunchuck Guy, with another concussion, so the odds were in my favor.

I was getting ready to clock out when Jocelyn came back around.

"Hey, Gibson wants to talk to you before you leave." Her eyes were sparkling. "This is it!" she sang. "He's giving you the position."

Gibson was the current chief of emergency medicine for Royaume Northwestern. He was retiring this month. Technically he'd retired almost a year ago. Alexis had gotten his job and he'd left. Then a month later she quit to move to her new husband's tiny town in the middle of nowhere and open her own clinic, so Gibson came back.

"There's no way the board has voted yet, so I doubt it," I said. "But I appreciate the confidence."

But then I thought about it, and maybe he *was* giving me the position.

Not one person other than me had raised their hand for it. Nobody else was running. Did they even need to vote? What else would Gibson want to talk to me about if it wasn't this?

I made my way down the hall toward Gibson's office, a little excited. I mean, taking on the new job was going to be a ton of work. Six days a week, eighty hours or more. But I was ready. My whole life was Royaume Northwestern Hospital. Might as well work to my full potential.

I knocked on his door frame. "Hey. You wanted to see me?"

Gibson looked up and smiled warmly. "Come in."

He sat behind his desk, his gray hair neatly combed back. He reminded me of a sweet old grandpa. I liked him. Everyone did. He'd been in the position forever.

"Close the door," he said, finishing something he was signing.

I slipped into the chair in front of him.

He finished his paperwork and moved it aside and gave me a full, toothy smile. "How are you, Briana?"

"Good," I said brightly.

"And your brother, Benny?"

I bobbed my head. "As well as can be expected."

"Well, I'm glad to hear that. Such an unfortunate circumstance. But he's got some great doctors."

I nodded. "Royaume Northwestern *is* the best. Speaking of which, I'm excited to get started—not that I'm looking forward to you leaving," I added.

He chuckled.

"Is there going to be a vote?" I asked. "Nobody else is running."

He threaded his fingers over his stomach. "Well, that's what I wanted to talk to you about. I wanted to tell you personally. I've decided to delay my retirement for a few more months."

"Oh." I tried to disguise my disappointment. "Okay. I thought you and Jodi were moving to some villa in Costa Rica."

He laughed good-naturedly. "We are. But the jungle can wait. I'd like to give everyone some time to get to know Dr. Maddox before we put forward a vote. It only seems fair."

I blinked at him. "I'm sorry. Who?"

He nodded in the direction of the ER. "Dr. Jacob Maddox. He started today. He was chief of emergency medicine over at Memorial West for the last few years. Great guy. Quite qualified."

I was rendered mute for a solid ten seconds. "You're holding off the vote? For *him*?"

"To give the team a chance to get acquainted."

"To give him a leg up," I said flatly.

He looked a little surprised at my reaction. "No, to make it fair. You and I both know these things can be a bit of a popularity contest, and he deserves a clear shot."

I stared at him in disbelief. "You're actually doing this. Delaying the vote so he has a greater chance at taking the position. I've been here *ten* years."

He looked at me seriously. "Briana, I have to consider what's best for the department. A broader pool to choose from is always preferable. There's no glory in getting the job by default—"

"It wouldn't be by default. It would be on merit. Ten years of merit."

He peered at me patiently. "You know, Alexis didn't run unchallenged. Competition is healthy. If the job is yours, it'll still be yours in three months."

I sat there trying to breathe calmly through my nose. It took everything in me not to blurt "They call him Dr. Death!"

"It's just three months," Gibson continued. "Then we vote,

and I'm off to drink from coconuts on a beach somewhere and hopefully you're right where you want to be too. Enjoy the calm before the storm, take it easy. Spend some time with Benny."

I let out a slow, centering breath.

Gibson probably knew this Dr. Death guy. They must be friends. They probably golfed or something. This whole thing reeked of nepotism. But what choice did I have? If Gibson had decided not to retire yet, there was nothing I could do.

"Thank you for letting me know," I said stiffly. I got up and let myself out.

The second I got in the car I called Alexis. "I hate the new guy," I said when she picked up.

"Well, hello."

"They call him Dr. Death. He killed seven patients today. *Seven.* First day."

"Well, it happens." She sounded distracted.

"And get this, Gibson is holding off on his retirement so the new guy can get a shot at getting the chief position. It's total boys'-club bullshit."

"Uh-huh," she mumbled.

I listened for a second. Then I recoiled in horror. "Oh my God! Are you guys making out? I'm on the phone!"

She and Daniel were always all over each other. I think they only came up for air to eat.

I rubbed my temple. "Can you please toss some cold water on him and talk to me? I'm having a crisis."

"Sorry, hold on." She whispered something I couldn't hear and giggled. Then *he* giggled.

I rolled my eyes and waited. This year was going to be my villain origin story, I just knew it.

A door closed in the background and she came back on. "Okay. I am here. Tell me all the things."

"Okay, so the new guy is some hotshot transfer from Memorial West. I guess he was their chief over there, so Gibson wants to delay the vote so everyone can get to know him better. The guy's a total dick, the nurses hate him—"

"Well, if the nurses hate him, you have nothing to worry about."

"That's not even the point! Do you think Gibson would do this if the transfer was a woman?"

I heard her pressing buttons on a microwave. "Eh, yeah. I do. Gibson's pretty fair. I don't picture him making this a gender thing."

"You are supposed to be on *my* side."

"I *am* on your side. Look, there is no way you're not getting it. He did you a favor. He just handed the summer back to you without you being tied to the ER for eighty hours a week. Benny needs you right now. It's better if you're free for the next few months while he gets adjusted."

I went quiet. The way things were going with Benny, I'd probably see him as much in the ER as I would at home. I pushed down the knot I always got in my throat when I thought about my little brother.

"So what does this new guy look like?" Alexis asked, clearly changing the subject.

"I have no idea," I mumbled. "He's like a shadow demon. Every time I'm about to walk into a room he's in, he steps out the other door. I've seen the back of his head a few times, but that's it."

"You didn't introduce yourself when he got there?"

"I mean, I was *going* to. But we got slammed the second I clocked in. And then when it calmed down, I couldn't find him. It's like the guy hides in a supply closet somewhere when he's not declaring people dead."

"Look," she said, getting back on topic. "Everyone loves you. You're going to be a shoo-in, no matter who runs against you. And that new guy? I give him a month. The nurses will eat him alive. You'll be the first Salvadorian chief in Royaume history by the end of summer, *te lo prometo.*"

Alexis was trilingual. English, Spanish, and American Sign Language. She was brilliant, a world-renowned philanthropist from a prestigious family—and an optimist to boot.

I heard her open the microwave door. "Hey, when I come up, I'm making you scones," she said.

Aaand now she was baking too. I had to smile despite my mood. Alexis making scones was comparable to me going out back and chopping wood—hell would freeze over first. She really had changed when she met Daniel, and for the better.

I rested my elbow on the car door and put my head in my hand. I felt myself calming down. My best friend always de-escalated me. Sometimes I hated that about her. There were times when I just wanted to be pissed off, careening forward on the strength of my pure rage. I was grateful for my ability to stay furious, especially over the last year. Anger is a powerful fuel. It can be very motivating. Fortifying.

The only problem with anger is that it burns hot and fast. It doesn't tend to burn long.

Sadness burns long. Grief. Disappointment.

I realized that's what I was afraid was going to happen on the nineteenth. My divorce would be final, my rage would finally burn out, and I'd be left with what was left of me.

And that wasn't much.

CHAPTER 2

JACOB

I pulled into the parking lot and sat there staring through the windshield, debating whether I should just go.

Amy and Jeremiah wanted to talk to me.

There really was only one reason they would need to at this point. I knew what it was. I'd been expecting it for months now. There was almost a morbid sense of relief that we were finally getting it over with. I looked glumly at the sign on the building.

BAD AXE GRILL.

That was where they'd decided to do this, a damn ax-throwing bar. This is where they were going to drop the bomb? The location of this meeting was only slightly less awful than the news I was about to get.

It would be loud. There would be drunks. People in wedding veils and birthday hats hooting and cheering, shouting over the music. It was the kind of place that felt thick, like everyone was sitting on top of one another. Strangers would bump into me, the bathrooms would be filthy and crowded, the tables would be sticky. Like an adult version of a Chuck E. Cheese with booze and obnoxious frat boys.

I felt my heart beginning to pound at the idea of being in there.

I never went to bars unless I was being dragged. Jeremiah should know better. He was my brother, he knew about my dislike for places like this, that I got overstimulated and overwhelmed. But my guess was he was deferring to Amy—and this was very, *very* her. She'd take me to a place like this and be bewildered when I'd want to leave as soon as humanly possible. She'd say something like, "But they're famous for their wings! You love wings, that's why I brought you here!" as if the right buffalo sauce could mitigate the rest of it.

No wonder she'd left.

I was boring and withdrawn and impossible to understand. Even after two and a half years together.

I shifted in my seat. I should just go. Tell them I'd talk to them later. I was so drained I could barely think straight. I'd started a new job today. Lost every patient who walked into my ER.

I rubbed my temples. I felt like the angel of death. People dying is inevitable in my line of work. You can't save them all, and it's naïve to think you have any control over what comes through those sliding doors. But on my first day?

The nurses hated me. I could feel the loathing dripping off them my whole shift. And none of the other attendings even came over to say hi.

I'd second-guessed everything in the last twelve hours. Quitting Memorial West to go somewhere new, giving up my leadership position, starting over. It had sounded like a good idea in theory, but I think I'd overestimated my adaptability. I felt unmoored, like I was being tossed around on some choppy sea and all the captains of the passing boats were sneering at me instead of throwing me a lifeline.

Being in this hellhole of a restaurant would suck the last of the energy from my already-depleted soul.

Maybe I could do this meeting tomorrow instead. But if I left, Amy and Jeremiah would assume I was hurt. That I wasn't over it. Couldn't handle it. Even if I explained it was the place and not the news, they'd never believe me. I'd dated Amy for years and hadn't succeeded in making her understand my anxiety, so why would she get it now?

I wished there was some sort of autopilot I could slip into, like I usually did at work. A muscle memory to move me through the motions. But it would have to be all me. I'd have to be awake for it. Fully aware.

I let out a long breath, turned off the truck, and got out to drag myself into the bar. A young woman with a nose ring was working the hostess stand and took me through to a table in the back where my ex-girlfriend and my younger brother sat side by side in a booth.

They were laughing and leaning into each other before they saw me, but the second they did they jumped apart.

My stomach twisted at seeing them together.

They'd been disinvited to the monthly family dinner at my parents' house, so I hadn't been forced to see this with my own eyes until now. I felt ill.

I sat down and tried my best to appear relaxed. "Hey. Sorry I'm late."

Amy chewed on her lip in that way she did when she was nervous. "It's okay. We figured you might go for drinks or something with your new coworkers. You know, for your first day?"

I scoffed to myself.

"Thank you for coming," she said.

I nodded.

Thump.

Thump.

Thump thump thump.

Axes hitting walls.

I could feel the tunnel vision of an anxiety attack plucking at the edges of my sight, and I wondered how long I had until I'd have to get up and go, whether it was appropriate or not.

They sat there, looking at me like they didn't know how to start.

I glanced at my watch. "I have an early shift tomorrow..." I lied.

Amy nodded. "Right. Sorry." She tucked her hair behind her ear. "So, I don't really know how to say this..."

"You're getting married," I said.

I could see the confirmation on her apologetic face before she uttered a word.

She nodded. "We're getting married."

Thump. Thump thump thump.

Laughing, shouting, the clink of forks on plates. Someone dropped a glass and it shattered and everyone cheered. The press of the room closed in on me, but I managed to smile in a way that I thought looked authentic.

"Congratulations," I said. "Have you set a date?"

She looked at Jeremiah, and he smiled at her. "We're thinking July," he said.

I nodded. "Good. It's a good month. Well, I look forward to being there." I was amazed at how stoic I sounded.

Amy licked her lips. "We, um...we haven't told anyone else yet. We thought you should be the first to know."

"Thank you," I said. "But that wasn't necessary. I'm sure everyone will be thrilled." I looked at my watch again. "It's a little loud for me in here. I think I'm going to get going. Congratulations. And let me know if I can help in any way."

They looked at me gratefully. I don't know what they expected. Maybe they thought despite the graceful way I'd handled everything else up to this point that this might be the thing that pushed me over the edge. But I was fully committed to maintaining my position on this. Being difficult and indignant wouldn't change it. And they didn't mean to hurt me.

Even if they did.

I got up and tried my best to walk at a normal speed out of the bar. The *thumps* chased me, each one like a gunshot to my heels.

I felt myself just outpace the wave of anxiety as I burst into the cool April air and leaned forward on my knees, gasping for breath on the sidewalk.

So it was finally happening. The woman I loved had moved on. She was marrying someone else.

And the someone else was my brother.

The next day I was on the hospital floor, in between patients, when my cell phone rang. It was my older sister Jewel. I stared at the incoming call with a resigned sense of dread.

I was going to deal with the shock wave of this news in layers. My own feelings about it, and then everyone else's, dumped on me like ice water over and over until I was drenched in it.

I slipped into a supply closet and hit the Answer button.

"Jewel."

"It's total bullshit," she said. "I'm not going, just so you know. Fuck them both."

"Fuck them both!" her wife, Gwen, parroted from the background.

I rubbed my forehead tiredly. "Gwen, it's fine."

"It's okay to not be fine, Jacob." Mom's voice.

"I'm not going either," a fourth called out. My other older sister, Jill.

"Me either!" The youngest, Jane.

Amy and Jeremiah must have told my family together.

"Your father's here," Mom said.

"Jacob, I'm here if you want to talk," Dad said from somewhere farther away than the women.

He'd probably been roped into this phone call. Dramatic declarations weren't really his style.

"They've made their bed," Jewel said. "No one from this family is going to be there."

"*I* will be there. I'm happy for them," I lied. "And I intend to fully support them," I said honestly. "And I hope you will too."

They gasped indignantly in unison. "How can you *possibly* be okay with this?" Jewel asked. "They started dating less than three months after you two broke up. It's disgusting."

"It's fucked up, man." Walter, Jill's husband.

The whole gang. Perfect.

I sat on a box of toilet paper. "I'm really okay," I said, pinching the bridge of my nose.

"You are *not* okay," Gwen insisted. "They're assholes! How can they expect you to be there? How can they expect *any* of us to be there?"

"I don't think they expect anything," I said wearily. "But you not supporting it isn't going to change it. As long as they want me there, I'm going to the wedding. Even if you're not."

"Jacob," Mom said carefully, "you have always been the diplomatic one. I love that about you, but you do *not* need to put yourself through this. It's fine to set boundaries."

"Mom, I'm really okay. I'm over it. I've moved on."

"Moved on *how*?" Jewel said. "You haven't gone on a single date since she left."

Jill whispered in the background, "Maybe he's finding himself. He doesn't need to date to move on—"

"Yes, he does!" Jewel hissed. "If he's not having sex with someone else, then he's still obsessed with *her*—"

"We don't know that he's not having sex," Mom said. "Just

because he hasn't brought anyone home doesn't mean he's not having intercourse—Jacob? While I think rediscovering your sexuality after a split can be wonderful for your self-esteem, risky sexual behavior is more common after a traumatic breakup. If you're having intercourse, you *are* using protection, right? Now you know how I feel about coconut oil as a lubricant, it's very healing for the vagina but it does cause condoms to break—"

"What about grape-seed oil?" Dad asked from somewhere far off. "Does that do the condom thing? I like the grape-seed oil. Silky."

"Okay, can we not?" Jewel said.

"Your father and I are sexual beings," Mom said. "Let's not pretend like we don't know how you kids got here."

I squeezed my eyes shut. I am in *hell.*

"Jacob, are you having sex with anyone?" Jill asked. "I feel like we should just clear this up."

I threw up a hand. "You know what? Yes. I am."

The lie was so out of nowhere it almost felt like someone else said it. And why *had* I said it? But then I knew why.

It was one of those falsehoods you told to make someone else feel better. Telling a dying man that everything was going to be okay when you knew it wasn't. It was a sort of mercy. For all of them.

I think deep down my family wanted to be okay with this wedding. They loved Amy, and they loved Jeremiah. They were upset on principle and for my benefit, not because they hated either of them. They just hated how they thought it made *me* feel. It was obvious that as long as I was unattached, I was the jilted ex in need of their protection and indignation. Amy and I would never get back together, so what was the point? Why make this stand in my honor? I didn't want it.

Amy and Jeremiah would get married with or without my family's support. And they'd have kids, and those kids would be blameless. Even if the whole family shunned my brother and my ex for the rest of their lives, it wouldn't change a thing. So if I had to tell a white lie to redirect the focus, that's what I was going to do.

"You're seeing someone?" Jill asked. "Who is she?"

"It's just someone I work with," I said, hoping they'd drop it.

"At Royaume?" Jewel asked. "Is that why you quit Memorial West?"

"Uh…"

"Because we all thought you quit so you wouldn't have to work with Amy because you were so heartbroken and sad!" Jill sounded excited. "But you quit because you're in love and you want to be close to her?"

I blinked. "Yes?"

Everyone made an *awwwwwww* noise.

"When can we meet her?" Jane asked excitedly.

"I…I don't know," I stuttered. "I'm not ready to introduce her to anyone yet. It's still new."

I could feel them bubbling on the other end of the line. Damn. They'd never let this go now.

"Listen," I said, putting the phone to my other ear. "I am okay with this wedding. I have moved on, and I am *happy* for them."

"Will you bring your girlfriend to the wedding?" Gwen asked, a smile in her voice.

"Uh…I guess. If we're still together, yes."

More squealing.

I heard Jewel sigh dramatically. "Okay," she said. "Fine. I guess, since you're okay with it, I hate it less. But I'm still not excited."

"I do like weddings, though," Jill said. "But you're right, I'm still mad at them," she added quickly.

I shook my head. "Don't be mad at them. Look, I gotta go. I'm on shift."

"Will we see you on the nineteenth for dinner?" Mom asked. "I want lasagna, but your father might smoke a pork roast."

"Yes, I will be there for dinner," I said.

"Can you bring a bottle of wine?"

"Yes, I will bring wine."

"Okay. Love you!"

They all said good-bye in unison and hung up. I set my phone on my thigh and put my palms to my eyes.

I'd have to say I broke up with my imaginary girlfriend when it came around to it. But hopefully it would take the pressure off in the meantime. Maybe everyone would finally stop looking at me like I was going to crumble into dust.

Granted, it *had* been a bad breakup. But at least I got the dog.

I dragged myself up and let myself out of the supply closet— and someone crashed into me. I let out an *oomph*, and my phone flew from my hand and went skittering across the hard floor.

The doctor who hit me didn't stop. She launched off me and continued running down the hallway toward the patient rooms.

"What the *hell*?" I muttered, picking up my phone. The screen was cracked.

"Watch where you're going!" I shouted after her, annoyed.

She didn't even glance back. A nurse gave me a dirty look like *I* was the asshole.

Was everyone rude like this here? What the hell was wrong with this place?

I peered forlornly at my cell. It still worked, but the corner was shattered. The perfect ending to the worst week ever. I gritted my teeth.

I stalked down the hallway in the direction the woman ran. I didn't know exactly what my plan was. Give her my thoughts on running in the halls? Demand she cover the screen repair?

I poked my head into the rooms one at a time until I spotted her. She was bedside, her back to me, talking to a young man.

The patient was gray. He had a dialysis catheter in his chest. The skin around it looked red and swollen.

"Why didn't you call me?" she asked the man in the bed. "This is totally infected." She fluttered around him, looking at his vitals. "You could have gone septic. This is so dangerous." She took a thermometer out of his mouth and shook her head. "You can't let things get this bad, Benny. You need to tell me when stuff isn't right."

I realized then that I was intruding on something and was about to make my exit, but a nurse came up behind me with a huge dialysis machine, forcing me fully into the room. I stepped aside and stood next to the wall as she wheeled it to the bed.

"It hurts..." Benny said quietly.

"I know," the woman said, a little softer now. "I'm getting you on some antibiotics and pain meds." She put a hand on his head. "In a few minutes you'll be sixteen again, passed out on Jäger in a cornfield."

I snorted from my corner, and she twisted and noticed me standing there. "Uh, can I help you?"

My *God*, she was beautiful. She was so beautiful it disarmed me. For a second I forgot what I was even doing there.

Long brown hair tied into a messy bun. Wide brown eyes, full lashes.

Then my anxiety lurched—some violent combination of a throwback to tenth grade, me nervous talking to a pretty girl, coupled with the stress of meeting a new coworker in a hostile work environment while I was in a room I shouldn't be in. I froze.

This didn't normally happen while I was on the job. My anxiety was well managed at work. I was assured and confident in my interactions with my peers and subordinates. I was an excellent physician. But she had me flustered just by looking at me—the *way* she was looking at me, annoyed and impatient. I felt my social skills drop off like a heart-attack victim flatlining.

I cleared my throat. "Uh, you bumped into me back there," I said awkwardly.

She blinked at me like I was telling her the most unimportant thing in the world. "Okay. Sorry?"

"You, uh, shouldn't run in the hallways."

She stared at me.

My mouth started to get dry. "It's just, I used to be head of emergency medicine at Memorial West and I know how easy it is for accidents to—"

Her eyes flashed. "Yeah, I'm aware of your résumé, Dr. Maddox. Thanks for the hot tip. Now, if you don't mind, I'd like to be alone with my patient?"

She cut daggers through me. Benny was staring. Even the nurse was glaring at me.

I stood there for another second. Then I backed out of the room. Hot embarrassment seared up my neck. What had I been thinking going in there like that? *Jesus Christ, Jacob.*

I went back to my side of the ER, running the whole awkward encounter through my head over and over, obsessing about what I should have said or should have done.

So *stupid.*

I shouldn't have broached it when she was with a patient. That was the first thing. Maybe I should have led with the fact that she actually broke my phone, so she knew I wasn't just there to give her a hard time about the running.

Maybe I should have just let it go.

Letting it go would have been better. Because then there would have been no encounter at all. I should have just said "Wrong room" and left.

God, I was a jerk. I was effortlessly succeeding in making myself the most hated person at Royaume Northwestern.

I knew from years of therapy that I was ruminating. That the encounter had probably been nothing to her, but to me it felt like the most embarrassing thing that had ever happened. A decade from now I'd be lying in bed and my eyes would fly open and I'd remember the incredulous way she'd looked at me—me, the guy who had the audacity to walk into her ER room and talk to her about running toward a critical patient, one she obviously knew and cared about.

I cringed through the second half of the day. My anxiety felt like electricity. A low, humming current under my skin, a survival instinct triggered and gnawing at me, telling me to flee. I couldn't escape it, and I couldn't calm it down.

Usually my anxiety meds leveled me out. But there was only so much meds could do. I had to manage stress, use the coping skills I'd learned in therapy. Most importantly, I had to live a lifestyle conducive to wellness. That's what I thought I was doing coming here, getting myself out of the unhealthy situation at Memorial West with Amy and Jeremiah, making a choice that was best for my mental health.

But now *this*.

I knew I was being quiet and taciturn and this wasn't helping to endear me to the already-cold nurses on my shift, but I was so in my head I couldn't stop myself. I'd managed to trade seeing Amy and Jeremiah every single day for a whole team of people who hated my guts instead.

I'd always had a hard time making new friends. I got nervous in unfamiliar social settings, so I would say the wrong thing or become withdrawn, so it took time for people to warm up to me. Maybe I just needed time here too. But something told me this place was different. They were too cliqued up. It felt like high school all over again. I was the outsider and I'd keep being the outsider, especially if I kept messing things up the way I'd been doing. And I didn't even know how to stop.

I had another hour of my shift, but I needed a break. My mental battery was empty again. I didn't want to run into that woman in the doctors' lounge, so I headed back to the supply closet.

Only when I got there, it wasn't empty...

CHAPTER 3

BRIANA

I got Benny situated and managed not to cry the whole time. Then, once he was comfortable, I made a beeline for my sob closet.

I liked to cry in the supply closet by Gibson's office. Quiet, low traffic. I had a toilet-paper box I liked to sit on, and the stuff on the shelves acted as sound insulation so nobody could hear me completely losing my mind.

I'd cried in this closet more times than I could count. I cried in here after losing patients. I cried here when they told me Benny was in end-stage renal failure. Cried here for Nick. I'd even cried in here a little bit for that backstabbing traitor, Kelly, the "friend" who spent two years sleeping with my husband in between meeting me for brunch. But never in all those times had anyone ever walked in on me. And today someone did.

The door opened and a man slipped inside. He shut the door behind him and turned around to see me sitting there, all snot bubbles in my nose and hair sticking to my cheeks.

Dr. Death.

We stared at each other in surprise for a split second—and then he fled.

I let out the breath I'd been holding and put my face back into my hands.

Of *course* this guy would violate the sanctity of this space. What an asshole.

He yelled at me earlier. I mean, I ran into him, so yeah, I got it. But then he followed me into Benny's room to give me some mansplaining dressing-down about running in the hallways. First he got the red carpet rolled out for him to try his best at taking my job, then this. I couldn't believe—

The door opened again. He came back in, shut the door behind him, crouched in front of me, and handed me a wet washcloth.

"For your face," he said gently. "It's warm."

There was something so kind and disarming in his light brown eyes that I almost forgot how much I disliked him. Almost.

I paused for a moment, then took it. "Thank you." I sniffed.

He smiled a little and nodded. But he didn't go. He sat down against the door.

I stared at him, wondering what in the world he thought he was doing. I wanted him to *leave*. The room was totally crowded with him in it, and I wasn't going to keep crying with him sitting here.

But then I realized that he probably wanted to make sure I was okay. I guess it *would* be weird if he just handed me a washcloth and took off, like "Enjoy your meltdown."

I let out a resigned breath and pressed the warm towel into my eyes. It *did* make me feel better.

"Are you okay?" he asked quietly.

I sniffled and nodded, looking anywhere other than his face.

The legs of his black scrubs were inched up and I could see his gray socks. They had tiny brown dogs on them. I guess he was a novelty sock kind of guy.

He had on a black smartwatch. Toned freckled arms like he

worked out. A stethoscope draped around his neck, his hospital badge clipped to his shirt. When I got to his eyes, he was gazing back at me. A five-o'clock shadow, a full head of thick reddish-brown hair. He wasn't bad looking. Like, at all.

I distrusted good-looking men on principle. Nick was good-looking, and look where *that* got me.

His eyes were red, and I wondered if his day was going about as well as mine. Maybe he'd come in here for a break too.

"So," he said. "Do you come here often?"

I let out a dry laugh at the joke. "Best place to cry in the whole hospital," I said, my voice raspy.

"I used to like the stairwell at Memorial West."

I nodded. "Also a solid choice. A little too echoey for my use, but a nice supply closet alternative if you're claustrophobic."

"On-call rooms are good too," he suggested.

"Too far from the ER. I like the sob closet. Close enough for a spontaneous midday breakdown."

"My favorite kind," he said tiredly.

So he *had* come here to hide.

He paused a moment. "I'm Jacob," he said.

"Briana."

Then we went quiet again.

There was something comfortable about the silence, a kind of understanding in it.

It reminded me of a backpacking trip I'd taken a few years ago. Nick hadn't wanted to go, so I was alone. I knew only too well now *why* he didn't want to go. His favorite time to cheat was when I was on a mountain somewhere without cell service—but anyway. I'd been on the Superior Hiking Trail right after dawn, and ran into a bear on the path. We both paused and just stood there, looking at each other. Him with his bear claws and bear teeth. Me with my bear spray. But neither of us moved to hurt the other, and I couldn't explain it other than to say that the bear and I agreed to be harmless to each other and share the space. That's what this felt like. A quiet, unspoken truce.

Maybe he wasn't so bad. He didn't *look* like an awful person. He looked tired. Sort of vulnerable.

"Is he someone you know?" he asked quietly. "The dialysis patient?"

I let out a slow breath. "My little brother," I said.

"What caused it?" he asked.

"An autoimmune disorder. Came out of nowhere."

We sat there quietly. Him against his door and me on my TP box.

"You know, it could be worse," he said after a moment. "You can live for decades on dialysis."

I was instantly snapped back into the room.

It could be worse.

I was so sick and tired of platitudes.

God has a plan.

Everything happens for a reason.

What doesn't kill you makes you stronger.

No, it doesn't, and fuck all of it.

There was no reason for this to be happening to Benny. It wasn't God's plan, and it wasn't going to make him stronger. And you know what? Maybe it *could* be worse. But who cares? That was the most unhelpful comment of all. Benny had every right to hate what was happening to him. He had every right to grieve the life and the body he'd lost and to be angry about it, no matter how many countless other scenarios sucked slightly more than this one.

"Why the fuck would he want to live for decades on dialysis?" I snapped. "He's twenty-seven years old. He wants to make spontaneous trips to Vegas with his friends, drink beer, meet girls, and have sex without being embarrassed about the tubes sticking out of his chest."

He put up a hand. "I didn't mean—"

"I really hope something like this never happens to someone you love. Or to *you*. And I seriously hope you never say stupid shit like this to your patients."

I got up. "Let me out."

He pushed a long breath through his lips and dipped his head between his knees for a second. Then he dragged himself up and moved away from the door.

I stopped right before opening it. "And another thing. I think it's completely unethical what you and Gibson are doing. But it's fine. Doesn't matter." I looked him in the eye. "This is *my* team. This is *my* hospital. You'll never get the job, no matter who pulls strings for you."

I slammed the door on my way out.

CHAPTER 4

JACOB

I had no idea what the hell she was talking about. None. And I wasn't going to ask her. I waited a few moments before leaving the supply closet to give her a chance to clear the area. Then I did my best to stay on my own side of the ER for the rest of my shift.

I wondered if I could keep doing this. I was miserable here. I was miserable at Memorial, and I would probably be miserable wherever else I went too. Maybe this was my life now, just existing and hating every minute of it.

It occurred to me that maybe Amy had been right to give up on me. How could I be lovable when I wasn't even likable?

I wrapped up my last patient and was heading to the locker room when Zander came out of room seven, the one Benny was in.

"Maddox!" He grinned at me. "There you are. I was gonna go hunt your ass down."

Dr. Zander Reese was a nephrologist. A kidney specialist and a good one. He was also my best friend. We'd been roommates in med school and through our residencies. He was one of the selling points of this move. Knowing someone here had been a plus. It was nice to finally see a familiar face, one that wasn't scowling at me.

Maybe Zander was Benny's kidney specialist? I peered past him to see into the room, but the curtain was across the sliding glass door.

I wondered if *she* was still there. Probably.

I felt like I should apologize to her for the comment in the supply closet, but it seemed like the more I talked, the worse things got.

Zander smacked me on the shoulder. "Hey, sorry I missed you yesterday, bud, I had rounds at the dialysis clinic." He nodded down the hallway. "Gibson sent me to look for you. You're off right now, right? Wanna get a drink? We're thinking Mafi's across the street."

I liked Mafi's. And I liked that it was a place I'd been to before. He'd probably picked it for that exact reason.

Places I knew were less stressful for me because I had a sense of how loud it was going to be, how crowded. I wouldn't have to ask anyone where the restrooms were.

Sometimes I'd Google a place just to see what I could before going. Figure out what I'd order, what the parking situation would be like. Or if there was a big dinner or a party I had to go to, I'd walk through the venue the day before, so when I got there, I'd feel more oriented and less stressed before having to deal with a large social commitment.

I'd done that here too. I'd toured Royaume twice before I took the transfer. Zander was here, I knew Gibson, I knew the job, I'd felt comfortable with the move.

But sometimes even the most thorough due diligence couldn't show you the heart of a thing…

Zander was waiting for my reply.

Normally after a day like today I'd just want to go home. But I needed to have a positive social interaction so the last one wouldn't be all I could think about. If I didn't put something between me and what happened, I'd fixate on it the rest of the night.

"Sure," I said. "Let me get changed. I'll meet you guys there."

I found them in the restaurant thirty minutes later. Gibson waved me over with a friendly smile. He was one of those easy people everyone liked.

Gibson and I went way back. We'd never worked together, but we'd had the same job for the last few years and ended up at enough of the same conferences to get pretty well acquainted. Plus he knew Mom. Most doctors did. She was a well-respected physician in her own right.

He smiled at me as I sat down. "Maddox. How's the new job treating you?"

"Good," I lied.

"And how's Amy?" he asked.

"Fine. We broke up eight months ago."

He arched an eyebrow. "Ouch. I didn't know that. I'm sorry. Is that why you transferred?"

I picked up a menu and looked at it, though I didn't need to. I'd already checked it out online. "In part, yes," I said. "She's getting married, actually. To Jeremiah."

Zander stared at me. "Are you kidding me?"

"I'm afraid not."

Gibson leaned back in the booth. "And what does your mother have to say about that?"

"Plenty," I mumbled.

Zander nodded at me. "At least you got the dog," he said.

"There *is* that."

I'd adopted Lieutenant Dan when Amy and I were together. He was my dog, but we'd shared him pretty equally, and Amy loved him just as much as I did. I half-expected her to ask for partial custody, but luckily she didn't fight me on it. She didn't fight me for much, come to think of it. There was nothing to fight over. We'd never lived together, didn't have kids.

I looked up at Gibson over the menu. "Hey, I wanted to ask you something. There's a doctor here, Briana—Zander, I think you're treating her brother?"

"Dr. Ortiz," Gibson said a little warily. "Is she giving you problems?"

"No. She said something to me about you pulling strings for me? She seemed upset about it. Do you know what that's about?"

He blew a breath through his lips. "She's up to replace me when I go. I mentioned to her that I've put off retiring to give the staff a chance to get to know you before we vote on the next chief. She was not happy with me."

I pressed my lips together and nodded. Well, that would do it.

"I have no interest in the position, Gibson."

He looked surprised. "No? I just assumed you'd take a stab at it. You took a pretty big step down coming here."

"My chief days are over. I came here to simplify my life." And was failing miserably...

He let out a sigh. "Okay. Well, I can respect that."

"Seems a little unfair to delay the vote on my behalf," I said. "I can understand why she'd be frustrated."

"Eh, it wouldn't have mattered," Gibson said dismissively. "No shade to you, I'm sure you'd put up a heck of a fight, but it'd be a landslide in her favor no matter how long I waited. Her team loves her and she's a hell of a physician."

"Then why bother putting off the vote?" I asked.

He picked up his menu and started to look it over. "I don't like the optics of her running unchallenged. It takes validity out of the win and I don't want anyone whispering under their breath that she got it because there was no one else. It's not fair to her and it's not a good way to enter a position of leadership."

Zander bobbed his head. "So you put her up against an obvious front-runner—and let her obliterate him." He looked impressed. "I like it." He nodded at me. "Fucked up for you, but I do like it."

I also liked it. Not the me losing part, but the reason for it. At least it had been well intentioned.

"As noble as it sounds, I'm still going to have to opt out," I said.

Gibson nodded. "Noted. Well, I'm sticking around anyway in case someone else brave enough to challenge her surfaces. And honestly, I'm happy for the extra couple of months. I'm not ready to leave yet. Quitting after twenty years is a lot. And spending all that time with Jodi? I don't know if I'm ready for it."

"You're not," Zander said. "Trust me. I look forward to my husband's curling trips all year so I can get some peace."

Gibson shook his head over his menu. "I suppose you don't take a job like this one if you're happy at home. Unless you're in your position. I'd imagine Amy didn't care, since she saw you at work anyway."

"She cared," I muttered. I didn't elaborate. "And anyway, I didn't really want the chief position then either. I was sort of pushed into it by the team. It's not really my thing."

Gibson waved me off. "If they pushed you into it, it's your thing. You're diplomatic, fair, and you don't lean toward drama. They respected you. Briana's the same way, actually. Though a little bit more of a bulldog."

Zander raised a finger at a server to call her over. "Briana will make a good chief—if you ever get the hell out of here."

Gibson chuckled.

"How's the anxiety?" Zander asked me. "Not easy being the new guy."

"It's been okay," I lied again.

"Starting a new job has gotta be like your own personal hell," Zander went on. "The grown-up version of standing up in front of the class and introducing yourself."

I scoffed. It was exactly like that. Only I was naked too and my dog ate my homework.

Luckily our server came over before I had to get more into it. Zander ordered one of every appetizer for the table, so the guys didn't order any entrées, but I got a salad. I'd try what came, but I wouldn't fill up on fried foods and sodium.

When my mental health was struggling, I had a strict self-care regime. The second I started to notice the glitchy, staticky feeling creeping in, I made a concerted effort to exercise and get enough sleep. I cut out alcohol, processed sugar, and carbs, tried to eat more whole foods. Journaled. It all helped. And right now I needed all the help I could get. I was teetering on some precipice, trying not to fall. Amy and Jeremiah, my family, my new job—all of it prodding me to the drop-off.

The guys' cocktails were delivered, and I got my club soda and lime. They went into stories about their patients as I sat back and enjoyed the distraction. I was glad I came. I needed this. A reminder that there were people who liked me.

Interactions like this one didn't wear me out. They knew me. They didn't take it personally if I slipped into silence and just listened. They didn't give me a hard time about not having any alcohol, which is something I never did either, to anyone. You never knew what someone's reason was for not drinking.

These friends were easy. Not all of them were.

Different people had different energy demands. Some people took more from me than others. Dad, for example, was low energy. I could spend days with him in his workshop and never feel like I needed a break. Jill and Jane were easy too. But Mom and Jeremiah and Jewel? They were high-energy people who could drain me in a matter of minutes. There was only so much of them I could handle.

Amy was the highest-energy of all. There was never silence. She had to fill every moment.

In the beginning, I liked it. I didn't have to be charming or force conversation. She'd do it all, and I'd get to sit and listen and laugh at her stories, and she never needed me to contribute. Listening was my contribution. When we went to parties, she handled all the small talk with everyone and I got to just be there. It took pressure off me. My family loved her. It was easy. I think my reserved personality made her feel listened to and the center of attention, the way she liked. And it made me the opposite. She made me invisible, the way *I* liked.

But then one day I realized I knew everything about her and she knew nothing about me. Nothing. And I was lonely, even though I was with someone. So I finally brought it up to her and...well. Here we were.

Gibson nodded to Zander. "Did I see Benny come through today?"

"Yeah. Infected catheter."

I sat up. "Briana told me about him," I said, suddenly interested in participating in the conversation. "Autoimmune disease."

"Man, shit luck for that kid. Zero to kidney failure in eighteen months."

"Is his sister donating a kidney?" I asked.

Zander took a swallow of his bourbon. "Not a match. So far nobody is."

Gibson shook his head. "Poor kid. Lost his job, girlfriend broke up with him."

"*That* pissed me off," Zander said, tipping his glass at Gibson.

"Why'd she break up with him?" I asked.

"Couldn't handle it," Gibson said. "No end in sight, didn't want to wait it out."

I shook my head. "How long does someone like that wait on the transplant list? It can't be that long."

Zander bobbed his head. "Depends. Can be anywhere from three to seven years. But he's got a rare blood type—the rarest blood type, actually. Might be longer for him."

I sat back in my seat. "Longer than seven years," I breathed. "God, I can't imagine." No wonder his sister was so upset.

I hadn't meant to be insensitive with my comment about dialysis. I'd meant it to be reassuring—because it was true. Dialysis would keep him alive. But the quality of his life would suffer in the meantime. Today had been a prime example of it.

Besides the health roller coaster, he'd be strapped to a dialysis machine for four hours a day every other day. He couldn't have too much liquid, since his body couldn't get rid of it. No soup or ice cream or watermelon. No drinks with friends. Not even a Coke. Nothing salty because he wouldn't be able to handle the sodium, nothing fried. He couldn't do the thing I was doing right now, eating random appetizers and thinking nothing of it.

"Will his autoimmune disease damage his new kidney when he gets one?" I asked.

Zander shrugged. "We got it under control. Only about a ten percent chance of recurrence. He'll have a normal life if he gets a donor. But I wouldn't hold my breath."

I went quiet for a long moment.

I thought about what Briana said, how her brother just wanted to be normal. I knew what it was like to have your life controlled by an outside factor. My anxiety was limiting too. But this? It had to be hard. Especially for such a young man.

What had *I* been doing at twenty-seven? I took that back-packing trip to Machu Picchu with Zander, went camping a lot. Things I took for granted. Things that wouldn't be possible on dialysis, that's for sure.

"He's got a better chance of getting a deceased donor," Zander continued. "But the organ won't last as long, and they don't take as well either. Higher chance of rejection. Ideally he'd get a living donor, but none of the family's a match, and with his blood type..."

"What's the recovery like for a living donor?" I asked.

"Not too bad. Couple of weeks. Why? You thinking about it?"

"I've always considered it after Mom."

"Oh, yeah, I forgot about that," Zander said. "That was—what? Twenty years ago now?"

I nodded. "Just about."

Mom had lupus. She'd gone into kidney failure when I was in high school. Never got to the transplant list, though, because her best friend, Dorothy, stepped in and gave her one of hers. Mom was lucky. She never even had to do dialysis.

We were all kids at the time, so none of us could help, and Dad wasn't a good candidate because of his high blood pressure.

I'd been deeply moved by the gesture.

"I always promised myself when I was old enough, I'd pay it forward," I said.

"What's your blood type?" Zander asked.

"O."

He sat up a little straighter. "Universal donor." He seemed to study me now. "Any health issues?"

I shook my head. "No."

"Want me to set up the labs? Just to see? No commitment. The family won't know."

I thought about it for a moment.

What was the harm in seeing? I might not be a match in the end, and I could always say no.

I shrugged. "Okay. Sure."

CHAPTER 5

BRIANA

I'd had a total breakdown last night when I got home.

I'd started to realize I would never really be happy again. Not the way I had been. I wasn't ever getting my life back, and it wasn't just the thing with Nick. Benny's condition had broken me. It was the final straw.

Benny was like my child. I was eight years older and had practically raised him while Mom worked and went to nursing school.

I could be the strong-ass woman Mom taught me to be. I could put myself through med school and support myself and live through my horrendous divorce. But I could not watch Benny deteriorate like this and hold the line. I just couldn't.

When I'd gone to his apartment yesterday after work to get his cat, there had been a three-day notice to vacate on his door. He wasn't paying his rent. Then I got inside, and it went from bad to worse.

His place had been trashed. He hadn't cleaned the litter box in weeks, the dishes in the sink had mold on them, the treadmill that he used to use religiously was covered in unwashed laundry. The cat practically dove into my arms when he saw me, like I was part of a long-awaited rescue mission and he was relieved I was finally there to save him.

Benny was clinically depressed. He'd been depressed since all this started last year, but it had gone from a functional depression, where he could still shower and take meds, to *this*. He just gave up when his kidneys did.

I think I needed to move him in with me. Either that or call Mom. He needed an adult-ier adult to take care of him right now. He was going to have to decide which overbearing woman he wanted in his life, because one was about to be assigned to him whether he liked it or not.

I'd gotten home last night and collapsed into bed and machine-gun sobbed into my pillow until I fell asleep—which didn't last long because Benny's cat woke me up. It took me a solid ten seconds of pure terror before I realized I had a cat in my bedroom and not a murderer. I couldn't go back to sleep after that.

I needed to not be at work today. I needed to sit around my house without a bra, my hair in a weird bun, watching reruns of *Schitt's Creek*. My eyes were still puffy, and I was a soft breeze away from losing it again—*and* I got my period. I get to bleed for a week without the sweet release of death.

I guess for the moment it *was* sort of good that I wasn't training for a new job—not that I was thrilled with how that whole thing went down and why. But at least I didn't have to be at the hospital eighty hours a week when I could barely handle the forty-eight I was currently scheduled.

It was six-thirty a.m. I was having coffee with Jessica before work today.

I didn't used to like her very much. She was good friends with Alexis at one point. They were neighbors before Alexis moved. I always found Jessica a little too bitter, but now that I was bitter too, I appreciated her burn-the-patriarchy energy.

I got to the hospital cafeteria and grabbed a triple cappuccino. I wished there was vodka in it.

I spotted Jessica at the table she'd picked in the corner and headed over, dressed in the baggy black zip-up hoodie I wore over my scrubs. The hood was on. That coupled with the sunglasses I was wearing over my puffy, bloodshot eyes made me look like I was about to drop the hottest hip-hop album of the year.

Jessica, on the other hand, looked great. Perfect hair and bright red lipstick at six-thirty in the damn morning. She was an OB-GYN. She was forty-six, perfectly put together at all times, and I'd never seen her smile. Like, ever. She was married to some big lawyer or something, but she hated him, which didn't surprise me because she hated everyone. It was currently my favorite thing about her.

When I dropped into the chair across from her like a human beanbag, she was looking at her phone. "And what happened to you?" she said without looking up, her tone bored.

"Why would you think something happened to me."

She set her phone down and looked at me like a parent talking to a petulant teenager. "You're wearing sunglasses indoors."

"Maybe I have pinkeye."

She waited.

I tossed my bag on the floor next to me with a thunk. "Benny's not doing great. And my divorce is final in two weeks."

"Good," she said dryly. "Free at last."

I rolled my eyes. "Free to do *what*? Date? Have loads of sex with hot singles? Have you *seen* it out there?" I leaned forward. "And believe me when I tell you that my standards are *low*. The bar has come *waaaaay* down. At this point I'd settle for a guy simply because he has a penis, more than one towel, and no flags hanging on his walls. I mean, do they actually expect us to have sex with them on a futon in their mom's basement? Like, actually?"

"Yes," she said flatly. "That is exactly what they expect."

I sat back heavily in my seat. "I'm beginning to think men are not sending us their best people."

She scoffed, which was Jessica's version of laughing. "All they do is lie and throw off your PH balance. They are a constant reminder that we don't choose our sexuality, because who in their right mind would choose to be attracted to *men*. They are completely worthless as partners. Did you know that when a wife becomes seriously ill, she is six times more likely to be abandoned by her spouse than a husband is?"

I stared at her. "Are you *serious*?"

She took out a compact and checked her teeth. "And the older the woman, the higher the rate of abandonment. I hear there's a saying up in oncology. When the wife gets sick, the husband gets a new wife." She clicked the mirror closed and gave me a pursed-lip can-you-believe-this-shit look.

I blinked at her in horror. "That is *disgusting*."

"Yes, it is." She agreed. "But remember, you can't spell disappointment without men," she sang.

I laughed a little too manically before putting my forehead into my hand. "That's it," I mumbled. "I'm giving up. I should just accept that I'm never having sex again. I'm canceling my bikini-wax appointments. Just gonna let the forest reclaim the land, succumb to my inner swamp witch."

I squeezed my eyes shut from behind my glasses. "I feel like if I died, it would take me a solid twenty-four hours to realize I'm in hell."

Then I groaned, remembering. "And then there's this asshole I'm working with, this new guy I can't stand—"

"Oh? Who?" she asked, looking back at her phone, only sounding mildly interested.

"Dr. Maddox." I made a face.

She paused and looked up at me over her screen. "Jacob Maddox?"

I rubbed my forehead tiredly. "Yeah. You know him?"

"Wonderful man," she said matter-of-factly.

I froze and blinked at her. "I'm sorry—*what?*"

Her beeper started going off. "I know his mother," she said, looking at her pager. "I've known the whole family for years. I have an emergency C-section, I need to run." She got up.

"Wait. Are you sure we're talking about the same Jacob?" I said, watching her grab her bag. "Brown reddish hair? Sort of yea high—"

"He was head of emergency medicine at Memorial West. He's an excellent human being."

I stared at her. An excellent—"Nobody likes him!"

She flung her bag over her shoulder. "Well, they're wrong. Drinks later?"

"I can't. But—"

"Text me when you're free."

She grabbed her coffee and I watched her walk off, high heels clicking. She dropped the cup into a trash can, turned a corner, and disappeared.

I sat there blinking after her from behind my glasses.

What the hell was *that* about?

She didn't say anything nice about *anyone*, let alone men. An excellent human being? Gross.

Whatever.

I was too exhausted to even think on this. I had to broach the Mom/move-in subject with Benny today. Then if he said yes, I had to actually move him in, which I doubted he'd be able to help with in his state. I didn't have time to ponder the benevolence of what's-his-face.

I finished my coffee alone and then went to the locker room to get rid of the hoodie and glasses and change my tampon. I felt surly and extra grouchy, so when I got to the ER and saw Gloria standing by a patient room with Hector, peeking through a crack in the curtain, I came up behind them like a cranky old woman getting ready to chase people off her lawn. "What are you doing?" I grumbled.

"Shhhhhh," Gloria whispered. "We're watching."

"Watching what?" I said, straining to look around them through the sliding glass door.

"Dr. Maddox," she whispered.

I groaned. "Oh God, what has he done now?"

I hadn't seen him for a few days since the supply closet Go Fuck Yourself. I think he was avoiding me.

Good.

Hector didn't look away from the window. "This little girl came in with a dog bite and he's sewing up her doll."

I wrinkled my forehead. "He's what?"

"Yeah. I was just in there. I guess the dog tore her doll and she was all freaking out and crying, and Dr. Maddox goes in there and starts talking all soft to her like, '*Mija*, let's take care of your baby, okay?' And then he gets his suture kit and starts working on the doll, while his resident started the kid's stitches, so she wouldn't notice it. *Dios mío*, I have never seen anything so sweet." He turned to Gloria. "Do you think he's single?"

"Yeah," she said. "I also think he's straight."

Hector shook his head. "No. No way. I seen him at the Cockpit."

"Where?" she asked.

He leaned to look around her into the room. "A gay bar in uptown. It was definitely him. I never forget a jawline like that."

"Just because he was at a gay bar doesn't mean he's gay," she said. "I heard he used to date some doctor at Memorial West. A woman," she added. She nodded at me. "Come look." She stepped aside so I could peer into the crack in the curtain.

I could see Dr. Maddox, the patient's mom, a second-year resident, and Jocelyn in the room. Dr. Maddox had his back to us, sitting next to the gurney. His scrubs were hiked up and he was wearing colorful socks again, though I couldn't make out the design from here.

He had the doll on a table, and he was stitching her up. The little girl couldn't have been more than four or five. She wasn't crying, she was distracted. He seemed to be telling her a story as he worked because she giggled. Even Jocelyn smiled, and she was one of his earliest and most dedicated haters.

"Well, I'll be damned," I muttered. "He's not Satan after all."

"What are you guys doing?"

We jumped at the voice. Zander was coming toward us from the double doors.

"Hey. Nothing," I said, putting my back to the glass. "Just watching a procedure."

Gloria and Hector took this as their moment to exit and left.

"What's up?" I asked.

"I came down to tell you, I'm releasing Benny today. He looks good. Ready to go."

I immediately perked up. "Great!"

"So who are you watching?" He peered around me into the room. "Oh, Jacob." He grinned when he saw what he was doing. "That son of a bitch, look at him in there. I always did like his bedside manner."

I cocked my head. "You know him?"

He nodded. "Yeah. We were roommates for years. One of my best friends. Great guy."

I made a face.

He eyed me. "What?"

"No, it's just I keep hearing that today, but nobody here likes him much."

He drew his brows down. "Jacob?"

"Yeah. He's kind of a dick."

Zander barked out a laugh so loud it surprised me. "Jacob is *not* a dick. That guy's the nicest dude you'll ever meet, trust me. He'd give you the shirt off his back."

"Jacob," I deadpanned, crossing my arms. "He's totally rude."

"If he's coming off that way, he's probably just nervous. He's an introvert, kind of shy." He looked at his watch. "Look, I gotta run." He started jogging backward. "Hey, be nice to him, yeah? He's one of the good ones." He turned and jogged the rest of the way to the double doors.

I gawked after him. One of the good ones?

I'd known Zander for years. I not only respected him as a doctor, but I also trusted his judgment in general. I didn't think he'd say that about anyone unless he believed it was true. I mean it *wasn't* true, Jacob was definitely an ass. And he was in cahoots with Gibson for the chief position, which I was still pissed about. But I did believe that *Zander* believed Jacob was a nice guy.

And Jessica also believed Jacob was a nice guy...

Gibson must like him too.

Huh.

I looked back through the glass. Jacob was finishing the doll. He wiggled it in front of the little girl and then bopped her gently on the nose with it before handing it to her. She clutched it and beamed.

I felt my face soften.

I mean, he *had* brought me that warm washcloth that day in the supply closet. He could have just taken off, especially after I snapped at him in Benny's room. And I never really apologized for running into him that day either. Now he was over here saving dolls from certain death...I guess he wasn't *all* bad.

I chewed on my lip.

If Jacob was shy, losing all his patients on his first day and then pissing off the entire nursing staff wouldn't help matters. No one really gave him a shot after that. If he really was "one of the good ones," like Zander said, that kind of made me feel bad, like it was his first week at a new school and *I* was one of the mean girls.

Maybe I *was* one of the mean girls.

I was so crabby lately I was probably shorter with him than I would have been if my life wasn't a dumpster fire.

Benny was an introvert too. He had a really hard time in school…

Through the sliver in the curtain, I saw Jacob get up and I started for the nurses' station, but I only got a few feet before I let out a groan and turned back around.

A moment later, when the door to Jacob's room slid open, I was waiting outside. I stepped in front of him with my arms crossed. "Hey," I said flatly.

He froze with his hand on the door. "Hello," he said, looking like a deer in headlights.

"Bring them desserts."

He blinked at me. "What?"

"You should have brought the nurses donuts on your first day. You showed up empty-handed, that was your first mistake. Cupcakes *might* save you, but not the cheap stuff. Nadia Cakes, two dozen, get a keto one for Gloria, at least four gluten-free ones, and one vegan. Hector doesn't do animal by-products. Bonus points if you get a doggie cupcake for Angelica's new puppy."

He stared at me, and I turned and walked away.

There. I was nice to him like Zander had asked. I gave him the tools to dig himself out of his nosedive with his team. Whether he chose to take my advice was on him. *My* conscience was clear. I was no longer a mean girl.

"Hey," he called after me.

I let out a long breath and turned back around. "What?"

He stood there with this earnest, hat-in-hand, puppy-dog look that made it hard to keep my flat expression. I registered again, almost to my own annoyance, that he was cute.

He had this super-sexy, strong-quiet-type thing about him. Deep, gentle brown eyes, a square jaw with just enough scruff to look a little rugged but still put together. He was maybe five-nine, five-ten, to my five-four. Mid-thirties, in shape. His hands were plunged into the pockets of his black scrubs and he had veins running down his toned arms. I *loved* well-hydrated veins.

I shook it off. Was he hot? Yes. Fine. Doesn't matter. Super annoying, though.

"Yeah?" I said impatiently.

"What about you?" he asked. "What kind of cupcake do you like?"

"Red velvet, and I don't want one," I said, turning back around.

I didn't want anything from *him*.

CHAPTER 6

JACOB

After my shift, I stopped and did the second round of labs Zander had ordered. Then I called in the cupcakes Briana told me to get for the nurses so they'd be ready in three days when I went back to work.

I didn't know why she was helping me. It clearly pained her to do it. Did Gibson say something to her? I hoped not. I didn't need some intervention from the boss on my behalf, some forced Play Nice.

I walked Lieutenant Dan and got something on Grubhub. I had dinner, took a shower, and had just sat down to journal in my plant room when my phone rang.

Mom.

I didn't answer it. I'd been ignoring everyone's calls and texts since the phone call last week. I knew what they wanted—to know about my girlfriend. I had no idea what to do about it.

I contemplated dragging it on. Making excuses for why she could never make it to anything and then eventually saying we broke up. Maybe I could suspend their disbelief right up until the wedding—which I would then show up to alone, for everyone to look at with pity as the newly single again, twice-jilted, brokenhearted ex of the bride.

Maybe I should just come clean. Or at the very least end the charade and "break up" with her now.

It was one thing to keep it vague. Say I'm seeing someone and leave it at that. But the details bothered me. I didn't like looking my family in the eye and giving them some made-up name and made-up background for a made-up woman who didn't exist. It felt wrong, even if my intentions were good. And I just didn't know how to get around this. Frankly, I was surprised nobody pressed me harder for her name when I'd told them the news. At the time, I think they'd been too shocked to dig for more info—but they were definitely ready to dig now. Even Walter had called me.

Mom's call ended. Then a text pinged through.

Mom: Jacob, will you be having a plus-one on the nineteenth? I have to know how many cutlets to make.

And then a moment later:

Ping.

Mom: Never mind, I'll just make my pesto pasta. There'll be plenty. Unless she's allergic to nuts? Is she allergic to nuts?

I pinched the bridge of my nose. *I don't know, Jacob. Is your imaginary girlfriend allergic to nuts?*

God.

How was I going to do this when I had all of them pecking at me in person?

Then I remembered that even the most unrelenting interrogation would be better than the alternative—everyone watching to see if I was unraveling, everyone blaming Jeremiah and Amy. I could feel the tension of that inevitable situation bearing down on me like radiant heat.

I just wanted to be invisible. I wished I could wipe everyone's brains and have them forget that Amy and I had ever been a thing.

Hell, I wished *I* could forget Amy and I had ever been a thing.

Lieutenant Dan got up from his spot by my feet and put his big head in my lap. He always knew when my anxiety was high.

Lieutenant Dan was a three-legged two-year-old Bernese mountain dog. He was also one of the many reasons why I wasn't interested in a chief position at Royaume Northwestern. When Amy and I shared him, he was never home alone for more than a few hours, even if I was working my eighty-hour week. But now he just had me. I wasn't interested in never being home anymore. I *liked* being home. These days, home was the only place I felt true peace.

Especially now that everyone at work hated me.

I sat back in my chair in my plant room and stared wearily into the succulents. I hoped the cupcakes helped. I didn't see how they could. The situation felt well beyond baked goods to me.

I looked back down at my journal. Journaling centered me, made me feel calmer. It was one of the skills I'd learned in therapy, and it helped me work through the events of the day and subsequent emotions when I transferred them onto paper. But in the end I didn't journal.

I wrote a letter to Briana Ortiz.

CHAPTER 7

BRIANA

You move in with me or I call in Mom."

It was seven p.m. and I was driving a discharged Benny home from the hospital after my shift.

He looked at me, horrified, from the passenger seat. "Why are you punishing me? Isn't my life shitty enough?"

"I'm not doing this to punish you," I said. "You need help right now, and I can't be over at your place cleaning for you and making sure you're taking your medications. You're not paying your rent and you just put yourself in the hospital. You're skipping dialysis. You're not even showering."

He leaned his forehead on the car window. He looked so frail and exhausted. So different from the healthy, fit, virile man he was just eighteen months ago, before this nightmare started for both of us.

You know what? Maybe Mom *did* need to tap in. I didn't know if I had the mental and emotional fortitude to take care of him *and* me. But then I wasn't sure I had the mental and emotional fortitude to deal with her either. Calling her was definitely the nuclear option, and I did *not* take it lightly.

When the lid blew off the Nick thing last year, Mom had flown in from Arizona, where she'd retired with her husband, Gil, and mothered me to within an inch of my life. I'd had to call Gil to physically retrieve her when she wasn't showing any signs of leaving when the one-month mark hit. She never stopped cooking. Not for a second. She filled my entire freezer, then bought a deep freezer for the garage and filled that too. The day she left, she cooked hot dogs, put them in buns, and wrapped them in foil in the fridge like I couldn't figure out how to assemble them once she was gone. I was *still* eating the leftovers a year later. It would be full-chaotic Mom energy if I summoned her home.

I turned onto the freeway. "It's Mom or my place," I said.

"I don't want to give up my apartment," Benny said tiredly.

"I know," I said, merging into the left lane. "But your apartment looks like shit. You're barely taking care of the cat. Just move in with me. It's only for a little while. You can have your old room. You can have *my* old room, it's bigger," I said, trying to sell it.

He paused before replying like it was wearing him out just to conjure sentences. "I don't want to mess up your dating thing," he mumbled.

"There's nothing to mess up. I'm like the most single person you've ever met. You seriously wouldn't be cramping any of my style moving in. I have nothing going on right now."

He didn't reply and I glanced at him. "This is only temporary, Benny. You'll get a transplant and you'll get your life back."

He stayed silent for a long moment. "I'm going to be dealing with this for the rest of my life," he said quietly.

"It won't always be this bad. Once you get a kidney—"

"I *won't*. You know I won't. You just don't want to admit it."

Now *I* went quiet. I didn't know what was better. Trying to keep his hopes up or managing his expectations.

"Okay," I said. "So let's say you don't get one and this is just your life now—it can still be a good life. It can be a *great* life. Why don't we get you a home dialysis machine? You can do it at night while you watch TV. You only need to do it for two hours if you do it every day."

There was no reply again, so I had to look over at him.

"I can do it from home?" he asked tentatively.

"Yeah, totally. You have a doctor for a sister. You can't do it when you're living alone, but if you move in with me, I'll be there to sterilize the equipment, monitor your vitals."

He looked slightly if not hesitantly optimistic.

"And if you do daily dialysis instead of three times a week, you can have restricted foods since the fluid won't build up."

He sat up. "I can have ice cream?"

I nodded. "Yup. We might even be able to get you off some of the meds with the more frequent dialysis. You'll feel better, you'll have more energy..."

I think this was the first time I saw him smile in months. Well, he sort of smiled. It was more of a neutral frown on the cusp of a smile—but still, it was progress.

"Benny, you can do this. You just need to get adjusted. I can help you."

Please let me help you.

The silence hovered between us.

"Okay," he said finally.

"Okay? You'll move in?"

"Yeah. I guess."

I let out a breath. I felt simultaneously relieved and sad. Relieved that I'd be able to take care of him, that I wouldn't get any more surprise ER visits, that him being with me would give him a better quality of life. And sad that a certain chapter was ending—for both of us. Because both of our lives had officially come to an abrupt stop. We were adults, regressing.

It was like the clock had just wound back twenty years. Suddenly I wasn't grown-up, thirty-five-year-old married Briana anymore. He wasn't bright, driven Benjamin working in IT, training for a 5K. I was the older sister again, in charge of watching a brace-faced Benny while Mom took night classes and worked a double. And I *was* going to have to watch him. Because I didn't trust him with himself.

I got him home to his apartment and made him dinner. He barely touched it and went straight to bed. I drove home after starting a load of dishes and watering his wilting plants that still looked twice as alive as my brother did.

I was so mentally drained by the time I got back to the house I just plopped on the sofa wrapped in a blanket and passed out there until the cat unceremoniously walked across my body at two a.m. Then I dragged myself to my room and stared at the ceiling in the dark, unable to go back to sleep.

I was getting further and further away from the me I'd planned. Of the *life* I had planned.

In two weeks, I'd no longer be married. I would, from this day forward, be alone.

I was never doing this relationship stuff again. Any of it.

I'd always told myself that what happened to Mom with Dad was isolated. That most men didn't walk out on their pregnant wife and eight-year-old daughter, leaving them homeless and destitute. I believed in love. And when I met Nick, I'd believed I'd found the one. I was almost snide about it. See? There are good men out there. I knew lots. Zander, Gibson, Benny—and now I'd found one to be the love of my life too.

But having men as friends and peers and family is very different than having them as partners.

Everything Mom had told me my whole life about being in relationships with men turned out to be true: They can't be trusted. They can't be relied upon. Men will always hurt you and leave you and let you down.

What Dad did cut even deeper now, because he'd given his son his rare blood type but didn't bother to stick around to give him a kidney when he needed one. The bitterness twisted in my gut like a knife.

I was done. *Done* with men.

From now on I'd use them the way they used women. For entertainment. For sex. For convenience. I would never live with a man I was dating and I'd sure as hell never get married again. Ever. And kids? No. Not if it meant I'd be attached to their father for the rest of my life.

I was so disgusted, so severely disappointed by what Nick and Dad ended up being. And it was reinforced daily, with every battered woman who came into my ER and every idiot I met on Tinder. It didn't even surprise me that I couldn't even find one decent enough for casual sex. The only ones on the dating apps who seemed to have their shit together always turned out to be married, which only further confirmed my opinion of dating men in general.

Jessica was right. I was better off with the cat.

For the next three days I packed Benny's apartment and moved him in. His best friends, Justin and Brad, came to help with the heavy lifting. They set up Benny's treadmill in the den, put his furniture in storage, and got him situated. Having his friends over at least got him to shower and put on clean clothes, so that was nice.

I made arrangements for a home dialysis machine to be de-livered. I spent a full day washing the trash bags of dirty clothes I'd packed up from his apartment while he depression-slept. Then I spent five minutes holding a cold cup of coffee and staring morosely at the giant hideous cat-scratching thingy that now lived in my living room next to the equally hideous pink floral sofa that Mom bought in 1994.

I currently lived in the house I grew up in.

When Mom married Gil, she refused to give up her house. Even when he retired and they moved to Arizona, she still wouldn't sell it. Mom said, with men you always need a fail-safe. To never put all your eggs in their basket.

Looks like once again Mom was right. When I left Nick, at least I had someplace to go.

I'd never decorated Mom's house when I moved in. I didn't really plan on still being here a year later, and decorating it made my situation feel permanent. So I just lived here in the faded remnants of my childhood. The whole place looked like a time capsule from the 1970s. Macramé wall art, oak cabinets and brass hardware, brown shag carpet, peeling linoleum in the kitchen. It was depressing. And now there was a cat tree the size of a real tree in here too.

Why did I *live* like this?

I could afford an apartment. I could afford a *house*. But I felt paralyzed by the idea of it. Like I'd had just enough strength to leave the home I'd made with Nick, but not enough to make a new one for myself. So I just squatted here like a castaway trapped on a deserted island.

Maybe a part of me was afraid to leave the island. Because then this was all real.

I took an extra day off work to finish moving Benny in. By the time I went back to the hospital on Wednesday, I was a zombie. I felt totally numb. Like the Nick thing and the Benny thing and the house thing were a horrible third-degree burn, so severe the nerve endings were gone and I could feel nothing.

It occurred to me that this was the worst time of my entire life.

I mean, when Nick cheated, yeah, that was bad. But at least

Benny still had his kidneys then. At least I still had Alexis nearby. I had *hope*.

Now I had a dialysis machine getting delivered in a few days, Benny wasting away mentally in a bed down the hall, and a litter box in my laundry room that only I was going to clean. My best friend was two hours away and too busy with her new life to be the diversion I needed to not think about all this.

There was nothing for me to look forward to. Even the chief position was at a standstill. I had no dating prospects. No joy in my life. Not a single distraction. I hadn't had sex in a year. I was just getting older. Heading in the wrong direction in every way, my life crumbling around me.

And I was bored.

That was the worst thing of all. The boredom. The monotony of my uneventful, unremarkable, depressing fucking life.

If Benny wasn't a factor, I'd do Doctors Without Borders or something, walk the earth. What was the point of being in Minnesota? It was cold here, everything reminded me of Nick, or, worse, Kelly. I was alone. I didn't even really want the chief position if I was being honest with myself. It just seemed like something everyone expected of me after Alexis left, and I figured why not, what the hell else was I doing? At least I'd be building my résumé.

This wasn't the life I wanted. And I didn't know how to change it. It was quicksand.

Jocelyn was at the nurses' station when I came onto the floor clutching a triple cappuccino and feeling as tired as I looked. I had no idea how I was going to make it through the day.

"Hey, someone left something for you." She nodded to a spot behind the counter.

I leaned over wearily to look. There was a jumbo-sized red velvet cupcake with an envelope taped to the container with my name written on it.

I smiled for the first time in days. Alexis?

"Who's it from?" I asked.

"Don't know. It was here when I got here yesterday." She tapped a pen on the counter and eyed me. "Hey, you okay? You called out."

"Fine," I said, leaning down to pick up the card. I set my coffee on the counter and slid a finger under the seal on the envelope.

It was a letter. A long letter. Handwritten.

From *Dr. Maddox.*

I blinked at it. Dr. Maddox? *Why?*

I looked around, like he might be somewhere watching. I didn't see him.

"Who's it from?" she asked.

"Nobody. I'll be right back."

I grabbed the cupcake container and hurried to the supply closet. I shut the door behind me, sat on my toilet-paper box, and pulled the letter from the envelope. It was in black fountain pen, clear and careful writing.

Briana,

I sometimes find that journaling helps me organize my thoughts. I seem to be having a hard time saying and doing the right things recently, so I figured writing this down might be best.

I wanted to thank you for the cupcake suggestion.

You are likely unaware of this, but I deal with some social anxiety. It's worse when I'm in a new situation with people I don't know. Interaction doesn't come naturally to me in those circumstances and I struggle. When I make mistakes, like I've done often since I got here, it makes me more uncomfortable and my anxiety gets worse. I get more nervous, and that makes me more withdrawn. It's a bit of a self-perpetuating cycle. So your help was deeply appreciated, even though I know you didn't have any reason to give it.

There are a few things I want to address.

You mentioned that Dr. Gibson was holding off the vote for head of emergency medicine in hopes that I might be up for the position. I have no interest in this job, nor did I convey any such thing to Dr. Gibson upon my arrival. I was unaware he was making this decision, and I have told him I do not intend to run. I'm sorry if you felt that the delayed vote was done on my behalf. I was not a part of it.

The other day when I came to your brother's hospital room I didn't mention that you broke my phone. I was frustrated and should have picked a better time to bring up you running into me in the hallway. But again, my anxiety sometimes makes it hard for me to gauge social cues, and I don't always express myself the way I hope to. It was poor judgment on my part, and I apologize.

Lastly, in the supply closet, when I said that your brother could live on dialysis—my mom had chronic kidney disease when I was a teenager. She received a kidney transplant before she required dialysis, but that period of my life was a terrifying time. I remember feeling comforted by the knowledge that if her kidneys failed before she got a donor that at least dialysis would keep her alive. It wasn't like losing your lungs or your heart. She would have time. She would have decades if she needed it.

I meant what I said to be reassuring, but I didn't

consider how insensitive it would come off without context. I in no way meant to minimize what was happening to your brother or invalidate what has to be a traumatic and life-altering diagnosis.

If any of my mistakes have brought you stress or unhappiness, please accept my deepest apologies. It was unintentional.

Again, thank you.

Sincerely,
Jacob

I set the paper down on my knees.

Wow. I was an *asshole*. I felt HORRIBLE.

I saw so much of the last few weeks differently now. I should have done more to welcome him here. I should have given him the benefit of the doubt or at the very least not been such a raging bitch.

I looked back at the letter resting on my thighs.

I don't think anyone had ever written me a letter before. It was shockingly effective. Way better than text or email, like it had a different weight to it or something. There's something about holding the paper in your hand, seeing the ink on the page, the press of the pen. He made this. It took effort. It was a physical act. He couldn't erase it if he made a mistake, he had to think about what he was going to say before he said it—or he said exactly what he wanted to and didn't need to change it.

I looked over at the cupcake. I didn't even want to eat it. I didn't *deserve* to eat it. Nadia Cakes didn't sell jumbos on a walk-in basis; they were a special order. He special-ordered this—for *me*. It was thoughtful.

It made me feel a thousand times worse.

I had to go back to the floor, but the letter gnawed at me all day. I kept thinking about it, about how to respond—because I *had* to respond. But in the meantime, I was going to avoid Jacob like my life depended on it, which wasn't too hard because I think he was avoiding me too—and why wouldn't he? I was the Wicked Witch of the ER.

Imagine being the reason why someone hated their new job. That was me. *I* was the reason.

On my lunch break I slipped into the supply closet with some paper I took out of the printer and wrote him back.

CHAPTER 8

JACOB

There was an envelope taped to my locker. My heart started to race before I even touched it.

Chances were good it was just a thank-you note from the nurses for the cupcakes. Chances were also good that this was Briana telling me to go to hell.

I shouldn't have written her.

I wanted to clear the air with her and tell her I was sorry for my comment about her brother. But maybe I should have done it in person. Maybe the formality of a letter was too dry for something like this and she hadn't taken it in the olive-branch spirit it was intended.

Maybe this envelope was *my* letter being returned to me unread.

I dragged a hand down my mouth before I plucked it off the door. I pulled it out and flipped to the last page to look for the signature.

It was from Briana. My pulse thrummed in my ears.

I folded it back up without looking at the rest of it and put it into my duffel bag to head home.

I felt like everyone was watching me on the way out, like they all knew I'd been given a letter and they knew what was waiting for me in those pages.

Maybe they *did*.

Maybe she'd read it to the nurses before she left it on my locker. Maybe she'd read them my letter too... Maybe they were all having drinks together, laughing about it *right now*.

I could feel the envelope next to me in my bag like it was a ticking bomb about to go off.

The cupcake I'd gotten her was gone at the end of her shift. Did she eat it? Or did she just give it to someone else? Or, worse, maybe she threw it away... She said she didn't want one, so maybe I shouldn't have gotten her one. But it had been my experience that most of the time when people say they don't want food, they actually don't mind it when it shows up.

Maybe she just didn't want it from *me*.

Maybe giving it to her anyway made her upset, like I was forcing baked goods onto her when she'd explicitly said she didn't want them. Was that rude of me? Presumptuous?

I got home and took Lieutenant Dan on a long walk, mostly to delay the inevitable.

For a split second I considered not reading the letter at all, which was ridiculous. I needed to know where I stood, especially because I had to work with her. But something told me that if this went badly, if the tone of this letter was what I was afraid it was, that would be it for me. I couldn't stay at Royaume. I'd just have to accept that I'd gotten myself into a situation that simply wasn't salvageable and move on. Quit and go somewhere else.

When I finally forced myself to sit down and look at the letter, it was almost ten o'clock. I took a deep breath and pulled it out of the envelope. It was two pages, written in blue pen on printer paper.

Dear Jacob,

Since I now know you have anxiety, I figured writing you back instead of talking to you in person would be the best and least stress-inducing way to respond.

I scoffed. Of course I'd managed to work myself up anyway.

I don't write a lot of letters. My hand already hurts, so I'm going to have to take lots of breaks, but here we go.

First of all, if you think for one second that I can be flipped with cupcakes and handwritten apology letters, then you are absolutely correct. I accept all your apologies and explanations. I also would like to apologize. I have been <u>awful</u> to you.

Awful was underlined twice.

So, I know that you don't know me, but I'm not usually like this. I know people always say stuff like that, but I'm serious. I'm not always like this. I'm not really the best version of myself these days. I know this isn't an excuse, but I've been having a pretty crappy year, and it's been wearing me down, and I think I took some of it out on you. That was really unfair and I'm sorry. Like, I don't even want to eat the cupcake you gave me because I feel like I don't deserve it. Nadia Cakes is too good for me right now. I'm going to put it in the freezer until I'm a person karmically worthy of cream cheese frosting.

I can't believe I broke your phone. I will absolutely pay for it. Please let me know what I owe you. And I'm sorry for the way I misjudged you—but to be fair, Gibson was very unclear about the whole chief thing, so I sort of blame him for instigating this. But I am sorry. I feel terrible.

I'd like to make you a peace offering. I think you probably want what every introvert wants—to be invited, even though you won't come. Grabbing drinks with everyone is probably not your idea of a good time, but whenever we go to Mafi's, I'm going to invite you anyway. This is going to be my way of making this up to you. Know that you are welcome and wanted, and if you ever do decide to take me up on it, I will sit next to you at the bar and I won't force you to make small talk with me and I won't let drunk extroverts anywhere near you. This is my solemn vow. Zero drunk extroverts.

I felt my smile reach my eyes.

Please know that—okay, seriously? Do you write letters like this often? Because my hand HURTS.

Then there was a word scratched out. There were a lot of words scratched out, actually. I think she was struggling with the lack of a Delete button.

All right, back to it. I took a five-minute break to do hand stretches.

If any of my mistakes have brought you stress or unhappiness, please accept my deepest apologies.

Regards (I've always wanted to end a letter with regards—oh, and to get one where someone signs it yours truly and calls me "dearest." It's so Mr. Darcy),

Bri
P.S. I need to get actual paper. I think lines would have helped.

I smiled softly at the signature on the page.

I couldn't explain the lift I felt in my chest. For the first time in weeks, the electric hum of my anxiety softened. I could actually feel the almost-constant flow of cortisol that I'd been dealing with shut off. I could breathe again.

Lieutenant Dan put his head in my lap and peered up at me like he sensed the shift in my mood.

I read the letter a second time. Then a third. Every time I read it, I felt myself getting lighter.

After the fourth time I read it, I pulled out paper and grabbed a pen.

CHAPTER 9

BRIANA

The day after I left my reply taped to Jacob's locker, I found an envelope with my name on it stuck to the backside of the supply closet door.

Dearest Briana,

I laughed.

Thank you for your kind reply and for offering to repair the phone. I had insurance and the cost was minimal, so that won't be necessary, though I appreciate the offer. I will however accept your invitation to be invited and never come. That sounds like an excellent time. I also enjoy not answering calls, not networking, never leaving the house, and hanging out with my dog.

I'm glad you were able to forgive me, and of course I forgive you as well. I understand what it's like to go through a tough time and the strain that it takes on your mental health and patience. I think you were generous in your interactions with me, all things considered, and I look forward to continuing to work with you. I hope you're not too hard on yourself over it and that you thaw and eat your cupcake.

I must return to my isolation now. I need twenty to twenty-two hours of alone time a day to function.

Sincerely,
Jacob
P.S. I'm only partly kidding.

I laughed. Then I read it again. I liked someone who could poke fun at himself.

An hour later, I left a yellow folded Post-it taped to his charting computer.

You have a dog? Can I pet it if I promise not to make direct eye contact with you or make small talk with you about the weather?

—Bri

An hour later there was a folded notepaper taped to *my* charting computer.

Dearest Briana,

Yes, you may pet my dog. But I should probably mention that Lieutenant Dan likes talking about the weather, so while you might not want to bring it up to me, maybe mention to him what a cold spring we're having?

Do you have any pets? I look forward to your reply.

Sincerely,
Jacob

We got super busy after that and I didn't have time to respond before I got off. I stopped at Target on the way home to get some nice paper and a better pen than the cheap Bic I'd been using, but I didn't really like the selection, so I Googled and found a stationery place called Paper Waits Cards and drove there instead.

For his letters Jacob used really nice heavy paper and this linen-type envelope. It was very fancy and it kind of made *me* want to be fancy.

It was a nice diversion going into a store I'd never had a reason to go into. It felt like a mission or a scavenger hunt or something. It felt like I had a project that I was actually into.

I went with pink-lined paper that had vintage flowers in the corners. The package came with three prints: roses, lilacs, and daisies. That way I could write him three different letters and they'd all be on different paper.

Once I got what I needed I hurried home. Benny's dialysis machine was getting delivered today.

It took me two hours to set it up and then a long training session with a dialysis nurse to make sure I knew how to use it. Then I had to hook Benny to it and get dinner going. I watched a movie with him while I monitored his vitals, so it was late by the time I sat down to write.

The writing was really relaxing. Cathartic.

I liked having something to do.

CHAPTER 10

JACOB

After I left the note on Briana's computer there was nothing else for the day. The next morning, however, I found an envelope taped to my locker again. I slipped into an on-call room to read it.

She'd gotten new paper and envelopes. She said she didn't write letters, which meant she probably got them just for this. The thought of her making that effort made me smile to myself.

Jacob,

Lieutenant Dan? Lol

I don't have any pets, but my brother and his cat have moved in with me, so I sort of have a cat I guess? His name is Cooter. He's really cute. My brother found him behind a dumpster by a gas station, which I'm told is where the best cats come from. Benny was a college student at the time and he lived in a house with his best friends, Brad and Justin, and they thought the name was hilarious. Now seven years later I have to make psps psps noises in my kitchen and call, "here, Cooter Cooter!" when I need to feed him.

Anyway, I've barely seen him in the week that he's been here. He's sort of freaked out being in the new place and he hides. I only know he's alive because he does this 3:00 a.m. zoomy thing where he tears through my house and somehow gets involved with the blinds?

I cracked up.

She was funny. I could see why Zander and Gibson—well, everyone—liked her. I went back to reading.

Okay, so this is going to be super random, but stick with me. I follow this travel blogger, Vanessa Price, and she's always got these wild stories. Once, before she was married and her husband went everywhere with her, she got locked in a tower in Ireland by this earl who thought it would be funny. She was sooo pissed. I guess towers are really drafty? Lots of bugs, not as romantic as they sound. He gave her this Shetland pony as an apology gift and she was like "thanks for the tiny horse, dick, I want my five hours back."

I barked out a laugh.

I was just thinking, what if I sucked at apologies and instead of giving you drunk extrovert protection, I'd just given you a small horse. Don't you feel lucky?

She drew a wide-eyed smiley face and a stick horse and signed it with the letter *B*.

I read this one twice before I left to start my shift. On my lunch break I grabbed a spinach wrap and some paper and wrote her back.

CHAPTER 11

BRIANA

Right before I left for the day, I found an envelope in my locker. I broke into a grin the second I saw it. It was a little long, and I got a flutter of anticipation when I saw all the pages.

This was fun. I was actually having *fun*, for the first time in I couldn't remember how long. I took the letter home and crossed my legs under me on the bed and unfolded the papers.

Dearest Briana,

While we're on the topic of insufficient apologies, a story for you if I may.

I have three sisters, Jewel, Jill, and Jane. And yes, my parents named all of us with J names. My brother is Jeremiah, my mom is Joy. Please do not hold any of this against me.

Jewel is a tattoo artist. She owns a parlor in St. Paul. She's very gifted.

A few years ago I lost a bet with her. If I lost, I had to let her give me a tattoo of her choosing.

I don't have any tattoos. I've always been too afraid

to commit to something so permanent. But Jewel is amazing at what she does, so I thought she'd give me something profoundly beautiful, an everlasting imprint that I'd cherish. Something I never knew I needed to carry with me through life.

She gave me a tiny lawn mower on my chest next to a small patch of shaved chest hair.

I *cackled.*

I laughed so hard I think I scared the cat in the other room.

It was sort of surprising how funny Jacob was. He seemed so uptight. But then I realized that it was probably the anxiety that made him come off that way. I felt like there was a lesson here about not judging books by their cover or something...

I read on.

The tattoo has since been lasered off, which cost me eight hundred dollars and was quite painful. She refused to apologize. Something about stupid games and stupid prizes?

If Jewel had lost, she had to shave her head. She shaved her head anyway. She's always wanted to, apparently, so my losing was a foregone conclusion. I should have known after a lifetime of experience that I am not capable of outsmarting the women in my family—which I suppose was the lesson.

I think I would have enjoyed the tiny horse.

Sincerely,
Jacob

That was it. No more letter.

I was starting to wish I had his number—well, I did and I didn't. Part of the fun was the letter thing. But then it was over so fast. Just a couple of minutes and then nothing for like a whole day. I wondered if I would have this much fun talking to him on the phone or texting him. I bet I would.

Benny was still sleeping. I had to wake him up for dinner and do his dialysis, but I decided to wait so I could write Jacob back really quick. If I didn't deliver a letter tomorrow, it would be longer until I got one from him again.

I was about midway done when Benny came dragging into the kitchen.

"What are you doing?" he asked, sounding so out of it I wondered if he'd even understand the answer.

He looked like a sleepwalker. He was wearing the same clothes as yesterday. A gray wrinkled T-shirt and checkered pajama bottoms. He needed to shave.

I'd known moving him here wasn't going to be a quick fix, but I was hoping he'd be doing a little better by now. He was taking his medications. At least he was this week. I'd been handing them to him myself. And he was back with his therapist now that I was here to make sure he went. She said he'd missed several weeks leading up to his ER visit, which explained a lot.

He wasn't alone anymore, and he was in a safe place. I was doing all the right things for him. But I wanted a sign that he was still in there. That some of this, *any* of this, was working. Even a little.

I cleared my throat and looked away from his haggard body. "I'm writing a letter."

He dropped into a chair at the kitchen counter.

I set down my pen. "Hey, what do you think about watching a movie tonight?"

He didn't answer, just stared into the kitchen.

"Benny?"

He didn't reply.

I reached over and put a hand on his wrist. "Hey, let's go for a short walk after dialysis. Just around the block. Yeah?"

He squeezed his eyes shut. "Just...stop *nagging* me," he whispered.

I had to swallow the lump that bolted to my throat.

There was this mother who came into my ER once. She'd ridden in on the same ambulance as her son after he made a suicide attempt. We weren't able to save him.

When I came out to tell her the news, she was so...*resigned.* Like she'd known this was coming for ages. Like she'd already cried about it and grieved him and this just made it official. She looked up at me with bloodshot eyes and said in the most sincere way I'd ever heard, "I did everything I could."

And it terrified me that now I knew what that meant.

There was nothing else I could do for my brother. There was nothing else to pull from my arsenal except for pleas to get him up and moving. He was already in therapy and on depression meds. I couldn't get him into an inpatient program unless he agreed to go, which he wouldn't. He couldn't be forced unless he was a danger to others or himself—which he wasn't. I didn't worry that Benny was going to hurt himself. Not directly, anyway. He was just going to give up on trying to stay alive.

He didn't want to live in this body. Not broken the way it was.

I knew many, *many* patients with disabilities and chronic illnesses who lived their lives with dignity and joy and purpose. I knew people in end-stage renal failure, just like Benny, who didn't even slow down. They took vacations and raised their families and had fun and made memories and plans. Jacob was right about dialysis. It was a gift. It gave you *time.* And I had hoped that Benny would get there, that he'd accept his new normal and find a way to keep loving life. But he wasn't. He was withering. It had all happened too fast and taken too much from him. He couldn't pivot. And the dialysis was the constant reminder that the worst possible thing had happened. Every time he sat down for it, he lost more of himself. Only a kidney could change this in any fast and meaningful way. And I couldn't get him a kidney. I couldn't even give him hope.

"Who you writing to?" he asked again, breaking into my thoughts. His tone was conciliatory. He probably felt bad for snapping at me.

I sniffed. "I'm writing to a friend. That doctor who came into your room that day in the ER."

"I thought you didn't like that guy."

I shrugged. "I like him. He's nice."

"Are you trying to date him or something?"

"No. We're just friends." I put the letter facedown and pushed up from my seat. "I'm going to fill up the tub for you."

He groaned. "What? *Nooo.*"

"Yes. I'll grab some clothes to change into when you're done."

He let out a resigned noise from the back of his throat. "No tub. I'll just...take a shower," he muttered.

"Cool. And shave. Then we'll go for a quick walk and watch a movie while we do your dialysis," I said, trying to keep my tone bright.

He sighed deeply and then got up and went upstairs. I watched him go and deflated as soon as he was gone.

It was hard to be strong for us both. I barely had enough for me.

The next morning, I left the letter peeking out from under the keyboard of Jacob's charting computer the second I got in.

Jacob,

Okay, but would you really enjoy the tiny horse? Really? I mean what do they even do? You can't ride them unless you're like seven or something. They're cute, but it's totally not practical.

It's like those little pet monkeys that wear the diapers. They seem so cool, but they bathe in their own urine and fling poo and unscrew all your lightbulbs.

I think I knew exactly the moment that he'd read this part because I heard a laugh come out of the supply closet. He liked to take his breaks in there.

Hey, you don't have a girlfriend, do you? It just occurred to me I never asked and me slipping letters into your locker might not be appropriate. I'm not hitting on you, in case you or your girlfriend are worried. I just want to be clear about that. I'm single and off the market, so no one can tell me who can write me letters or what kind of exotic pets I'm allowed to bring home. Might get wild and start realizing my dream of running a skunk rehab. They're supposed to be good to cuddle once their scent glands are removed.

I'd signed it with a terrible drawing of a skunk.

I figured I should make it clear that none of this back-and-forth was in anything other than the spirit of friendship, just in case he thought I was flirting.

I didn't date men I worked with. That was a personal rule for me—even if he *was* exceptionally attractive. Maybe *especially* because he was exceptionally attractive...

His personality really took it up a notch.

By lunch, I had a letter on my charting computer. It was on

the stationery he used when he wrote from home, which meant he brought it to work just to write me. I grinned.

Dearest Briana,

I'm single as well. My ex and I broke up last year. I didn't mistake your friendship for anything other than what it was, but I suppose it's good we clarify, especially since we work together.

I think I could handle a Shetland pony. I have a bit of experience with hard to manage animals. Lieutenant Dan was a rescue with behavioral problems, and I grew up with a parrot. A thirty-year-old African gray named Jafar. He's a bit of a jerk. He knocks things over and then blames the cat. He also likes the word (and you're going to have to excuse the language here) "motherfucker," so sometimes we're treated to the sound of shattering glass followed by "The cat did it, motherfucker!"

I was laughing SO HARD.

Jafar just added "bullshit," "cocksucker," and "you're sitting on the remote" to his twisted repertoire. We have no idea who taught him this, though I suspect it was my grandfather, who seems to enjoy a certain level of chaos at elegant family gatherings.

I replied on my lunch break with a hurried story about a patient I'd had that day who cut off his own pinky toe to prove to his friend we could reattach it. We did, so I guess he was right, but still.

Jacob wrote back by five about a guy who won a bet that he couldn't eat a whole container of sugar-free gummy bears. He had severe diarrhea. Jacob had to prescribe him Desitin for his diaper rash, and the guy's friends were cracking up so hard Jacob had to kick them out.

Then our shifts were over. We went home and now both had four days off because Jacob and I had the same schedule: twelve-hour shifts for one week with four days on and three days off. Then the next week it was three days on and four days off.

Four days, no letter. It *sucked*.

Now I *really* had nothing to do. I was so bored.

My first day off, the weather was nice so I took Benny out for ice cream, which I hoped would cheer him up, since he hadn't been able to have any for the last six months. He just poked at it and said it tasted weird. Probably his meds affecting his taste buds. I stopped at a park on the way home and made him walk with me around the lake. He acted like he'd been kidnapped, and he looked miserable the whole time. When we got back, he went straight to his room.

If I didn't have to be here, I'd probably drive down to see Alexis for the long weekend. I guessed I still could. Do Benny's dialysis now, get back by tomorrow night in time for it again. But I didn't really feel good about leaving him alone, even if he didn't care if I was here. So I just stayed. Doing nothing.

The next day off, I did laundry. I did the dishes. I cleaned the litter box. Then I lay on the sofa and started scrolling through TikTok.

I realized that the only thing that I looked forward to these days were the letters with Jacob. He was so interesting. And fun.

I wondered what *he* did on his days off. Maybe his letter would be about how he spent the long weekend?

I wondered if he was on TikTok. I typed his name into the search bar, but nothing came up except a slightly viral video with a couple thousand likes on it. Some patient a few months back at Memorial West, recording Jacob from across the ER, talking about how hot her doctor is. I went *straight* to the comments, and they did *not* disappoint. I think I laughed for a solid five minutes.

"I know where I'm getting my next Pap smear."

"This is why your grandmother always told you to wear clean underwear in case you're in an accident."

And the top comment said:

"As if Minnesota isn't wet enough already."

I *died*.

I hoped Jacob didn't know this existed—he would probably be mortified. I hearted the video *and* the comments.

I continued my quest still smiling and went to Google, but all I got was his bio on the Royaume Northwestern website. No Facebook or Twitter. I went to Instagram. He didn't come up on a search, but when I combed through Zander's friends, I found him.

His page was private. I immediately sent him a friend request. A few minutes later he approved it. I sat up with a smile and went right to creeping on his wall.

He only had twenty-three friends, but there were a ton of pictures. I scrolled down and went all the way back to the beginning, about three years.

Most of it looked like family photos. Shots at Christmas, barbeques, lake pictures. Jacob wasn't in most of them and he didn't seem to take selfies. Even his profile picture was just a nature shot.

There were lots and *lots* of Lieutenant Dan. His dog only had three legs.

I burst out laughing the second I saw it. He'd named his dog after the amputee in *Forrest Gump*. Jacob had never mentioned the missing-leg thing. He was surprisingly funny, in this self-deprecating, understated kind of way.

I think one of the best parts of this new thing with Jacob was drawing him out. I wanted to unravel him, find out more about who he was. I felt like I was peeling his layers back one letter at a time, getting these little glimpses of someone I could tell was highly private and super reserved. I liked people like that. Benny was like that. You had to *earn* their friendship. They didn't just fling it all over for anyone who was interested, and when they gave it to you, it meant something.

He seemed to be renovating a small cabin somewhere. He shared a lot of pictures of that.

No ex-girlfriend pics. Maybe he'd deleted them. God knows I'd deleted every picture of Nick after we broke up. It took me like a million years to get rid of them all. Probably would have been easier to delete the whole account and start over, but I refused to delete my non-Nick-related memories on principle.

They should make an app for that. A facial recognition one that could detect and delete photos of your ex. One click and your whole device is wiped clean. And it should delete all their comments too, so you don't have to see things like "hot mama!" on a picture of you in a bathing suit at your best friend's house on a day when I now knew for a fact he was at home having sex with Kelly, in our bed.

Nick and his lies tainted everything. Even the memories he wasn't in.

I shoved the dark cloud down and kept scrolling.

Jacob had a shot of Gooseberry Falls and Split Rock Lighthouse up by Duluth. A hiking trail. About midway through, there was a rare picture of him. He was in a kayak with a blond woman.

Maybe that was her? They had on life jackets. I couldn't really make her out. Another shot of him kneeling with an arm around two little kids on either side of him. A girl and a boy. He was really smiling in this one. It made *me* smile. He looked so happy. The opposite of how he looked at work, I noted.

Hector mentioned seeing him at the Cockpit. After seeing Jacob's wall, I was almost certain Hector had been mistaken. None of his pictures were of any places remotely like that, plus I didn't picture a man with social anxiety being in a rowdy bar getting drinks from a server blowing on a whistle while you took shots.

I scrolled through for a few more minutes. He hadn't posted anything in the last few days. No clue where he was today or what he was doing. When I got to the last picture, I sighed.

I was beginning to feel like letters were not enough. It was fun, but they couldn't keep up with the demand. We'd passed four letters back and forth on our last shift alone, and I still felt like I had more to say and so did he.

I wanted to hang out with him. I wondered if he'd be open to that. I'd have to really reiterate that I wasn't hitting on him, though. Hanging out seemed a little line blurring, especially if it was going to be outside of work and only the two of us. But maybe I could get him to come to Mafi's the next time everyone else went. That would be okay.

I liked the last picture he posted, a shot of his dog sleeping on a wooden porch, and I posted a little comment. A few minutes later he hearted it.

That was all I'd get of Jacob until work on Monday.

Unless...

CHAPTER 12

JACOB

I t was Saturday, the second of four days off, and I was up at the cabin working on the yard. It was overgrown and I'd spent the day before cutting down a few maples that were blocking the view to the lake. I had my shirt off and Lieutenant Dan was watching me chop one of the trees into firewood from the porch. I was stacking the logs to dry out when the notification pinged on my phone. When I swiped it open, I stared at it for a solid minute, my heart in my throat.

Briana sent me a friend request.

Instant jolt of adrenaline.

My social media was not easy to find. She'd had to have gone looking for it. Why?

We'd been passing notes back and forth—it wasn't flirting. She'd been clear with me on that. I'd actually felt a twinge of disappointment when she'd said it.

I mean, I guess *I* wasn't really flirting either. It wasn't that I wasn't interested, I just wasn't that bold. It took a lot for me to make a first move or even to accept that a woman might be open to that. Everything we were doing was more forward than I was usually comfortable with, even on a friends-only level. Maybe it was easier because we didn't speak to each other? Just the letters. It felt like speaking to each other wasn't allowed, like it wasn't part of it. Was this? Being friends on Instagram?

I wasn't one of those people who collected followers. The only people I let follow me were my closest friends and family. Not acquaintances, not people from high school. Close. The photos I shared were for those who knew me better than anyone, so I never worried about what they thought. But I cared what Briana would think. I cared a lot.

What if I accepted this friend request and she realized how boring I am? Or I somehow failed to meet some expectation of who I was outside of work? What if she simply didn't like me once she knew me better?

I dragged a hand down my mouth and sat on the back steps. Why was a woman like her even engaging with me in the first place? I wasn't interesting, I wasn't fun.

Still, she'd sent the request. She must want me to approve it.

I stared at the notification for another long moment. Then I swallowed hard and accepted it.

I went straight to look at her wall. Her first picture was of her with a calico cat on her lap. He was rubbing his head affectionately on her chin. The caption said "my new roommate." That must be Cooter.

Farther down the timeline there were a few pictures at a wedding. She was in a black dress, posing with the beaming bride, a redhead.

There were some nature pictures. A trail with light green leaves on the trees. A selfie in front of Minnehaha Falls. She was wearing sunglasses and a gray baseball hat in that one. She liked to hike, like me. There were a lot of pictures in the woods, camping. Superior Hiking Trail.

There was one of her in a bathing suit in a pool. I looked at this one longer than I probably should have. She had a nice figure. It was hard to tell under the scrubs, but she did. She was a very attractive woman.

There was a shot of her in a blue ballgown, like she was headed to an event, seven months ago. She looked beautiful.

As I scrolled down, I spotted a picture of her with her brother from two years ago. The difference was stark. The before-and-after of his illness. He was tan and fit. She looked happier too. She was wearing a wedding ring in this one.

She was married before? Maybe this is what she meant about the last year being hard.

If I didn't know the situation with Benny, I might not have noticed the weariness in her now. She was beautiful then and she was beautiful today. But I could see the toll it had all taken.

I got a notification that she'd liked one of my pictures. Then another one that there was a comment. I tapped on it. It was my last picture of Lieutenant Dan. She'd written "he's so cute! 😍" I smiled.

Maybe she'd like to meet him. I thought about asking her if she'd like to go to the dog park with me after work one day. I could DM her.

We could message back and forth. Right now. I wanted to.

It was hard to have a running conversation via letters. It took too long. Even on days when we passed three or four notes, I had to wait all day to get a written response to just one question. And then on our days off, there were no notes at all.

The days where there were no notes felt particularly long.

But what to say? What message would I send? "Hey"? I couldn't send Hey. It had to be something smart. Or funny. Not Hey.

A notification popped up. I had a message. From Briana.

My heart lurched. I hurried to click on it.

Briana: Hey

My mind started to race. What should I reply? Hey too? Maybe I should ask an open-ended question. That way she'd have to respond so it wouldn't just be Hey Hey and then nothing.

Another message popped up.

Briana: What r u doing?

Panicking???

I stood and started to pace. I typed into the message bar.

Me: Not much. At my cabin this weekend. You?

I read it over five times before deciding it was good. I changed You to U and then back again. I hit Send and stared at the screen.

No new message came through.

I waited a few minutes. Then I decided to go back to her wall, just to have something to do. But when I got there, I saw a red #1 on the message arrow telling me there was a DM. I went to tap it, but there was nothing there.

Shit. It was the Wi-Fi. My messages weren't loading. *Noooooo.*

The cabin had crappy internet. Crappy cell service too. In fact, this was one of the reasons I came up here this weekend, to have plausible deniability when my family couldn't get in touch to interrogate me. I knew if I'd stayed home, they would have shown up to corner me, so I fled up north. Only now my plan was backfiring because the only person I actually wanted to be able to talk to couldn't get through.

There were times when I couldn't get Instagram to load for hours. My cell phone had only one bar unless I went over to the little cabin-themed restaurant down the street to get a signal.

I was going over to the little cabin-themed restaurant down the street to get a signal.

I pulled on my shirt, grabbed my coat and wallet and Lieutenant Dan's leash. I clipped it to his collar faster than I've ever moved in my life and then started running with him the quarter mile to the restaurant. As soon as I made it to their patio, their Wi-Fi connected to my phone and her message pinged.

Briana: Nothing. So bored.

I stood there, panting.

A server nodded to an empty table and I realized how I looked—sweaty and out of breath, like I went jogging in my jacket and work boots.

The server set a menu on the table and I took a seat and stared at the screen wondering what I should reply. But before I got the chance to, she sent another message.

Briana: Can I just call u?

She wanted to talk? On the *phone*?

I raked my hand through my hair. I did want to talk to her. But this didn't really give me the time to change mental gears and get used to the idea that it was happening *right now*. I didn't really do spontaneity, especially in social situations.

But I *did* want to talk to her... I wanted to talk to her a lot.

Me: Sure.

I typed in my phone number.

My cell rang immediately. I picked up on the first ring, and then kicked myself for looking so eager.

"Hey," she said brightly.

This was the first word she'd spoken to me in person since the day over a week ago when she'd told me what cupcakes to bring.

"Hey," I said back.

"Sorry, it's just typing takes so long. Better just to talk to you," she said.

"Yeah. No problem."

"Okay, so I have to ask," she said. "And I need you to be super honest. Are you sending me all the butt stuff?"

I choked out a laugh. *"What?"*

"I have gotten *all* of the weird butt-stuff patients this week. A zucchini, a headless Barbie, an antique candlestick—and the guy asked me to be careful pulling it out because it was his *mother's*—are you sending me these? Do you have an arrangement with the charge nurses?"

I shook my head with a chuckle. "No. But if it makes you feel any better, I've gotten all the drunk frat boys this week. One pulled out his IV and stripped naked and took off and I had to tackle him before he escaped. Do *you* have an arrangement with the charge nurses?"

"Of course. But I'm not sending you all the naked drunk frat boys. I'm only sending you the runners."

I laughed so loud the waitress looked over at me.

"The last drunk frat boy I got thought he was in a drive-through," she said. "I had to be all like, 'Sir! This isn't an Arby's!'"

I had to pinch tears from my eyes. God, she was funny.

"Every day is a full moon around here," she said. "Was it this busy at Memorial West?"

I shook my head. "No, not this bad. But then they weren't a level-one trauma center, so…"

"Yeah, it keeps us from getting bored for sure. Do you like it better?"

I nodded. "I think I do. Never a dull moment."

She sounded like she was stretching. "Why'd you pick emergency medicine? I'd think it would be a hard specialty with your anxiety."

This was a common misconception. And I understood it—high-stress job, not great for the nerves. But it was perfect for me.

I'd always known what I was and was not capable of, even as a child. Your parents tell you that you can grow up to be anything. But I knew from the earliest age that wasn't true. I remember my teacher telling me I could be president one day, and me replying that I didn't want to because I didn't like parades.

"I did a short stint in the emergency department when I was in residency in Las Vegas," I said.

"You lived in Las Vegas?"

"Just for a few years. Zander and I were roommates—I don't know if you knew that. We go back a long time, he's one of my oldest friends. Anyway, he wanted to live there. It was close enough to Utah and I wanted to hike all the parks there, so I went with him. It was between pediatrics and emergency services, but I ended up picking the ER. It's so fast paced it makes me focus. It's like my brain gets quiet because it only has time for the task at hand. It's actually pretty relaxing."

"I guess that makes sense," she said. "You get in the zone. It makes work go by so fast. God, could you imagine being a surgeon? Nothing to do but think?"

"I would *hate* it."

"Did you ever see any celebrities over there?" she asked.

"Oh, yeah."

I couldn't tell her who because of HIPAA and she wouldn't ask for the same reason, but I could give her broad strokes. "Lots of performers," I said. "Mostly drunk. Contusions, lacerations. Once I had a big musician come through. He had a bruised hand, but I wrote it up as a fracture."

"You did? Why?"

I shrugged. "Something told me he needed to take some time off."

"That was nice of you. But what if you'd gotten busted?"

"I'd just do what our residents do to us. Act like I don't know what I'm doing."

She laughed. "It's a time-honored tradition."

I smiled. Then the server approached the table.

"Can you hold on a second?" I asked.

I put her on mute and ordered a salad and a club soda with lime. I wasn't hungry, but I was taking up the table. And I got Lieutenant Dan a grilled chicken breast with no seasoning and a bowl of water.

"Okay, I'm back," I said.

"So, what do you do for fun?" she asked. "Hector said he saw you at the Cockpit. Do you like bars?"

I shook my head. "No, definitely not."

I'd had a nightmare once about being in a crowded bar that didn't have table service and I had to order at the packed counter, squeezing in and shouting at the bartender. I'd woken up in a cold sweat.

"He must have seen me there last summer," I said. "I've only been in there once. Jewel's wife, Gwen, owns that bar. I went to the farmers' market with her. She wanted to bring stuff back, I carried a watermelon."

"You carried a watermelon?" She sounded amused.

"Yup. Nobody puts Baby in a corner."

She laughed at my *Dirty Dancing* reference and I smiled at making her do it.

"So if you don't like bars, where do you take dates?" she asked.

"I'm not dating. I'm just trying to get used to the new job right now. You're not dating either, right?"

She sighed. "I was trying to date for a little while. But it's bad out there."

"Really?" I asked. "How bad?"

"Oh boy, strap in. *Bad.* There was the guy who brought his three cats with him—"

"He brought his *cats?*"

"Yeah. I told him I like animals, so he brought his three tabbies. They were loose in the car. Then he realized they couldn't stay in there while we went to go eat, so he tried to get me to come back to his house to drop them off and see his custom catio."

"A what?"

"An enclosed patio for a cat. Which I *was* interested in seeing if I'm being totally honest, but I wasn't going into some rando's cat house to get murdered. The whole time he was trying to convince me to come he was wearing one of the cats around his shoulders like a shawl. It was so weird. Then there was the guy who wanted me to look at his rash—"

"I've had that date. Before my ex."

"Why is it always a rash?"

"Sometimes it's a mole."

She laughed, *hard*.

She continued, still cracking up. "One time I met this guy online and he was just like you. Handsome, smart, funny—*normal*. I kept wondering what the catch was. We made plans to go to dinner and the second we got our drinks he went into a pyramid-scheme pitch."

I chuckled. I also tried to hide how much I liked that she thought I was handsome and smart and funny.

"God, sometimes I think I only attract the weirdos," she said.

"You're a beautiful, intelligent woman," I said. "You attract everyone."

She went quiet at this and I wondered if I'd said something I shouldn't have. It just sort of came out. Maybe it came off as flirting and she didn't like that? But when she started talking again, she had a smile in her voice.

"It's amazing how much this dating stuff wears you down after a while. I'm over it. At this point I'd be excited if someone just had their shit together enough to have a headboard."

"Ha."

"Do *you* have a headboard?" she asked.

"Yes. Absolutely."

The server set my drink down in front of me.

"Congratulations. You're the one percent."

I was happy I seemed to have fallen into a category that she approved of, a man in possession of complete bedroom furniture.

"I'm a hair's breadth away from just finding other like-minded women and starting a coven," she said, going on. "Anyway, Lieutenant Dan is pretty cute."

I looked down at my dog, sleeping under the table at my feet.

"The rescue almost didn't let me have him."

"Why?"

"He didn't like men. We think he was abused by a man when he was a baby. He wouldn't even let me get near him."

"How'd you work through *that*?" she asked, sounding impressed.

"I showed up every day. I'd bring food for him and sit down on the floor and talk softly to him until he trusted me."

"*Awwwwww.* And were you the one to name him?"

"I was. It seemed appropriate."

"What happened to his leg?"

I squeezed lime into my club soda. "We think he was born that way. Probably at a puppy mill."

"Ugh. That's so sad. I used to get all the abused/neglected animal videos on TikTok before the algorithm realized I didn't like them. Animals adopting orphaned babies or military service members coming home and surprising their dogs—I am not emotionally equipped to deal with that kind of energy right now. Are you on TikTok?"

"No," I said. "Well, sort of. I watch videos on house restorations, but I don't post anything."

"I'm on lesbian TikTok right now and it is the most glorious place on earth."

"Really? I get a lot of Fail videos on my For You page, for some reason," I said. "I hate those."

"Me *too*. Like, how are you just gonna show us the accident and not give us the follow-up. I need a Six Months Later Where Are They Now video with a list of the injuries."

"*Yes*. It feels like a documentary that stops just as it's getting interesting."

"Right? Anyway, you have to engage with the app," she said. "Swipe away videos you don't like, like right away so they know what you don't want to see. You'll be in the warm embrace of lesbian TikTok with me in no time."

"Do the TikTok lesbians know how to remove old wallpaper? Because that's the kind of content I need at the moment."

"Oh, yeah. They know *everything*. It's where I learned how to fold a fitted sheet."

I made a *TikTok lesbians* mental note.

We stayed on the phone and talked about nothing like this for *hours*. The time just flew by. Talking to her was easy in a way I wasn't used to.

She drew me out. Made me feel comfortable. And the words just flowed. She made me feel interesting, like she wanted to know about me and what I had to say. And we had a lot in common too. I guess that made sense, we had the same job. But we both liked being out in nature. We liked cultural vacations over relaxing beach ones, and we liked the same movies. We even had the same Lola Simone songs in our phones.

About an hour into the call, it started to drizzle. I squeezed in under the not-big-enough table umbrella. I'd been in such a hurry I hadn't considered the logistics of bringing my dog. I couldn't go inside the restaurant because of Lieutenant Dan. I could hang up with Briana and run home and drop him off, then come back. But I got the feeling if I asked to call her back, she'd just say she'd talk to me on Tuesday, and I didn't want to risk it. So I huddled under the umbrella with rain soaking through the back of my jacket and Lieutenant Dan hiding under the table, drier than I was. The waitress looked at me like I'd lost it.

After three hours, a slice of rhubarb strawberry pie, and the sun starting to set, Briana hung up with me to go do Benny's dialysis.

The mosquitoes were eating me alive, so it was probably a good thing—but I still wouldn't have hung up with her first.

I liked her. A lot.

The weird thing was, she seemed to like me too, for some reason. I couldn't imagine why.

It filled me up. It made me smile when I thought back on it. Probably because I'd been feeling so flawed and rejected for the last few months and suddenly I wasn't. At least to her.

I didn't hear from her again for the rest of the weekend, but it didn't matter because I knew when I went back to work, we'd resume our back-and-forth. I looked forward to it. A little more than I wanted to admit.

On my way into the hospital on Tuesday, I ignored another call from Jewel. I still hadn't decided what I was going to do about the situation with my family. Call and cancel on family dinner tomorrow was about all I'd worked out.

Just as the stress of my new job and coworkers began to mercifully quiet down, the stress of my family began to ratchet up.

I made my way down to the ER for my shift, putting Jewel's number on mute so at the very least I wouldn't be alerted to exactly how many times my sister was trying to get me on the phone. I was coming down the hallway focused on this when Briana flew around the corner.

"There you are! Come on, you'll miss it!" She grabbed me by the elbow.

This was the first time she'd touched me outside of crashing into me. It made me feel a little breathless—the unexpected interaction *and* the contact.

"Miss what?" I asked, letting myself be dragged along.

"Opera Lady."

"Who?"

"There's this group of opera singers who come in drunk like once a month and they always sing in the ER. You *have* to see it. I was looking for you everywhere."

I stifled a smile.

We went through the double doors to the ER. There was already a small crowd hanging out outside room six when we sidled up to the front. An aria in a high soprano belted out of the room. Everyone stood silent, listening.

I knew this one. "Der Hölle Rache" from *The Magic Flute*. Mozart. Breathtaking high notes that rose like fiery sparks. I could hear the missing instruments in my mind. Flutes, oboes, violins, clarinets. I melted into the poignant vocal gymnastics of the piece. It was beautiful.

I glanced over at Briana while we listened. I'd noticed the way the staff had made a space for us, parting to let us through so we could be closer to the door. It was a sign of respect—and it wasn't for me.

I'd gotten more friendly nods since the cupcakes. The nurses weren't as cold to me anymore. But this reception to our arrival was for Briana. Her bringing me sent a message to everyone that I was liked by someone they loved and respected. Maybe she even went to get me in part to let everyone know this.

I felt myself soften. Like the fight-or-flight instinct this place had activated was finally dismissed.

I was always braced here. Braced for confrontation, braced for open dislike. Braced for unpleasantness in general. Only just now did my brain decide that I didn't need to be. And that was because of *her*.

I *liked* coming to work now. I looked forward to it. I got a little jolt of dopamine every time I saw a letter.

I got a little jolt of dopamine every time I saw her across the ER...

I knew for her they were probably just notes. She was likable and easy. She probably had this fun little back-and-forth with everyone in one way or another. But for me it was a lifeline. An outstretched hand while I was falling, an umbrella in a downpour. Friendship in a hostile place.

I'd been doing something for her the last few days. I'd been watching *Schitt's Creek*.

I didn't usually watch new shows. I just rewatched the same ones over and over. I liked the familiarity, the predictability. If I rewatched a show, there were never any surprises. No emotional jump scares. I didn't have to process new feelings or stress over cliffhangers. I knew where it was going and how it would end. Music too. When my anxiety is extra high, new music is too draining to process. I'd lean on old playlists. A lyrical safe space, the comfort of repetition. And my anxiety hadn't been as high as it was right now in longer than I could remember.

But I'd been watching *Schitt's Creek* because Briana had mentioned it on our phone call the other day, and I wanted to understand her references. I wanted to have things in common with her. I wanted to try the things she liked.

It was a small, invisible gesture of friendship from me. Something she'd likely never even fully appreciate because she didn't know the effort that came with it. She'd just think I watch the same popular show she does and that would be it. This was me making space for her, even though she would never know it. My way of saying thank you for her friendship, even if it was too quiet to hear.

The singing stopped. Half the group was dabbing at tears.

Everyone started dispersing and I turned to Briana. "She's good," I said. "Amazing she can do that drunk."

"You should hear the tenor."

Then we just sort of stood there, like we weren't sure how to proceed now that the distraction was over.

God, she really was beautiful. She had her hair up in a loose ponytail, reading glasses on.

I cleared my throat. "Thank you for getting me. I appreciate it. It means a lot to be included."

"I told you I was going to." Then her brows drew down. "You are *covered* in mosquito bites."

I looked at my arms. "Yeah. The cabin's buggy." *Or rather the table on the patio of the restaurant I talked to her at was buggy...*

She put a thumb over her shoulder. "So I was going to go visit the sob closet around noon today—"

"Oh. Good to know," I said. "I'll schedule my breakdown around two to give you a chance to finish up."

She laughed. "No. Do you want to meet me? I was just going to have my lunch in there. There's a new box of paper towels, so we both have a seat now."

The corner of my lip twitched. "I could eat at noon. You don't want to eat in the doctors' lounge, though? Or the cafeteria?"

Not that I wanted to. Frankly, I preferred the supply closet. Most days I ate lunch there or in my truck. I liked the quiet. But it was an odd choice for her.

She shook her head. "The closet's quiet."

"The closet *is* quiet," I agreed.

She smiled. "Cool. See you at noon."

She made a finger gun at me and joined a small group of nurses who were waiting for her. I watched her walk down the hall and turn a corner.

Then the panic set in. I obsessed over what to eat for the next four hours.

I didn't want anything that would stink up the small space. No feta cheese or heavy garlic. We wouldn't have a table, so nothing that required silverware. Soup was out of the question. I didn't want anything crunchy since it would be amplified in the tiny room. No apples or chips. I finally decided on a sandwich—no onions and no spinach in case it got stuck in my teeth—with a fruit cup.

It occurred to me that this overthinking was very likely *not* happening on her end. But I was too self-conscious for this.

Eating was intimate. It took me a long time to truly feel comfortable doing it in front of someone.

It took me a long time to feel comfortable doing a lot of things in front of someone.

At noon I let myself into the supply closet with my food. She was in the same spot as last time, looking at her phone. When she saw me, she peered up and smiled warmly. "Hey."

She had a Cup Noodles on the floor next to her and she picked it up as I shut the door. "I waited for you to eat," she said.

"You didn't have to do that," I said, sitting on the paper-towel box.

She pulled out a plastic utensil and took the cover off her noodles. "So what'd you get?"

"Just a sandwich," I said, leaving out the part where it took me all day to decide on it.

I unwrapped it on my lap and felt a twinge of dismay as I realized they'd put vinegar on it. I looked up at her to see if she had any reaction to the smell, but she was twisting noodles around her fork and pulling them to her mouth, catching the fallout in the cup—and I realized this woman didn't care. She didn't care what she looked like eating and she probably didn't care what my damn sandwich smelled like either. Hell, the whole room smelled like soup.

I relaxed a little. I had to remember that not everyone over-thought everything the way I did.

Wouldn't it be amazing to live like that? To not carry that burden around with you. To not feel constantly overwhelmed and overstimulated and second-guess every little thing.

It got better the more I got to know people. At Memorial West my anxiety was hardly a problem at all. They were my friends there, my team. I was used to them and comfortable around them.

All things considered, I was comfortable around Briana too, I realized.

Briana made me nervous, but she didn't make me uncomfortable. That was a big distinction. For me, nervousness usually got better with time. Uncomfortable didn't.

At least it didn't with Amy.

Amy never stopped making me uncomfortable. She still did. Mostly because I don't think she knew me well enough to know how not to.

I took a bite of my sandwich while Briana ate her noodles, and we fell into a silence. But unlike most silences, this one didn't feel awkward. It was like the pause between our letters. Just a small break in the dialogue.

Briana reached down and picked up a Snapple. "What's on your socks?" she asked, nodding at my ankles.

I pulled my pant leg up to look. "Elephants."

"Do you always wear animal socks?"

"I do it for my niece and nephew. They like them."

"Are you going to see them today?"

I shook my head. "No. But kids like them, so I always wear them to work."

She smiled. "Can I ask you a question?" she asked, putting the cap back on her drink.

I wiped my mouth with a napkin. "Sure."

"You said your mom had a kidney transplant?"

I nodded. "She has lupus. Her best friend donated."

She paused for a moment. "How is she?"

"She's great. Healthy. Her lupus is managed for the most part." I peered at her. "How's your brother?"

She shrugged, looking into her soup cup. "He's not really thriving on dialysis. I thought by now he'd at least be getting adjusted, but..." She went quiet again. "He's so depressed I'm beginning to think that his infected catheter was on purpose."

I blinked at her. "You think he's suicidal?"

She poked at her soup. "I don't think he wanted to die so much as he just doesn't have any interest in living like this anymore."

I stared at her. I had no idea it was that bad.

She still didn't look at me. "I think if it had been more gradual, it wouldn't have hit him so hard. But it all happened so fast. He lost his job because he couldn't work with his health issues. Then his girlfriend broke up with him a few months into it, which didn't help."

I knew this. Gibson had mentioned it. But having it confirmed was upsetting all over again. "Because he was sick?" I asked, incredulous.

She gave a one-shoulder shrug. "I don't know that she left because he was sick, or more that he stopped being the person she knew he once was. He got moody and short with her, self-conscious about his body. He didn't want to be touched. Maybe he pushed her away. I don't know."

Not a good enough reason. I could never leave someone I love when they need me—especially if they were sick.

I studied Briana's face. She looked so tired when she talked about her brother.

"Any status on a donor?" I asked.

She shook her head. "No. I have a website for it, and we all have HELP BENNY FIND A KIDNEY. YOU COULD BE THE MATCH! stickers on our cars. But it's been eight months since I started looking for someone."

"Do you have any more stickers? I'll put one on my truck."

She looked up at me and brightened. "You will?"

"Yes, of course."

She beamed at me like this tiny thing was everything. "Thank you. And thanks for having lunch with me," she said.

"Anytime," I said, meaning it more than I think she knew. "Maybe next time we can do the cafeteria."

She laughed a little. "I know you don't like loud, crowded places. I never see you in the lounge. I just figured you'd be more comfortable here."

Now *my* face went soft.

She'd picked here on purpose? For *me*?

Briana had just managed to do what Amy never could after almost three years together. She took me someplace to meet for lunch that wouldn't make me anxious.

It wasn't Amy's fault I was like this. But I wondered if we'd still be together if every date with her didn't wear me out. Would we have seen each other more if it wasn't so exhausting for me? Maybe she would have known me better if she'd understood *how* to get to know me better. Like this. Putting me at ease. Meeting me halfway.

Someone knocked on the supply room door. I was sitting against it, so I had to get up to open it.

"Expecting someone?" Briana teased.

I was smiling at this when I opened the door, but the second I saw who it was, my expression flatlined. It was *Jewel*.

"What...what are you doing here?" I asked, confused.

She crossed her arms over her hot pink T-shirt. "I had to do a wellness check since nobody can seem to get you on the phone. Some nurse told me you were eating lunch in a closet?"

Then she peered past me at Briana. A huge grin ripped across my sister's face.

"Hey," Briana said, getting up with a smile. "You must be Jewel."

My sister had a shaved head, she was covered in tattoos, and she looked just like me. She wasn't hard to spot based on my brief story about her.

Jewel looked positively elated. "I am. And you are?"

"Briana," she said brightly, offering a hand.

"Briana. Very nice to meet you." My sister shook her hand, beaming. "So what are you two doing in here?" she asked, looking back and forth between us.

"We're just having lunch," I said.

"I see. Well, now that I know you're alive, I'll let you kids get back to it. Call me after work."

"Yes, sure."

She gave me a smile I couldn't interpret and left. I shut the door and sat back down.

"She's nice," Briana said, picking up her Snapple. "In an I-gave-you-a-lawn-mower-chest-tattoo kind of way."

I scoffed.

"Does your family do these wellness checks often?"

"She's very in my business right now," I said. "They all are."

"Why?"

"Eh, it's a long story."

She looked at her watch. "We have fifteen more minutes."

"It's going to take longer than fifteen minutes."

"Okay. Want to meet for drinks after work? Everyone's going to Mafi's for Hector's birthday. We can get our own booth while we do our part to keep the liquor industry strong."

I laughed. Then I immediately wondered if she really wanted

me to go, or did she invite me because she didn't think I'd actually come? I studied her expression. She looked almost hopeful. She really *was* trying to include me.

"I'm actually going anyway," I said. "With Zander." He'd texted me earlier for drinks after work.

"Perfect. I'll come say hi."

When our break was over, I held the door for her to let her out. "See you tonight," she said before heading back to her side of the ER. As I watched her go, my cell pinged from my pocket. Then it pinged again and again and again in quick succession.

I pulled out my phone to see what was going on, and the second I saw it, my smile fell.

Oh *no*...

CHAPTER 13

JACOB

I stared at the string of texts from my family that had been streaming in since lunchtime. Everyone but Dad. Lots of exclamation marks and heart-eye emojis. I dragged a hand down my mouth.

I was sitting at Mafi's with Zander having the after-work drinks I'd promised him earlier. Briana was across the restaurant with the birthday crowd. I could see her laughing with Hector against the bar.

"This is so bad," I muttered, putting my phone facedown and my palms to my eyeballs.

Jewel thought Briana was my girlfriend.

It didn't even occur to me at the time how that whole thing had looked, me alone in a supply closet with a woman, Briana knowing my sister sight unseen, like a girlfriend would. No wonder Jewel'd been so smiley.

She told everyone she'd met my girlfriend. She'd even gone so far as to search the Royaume Northwestern website to get Briana's bio and photo, which she then shared in the group text.

"What's bad?" Zander asked.

I sat back in my seat and paused for a long moment. "I messed up," I said finally.

"With what?"

"My family. I told them I have a girlfriend."

He blinked at me. "Why the hell did you do that?"

I blew a breath through my lips. "They're worried about me. Jeremiah and Amy getting married. I just wanted them to think I was okay."

His smile moved into a low chuckle. "Damn. Your mom's going to lose her *shit* when she finds out about this. You're gonna get psychoanalyzed within an inch of your life."

"I know," I said. "But it gets worse. They think it's Briana."

"*Our* Briana? *That* Briana?" He nodded to her sitting at the bar with Hector.

"Jewel came to see me today and I was eating lunch with her in the supply closet by Gibson's office. She assumed."

"Well, what are they saying?" Zander asked.

I glanced at my phone. "That my girlfriend is beautiful. That they can't wait to meet her. That we were making out in a supply closet."

He practically howled.

"She *is* single, you know," he said, still cracking up. "Check this out. The jackass she was married to? Cheated on her with her friend." He shook his head. "Idiot. You should have seen what she did to him when she caught him."

I wrinkled my forehead. "What did she do?"

"Not my place to tell you. You should ask her. Let's just say he got what he had coming, and I hope I'm *never* on her bad side." He laughed again.

I took a deep breath. "I'm calling my family." I picked up my phone and went to dial, but he stopped me.

"Just hold up a second. Hold up," he said. "Why don't you just ask her?"

"Ask her what?"

He shrugged. "Ask her to be your date to the wedding stuff."

"They think she's my *girlfriend*. A date isn't going to do it."

He shrugged again. "Well, ask her to be your girlfriend."

I stared at him incredulously.

"Not for real. Ask her to help you out."

When I didn't reply, he leaned forward on the table. "Look, Briana is cool as hell. She'd probably do it. Especially if you're her brother's kidney donor—" He bounced his eyebrows and grinned.

I stared at him a second. "I was a match?"

He shook his head. "You didn't just match. It was perfect—well, as perfect as it can get, outside of growing your own organs. I mean this kid's not gonna find anything better, I'll tell you that."

A match.

In the last two weeks Zander had sent me for a physical and a mental health evaluation, in addition to the labs. I guess that should have been a good indication that things were lining up. Still, the news surprised me.

"Give me the broad strokes."

"Okay," he said, leaning back in the booth. "Well, all the standard surgical risks. Pain, infection, hernia. Bleeding, blood clots. General anesthesia, two- to three-hour surgery for a laparoscopic nephrectomy. Afterward, a couple of follow-up visits. No driving for two weeks, no lifting anything over ten pounds for a month. That's it. Donors have the same life expectancy as non-donors. You'll go on with your life."

I sat back in my seat. "I need to think about this."

"Of course."

"It's not really a good time for me. I've got wedding stuff for the next few months."

"We can schedule it when you want."

"And I don't know if Gibson will give me the time off—"

"He will. I already asked him."

I snorted.

"Look, I'm not trying to pressure you," he said. "But I'd be lying if I said I didn't hope you did it. This is the best possible scenario for this kid. And Briana's a friend of mine, and I want to see her relax a little bit. It's been hard on her."

Briana. That was a bonus to doing this, if I was being honest. I liked her. Not that she'd know it was me if I did decide to do it. I wanted to donate anonymously.

"I need to think about it," I said. It was a big decision.

He nodded. "Okay. But I'm just sayin'. This would definitely get you a wedding date."

"If I do it, I don't want anyone knowing it's me."

He looked at me like I was speaking in tongues. "Why not? Man, you'd be the hero of the whole ER. They'd probably throw you a damn parade—"

"That is exactly why I don't want anyone to know. I wouldn't be doing it for the recognition. I'd be doing it to help him. I don't like that kind of attention."

I didn't even tell anyone it was my last day at Memorial West. I didn't want anyone to make a big deal about it. I didn't even like people singing "Happy Birthday" to me. Getting tearful thank-yous from Benny's family and backslaps and handshakes from strangers was my idea of hell.

"If I do it, we're doing it anonymously and we're doing it at the transplant center down at the Mayo in Rochester, not here. I don't want anyone poking their head into my recovery room."

He let out a sigh. "All right, all right. It's your thing, I will respect it. But I still think you should ask her."

I rubbed my forehead tiredly. "I can't ask her to do this," I mumbled.

"Why? What's the worst thing she can say? No?" He took a swallow of his old-fashioned. "Just tell her what you told me. Level with her. Plus your family's fucking hilarious. She'd probably have the time of her life over there."

I let out a long breath. "She'd probably think we're a bunch of weirdos."

The idea of her being submerged into that chaos was enough to give me heart palpitations. Grandpa trying to run people into the bushes in his electric wheelchair, Mom talking about sex toys and lubricants, while Jafar squawked profanities. No. God, no.

Zander swayed his tumbler at me. "Your family is *awesome*. Hell, *I'd* be your date if I could. And I wanna see if you can pull this shit off." He chuckled into his glass.

I looked at my phone and the string of texts. They didn't even need me for this conversation, they were off to the races all on their own. They bought this hook, line, and sinker. And why wouldn't they?

It felt like some strange self-fulfilling prophecy, like I'd created Briana by speaking the lie into the universe. She was exactly the kind of woman I would like to bring home to my family. Smart, successful, likable—beautiful. And she worked with me, just like I'd alluded to when I told them I was seeing someone. Absolutely nobody would feel sorry for me because my ex was marrying my brother if I showed up with this woman on my arm. She was, for all intents and purposes, perfect.

But I had no idea how to broach this subject with her. At *all*. And part of me worried that if I did, she'd be so turned off or weirded out by it that she'd stop talking to me altogether.

This new friendship was the only good thing happening to me at the moment. I didn't want to jeopardize that.

Still, the idea of admitting to my family that there was no girlfriend...I couldn't tell which scenario was worse: the one where I maybe scared off the only friend I'd made since coming here, or the one where I showed up alone while Amy married Jeremiah and everyone watched to see if I'd die of a broken heart.

"How did I get myself into this situation?" I breathed.

Zander shook his head. "Just *ask* her. Trust me. She's one of the coolest people I know."

I glanced at my phone again. This time Dad had texted. Can't wait to meet her.

Everyone wanted me to be okay. They were so happy because this was *proof* that I was okay, that I'd moved on, that I was whole. It was permission for them to let the Amy/Jeremiah thing go, to be excited for them, to accept this new reality. I could feel the elation coming through my phone, the collective sigh of relief that this was a real thing, a real woman—real closure to what had happened.

If I'd had any doubts about how badly my family needed this, this was the answer.

I glanced at Briana across the restaurant. This time she was looking back. She waved, and leaned in and said something to Hector. He looked over at me and waved too. Then she jumped off her barstool and headed in our direction.

I got instantly nervous. Like she'd somehow know about the miscommunication with my family and demand an explanation. I felt myself clamming up the closer she got, like my ability to speak was being sucked into a vacuum.

"Hey," she said as she got to the table. "You came." She smiled at me in a way that made her whole face light up.

Luckily I didn't have to answer, because Zander broke in. "Sit," he said, scooting over.

She slid into the booth, set her purse next to her, and plucked one of Zander's french fries off his plate and ate it. "What are you guys talking about over here?" she asked, chewing. "I can hear you laughing across the restaurant."

Zander pushed his plate toward her and nodded at me. "Talking about the time Jacob carried an injured ATV driver out of the woods a few years ago."

I blinked at him. That was *not* what we were talking about. It was a true story, but we hadn't brought it up in years. What was he doing? Was he wingmanning me?

Briana arched an eyebrow at me. "Oh yeah? What happened?"

I cleared my throat. "He crashed it. Broke both feet. We couldn't get a signal to call for help."

"And you piggybacked him?"

I nodded. "It took three hours."

"And that was *funny*?" she asked, looking back and forth between us.

Zander didn't skip a beat. "The guy threw up down his back on the hike out."

Briana choked on her giggle. Well, so much for the wingmanning.

"That was nice of you, though," she said, still cracking up. Then she leaned in a little. "Just so you know, I forbade Hector to come over here." She nodded back to the bar. "That's today's drunk extrovert."

I laughed a little.

Then she seemed to remember something, and she reached down next to her and started rummaging in her purse. "I forgot. Here's the sticker for your car," she said.

She slid it facedown across the table toward me. "Thanks for taking one."

I put a hand on top of it. "Of course."

"I have to get back over there," she said, looking at her watch. "Hey, why don't you tell me that family-story thing at lunch tomorrow? Supply closet? Noon?"

I nodded. "Sure."

"You guys have fun!" she said, plucking another french fry off Zander's plate. Then she slid out of the booth and was gone, back to her side of the restaurant.

"See? She's cool," Zander said, taking his fries back. "I'm telling you, ask her."

I watched her walk back to the bar and hop onto the barstool next to Hector.

I picked up the bumper sticker and looked at it a moment. It was white with blue letters. It said Help Benny Find a Kidney. You Could Be the Match! There was a website under it.

It felt so futile. Like a shout into the void.

This kid was never going to find someone. It was going to take him years.

I'd never imagined donating a kidney to someone I didn't know. I'd figured if I ever did it, it'd be for someone in my life, not a stranger. A part of me even thought I should hold off in case Mom needed another transplant—though I knew she had four other kids who would gladly step in. She didn't need me to save mine.

I stared at the sticker.

I didn't know Benny. But I *did* know his sister. If I did this, it wouldn't just change his life. It would change *hers*.

I looked across the restaurant at Briana. She was laughing with some of the nurses. But I remembered the look on her face earlier when she talked about her brother. I remembered the day he came into the ER and the panic in her voice when she was treating him. I remembered the way she cried in the supply closet that time I walked in on her...How despondent she was. How helpless she probably felt. It was how I would have felt if Mom hadn't gotten a donor when she did.

She must have sensed me looking at her, because she peered up at me and smiled. A beautiful, genuine, friendly smile.

And in that instant I decided.

"I'm in," I said, talking to Zander but looking at her.

There was a moment of silence next to me. "I'm sorry, I didn't get that."

I looked at him. "I'm in. I'll do it. I'll donate."

He smacked a hand on the table. "All right! Yes!" Then he paused. "You're sure?"

I nodded. "I'm sure."

He grinned. "I'll tell him tonight. That kid's gonna lose his shit. Seriously, man. You have no idea what this means to them. You're doing a good thing." He paused. "And you're *sure* you wanna do this anonymously?"

I nodded. "I'm sure. Don't tell anyone. No one. Not even my mom."

"You're not telling your *mom*?"

"No. I'm not telling anyone."

It wasn't that I didn't want my family to know. It was that I didn't want *Briana* to know. I didn't want her to feel like she owed me anything or was obligated to be my friend because of this. I didn't want strings or the recognition. I just wanted to help her, and I wanted to do it in secret, and my family knowing was too risky. Contact with her had already been breached. I couldn't trust that Jewel wouldn't show up at my work again and casually mention me donating a kidney to someone. And Mom too. She knew too many people and there were too many opportunities for this to leak. I wanted it quiet and confidential, at least for now.

And then I had to laugh, because it occurred to me that

it was easier for me to donate an entire organ than it was to ask a woman to pose as my girlfriend and come with me to a few family gatherings. My fear of rejection and judgment was that acute.

I guess I just had to decide what scared me the most. Showing up to this wedding alone, or making Briana Ortiz an indecent proposal.

CHAPTER 14

BRIANA

When I got home, Alexis was sitting on the porch swing in front of my house.

"What are you doing here?" I said, closing my car door. "I thought you weren't coming until tomorrow!" I ran to hug her.

"I'm staying the night," she said with her chin over my shoulder, her pregnant belly pressed into mine. "Figured you needed emotional support. Jessica came down today to do a free clinic at my office and she mentioned something about the forest reclaiming the land?"

I laughed and let her go.

"You all right?" she asked, eyeing me.

I sighed. "I'm fine. Sort of."

As fine as anyone could be on the eve of their divorce.

Tomorrow was the nineteenth. It was finally here. D-day. I'd planned on working and acting like it was any other Wednesday. I'd told Alexis numerous times over the last two weeks not to come. But she came anyway.

I loved her for it.

She looked great. Her red hair was in a ponytail, and she had on a dark green fitted T-shirt and jeans. Small baby bump. No makeup. Everything about her was relaxed. So different than she used to be, back before Daniel. I was *also* different than I used to be, but not in a good way.

She grabbed a duffel from the swing bench and a brown paper bag. "I brought you muffins," she said. "I made them from scratch."

"Of course you did. You're a country girl now. Did you churn your own butter?"

She laughed. "Shut up," she said, following me in.

Justin, Benny's friend, met us at the door on his way out.

"Hey," I said, surprised and happy that someone was here.

"Hey."

Benny was in the living room behind him on the sofa. He looked up at Alexis with that flat expression he always wore these days before staring blankly at the TV again.

"Did you guys have a good day?" I asked Justin, my voice hopeful.

He pressed his lips together in a way that meant no.

"We're gonna go to GameStop tomorrow, right, buddy?" Justin called over his shoulder.

Benny didn't answer. Justin looked back at me as if to say, This is how he was all day.

"Thanks for trying," I said quietly.

"Yeah. Of course." He glanced at Benny again. "We'll try again tomorrow."

Justin was a good friend. Brad too. The three of them were tight. Justin's dad had died a few years ago and Benny and Brad had been there for him during that, and now the guys were here for Benny. Both had been tested to see if they were a kidney match. All of Benny's friends had. But after that, they started to drop off one at a time. With the exception of Justin and Brad, no one else really came around anymore. I was infinitely grateful to the ones who did.

Justin left. I put Alexis into the guest room, and then we went to set Benny up on dialysis. Alexis helped me get him situated. We spoke without saying a word the whole time. After ten years of working together plus med school, we had our own language. She was concerned about him.

His physical deterioration had to be shocking for her. He'd lost at least thirty pounds in the six months since she'd last seen him. He was in shorts. His legs were so thin they looked like ropes with knots in the middle. He hadn't shaved, his eyes were sunken. He'd barely said two words to us the whole time we were setting him up.

Alexis made eye contact with me while she checked his blood pressure. It was the same look she gave me back when we worked together, the one that meant we needed to discuss the patient in private.

I had to look away from her.

I hated that this was the state of things now. That I didn't have a better life to show her, happy news to share. That she had to come here because I was going to be divorced tomorrow and she didn't want me to be alone and then when she got here, this was my life. This old, worn-down house, my sick brother. My broken heart.

It was pathetic.

I peered around my living room, trying to focus on anything other than my best friend's worried gaze and my languishing patient, but the rest of the scene wasn't any better—the ugly, tired couch, the brown shag carpet, the fucking cat tree.

A sudden surge of despair washed over me.

There were times when my protective shield cracked down the middle. When the anger parted and the sad seeped through. I *hated* when it did. At least when I stayed mad, the emotion was directed outward and not in. But it was too heavy today. The feelings collapsed onto me and I broke.

I pretended I needed to go get a blanket for Benny in the linen closet and excused myself. The second I got around the corner I stopped in the hallway and burst into muffled tears.

What was my fucking life? How had I ended up here?

Everything had gone wrong.

Once the tears started, I just couldn't get them to stop. It was an avalanche. A tidal wave. Proof that I really, *really* wasn't okay.

Nick.

It was over. It was officially over.

I didn't want to celebrate my divorce. I didn't want to pop champagne or hit the town and act like I was happy to be done with my marriage. I wasn't happy. I was living a nightmare. Some alternate reality that I was never supposed to know.

Nick and I were supposed to grow old together. It was *good*. We were happy.

But I just wasn't *her*.

I think I always knew something was there. She was his partner at work. They'd never dated. She had a boyfriend when I met Nick and then she had a husband. We went to BBQs at each other's houses, we went on couples' trips together. I *liked* her. She was my friend.

And now I saw the truth I couldn't recognize then.

I saw Nick at her wedding, drinking more than I'd ever seen him drink and passing out on the bed in our hotel room, still in his clothes.

I saw them whisper-arguing in the kitchen the night of our ten-year anniversary dinner, and he said it was about work and I believed it because I wanted to believe it. I saw all the times he was moody and distant because I wasn't her and that annoyed him.

It was like finding out you have cancer and finally connecting all the dots and realizing you've been seeing the symptoms for years and wondering how something so horrible could be something you missed. And now I wondered how I'd been so stupid. How I didn't know until that day.

Mom was right.

Only an idiot puts all their eggs in a man's basket. And I'd given Nick everything. Now I had nothing, not even hope. Because he broke the trust in men that I'd need to ever be with one again. There wouldn't be a next time for me. There wouldn't be a second husband, another love of my life. There would only ever be this.

"Hey. You okay?" Alexis asked gently from behind me.

I turned around, wiping under my eyes. "Yeah. Sorry. I just..."

I shook my head, doing my best to regain my composure. "It just all sort of hit me."

She reached into the bathroom and pulled some tissues from a box and handed them to me. Then she leaned on the wall opposite me.

"Thanks." I sniffed, dabbing at my eyes.

She waited, peering at me quietly.

I took a deep breath and let it out slowly. "Do you remember teleporting when you were little?"

"What?"

"You know, when you were a kid and you'd fall asleep in the car and your dad would carry you to bed and you wouldn't remember it? You'd just have a foggy memory of floating through space. And then you'd wake up in bed the next morning not remembering how you got there, but sort of remembering it at the same time?"

She narrowed her eyes like she was thinking. "Yeah. Only it was never my dad. It was the nanny. But yeah."

I sniffed. "My dad was gone by the time I was eight. I never teleported again after that. There wasn't anyone strong enough to carry me." I paused for a long moment. "Men have only ever left me, Ali," I said quietly.

She waited, silent.

"You never realize you're living the best time of your life," I said softly. "It happens and then it ends, and you only see it for what it was after. I gave Nick the part of me I don't give anyone. I gave him the kind of stupid, innocent love that you can only give before you know better. He got the best of me. And I'll never find that me again."

"Yes, you will—"

I shook my head. "No. I won't. Because I'll never be that trusting again. I'll never give myself to someone else with the complete abandon that I did with Nick. I don't have it in me. He was the exception. He was me saying 'Okay, so Dad left. But this one won't. I picked right, not all men are like Dad. This one's going to carry me. All my broken pieces.'" I paused. "And he didn't. He did *exactly* what Mom always warned me that men do. He validated every cautionary tale I grew up hearing. Always have a separate bank account. Make sure your name is on the house. Trust but verify." I shook my head again. "I didn't listen," I whispered. "And now I'll never teleport again."

She looked at me, her eyes sad. "This isn't your life, Bri. This is just a shitty chapter in your story. You know, I didn't think I'd ever date again after Neil, but then I found Daniel. There are good men out there, you'll find someone too."

I scoffed dryly. "That ship has sailed. I am no longer a reliable source of judgment when it comes to picking men." I wiped under my eyes and took in a deep breath.

"Speaking of husbands," I said, changing the subject. "I can't believe you actually left yours home alone."

"The sex is better when I'm gone for a bit."

"Oh, so *now* I get why you came to see me. This is foreplay."

She laughed.

I sighed. "I wish marriage came with an app that makes it so your husband's penis only works for one user. Like a phone that only you can unlock? I would have given it to you as a wedding gift."

"I don't think I have to worry about that with Daniel."

I nodded. "You're probably right. He'll make a good teleporter one day—but just keep a separate bank account. Trust me on this one."

She smiled. Then she gave me a playful eyebrow. "You know, Doug is still single."

I gagged and she cracked up. Her husband's crusty best friend had followed me around with a guitar at their wedding.

"I'm not that desperate," I said. "Yet."

We were giggling at this when the screaming started.

Benny.

Alexis and I looked at each other for a split second before we bolted.

Everything moved in slow motion after that.

Down the hallway, around the corner, into the living room— I was braced for something awful. A disconnected tube, blood everywhere. But when I got in the room, he was right where we left him, still hooked up to the machine.

He was crying, hysterical.

Alexis and I both darted to his side, going into ER mode, frantically checking wires and screens on the dialysis machine while he screamed.

"What's wrong?" I said, touching dials. "Benny!"

He was so worked up he couldn't even form words.

Alexis shook her head. "This looks fine. It's not the machine."

I turned to my brother, frantic. "Benny, what is it?!"

And then I saw he wasn't just crying. He was *laughing*. Manic, high-pitched laughing between sobs.

"Zander..." he managed, looking up at me with tears in his eyes. "He just called...I...I have a donor."

CHAPTER 15

JACOB

I could feel the buzz before I even walked into the ER. The mood on the floor was palpable. Everyone was happy and chattering. And when I saw Briana by the nurses' station, a group huddled around her, I knew why. Zander must have told Benny.

I smiled and stood back and watched, my hands in my pockets. Briana was glowing. Laughing, smiling. Someone hugged her. Then someone else.

My own smile reached my eyes.

She looked up and saw me and waved excitedly. Then she said something to everyone and jogged over to me.

"Did you hear?" She was beaming.

"No," I said, playing dumb. "What's up?"

"Benny has a kidney donor."

I grinned at her. "That's wonderful."

She bit her bottom lip and bounced a little. "Thank you for putting the sticker on your car. I mean I know it wasn't from that. Too soon. But stuff like that made this happen. So thank you."

"Of course." I just stood there, smiling.

She started to tear up a bit and wiped under her eyes. "I'm sorry.

I'm so emotional. This was so unexpected. I can't do lunch with you today, my best friend is in town. Tomorrow? Supply room? You have to tell me that family thing."

I nodded. "Yeah. Sure. See you then."

Then I watched her go back to a group of waiting nurses.

I didn't even realize how good this would feel. I was glad to be the source of everyone's happiness, even though they didn't know it was me. But mostly I liked seeing Briana so excited. I couldn't have anticipated how much joy that would bring me.

It occurred to me that the same way Briana had shut off my anxiety by welcoming me to Royaume, I had probably just done the same for her. An instant relief. It made me smile to think of it like that. Like I'd paid her kindness forward, even though it was in secret.

I hoped Benny was celebrating today. But I had to admit, I was more invested in how Briana took it. I was stressed about the dinner tonight with my family, but I was in a good mood all morning anyway.

My life was a mess. But at least Briana's was the way it should be.

CHAPTER 16

BRIANA

I'd just finished lunch in the cafeteria with Alexis, and she'd gone back to my house. I swung by Gibson's office on the last ten minutes of my break and knocked on his door frame. He held up a finger, asking me to wait while he wrapped up his call.

I needed to ask for the days off for Benny's transplant in July. I was practically bouncing. I'd been like this since last night. I couldn't stop smiling.

It was like a light had switched on inside my brother; the change was instantaneous.

He'd stayed up with me and Alexis celebrating. Brad and Justin came over, and my brother was joking and laughing and was *Benny* for the first time in so long, I wanted to cry even thinking about it. This morning, he was on his treadmill when I got up. He said if he wanted to be ready for the next marathon, he had to start training now. Then he ate a full breakfast. All of it. I'd had to muscle down the happy sob that came out of my mouth.

Someone had given me my brother back.

I didn't know who the donor was or how they found us. All we were told was that they were available for a late July transplant, they wanted to do it at Mayo Clinic, and that they wished to stay anonymous. Zander said they were a perfect match.

A *perfect* match.

I'd been braced for today to be so shitty. And now I didn't even care that I was officially divorced. Didn't care. Nothing could cast a shadow on this moment. Not even Nick.

Gibson hung up the phone and motioned me inside.

I stood in front of his desk feeling buoyant and light. "I need to request two weeks off in July," I said.

"All right." He logged on to his computer. "Going anywhere fun?" he asked, tapping into his keyboard.

"Rochester. To the transplant center."

He stopped and looked up at me over his glasses with a grin. "Well, I'll be damned. You see? Everything happens for a reason." He went back to tapping. "And to think he might have gone to a different hospital."

I laughed a little. "Why would Benny go to a different hospital?"

"Not Benny. Jacob. He'd never have met your brother if he had. Look at that, everything works out." He shook his head with a smile and went back to the screen.

I stood there, my brain trying to make sense of what he was saying. "Jacob?" I asked.

"He's doing it for Joy," he said, talking to the screen. "Did he tell you that? His mother had a kidney transplant when he was a kid. Always dreamed of paying it forward. At least that's what he said when Zander asked him if he wanted to run the labs. Glad it worked out."

My soul. Left. *My body.*

"*Jacob* is my brother's kidney donor?" I breathed.

Gibson looked up at me. "What's that?"

I swallowed. "The donor is anonymous..."

I watched Gibson's smile melt, then morph into sheer panic.

"It's…he didn't…Briana, I had no idea." He stuttered. "He spoke about it freely, the…the two of you seemed to be friends—you…you were eating lunch together yesterday. I—I didn't know, I just assumed…"

I turned and ran. I had to find him. Now. *Immediately.*

I threw open the door to our supply closet as I darted past. He wasn't there, so I bolted to the ER floor dialing his number.

My heartbeat was thudding in my ears, my mind careening forward faster than I could keep up, the details shifting and reconfiguring.

Jacob was Benny's kidney donor.

Jacob. Was Benny's. Kidney. *Donor.*

How???

I'd been so mean to him.

I wasn't even nice to him in the beginning. I was a total nightmare. And he'd have to have been working on this even back then because it takes weeks for the labs and the tissue samples and the medical and mental health evaluations, and I knew they took that long because I'd done them myself once when *I* was trying to see if I was a match.

I pulled back sliding glass doors to patient rooms and yanked away curtains with my phone to my ear, his number ringing. He didn't answer, so I ran through the doctors' lounge and checked the stairwell and the cafeteria.

Then I started to cry.

He didn't want me to know.

He didn't want *any* of us to know. He just wanted to do this in secret when he could have done this in the open and let everyone love him for it—and they would have. Every single person who worked in this department would have instantly adored him for his selfless act, worshipped the ground he walked on. He would have been beloved, forgiven for anything, a hero.

But Jacob wasn't like that. He *was* a hero, but he was the kind that never let anyone know.

A sob burst from my mouth, and I had to cover it with a hand.

Jessica was right. He was an excellent human being.

I felt my chest filling up, like love and gratitude and appreciation were solids that took up space inside me. I could feel the emotions pouring from my heart, streaming from the tips of my fingers, bursting from my mouth like a shout.

I would jump in front of a bus for this man. Take a bullet. Fight a mob. I would defend him to the death, kill someone for so much as looking at him wrong.

I wanted to go back in time and punch *myself* in the face for causing him even a moment of unhappiness. My devotion to him shot adrenaline into my system, made me feel frantic to find him so I could thank him, even though thanking him wasn't and never would be enough.

I must have looked hysterical, tearing through the hallways sobbing, throwing open doors, mascara running down my face. It felt like a dream. One of the ones where your legs won't move fast enough and you can't find what you're looking for.

And then there he was.

He was coming down the hallway from the direction of the locker rooms. This beautiful, benevolent angel of a man.

I ran at him, grabbed him by the hand, and yanked him toward a supply closet.

"Uh . . ." he said, letting himself be dragged. "What are we—"

I pulled him into the small room and shut the door behind me, panting.

He stared at me. "Are you okay?"

I gasped for a moment before blurting it out. "Are you Benny's kidney donor?"

I watched the question move across his face.

I shook my head. "I know you don't want anyone to know. And I won't tell anyone. Not even Benny. But I have to know, for myself, if it's you. Please. Is it you?" My voice cracked on the last word.

He peered at me quietly. The moment stretched a thousand years.

I tried to read his expression, tried to glean the answer from the tic in his jaw or the resigned set of his eyebrows, the searching in his kind brown eyes. I had to know, I *had* to know.

I watched his lips part and then he said it: "Yes."

I *threw* myself at him.

CHAPTER 17

JACOB

She dove at me.

I caught her and staggered back a few feet before I regained my balance.

She hugged me like I've never been hugged in my life. It was like she was collapsing at the end of a finish line.

"Thank you," she sobbed. "Thank you thank you *thank* you."

"I...it's okay," I said. "I wanted to."

She wept into my neck, and my instinct was to wrap her in my arms and comfort her, even though I knew these weren't sad tears. And when I folded them around her, she clutched me tighter and everything I was going to do, the organ donation, the surgery, the recovery, was worth it for this one moment alone.

I'd thought that any show of gratitude would make me uncomfortable. But for some reason I didn't mind it now that it was happening, and I think it was because it was happening with *her*.

I liked her.

And I liked making her happy and I liked seeing her this way and I *liked* this hug.

It occurred to me that I hadn't been hugged—really, really

hugged—since Amy. And even then, I couldn't remember the last time we'd held each other in any way that felt like this. She'd been so frustrated with me and I'd felt so distant from her, the intimacy had ended long before the relationship did.

I'd been deprived of this basic human contact and now that I had it again, I realized how much I needed it. As I breathed out, Briana filled in the space and I just felt... still. Calm. Grounded.

"I wasn't even nice to you," she whispered into my neck.

"You're nice to me," I said quietly.

She pulled away and peered up at me with wet eyes, her chin quivering. "Jacob, how can I ever thank you for this? There are no words."

I dug in my pocket and handed her a tissue from the pack I always carried.

She took it and dabbed under her lashes. "Thank you."

She was calming down a little. Catching her breath.

I studied her while she regained her composure. So beautiful. Even crying, she was beautiful. I felt like I should look away from her, but I didn't even know how. I still felt the hug, even though it was over, and it disabled something inside of me again, just the way she did that first day in Benny's hospital room. I was rendered frozen and speechless and completely at her mercy, and I had to wonder with a touch of awe and amusement if she had bewitched me. If I was under some spell. Because I'd never felt like this before, this compelled to do something for someone I just met, this drawn to anyone.

Maybe she'd started that coven after all.

She sniffled and looked up at me. "Jacob, you have changed his whole life. Like, I know you know, but you *don't* know. My brother is alive again. He's *him* again."

I gave her a soft smile. "Good." Then I tilted my head. "How did you find out?" I asked.

She wiped under her eyes. "Gibson. I think he slipped."

I nodded. "Ah."

I guess that was a fair mistake. He didn't know I was donating anonymously. I hadn't even seen him yet today.

We'd managed to keep this under wraps for an entire twelve hours.

"I would really appreciate it if you didn't tell anyone else," I said.

She shook her head. "I won't. I promise you I won't. Are you mad at him for telling me?"

I slipped my hands into my pockets. "No. It was an honest mistake."

"You should text him and tell him. He's probably freaking out." She sniffed.

I nodded. "Okay."

She gazed into my eyes. "Do you know what today is, Jacob?" she asked, peering up at me. "It's the day my divorce is final. I don't know if you knew that, that I was married?"

"You had a wedding ring in some of your pictures."

She nodded, looking down at the tissue in her hands. "I didn't think that there was anything that could have made today okay." Her eyes came back up to mine. "But then this happened." She smiled up at me, blinking through tears. "This is one of the best days of my life, on one of the worst days of my life. And all I'm going to remember when I think about it is you and what you've done. Thank you so much." She choked on the last word.

I didn't know what to say. So I didn't say anything at all.

Silence was always my default response. Sometimes things are easier to understand when unsaid. Sometimes words complicate things and make them murky. This moment didn't need them.

We just stood there. Me with my hands in my pockets and her dabbing at her eyes, gratitude coming off her in waves.

For so long I'd wanted this kind of admiration from Amy—and

even this wasn't really real. Briana was just grateful and excited, and it would wear off. But it felt good anyway.

My phone chirped in the silence.

I cleared my throat. "That might be Gibson. I should probably check it."

I pulled out my cell and sighed looking at it. A missed call from Briana that I hadn't heard and five texts from Mom. She was asking about tonight.

I must have been making a face, because Briana said something. "Everything okay?"

I dragged a hand down my mouth. "No. It's just that family thing I was going to tell you about."

"What? What is it? Anything I can help with?"

I barked out a laugh. The irony.

"What?" she asked.

I shook my head. "Nothing."

"No, what?"

I tipped my head back and stared at the ceiling. "This actually is something you could help me with. But there's no way I'm asking you."

"Uh, the hell you aren't," she said. "Like, I don't want to be dramatic, but I would literally die for you right now. What do you need?"

I looked back at her. "I can't. It's too ridiculous to entertain."

"Try me. Entertaining ridiculous is my specialty. I'm *really* good at it."

I laughed a little. Then I let out a breath. "I need a girlfriend for a few months."

She stared at me.

I put up a hand. "Not like that. To come with me to some wedding stuff. I need my family to think I'm in a relationship. My brother is getting married. To my ex-girlfriend."

She gave me a weird look. "To your...ex-girlfriend."

"We dated for a little over two and a half years. Broke up last year. They started dating three months later and got engaged a few weeks ago. The wedding's in July. I need them to think I've moved on."

"Why?"

I looked away from her a moment, trying to figure out how to explain it. When I came back to her, I held her gaze.

"Leaving me, choosing *him* was not easy for her. My sisters didn't speak to them for six months, and my parents almost disowned him. It tore my entire family apart for the better part of a year. They're all going to look to *me* to decide how to act. If I'm upset, they'll be upset, and I'm already doing everything in my power to hide my feelings. They need to think I'm happy and moved on. If I'm alone, they'll spend the next three months waiting for a crack in my façade to decide to hate them both. It will take away from her happiness. And I don't want that."

She looked at me incredulously. "She waited three whole months to start dating your brother and you want her to be *happy?*"

"I love her," I said. "Of course I want her to be happy."

Something in her expression went soft. "Well, you are a much nicer person than I am, Jacob Maddox. When people go low on me, I go lower."

I laughed despite myself.

"So you're not over her, then," she said. It wasn't a question, it was a statement.

I paused. It was complicated and, to be honest, even I wasn't entirely sure of the answer.

My feelings were muddied by too many things. The incomplete way it ended, the rejection I felt, the betrayal of her dating someone else so quickly and that man being Jeremiah. But for the sake of simplifying, I said, "No. I am not."

She pursed her lips and nodded. "Okay. So you think they'll buy it? Us dating?" she asked.

"They already do. When my sister saw us in the supply closet, she assumed. I didn't correct her. I sort of panicked. I'm sorry."

She crossed her arms. "So what exactly would I need to do?"

"Meet my family. Come with me to monthly dinners at their house. Then the engagement party, rehearsal dinner, wedding. That's it."

"I'm in."

I blinked at her. "I . . . you are?"

"Totally. And it's not even the kidney thing. I would have done it anyway."

I pulled my face back. "You would? Why?"

"I would have given an eye to have a date to my best friend Alexis's wedding last year. Some rando named Doug followed me around the whole time with a guitar. He sang me 'More Than Words' by Extreme. Twice. I seriously debated faking my own death just so it would end sooner. Nobody should ever be forced to go to a wedding alone."

She drew a smile out of me, but then I went serious again. "Are you sure?" I asked.

"Very sure."

I peered at her. "Thank you," I said. "This takes so much stress off of me."

"Good. We gotta take care of that kidney."

I made an amused sound and she grinned.

"So when's the first thing?" she asked.

"Tonight."

She blanched. "Tonight?!"

"It's family dinner night. Jeremiah and Amy won't be there. They're invited, but it's her dad's birthday. It's the only event where you won't have to meet my family and my ex at the same time.

We can wait until the engagement party if you want, but it might be a lot, meeting everyone at once."

She pursed her lips, thinking, then nodded. "Okay. I can do tonight. Are you picking me up?"

"I'll pick you up."

She took a step closer and looked at me. "Jacob, I am going to be the best girlfriend you've never had."

CHAPTER 18

BRIANA

I'd had to cancel on dinner with Alexis. I couldn't explain to her why I was suddenly honor bound to be somewhere else tonight, so I just told her the second truth. I had a date with a hot guy. She was more than happy to go home early on those grounds. Plus I think she missed Daniel.

I ran home after work and got ready. Alexis had done Benny's dialysis for me before she left, which was perfect because I was on a tight turnaround. I picked a cute gray top with some jeans. Did my hair and makeup, and Jacob picked me up in a black F-150 at exactly eight o'clock.

I was going to do *anything* he needed to make this fake-girlfriend thing work. I was about to put on an Oscar-worthy performance the likes of which Hollywood has never seen. I was so committed I would tattoo his name across my boob. Pose for fake engagement photos if he wanted them. Hell, I'd fake a damn wedding.

I saw him arrive in the Ring Doorbell, so when Jacob came up the walkway to get me, I was already coming out. I didn't want to invite him in to see the time capsule I currently lived in.

"Hey," I said, squeezing out the crack in the door and closing the screen behind me.

"Hey. Ready to go?"

He was wearing jeans and a thin black V-neck sweater with the sleeves rolled up. Very handsome.

"I brought a bottle of wine," I said, holding up a chardonnay.

"They'll love that," he said, slipping his hands in his pockets.

He looked a little nervous. His jaw was tight.

I peered around him at his truck. Lieutenant Dan had his head out the open back window.

"You brought your dog!"

Jacob looked over his shoulder. "Yeah. I take him everywhere."

I jogged down the walkway to pet him with Jacob following behind me.

"He's so cute," I said, ruffling the dog's head. He wagged his tail and made an excited puppy noise. "I didn't really take you for a truck guy," I said, scratching Lieutenant Dan's ear.

Jacob was smiling a little, but it didn't reach his eyes. "I'm fixing up the cabin. I needed the bed."

He looked at his watch. "We should get going. I think we're going to be the last ones there."

"Okay."

He opened my door for me and then went around to the driver's side and got in.

"So where's your parents' house?" I asked, getting buckled.

"Edina," he said, firing up the engine.

I nodded. "Hmmm. Fancy." Probably a nice house. Not like where *I* lived.

The outside of my house was just as ugly and dilapidated as the inside. The lawn was all crabgrass and cracked walkway and old paint. I was sort of glad Jacob didn't say anything about it.

"Where do your parents live?" he asked, making a left out of my neighborhood.

"My mom lives in Arizona with her new husband, Gil. I don't

have a relationship with my dad. This is good," I said. "Ask me more questions. We should try to know as much about each other as we can before we get there."

"Good idea."

"So how did we meet?" I said. "They'll probably ask us."

"I told them I moved hospitals to be closer to my girlfriend. So that means we had to have met a few months ago and we couldn't have met at Royaume."

"Okay. Why don't we say that Benny came into your ER at Memorial West and that's how we met."

He nodded. "I like that. But let's not say which ER so technically it's the real story. I think we should try and stick to the truth as much as we can. Keep things as simple as possible."

"I agree. Do they know you're donating a kidney?" I asked, looking over at him.

He shook his head. "I wasn't going to tell them. But only because I didn't want it to get back to you. My mom is friends with Jessica. And Zander. And Gibson."

"Are you going to tell them now?"

He shrugged. "I guess I could," he said, getting on the freeway. "No reason to hide it from them at this point. Hey, are you allergic to nuts?" he asked.

"No. How about you? Any food allergies? Stuff you don't like?"

"I hate well-done eggs. Can't stand the smell. And I don't like dill. Other than that, there isn't much I won't try. What about you?"

"I think yogurt is gross. And cantaloupe makes my throat itch."

"No yogurt, no cantaloupe." He glanced at me. "So what time do I need to have you back? Are you doing Benny's dialysis?"

"My best friend did it for me before she left." I smiled. "Benny was gone before I got home. He's out with friends celebrating. He shaved and everything. There was beard hair all over the sink.

I didn't think I'd ever be so excited to have to clean that shit up again."

"He doesn't clean up his own beard hair?" he asked, changing lanes.

"Does any man? I mean, you guys *think* you do. You do the wet-toilet-paper wipe-down thing and call it a day."

"I actually *do* clean up my beard hair," he said.

"Uh-huh. I'll believe it when I see it. Which reminds me, what's your house like? I should probably know."

"Small. One-bedroom and a room for plants."

"For *plants*?"

"I like plants," he said. "Do you like plants?"

"I mean, yeah. As long as it's not me taking care of them. I've killed a cactus."

"Did you overwater it?"

"I didn't water it at all. I forgot it existed. My kitchen windowsill is more uninhabitable than a desert, apparently."

He looked amused.

We drove for a few more minutes and pulled into a nice neighborhood. Lieutenant Dan got up and put his face between us to look out the windshield like he knew where he was.

"Do you come to your parents' house a lot?" I asked, petting the dog.

"We're a close family. I go there, they come over."

He rubbed his forehead and I eyed him. "Are you okay?"

He let out a breath. "Just getting a little headache. Grinding my teeth."

Then he did a sudden double take out the windshield. He pulled the truck over immediately and put it in park.

"What's up?" I asked.

"I have to get something." He pulled some rubber gloves and a trash bag from the glove box.

"Uh...what do you have to get?" I asked, looking around the street he'd stopped on. It was residential. Nothing of note.

"I'll be right back."

He got out, and I turned to watch him come around the rear of the truck. I stared perplexed as he crouched and started looking at a raccoon carcass in the gutter. He was lifting the arms and turning it over. Then he put it into his trash bag.

I rolled down my window. "Uh, they have people who take care of that?"

"It's fresh, it's a good one," he called.

"Okay? And that's important *why*?"

He tossed it in the bed of the truck and came back around to the driver's side and got back in, peeling off his gloves. "Sorry. I needed to get that for my dad."

I stared at him. "You needed to bring your dad an unalive raccoon," I deadpanned.

He put on his seat belt. "My dad's a taxidermist. He's been looking for a good raccoon to mount."

I blinked at him. "And you couldn't have led with that so I wasn't afraid I was on a drive with a serial killer?"

He glanced at me and just now seemed to notice the look on my face. "I'm sorry. That was weird." He looked a little embarrassed. "I should have explained it before I got out. Sorry. I just...I'm nervous and when I'm nervous I...I sometimes miss steps."

He had his hat-in-hand, puppy-dog look again. That vulnerable expression like he'd done something wrong.

I felt my face soften. "Don't be nervous. We've got this. It's going to be fine."

He looked at me like he didn't believe me.

"It will. And don't worry about the raccoon thing. To be honest, this isn't even the creepiest thing I've ever had happen on a date. You're all good."

He laughed despite himself. Then he went a little serious again and looked away from me. "I don't want you to think that I do this often."

"Roadkill?"

He came back to me. "No. Lie to my family."

I pivoted in my seat to look at him straight on. "Jacob, you do *not* need to tell me what kind of person you are. I know."

He gazed at me a long moment. That quiet, thoughtful look he gave me sometimes, and I realized that behind that expression was probably the wheels of his brain, working overtime. Trying to assess the situation, worrying, overthinking like I knew Benny always did. His anxiety pinging around. A clawing internal panic nobody else could see.

But *I* could see it. Because I'd seen it in my brother his whole life.

I think that's why Benny's diagnosis was so hard on my brother. He wasn't just living what was happening. He was living what *might* happen. An infinite number of what-ifs, fueled by his anxiety, each one experienced like they were going on simultaneously, eating away at him, terrifying him, tormenting him. And once he started down that path, it was so hard to stop the progression. It was a self-perpetuating cycle of emotional destruction.

One that Jacob's selfless gesture had knocked off its trajectory.

Jacob had given Benny a reason to stop the inside screaming and look at just one way forward instead of all the possible worst-case scenarios his brain could conjure. He'd given him *hope*. And in doing that, he gave his restless mind peace.

And I could see, in this one quiet moment in this truck, that the screaming was going on inside of Jacob. He didn't have to say a word for me to know it. He was worried what was going to happen with his family today. He was worried what I thought of him. He was dealing with the fact that his ex was marrying his brother, and he was probably afraid we'd get caught in this lie.

I decided right then and there that my job was going to be to quiet it all down. I would be a buffer. An emotional support person. I would throw myself over him like a bulletproof vest. Wrap him up in my protection.

"Look, everything is going to be okay," I said. "We're ready. My cheekbones are contoured. We've got wine and the dead thing…"

The corner of his lip quirked up the tiniest bit.

"We're going to smile, and eat, nobody is going to know what we're doing, and it's going to be *fine*. Trust me."

He let out a long breath through his nose. "Okay."

This time he seemed to believe it. Or at least he appeared to *want* to believe it.

He drove us another few blocks, and we pulled up in front of a nice two-story house with half a dozen cars parked in the driveway. He sat staring up at the home through the windshield.

"It's going to be chaos in there," he said almost to himself.

"Okay. I'm good in chaos."

"I'm not," he mumbled.

I cocked my head at him. "Do you want to play a game?"

He arched an eyebrow. "A game?"

"Yeah. I think you'll like it. I used to play it with Benny when we'd go to stuff like this."

"Okay…"

"I give you a catchphrase. And you have to work it into a conversation. The second you do, you're allowed a time-out from peopling. We go sit on the stairs with the dog or something."

He eyed me. "A catchphrase? Like what?"

I twisted my lips and looked sideways. "Liiiike, 'Not on my watch,'" I said in a fake British accent.

He smiled a little.

"Benny liked it because it gave him a goal and it forced him to talk to people."

He seemed thoughtful. "All right. I'll try it."

"Sweet!" I got unbuckled. "Any last-minute tips?"

"Yeah, don't give Grandpa any cigarettes, no matter what he says. He's very convincing. And do not under any circumstances bring up sex toys to my mom. You will never escape the conversation. No one will be able to save you."

"Uh, I somehow don't think sex toys are going to come up while I'm talking to your mom."

"I think you'd be surprised how easily she works it in," he muttered. He put his shoulder to the door and got out to get Lieutenant Dan.

I grabbed my purse and met him around the front of the truck. "Should we hold hands?" I asked, my voice low. "Like, coming up the walkway? In case someone's looking out the window or there's a Ring Doorbell or something?"

He shook his head. "I don't think you should have to touch me as part of this deal. I think we can pull this off without it."

"I don't mind it."

He shook his head. "I think we'll be all right."

When we got to the front door, he didn't knock. It was unlocked and he let us in. It was like stepping into a Dave & Buster's. Music, laughing, kids screaming, a video game turned up too loud, a blender running. The warm smell of cooking food.

A parrot flew through the vestibule and I ducked. "Whoa!"

It landed on top of the coatrack and squawked, "MOTHER-FUCKER!" at the top of its lungs.

"Sorry," Jacob said, already looking flustered. "That's Jafar."

Then two children darted to us from out of nowhere. "Uncle JJ!" they called in unison.

Jacob smiled and crouched to catch them in a bear hug and hoist them up. The kids wrapped their arms around Jacob's neck. "What socks?"

Jacob smiled, his honey eyes creasing at the corners. "Frogs, like you said."

"Yay!"

He turned so they could see me. "Carter, Katrina, this is Briana."

The little boy looked over at me. "Hello."

I smiled. "Hi."

The little girl peered at me curiously. "You're pretty."

"Thank you," I said. "I like your necklace."

She didn't reply. They wiggled out of Jacob's arms like they'd exchanged some unspoken agreement to take off. They hit the floor and were gone, yelling like town criers that Uncle JJ was here with some girl with long hair.

Jacob looked at me. "Those are Jewel and Gwen's twins. And that's going to be the easiest introduction of the night."

"The animal-socks thing is *very* cute," I said.

"Sometimes they can't agree, and I have to wear two different ones."

I laughed.

Then adults started streaming into the vestibule. They came down the hallway in a wave of humanity and fanned out around me, all smiles and excited greetings.

I could practically feel Jacob's body tense next to me, and I had a knee-jerk urge to reach over and squeeze his hand to let him know I was okay, but I didn't get the chance because they edged him out to get close to me. I was completely surrounded. A cat started rubbing on my legs, the twins skipped around the throng, and Jafar squawked obscenities from the coatrack as people started shaking my hand, introducing themselves faster than I could keep up.

A young, pretty girl named Jane in a pink sundress. Jewel, who I'd already met; her wife, Gwen, a blue-haired Asian woman with a nose ring. Jill, a petite woman with Jacob's auburn hair in capri pants and a conservative white blouse, and her burly husband, Walter, a Black man wearing a T-shirt for a pit-bull rescue. An old man on oxygen in an electric wheelchair rolled in and bumped into my leg and then sat there glaring up at me in silence. Someone introduced him as Grandpa. He ignored me when I said hello.

The man who I assumed was Jacob's dad hovered behind the crowd like he was waiting for the chaos to settle before he said hi. And then an older woman in a flowing paisley top with dangling earrings and arms full of jingling bell bracelets parted the crowd and came right in for a hug.

I'd say that all of this would be overwhelming, except that when Mom took us back to El Salvador to visit, I did this exact thing times a hundred at every single family gathering. It took a full hour just to walk around and say hi to all my cousins and their families. This was nothing. And the rules were universal and simple: You smiled, acknowledged everyone, and asked how you could help with whatever they were doing. I knew how to handle this and was completely relaxed. But a glance at Jacob told me he was on the verge of a panic attack on my behalf. I gave him a reassuring smile over his mom's shoulder before she pulled away.

"I'm Joy," the woman said, grinning warmly at me. She looked a little familiar, but I couldn't place it. Maybe she just looked like Jacob? "It's such a pleasure to meet you," she said.

I smiled. "You too."

The older man made his move as the rest of the crowd started to disperse back into the house. He came up next to his wife. "I'm Greg, Jacob's dad. So pleased to have you."

Jacob looked a lot like his dad. They sort of had the same mellow energy.

I nodded to Jacob, who had stepped in to stand next to me now that there was room. "We picked up a raccoon for you on the way over," I said.

Greg lit up. "You did?"

"It's in the truck," Jacob said.

His dad rubbed his hands together. "Well, let's get it."

Greg edged past me and left out the front door with Jacob, leaving me with Grandpa, the dog, and Joy.

A timer went off somewhere.

Joy looked toward the sound. "Oh, I need to go pull that." She gestured for me to follow. "Come on, we'll get you a drink," she said, already heading down the hall with Lieutenant Dan at her heels.

I snapped my fingers. "Shoot," I said, remembering. "We left the wine in Jacob's truck. Let me run and grab that real quick."

"Okay. Kitchen's down this hallway," she called, still walking. Then she disappeared around a doorway and I was alone with the old man.

I smiled at him and he glared at me. "Give me a cigarette or I'll tell Jacob you're hittin' on me. You got five minutes."

I choked on a laugh. "What?"

"One cigarette and you roll me out to the gazebo and cover for me."

I shook my head at him. "Sir, you are on *oxygen*."

"What the hell is it to you? I'm gonna kick the bucket anyway! I'm half dead already. One cigarette. If you get me a whole pack, I'll give you my Purple Heart."

I had to fight to keep my face straight. "I'm afraid I can't do that for you."

He narrowed his watery eyes.

Just then Jacob let himself back into the vestibule holding the wine from the truck. His dad wasn't with him. Grandpa jabbed a finger at me. "She's hittin' on me!"

Jacob paused, looking back and forth between us.

"It's true," I said. "He's handsome. I can't help myself."

The old man scowled. He made a little fake lunge at me with his chair. Then he turned, pinning me with an impressive nonblinking glare, and left the room.

I turned to my fake date and smiled. This was seriously *so* much fun.

Jacob set the wine down on the bench by the door, looking exhausted. "I'm sorry."

I laughed. "For what?"

"That?" He nodded in the direction Grandpa had wheeled off in.

"Who says he's lying?"

He let out a snort.

"I told you it was going to be a lot," he said.

"Jacob, I have twenty-two first cousins in El Salvador," I said, taking off my shoes and setting them next to everyone else's. "This is *nothing*. You should just relax."

I nodded to the way he came. "You should go do stuff with your dad or something. Skin your dead raccoon. I'll hang out with your mom in the kitchen."

He shook his head. "No. I don't want to leave you alone with them."

"What's gonna happen?"

He slipped his hands into his pockets and peered at me wordlessly, and I imagined those wheels turning again, running through every scenario that could possibly end in disaster.

"Okay," I said. "Then come with me. But chill out. I'm having a good time."

He clearly didn't believe me.

I sighed. I was glad I'd made tonight work because if this was too much, the next one with the brother and the ex would have been a disaster.

This place was an introvert's nightmare for sure. Loud, overcrowded. Lots of social expectations crammed into a tiny window of time coupled with the stress of introducing a new person to his family. The worry that we wouldn't pull off this charade.

The next time he wouldn't have that pressure because we will have gotten it out of the way. He'd still have to deal with all the rest of it, but at least the two of us would have worked out the kinks of this arrangement by then.

I nodded to the house. "Come on. Give me a tour."

I suggested this on purpose to give him a chance to decompress before we joined the group again. I could tell immediately it was the right thing. He let out a breath that sounded relieved and nodded for me to follow him.

The house was enormous. I got the feeling it was the family hub. It was built for entertaining. The basement had a full bar and so did the pool. There was a water slide and a pool house with a nice outdoor BBQ. They had a movie room and a very comfy, very large living room where the twins were playing on a PlayStation. A big dining room with a table that seated twenty and lots of guest rooms.

"Did you ever live here?" I asked as we strolled past the open door of a guest room strewn with the twins' toys.

"I grew up here."

"Ohhhh," I said, turning to smile at him. "Show me your room."

"It's not the same as when I was a kid. Dad uses it now," he said.

"I still want to see it."

I stopped at a bookshelf off the hallway. There were framed photos tucked in with the books—a picture of Jacob in eighth grade. His hair stuck up every which way and he had braces and an overbite.

Damn. Puberty hit this man like a *bus*. The glow up was un*real*.

"Oh, look at that," I said, spotting a book I knew. "*Love Shows Up*. I read this." I tapped the spine.

"Mom wrote that."

I froze. *"What?"*

"She's a couples counselor and sex therapist. Bestselling author. She has a PhD in clinical sexology. She's also a board-certified OB-GYN."

I turned slowly to stare at him in horror. Then I hustled him into the nearest room and closed the door behind us.

"Please tell me you're kidding," I whispered.

He blinked at me in confusion.

"Your mom is Dr. J. Maddox? A world-renowned relationship expert? Are you serious, Jacob? You didn't feel like this was something you should have mentioned?"

He looked positively baffled.

I shook my head at him. "It is literally her *job* to call bullshit on us."

"I told her we were new—"

"Jacob, I don't even know what your penis looks like."

"Well, I'm not showing it to you—"

"I'm not asking! I'm making a point!"

I put a hand to my chest. "I thought I was gonna get here and your dad was going to call me Brenda or Bianca the whole time and they'd make small talk with me and then I'd go home and we'd have three more weeks before the engagement party to perfect our act. And instead we're in a two-hour couples-counseling consultation with a bestselling *sex* expert. She's going to take one look at me and know I've never seen you naked. She's gonna see it all over my face!" I looked at him bleakly.

He seemed to mull this over. "Maybe we haven't had sex yet. Maybe we're taking it slow."

I shook my head. "No. No way. We've *definitely* had sex. You supposedly moved to Royaume to be closer to me and we haven't even slept together yet? How is that in any way believable? The whole point is to make them think we're super into each other. How are you going to be over Amy if you're not having hot, kinky sex with your new girlfriend?!"

He started smiling.

"This isn't funny!"

"It's a little funny."

"No! And what is this room?!" I asked, throwing my arms out.

A thousand marble eyes stared out at me. It was full of taxidermy. FULL. And it was *weird*.

A squirrel in a cowboy hat and chaps riding a turtle. A white mouse dressed in a wizard robe and glasses reading a book, a rabbit with antlers, a ferret in a little bathtub scrubbing his back with a loofa. A dead coyote dressed like Flo from the Progressive commercials. She had the bouffant haircut and red lipstick and everything. It was pretty hilarious, but still.

"This is my old room. This is Dad's stuff," Jacob said. "It's where he keeps his novelty pieces."

I bounced back to the problem at hand. "This is a catastrophe, Jacob," I whispered. "What if your mom sends me a friend request on Instagram? There's not one picture of us together. It literally looks like I didn't exist until today." I shook my head. "We just walked in here like renegades. I don't know enough about you to pull this off. I don't even know how old you are. Do you sleep with the fan on? How do you take your coffee? Do you snore?"

"I'm thirty-five. I sleep with the fan," he said calmly. "Decaf when my anxiety is high, cream and sugar, and not that I am aware."

I shook my head at the gorgeous, oblivious man standing in front of me, who was totally not getting the gravity of this situation. "You said your mom knows Jessica?" I asked.

"Yes. And Zander and Gibson."

"We're going to have to be together in front of everyone. We're going to have to maintain that we're dating at work. I'll have to tell Benny. We'll need to disclose the relationship to HR."

His face fell.

"It's fine, I'm okay with it," I said. "It's just bigger than I thought."

Hopefully Jessica didn't talk to Joy too much and the jump from I Hate Him to I'm in Love with Him didn't come up.

"We're going to have to step up our game, Jacob. Big time. In your mom's book she said intimacy is in the small things," I whispered. "It's putting a hand on my lower back when we walk into a room or facing in my direction when we're together. You're going to have to touch me. You have to do it on purpose, but it has to look like you're not even thinking about it, like touching me is just natural for you because you like it. And I'm going to have to do the same thing."

He put his hands in his pockets. "Okay…"

"We're going to need to spend a lot more time together," I whispered. "If your mom doesn't call bullshit by the end of the night, Amy will in three weeks if we don't get good at this. I'm going to need to see your house. You're going to need to see… *mine.*" I gulped on the last word. "You have to have lunch with me every day."

I thought I saw the corner of his lip twitch.

"Maybe you should come up to the cabin," he suggested.

"YES. *All* the things."

I let out a slow breath. "God. No wonder you warned me about sex toys." Though I might actually want to talk to her about that...

I'd read Joy's book. Twice. It was good. She knew her stuff. It was also the book that made me realize how little I'd been getting from Nick. How wrong things had been for so long. I'd thought it was me. I was trying to fix something when I didn't know where the break was.

And then I'd found out.

"We should go back out there," I said, chewing on my lip.

Great. Now *I* was nervous. We both were. Perfect.

"I'm sorry. I don't know why I didn't think of it," he said forlornly.

I waved him off, trying not to freak out over the fact that I was in Dr. J. Maddox's house. Leave it to a man to completely miss the broad strokes.

He stood there for an awkward moment like he didn't know what to do now. Then he put out a hand, offering it to me like he felt sorry that I had to take it.

I breathed a sigh through my nose at his apologetic expression. I didn't want him to feel bad about this situation. I would have agreed to help him even if I'd known about his mom. Telling everyone I knew that I had a boyfriend was just an unexpected pivot. I hadn't been ready for how far this performance needed to stretch. And I'd meant what I'd said outside: I didn't mind the touching part, that wasn't an issue for me at all.

I gave him a reassuring smile. "It's going to be fine, Jacob. We'll work it out."

I slipped my hand into his waiting one and was surprised when I got the slightest flutter in my stomach at the contact.

It wasn't the first time I'd touched him. I'd hugged him earlier in the supply closet, but this felt intimate, even though it was just for show. I felt a tiny blush creep up my neck.

I cleared my throat. "No kissing on the lips," I whispered.

"No kissing," he agreed.

Then my "boyfriend" led me out.

CHAPTER 19

JACOB

We were in the kitchen. Jill, Jane, Jewel, and Gwen sat at the counter drinking wine and cutting pasta from scratch and hanging it on a drying rack. Walter was washing dishes, and Mom was stirring a pot. Dad had come back in from his workshop and was making garlic bread. Grandpa sat in his chair staring at the yard through the window. There were appetizers set out. A penis-shaped charcuterie board that Mom got for Christmas from her best friend, and an Edible Arrangement.

When we came into the kitchen, Briana had immediately started drying dishes.

The second she did, I relaxed a little. She seemed to inherently understand the communal effort that was the family dinner.

She seemed to understand a lot of things.

My anxiety had careened back in full force over the last few hours. A snowball gathering momentum at each unexpected development that was this day.

I hadn't been braced to be outed about the kidney donation. It was fine, but it was a mental gear change that I wasn't ready for. And so was this "date" we were on.

I hadn't planned on asking Briana to do this for me, and now it was happening, and I hadn't gotten the chance to process any of it or get used to the idea that I was actually going through with this farce. And on top of that, I hadn't anticipated how much I was going to dislike what we were doing.

I'd never lied to my family before. And while I knew I was doing it for a good reason, the fear of being discovered was enough to send me into a spiral.

If we pulled it off, the deception would serve everyone. But if we got caught, my family would know how desperate I was. They'd think I'd lied because I wasn't over Amy and I wasn't okay. That I'd had to make up an entire girlfriend because I couldn't find a real one. The pity would be unbearable. The stakes were unbelievably high. And on top of that, I felt horrible for asking this of Briana.

A part of me knew she felt obligated to me, and I didn't like that because I'd never know how she really felt about agreeing to do this. Was it an inconvenience for her? Was she gritting her teeth and bearing it? Cringing at having to hold my hand? Wishing she didn't know who Benny's donor was after all, so she wouldn't feel honor bound to entertain this ridiculous request?

I would have rather she'd made this decision before she knew, because then I'd know she actually wanted to do it. I was so worried she was being put upon that I'd almost called off the whole thing right up until I picked her up.

And now we were in it. And there was no going back.

Even if we "broke up," we'd already taken the lie beyond the point of inception—we'd actually seen it through. Put on the charade. And, worse, I'd asked her to participate in it. I'd made her an accomplice in my deception. I'd made her a liar.

But it was done. And so there was nothing left but to feel guilty about it, while also acknowledging that it was probably the right thing. At least for my family.

The stress of all this brought the live wires back. They cracked and sparked and shot through my fingers, and it had gotten worse the closer we got to the house. And then I'd stopped and picked up *roadkill*, because of course I'd do something on autopilot that made me look even weirder than I was. Then all the eccentricities of my family met us right at the door. Jafar and Grandpa and the mob of my overzealous family. And I could feel it all pressing on me from the inside, like a scream trying to get out.

But she was drying dishes. And my family was chatting with her and laughing.

If she was nervous after she found out about Mom, she didn't show it. I don't know why I didn't think of it. Maybe I was so busy overthinking everything else, the most important thing slipped. But Briana seemed to have rallied. She seemed comfortable and this thing we were doing felt easy and believable, and for the first time I started to feel the relief I'd imagined I'd feel when I'd come up with this plan. At having this weight lifted off me. Having everyone believe I was okay. And it actually *did* make me a little okay. Because I wasn't going through it alone anymore.

I started filling a pot of water for the pasta and Briana smiled at me.

I smiled back.

It was funny because it was easier to believe I was donating an organ than it was to accept that Briana Ortiz was currently in this kitchen with my entire family, pretending to be my girlfriend. Even broader still, it was hard to believe that she was doing it because Amy was marrying Jeremiah. I think if the me of a year ago had the ability to jump into the consciousness of the me of today for just thirty seconds, the what-the-hell would kill me.

"So," Jewel said, rolling out more pasta. "You guys gonna tell us how you met or what?"

Briana grinned. "Oh, this is *such* a good story. Jacob, do you care if I tell it?"

I set the pot on the stove and turned the flame on. "No. Go ahead."

She bounced a little and turned to face the room, dish towel still in hand. "So my brother was in the hospital and I was running down this hallway to his room and I crashed into this guy coming out of a door. I broke his phone."

I choked a little on my laugh.

Everyone looked at me. "It's true," I said. "She did."

She went on. "I didn't even stop to apologize, I was in such a hurry. I didn't really get a good look at him. And then five minutes later this doctor walks into my brother's hospital room—and it was the guy I knocked into and he was *so* cute. Sort of awkward? But in this really adorable 'I don't realize how handsome I am' kind of way?"

I felt my cheeks flush. I had to pretend to be looking for a pot lid so nobody could see.

"What'd you think of her?" Jane asked, looking over at me when I came up from the cabinet, lid in hand.

Briana peered at me, waiting.

I paused for a long moment, debating what to say. Then I decided the truth was best.

"I thought she was the most beautiful woman I'd ever seen."

"Awwwwwww!" my sisters said in unison.

Briana smiled. "But I didn't give him my number," she said.

"Why not?" Jane asked.

Briana threw up her hands. "He didn't ask for it."

"He's *so* shy," Jill said.

Jewel nodded. "Totally."

Briana gave them a mischievous grin. "But you know what he did? He wrote me a letter."

Jill gasped. "He wrote you a *letter*?"

Briana nodded. "Yup."

"That is *so* romantic," Jane said.

"Jacob has beautiful handwriting," Mom said, stirring the pesto. "I've always thought so."

"Why a letter?" Dad asked.

Everyone looked at me.

I thought carefully about the answer. Then I decided again that truth was best. "I wanted to talk to her, but I didn't know how."

Briana smiled. "So I wrote him back. Then he wrote me back. And then all I could think about was when was the next letter... Then I stalked him on Instagram and DM'd him for his number. He was up at the cabin. I called him and we spent half the day on the phone."

Jill looked confused. "He talked to you while he was at the cabin?" She turned to me. "You don't get cell service up there."

I cleared my throat. "I was sitting at the restaurant down the street."

Now Briana looked confused. "You were at a restaurant? But... we talked for like three hours."

I cleared my throat again. "I know." I paused. "I wanted to talk to you."

She held my gaze for a long moment. Then she seemed to decide to drop it and continue the story.

"So he never asked me out," she said, still giving me a searching look. I had to turn away from her. "So finally I just asked him to lunch, and the rest is history."

All the women smiled at me and sighed.

Well, so far so good.

Everyone chatted casually for the next half an hour. The water boiled, I started the pasta, the sides were placed on the table, and then we took a seat for dinner.

Grandpa sat next to Mom as usual, but this meant he was right across from us and used this position to glare at Briana. To her credit, she didn't seem bothered.

"So, what do you do?" Mom asked Briana, passing her a plate of garlic bread.

"ER physician, like Jacob," she said, taking two slices and passing it to me.

"You know, he didn't always want to be a doctor," Mom said. "He wanted to be a veterinarian."

Briana looked at me. "I could see that. Why didn't you?"

I passed the garlic bread to Jane. "I couldn't deal with seeing abused or neglected animals."

Briana laughed. "We just deal with abused and neglected humans instead."

"There's a little more recourse for it when they're humans."

She bobbed her head. "True."

"And what do your parents do?" Dad asked her.

"Well, my dad left when I was eight. But my mom is a nurse. She's retired. She immigrated here from El Salvador when she was eighteen."

"Oh! Do you speak Spanish?" Dad asked.

It occurred to me that I didn't know the answer. Briana was right. We hadn't been ready.

Briana nodded. "Yeah. It was my first language."

"Hmong was my first language," Gwen said. "It was so hard in school."

"I did okay," Briana said, shrugging. "I think it was harder for my mom. She didn't have any family here or anything." Briana turned to Walter and nodded at his shirt. "Do you work with that rescue?"

"I own it."

Briana beamed. "That's awesome."

"Yeah, we got almost thirty dogs right now. Springtime's the worst."

"I'll make a donation. What's your Venmo?" Briana asked, pulling out her phone.

Walter was directing her to the rescue's website when Jafar started weaving through our feet under the table. He was talking to himself, reciting every bad word he knew, interlaced with the word *Bieber*. This was particularly horrifying, since, according to my sisters, that was my parents' safe word. I prayed to *God* Briana didn't ask about it.

You could feel him climbing over your toes. I knew exactly when he got to Briana's because she made a little surprised squeak noise next to me.

"So do you have any baby pictures of Jacob?" Briana asked, trying visibly not to react to the parrot on her foot.

"Oh, *lots*," Mom said, serving Grandpa. "I'll show you after dinner. Wait until you see his third-grade Halloween costume. *So* cute."

I internally groaned.

Briana was trying to seem interested in me, which I was certain she wasn't. I felt bad she had to sit through this. I was *not* a good-looking kid. I was awkward and had acne. I didn't hit puberty until I was fifteen.

I bet Briana was one of the cool kids in school. I couldn't picture her ever having an awkward phase. She probably ruled her high school the same way she ruled the ER. Popular and well liked. Girls like that never talked to me—or maybe I was too afraid to talk to them.

Not much had changed.

"So what was Jacob like when he was young?" Briana asked Mom, twisting her pasta around her fork.

"Oh, he was such a good little boy," Mom said, putting salad on her plate. "So self-contained, even at a young age. He could play by himself for *hours*. He loved to be held—a very sensitive child. Couldn't stand tags on his clothes or wet hair. Do you remember that, Greg? He couldn't wear anything scratchy."

Dad nodded. "Yeah. I had to buy the underwear that didn't have a label in it, or he'd take them off and run around naked."

Jewel laughed. "I just remember him pooping his pants at school."

"Jewel!" Jill snapped.

I shot Jewel a look.

She rolled her eyes. "What? It was like twenty-five years ago. Get over it."

"It only happened like eight or nine times," Jill said. "You make it sound like he did it every day."

"You guys…" Jane said, looking embarrassed for me.

I flushed and Briana took an extra-long swallow of wine next to me.

"He had a nervous stomach," Mom explained. "He was always in the nurse's office, poor thing. It made him a little hard to potty train. But such a sweet boy, truly."

Jafar shrieked "BIEBER!!!" from under the table at the top of his lungs, and everyone started tittering.

Between this, tagless underwear, and the grade-school diarrhea story, I wanted to curl up and vanish. It was like my family had a competition going for who could embarrass me the most, and even the parrot was in on it.

Lieutenant Dan got up from where he was lying next to me and put his head in my lap. But when I went to pet him, Briana's hand came down on top of mine and gave me a reassuring squeeze. My heart jumped the way it had in Dad's taxidermy room.

I glanced at her, and she smiled gently at me.

"You know," she said, turning back to the table. "I read this study that said highly intelligent children are harder to potty train."

Jewel seemed to think about this. "Yeah. I could see that. He's pretty fucking smart."

Jill nodded. "Totally."

"I used to tell my friends that my older brother was a genius," Jane said. "He's like, the smartest person I know. Didn't he skip a grade?"

"Yup," Dad said. "And breezed through med school."

Briana squeezed my hand again. I let a small smile crack. My parents shared some sort of private look that I couldn't interpret from across the table.

An hour later, the night was over. Mom put Briana through only one photo album. I managed to work our catchphrase into the conversation when Mom passed Briana the Edible Arrangement at dessert and it had cantaloupe on it. I blurted, "Not on my watch!" before diving for the fruit like it was going to jump up and bite her. That was my grand awkward finale of the night.

After that, Briana made good on the promise of giving me a break and announced she had to get home to feed the cat so we could leave.

They all hugged her on the way out. They seemed to really like her, which I knew they would. So we pulled it off. At least today we did.

And I wondered how much she regretted agreeing to this…

CHAPTER 20

BRIANA

It was almost ten-thirty when Jacob walked me to my door.

"Well, that was a nightmare," he said, slipping his hands in his pockets. "Thanks for sticking it out."

"What?" I said, digging in my purse for my keys. "I had *so* much fun. And I think we did pretty well. I mean, the phrase drop was a little rough." I pulled out my keys and turned to him. "I think you could work on your transition next time, but I still gave it a solid six out of ten."

He looked amused.

"Also, those Halloween pictures of you were *so* cute. I can't believe you were a mermaid."

"A mer-*man*," he said with mock seriousness. "I was a mer-*man*."

I laughed and it made him laugh and his eyes wrinkled at the corners. I liked it when he loosened up. He seemed lighter now that the whole thing was over. He had that relieved, saved-from-a-near-death-experience thing about him.

"Thanks for the potty-training thing," he said. "Making fun of me is part of the family initiation process, apparently."

"Yeah, I totally made that up. But contextually it's true. You *are* highly intelligent."

"I want you to know that I have been fully potty trained for quite some time now. I'm pretty proud of it."

I laughed again and he gave me a bashful smile.

Damn, he was handsome. It seemed cliché, but his smile really did light up a room. Bright and dazzlingly gorgeous—and he didn't do it a lot. You really had to draw him out and earn it.

I enjoyed earning it.

It occurred to me that if this was a date, I'd be having a really good time. Like, *really* good. I'd go home with this one.

Why weren't guys like this on the dating apps?

But then I knew why. Because Jacob was way too introverted to put himself out there like that. And even if he did, something told me he wasn't the friends-with-benefits, casual-hookup type— which was the only type I was interested in. His profile would probably say he was looking for a life partner. That he wanted to get married and have kids. I would have swiped left.

But I could still appreciate the view.

"So tomorrow we tell everyone at work," I said. "I'll probably do lunch with Jessica to let her know."

He nodded. "Okay."

"When do you want to come over and see my house?"

He looked at the door. "I can't see it now?"

"Noooo." I shook my head. "No no no. I have to clean first."

And burn some sage, rip up the flooring, and take down the posters from my room that I put up in the eighth grade.

"Okay," he said again. "How about Friday after work?"

"Sure."

Then we just sort of stood there, looking at each other. The same way we did that day in the sob closet.

Agreeing to be harmless to each other.

The night was warm and still. Frogs and crickets were chirping from somewhere. Moths fluttered in the porch light, and the overgrown lilac bush by the light post that I really needed to deal with was in full bloom.

The porch swing looked sort of inviting. I kind of wanted to ask him to stay and just sit with him a bit and talk. But we both had work in the morning, and he was probably tired from all the peopling. But I could totally hang out with him longer. I liked him.

He glanced at the swing like he was thinking the same thing. Then he cleared his throat and put a thumb over his shoulder. "I should get going."

"Yeah. Right." I tucked my hair behind my ear. "I'll see you tomorrow."

"See you tomorrow." He paused at the top of the steps a moment like he was going to say something else. But then he seemed to think better of it and started for the truck.

I crossed my arms as I watched him go. "Jacob?"

He stopped in the walkway and turned back to look at me, those gentle brown eyes.

"Did you really sit at a restaurant for three hours just to talk to me?"

He did that thing where he went quiet.

I was starting to realize these pauses were a protective reflex. He always thought about what he was going to say before he said it. Like he was weighing it, deciding what he should reveal.

Jacob was a fortress. And I got the sense he didn't let people in very often. But it was *imperative* that I get in. One, to make this all believable to his family. But two, because I *wanted* in. I really did want to get to know him.

He intrigued me.

What kind of person protects his ex and his little brother from the consequences of their own fucked-up selfish choices? Thinks of his family's feelings before he thinks of his own.

Anonymously donates a kidney to a stranger.

Zander had said Jacob would give you the shirt off his back and that whole analogy seemed wildly inadequate now that I knew what Jacob was really like.

He had his own private code of ethics.

I didn't have that kind of grace. My high road was currently under construction.

But it made me like him so much. And all the stories his family told did too. I wanted to go back in time and hold baby Jacob. Be his friend in high school and tell all his bullies to fuck off. I sort of wanted to tell Jewel to fuck off too...

He waited another beat before replying to my question. "Yes," he said. "I sat at a restaurant for three hours."

I shook my head at him. "But... *why?*"

He fiddled with his keys, looking down at the walkway. "I wanted to talk to you," he said simply, the same answer he'd given earlier. He looked back up at me and we stood there, peering at each other.

Being harmless to each other.

It didn't mean anything. I'd wanted to talk to him that day too, and I'd had no agenda. And he was in love with someone else. That was literally why we were here. But it made my stomach do a little twisty thing anyway.

Maybe it twisted because for whatever reason, Jacob liked me. And being liked by Jacob meant something because he was so shy. It's like when someone's pet comes to sit with you instead of their person, and you feel like the chosen one. It made me feel a little special, like he saw something in me. Though I couldn't for the life of me imagine what that was.

"Okay," I said. "Well, good. I wanted to talk to you too."

The corner of his lip twitched and he looked down at his shoes. "Good night."

"Yeah. Good night."

I watched him get in his truck and drive off before I went inside.

"I thought you hated him," Jessica said flatly.

We were sitting in the cafeteria at lunch the next day. She had a chicken salad and I was eating a Caesar wrap.

"I think it was just all the sexual tension?"

She narrowed her eyes at me.

"Yeah, you know how thin the line is between love and hate? That whole thing? Turns out it's true. Who knew."

"I thought you said you'd never date a coworker."

"That was more of a guideline than a rule."

She pursed her lips and skewered a cherry tomato with her fork and chewed it slowly, eyeing me.

We'd made the official announcement this morning. Told Gibson, who seemed one part surprised by it and one part relieved, because even if he hadn't slipped about the kidney thing, this now meant Jacob would have told me himself, being my boyfriend and all.

The only person in on the scheme was Zander, who I guess Jacob had talked to about his situation. So I asked Jacob if I could tell *my* best friend, which he agreed to, since it was only fair.

That was an interesting phone call.

Alexis said it sounded like a romcom and to let her know when I got to the Only One Bed scene.

Jacob's whole family had sent me Instagram requests. We'd have to start posting pictures of us on there, now that we'd gone public with our "relationship."

When I got home from work, I started in on the house. Jacob was coming over tomorrow to see my place. Honestly, there wasn't much I could do about the way it looked. It wasn't dirty, it was just freakin' old.

But I could make some improvements on my room. For one, I didn't need to sleep under the ratty bedspread Mom got me for my fifteenth birthday. The glow-in-the-dark stars could come off the ceiling. I also didn't need all the *Smallville* posters hanging everywhere. I'd been seriously obsessed with Tom Welling and in a really creepy way.

I started by taking all those down. The teal paint I'd insisted on when I was fourteen had faded around them from twenty years of sun. All the spots looked horrible, but I didn't have time to paint. I wanted to buy a new bedspread, but I didn't have time for that either.

I stood back and looked at my pathetic room and realized how it would look to him. It was embarrassing. It was *sad*.

I tossed the posters in the trash and gave up.

My cell phone pinged as I flopped onto my bed.

Jacob: What's the dinner plan for tomorrow night?

Me: I don't know. We can just order DoorDash or something.

...Jacob is typing...

Jacob: I need more information than that.

I called him. He answered immediately.

"What do you have in mind?" I said without saying hello.

"I don't really care. I just like knowing what we're eating."

I bet this was his anxiety. He probably felt better when he knew what to prepare for. I filed that away.

"Very well," I said. "What about Taco Bell."

He groaned. "Do we have to?"

"What? Why not? It's been ages since I've had Taco Bell. Nick used to surprise me with it on his way home. He'd bring it with flowers."

"Taco Bell? This was his idea of a romantic evening? Everyone getting diarrhea?"

"I happen to *like* Taco Bell. And just so you know, there is no greater show of love than someone bringing you food without being told. A man who brings you food without you asking is thoughtful and considerate. He's a natural nurturer, he's taking care of you. It's extremely telling. Even if it *is* Taco Bell."

"He sounds nice."

"He's an asshole."

He let out a laugh.

"What do you get from there?" he asked, a chuckle still in his voice.

I shrugged. "A chalupa and two Taco Supremes with fire sauce."

"Those tacos are objectively the worst tacos ever created."

"The heart wants what the heart wants, Jacob."

There was a smile in the pause. "May I make a counteroffer?" he asked.

"You may."

"Juicy Lucy's. I'll pick it up. By the time I get to your place, the cheese will be cool enough to eat."

This was a key consideration when eating a Juicy Lucy. It was a burger with scalding cheese stuffed inside the patty. They took forever to cool down.

"This could work," I said.

"Okay. I'll send you the menu. What else are we going to do?"

I rolled onto my back and stared at the ceiling, an ancient brass and faux wood fan directly overhead. "I don't know. Watch TV? It's going to be very casual. I'm going to be in my pajamas. I will not be wearing makeup or a bra, so don't come overdressed. You can bring Lieutenant Dan if you want, the cat isn't afraid of dogs."

"All right."

"I need to warn you, my house is *very* ugly."

"Noted," he said. "Where do I park?"

"In front of the garage behind the small car stall."

"Okay. You're not upset I'm not bringing the diarrhea food, right?"

"I am very upset. But whenever I'm mad at you, just pull the kidney card."

He laughed and we hung up.

Then a minute later he sent me a picture of Lieutenant Dan. His tongue was lolled out and he looked like he was smiling. I grinned. I replied with a blurry photo of Cooter streaking through the hallway in one of his rare daytime appearances since the move. He still hid most of the time.

Jacob sent a cat heart-eye emoji. That was the last I heard from him for the night.

The next day Jacob and I were the only two attendings on the ER floor, which meant we couldn't take our lunches together since there was nobody to babysit the residents. He did however leave me a letter around noon, next to my charting computer, taped to a brown paper bag.

Dearest Briana,

There is no accounting for your poor taste. But the heart wants what the heart wants.

Sincerely,
Jacob

I opened the bag. It was Taco Bell.

I barked out a laugh and looked up to see him across the ER watching me with a smile. I blew him a kiss and he pretended to catch it—a very uncharacteristically playful move by Jacob standards. It cracked me up. Several nurses and a few patients made *awwwwwww* noises.

We were doing a *wonderful* job looking like we were in love. Everyone was eating this up.

I left him a note on his computer after I took my break.

If I'm in the bathroom later while you're over, just know that I died eating what I love. And also that you are an enabler.

Regards,
Briana

He'd even gotten me fire sauce.

CHAPTER 21

JACOB

Once I knew we were eating Juicy Lucy's, I carefully planned when I'd have to leave to get the food to get to her house on time. I Google Mapped it. I didn't want to show up early in case she wasn't ready for me. If I did get there early, I planned to wait in my car until it was time—but not in her driveway. Down the street somewhere. If I waited in her driveway, she might see me pull up and then it would stress her out that I was outside, even though I hadn't knocked—and thinking that I was stressing her out would stress *me* out.

But in the end, I ended up showing up late because my very last patient vomited all over me.

It pushed my entire plan back by twenty-seven minutes. I was twenty-seven minutes late. This made me flustered, so I was anxious when I pulled up in front of her house, even though I'd texted and told her what happened and she didn't seem to care that I wasn't there yet.

When I knocked at almost eight o'clock, my anxiety was at a low hum. But when she opened the door, it quieted down and then disappeared with a blip.

She was in black fleece skull pajama bottoms and a navy shirt that said *Everything Is Terrible* on it. Her hair was piled on top of her head in a messy bun and, as promised, there was no bra.

It was hard to feel anxious when the situation is so informal. And I was starting to realize it was hard to feel anxious around her in general. Most of the time when I did, it was in the lead-up to seeing her, not the actual spending time with her, and it was my own overthinking that got me there.

Speaking of overthinking...

There was something I kept going back to from the other night at my parents' house. She'd said she really looked forward to our letters. I wondered if she just made that up for the story. Because *I* had looked forward to those letters. A lot.

I think it mattered to me so much because those were before the news about my kidney. How she felt about the letters wasn't because of what I was doing for Benny, it was just between us. Unadulterated by gratitude.

There wouldn't be anything that was untouched by that now. Now I wouldn't know if anything she was saying or doing was because we were pretending or she was just feeling indebted to me.

I wished I could navigate it better and know what was what.

Had she really liked the letters? If she wasn't trying to make our relationship look authentic, would I even be here tonight? Would we have talked on the phone like last night? How much bonus time was I getting from her because of our fake dating, because she felt obligated?

I hated that I didn't know.

"Hey," she said, pushing the door open to let in me and Lieutenant Dan. I stepped into the entry and she crouched to pet my dog and he bounced on his lone front leg and made puppy noises. He liked her.

I looked around while she was ruffling his head. She hadn't been kidding about the house. It was... *old.*

I liked old. My cabin was old. But this wasn't the nostalgic kind of old that had aged well. This was the kind that was dated and in need of serious renovating. The carpet was brown shag, the ceiling was popcorn. There was a glass coffee table with shiny brass legs. A huge cat tree was in the corner next to a window covered in cheap, bent blinds. The pink floral sofa in the living room had thick plastic on it and a huge glittery framed painting of the Virgin Mary hanging over it.

Briana put her hands on her hips and surveyed the house with me. "Well, here it is."

"It's..."

"Don't lie to me. Actually—yes. Lie to me."

I laughed a little.

She nodded to the sofa. "Let's eat. I'll give you the grand tour later."

I took off my shoes and she made her way to the sofa. Her pajama bottoms were inside out.

"Your pants are on inside out," I said, following her.

"I know. The outside was fuzzier. Follow me for more fashion tips."

I smiled.

I'd settled on wearing my workout clothes—a gray T-shirt and some black Nike training pants.

It took me a day of planning just to decide on it.

She dropped onto the sofa and patted the spot next to her. I sat down and the plastic squeaked under me. I started unbagging the food onto the coffee table and she turned on the TV while Lieutenant Dan nosed around. He started sniffing under the dust ruffle of the sofa and wagging his tail. The cat was probably there.

I eased myself down onto the floor and put my back against the seat cushion.

"What are you doing?" she asked.

"Trying to meet your cat."

"Is he under there?"

"I think so."

I handed her a burger. She grabbed a blanket and pulled it over her lap. Then she crossed her leg under her, and her knee pressed into my shoulder.

I pretended like I didn't notice it, but I did. I *really* did.

There was going to be touching now. Obligatory touching, but touching nonetheless. We'd have to in front of my family.

I felt the same way about this that I felt about the rest of it. I liked it, but hated that I didn't know if she did.

She turned up the volume on the TV. Two actors walked through a parking lot as a building blew up behind them. "That stuff kills me," she said, setting down the remote and opening her to-go container.

"Total bullshit," I said.

"They wouldn't be walking away like that. Blown eardrums at the very least," she said.

"The shift in pressure would rupture a lung. Soft tissue damage."

She ate a fry and smiled at me like she liked that I knew this and we could complain about it. I liked it too.

"So I was Googling get-to-know-you games," she said. "And I think we should play Would You Rather."

I let out a dry laugh.

"What?" she asked.

"The last game Amy wanted to play was Penis," I mumbled, tearing the corner of a ketchup packet with my teeth.

"The game where you take turns shouting penis in a public place louder and louder until one of you gives up out of embarrassment? That's like your number-one idea of hell."

I nodded. "Yes. Yes, it is. I'm not very fun, unfortunately."

She scoffed. "You're fun. That game fucking sucks. What other torture did she subject you to? Did she like to text you 'We need to talk' too?"

I paused. "She did, actually."

Briana rolled her eyes.

"She threw me a surprise birthday party last year," I said. "She didn't understand why I was so mortified, since it was just my family and Zander there and she got my favorite cake." I shook my head. "I don't like parties. I especially don't like parties for me, and I definitely don't like them when I don't have a chance to mentally prepare for them. It was like my nightmare trifecta."

Briana bit the tip off a fry. "What the heck was wrong with her? I've known you like three weeks and even I know you'd hate that."

I pinched off a small piece of hamburger and held it under the couch. A moment later a soft mouth took it. "It's not her fault. She always meant well. She's just a people person, she likes parties. I was the one who always ruined things."

I felt Briana studying me and I looked up. "What?"

"You know that it's not your fault that you don't like that stuff, right? There's nothing wrong with you."

I didn't know what to say in response to that.

She pivoted to look at me straight on. "Have you ever heard that quote if you judge a fish by its ability to climb a tree, it will live its whole life believing that it's stupid?"

"Yeah..."

"Sounds like Amy really likes hanging out in trees."

I laughed a little.

"I will never judge you for how you climb a tree, Jacob. And you should know that you are an *exceptional* fish."

She held my gaze, and I smiled and looked down at my lap. I didn't know that I needed to hear this. But I did.

I put so much of the blame of what happened between me and

Amy on myself, it didn't even occur to me to look at it another way. And for just a moment, I allowed myself to believe that maybe I really was a fish put in a tree.

"All right," Briana said, sitting back into the sofa. "Would You Rather. Are you ready?"

I pinched off another piece of burger and held it under the couch. "I'm ready."

"Would you rather be a reverse centaur or a reverse merman?"

"Like, a man with a horse head or a fish head?"

"That is correct."

I thought about it. "A centaur. I don't love the idea of not being able to blink."

"Or breathe. You'd have to live in the water. Things would be *very* shrively."

I chuckled.

"Your turn," she said, taking an exploratory bite of her burger.

"I need to Google questions. I can't just think these up on demand," I said, pulling out my phone.

I scanned a Would You Rather question list. "Okay. Would you rather fight flying monkeys or infinity ants?"

She swallowed. "Flying monkeys," she said without thinking about it. "The ants won't ever stop. That was too easy, give me another one."

I looked again. "Would you rather know the history of everything you touch, or be able to talk to animals?"

She scrunched up her face. "I don't like either of those. Either way I'm going to be honor bound to solve unsolved mysteries for the rest of my life. But if I had to choose, animals."

"You don't like unsolved mysteries?"

"I do, but I don't want that to be my job. I only solve murder mysteries for fun."

I gave her an amused look.

"My turn," she said. "Would you rather name your kid whatever you want, or name your kid after an internet provider in exchange for eighteen years of free Wi-Fi?"

I laughed. "What? Like, Xfinity or something?"

"Yeah."

"Xfinity isn't awful," I said.

"So it's a yes? You'd do it?"

"How much is this free Wi-Fi I'm getting?"

She bobbed her head. "Well, assuming you're getting the premium plan for bequeathing them your firstborn—seventy-five, maybe a hundred dollars a month?"

"Over eighteen years that's probably about twenty thousand dollars in savings. Yeah. I'd do it."

She gawked at me. "You'd make your kid live their whole life with that name for twenty thousand dollars in savings? I'd pay twenty thousand dollars for my kid *not* to have that name."

"What? It's not like I named her CenturyLink. Xfinity's a nice name."

"If you're a horse in a Disney movie."

I twisted to look back at her and made my face serious. "There is nothing wrong with Xfinity pulling her weight around here. Childcare is expensive."

"Wow. It is sad how easily bought you are. At least she'll be able to Google therapists."

"We could call her a nickname and she could legally change it once she turns eighteen."

"What's her nickname? Password?"

I grinned. "Well, what nickname would *you* give her?"

"Ava," she said without even thinking about it.

"Why Ava?"

"Because I like that name. If I ever get a dog, I'm going to name her Ava."

The cat slid out from under the sofa.

Briana blinked at it. "Well, I'll be damned..."

Cooter sniffed me. Then sniffed Lieutenant Dan. Then the cat came back around and rubbed his head on my hand and let me pet him. "Hey, there."

She shook her head. "How did you *do* that?" she asked, her mouth open. "He's been hiding for weeks."

"Move slowly, talk softly, and offer food," I said, talking to the cat in a low voice.

She grabbed three fries, dipped them in ketchup, and bit the tops off. "I am impressed."

I looked up at her and smiled, liking that I did something to impress her.

"So what's your dream date?" she asked, taking another bite of a fry. "What kind of stuff are we doing in our pretend time together?"

I shrugged. "This."

She looked at me. "Really? You like this? Just hanging out?"

"I love this."

She nodded. "Me too. It's so underrated. And hiking and camping."

"Yes."

"Nick never wanted to go with me," she said. "I always had to go alone."

"I'll go with you," I said, a little too quickly and immediately regretting it. She wasn't asking me to join her.

"Oh my God, I would *love* that."

The corners of my lips turned up. "There's a lot of good trails up by the cabin."

"All right, it's a date. Oh! That reminds me. I should probably delete all my dating apps. I don't want someone seeing me on Bumble or something and think I'm cheating on you." She pulled out her phone. "You should delete yours too. In case you match with one of the nurses or something."

"I don't have any."

She looked at me over her phone. "Really? None?"

I shook my head. "No."

"Well, where'd you meet Amy?"

"At work. And my girlfriend before that too."

"Wow. Spared the horrors of online dating," she said. "Lucky you."

"I don't even know what they're like. I've never been on one," I said.

"Wanna see mine?"

"Sure," I said, getting back up to sit next to her on the sofa. The cat followed me and jumped up on my lap.

Briana did a few swipes and then handed me her phone, open to her profile.

Her main picture was the one of her at Minnehaha Falls in the gray baseball hat and glasses.

Her info was sparse. Drinks socially, never smokes, no kids and don't want any. Her bio read:

Looking for something casual. Someone to do fun things with. Must love tacos. And be advised I will be Googling you and I'm very good at it, so don't bother if you're not who you say you are. I don't want anything serious and you're not going to convert me, so don't fall in love.

"You don't want anything serious?" I asked, looking over at her.

"Nope."

"Now? Or ever?"

"Ever."

Oh.

Had her divorce been that bad? Amy hurt me too, but I wasn't ready to give up. I wasn't ready to date yet, but eventually.

I handed back her phone. "You lied on there."

"Uh, about *what*?"

"You said you like tacos. Those are not real tacos you like."

She made a fake indignant face. "Oh, stop."

"How's your stomach? Everything okay?" I asked, grinning at her with my hand on the cat's back.

"Mind. Your. *Business*, Jacob. Cat whisperer. I'm taking you to Taco Bell with me one day and I'm gonna eat ten of those and you're going to be impressed and not at all grossed out."

I cracked up and she laughed with me.

God, this was easy.

I wondered if she saw how easy it was too. Or maybe for her all her friendships were like this. Mine weren't. To have this kind of rapport with someone so early on was unusual for me.

Briana made me the best version of myself when I was with her somehow.

She stopped laughing and smiled at Cooter in my lap. "Why did you and your ex break up?" she asked, petting the cat.

I blew out a breath. "It's hard to explain."

She waited.

"It's like . . . I was a prop."

"A *prop*?"

"Yeah. Like she was the main character, and I was her sidekick. It was always about her. What she wanted to do, what she liked. I was there just to be there. And when I finally said something about it, she left." I laughed a little dryly. "The funny thing is, Jeremiah really *is* her sidekick. And he likes it. They like all the same stuff and he's perfectly happy just facilitating whatever it is she wants."

"Oh, I totally get that. That's what it's like with my mom and

Gil. He follows after her like a puppy dog. How did your brother and Amy meet?" she asked.

"They work together. They actually knew each other before we met. She's a pediatrician and he's a nurse practitioner in the pediatric department at Memorial West."

"Is that why you left the hospital?"

"That is why I left." I let out another long breath. "What about you?" I asked. "What happened with you and Nick?"

She pressed her lips together and looked at the cat instead of me. "Well. We were together for twelve years. Married for ten. And he spent two years of that having an affair with a friend of ours. So."

I peered over at her. "I'm sorry."

"Yeah. It was pretty messed up. Kelly and I hung out. She texted me almost every day, which just made the whole thing so much more disgusting. I'm pretty sure the emotional affair went on a lot longer than the physical one. I think he basically wished I was her for most of our marriage." She laughed a little. "I've never said that out loud to anyone else but Alexis. It's embarrassing."

"No, it isn't. It's just poor taste on his part and poor character on hers."

She nodded, but she didn't look at me.

"Anyway. Then he proceeded to fuck me over in every way possible. The house was his from before we got married, and my name wasn't on it. It was his grandmother's and he had me sign a prenup for it, so I got nothing there. Half the stuff inside of it was mine. I got awarded that. But they were living there, so it was all tainted and gross and I didn't want it anymore, so I had to fight him for over a year in court to get a payout for it."

Her face had gone flat.

"It's hard to find out that someone you love is fine with just setting your life on fire and walking away."

I studied her face. "I know what you mean. Amy never even tried. We went to one therapy session. She walked out and that was it. Broke up with me."

She blinked at me. "The same *day*?"

I nodded. "Same day. Never looked back."

"What the hell happened in that therapy session?"

"I was honest about how unhappy I was."

"And her response to that was to just give up?" She shook her head.

I looked away from her. "I felt betrayed for a really long time," I said. "And then she started dating Jeremiah and I felt betrayed again. And then they got engaged—and I realized that I had surpassed my ability to be hurt more than I already had been."

She went quiet for a moment. Then she looked over at me. "You know what I think about? I think about perfect matches. You know how with an organ donation a perfect match isn't really perfect? There's still a chance of rejection, even if all the stars align like they did for you and Benny. Nothing is *ever* perfect. There's just matches that have a higher chance of working than others. Maybe you guys were like that. It could have worked, but you'd spend your whole life forcing it."

"Maybe. You're probably right." I glanced at her. "What if your perfect match is out there? You're not going to look?"

She scoffed. "It's too late. I'm done. I've had enough heartache for a lifetime." I held her gaze, but she turned away from me.

"Anyway. Is it sad that I want Amy to be jealous?" she asked. "Maybe I'm just projecting my own bitterness onto this, but I kind of want her to rue the day she let you go. We need to put out some serious Morticia and Gomez Addams vibes when I meet her. Like we can't get enough of each other, like we stopped on the way over for a quickie."

"I think she's a little beyond caring what I'm doing at this point. But I appreciate your commitment."

A door closed somewhere in the house. Stairs creaked and Benny came down the hall.

Briana lit up. "Hey, where you going?"

He stopped on the other side of the coffee table. "Justin's. He got a PlayStation. Hi, I'm Benny," he said to me with a small wave. "Nice to meet you."

"Jacob. Nice to meet you."

He looked better than he did the last time I saw him. He was still frail, but Briana was right, he seemed brighter, more put together.

It was a little strange looking at this person, knowing that in a few months he'd have one of my kidneys in his body. But I didn't have too much time to ponder this because Briana scooted over and snuggled up next to me.

I couldn't even breathe.

"We're just gonna watch a movie or something," she said, putting a hand on my chest. "Set the alarm if you come home after I'm in bed, okay?"

"'K. Later." He nodded at us and left.

When he shut the door behind him, Briana tipped her head up to smile at me. "How was that? Was it good?" Her lips were *very* close to mine.

I cleared my throat. "It was good."

"Yay!" she said brightly.

Then she moved away from me. "We need to practice touching before the Amy thing. That way we're not all stiff and weird."

"Right. Good idea."

My heart was still pounding. The whole thing flung me into silence. Briana had rendered me mute, yet again.

I pretended I needed to eat my fries all of a sudden and leaned forward to grab them from the coffee table. We ate without talking while we watched TV and my heart rate finally stabilized.

After a few minutes, she finished her burger and put down her to-go container and wiped her hands with a napkin. Then she pulled her legs up to her chin and put her cheek on her knees and peered at me. "You know what these silences make me think of?" she said.

I looked over at her. "What?"

"I always think that when we're quiet, we're agreeing to be harmless to each other. That we're just sharing the same space and letting each other exist exactly as we are, and neither of us would hurt or upset the other one."

"Harmless to each other?" I looked at her earnestly. "I do agree to that."

She smiled a little.

"Good. I agree to that too."

CHAPTER 22

BRIANA

Three weeks. Jacob and I had been in our fake relationship for three weeks. And I *loved* it.

God, I liked him. Like, I really *really* liked him.

We spent pretty much every day off together—mostly with his family or places where we could take good selfies for Instagram. We'd met Jill and Walter for dinner at Outback. Stopped by Jane's work, where she managed a small cat café, to get lattes and say hi. Last week, we'd taken the twins to the park so Jewel and Gwen could have a few hours alone—Carter rolled down a hill and got dizzy, then barfed *alllll* over Jacob. It was hilarious. Jacob was such a good sport. I loved watching him with the kids. He was so patient and sweet with them.

We went for walks and to coffee shops, took Grandpa to lunch. He harassed me for cigarettes the whole time, but it was still fun.

Every time Jacob's truck pulled into my driveway, I got excited. I had someone to do things with again. To share my day. To eat out and see a movie and hang out with on my days off.

I hadn't had that kind of companionship in *so* long. Even before we separated, Nick had been so checked out.

Jacob and I texted when we weren't together, or we talked on the phone or wrote letters. We were so ready for the engagement party tonight it wasn't even funny. We had the PDA thing down pat. He was pretty affectionate once he was comfortable. Whenever anyone was around, we just held hands or stood extra close. It was super easy. Especially because I adored him. I literally *adored* him.

He was so sweet, and kind, and funny, and self-deprecating, and awkwardly lovable. I had this deep urge to take care of him and baby him and just love all over him.

Tonight I was going to his house for the first time. He was picking me up and we were stopping there first, then going to his parents' house for the engagement party. I hadn't been over to his place yet. I had to see it before I met Amy just in case it came up. I was super excited.

He picked me up at four, and I jogged out to the truck to meet him.

"Hey." He smiled as I tossed my purse onto the seat and got in. He held up a bag. "I got you a red velvet donut."

I grinned. "You did?"

"I have to feed you or you get crabby and nonproductive."

I gasped dramatically. "I am *never* nonproductive."

He laughed as I got buckled in. Then he backed out of the driveway while I dug in the pastry bag.

"Where's Lieutenant Dan?" I asked.

"At home. I didn't want to leave him in the truck while I ran in to get your donut."

He glanced at me. "You look nice."

"Thanks." I looked down at the red floral, knee-length halter dress I had on. The engagement party was a luau. I had a big fake red hibiscus flower in my hair. Jacob wore a black Hawaiian shirt with large birds-of-paradise on it. It was very hokey and *very* not Jacob. He'd probably had to go buy it.

According to him, this party was exactly the kind of crap Amy loved. Themed, loud, and lots of people.

I took a bite of the donut. Then I held it out in front of him and he took a bite too.

"So what's the plan?" I asked, licking frosting off my thumb. "What time is everyone getting there?"

He chewed and swallowed. "The party starts at six. Amy's family will be there and some of her friends. My parents are having it catered. It'll probably run until nine or so. We should stay the whole time."

"Got it. Are you nervous?"

He paused. He was nervous.

I had gotten to know him so well over the last few weeks he didn't even have to tell me. I knew his body language, and his facial expressions, and all of his quiets.

"Look," I said. "I'm not going to lie to you and tell you this isn't going to suck. But we've got this."

He glanced at me with a grateful but not entirely convincing smile.

I hated that he had to go through this. *I* wouldn't have been able to do it. If I had to go to Nick and Kelly's engagement party, I'd show up in my wedding dress to burn the venue down.

Jacob wasn't like that, though. He was diplomatic and not in the least bit petty. He was more inclined to take the high ground, put the blame for someone's bad treatment of him on himself rather than publicly admit someone had done him dirty.

I had *noooo* problem telling everyone Nick did me dirty. Fuck him.

We pulled onto Jacob's street and I craned my neck to see. He lived in a quiet wooded neighborhood in Minnetonka, a few blocks from the lake. I didn't know what I'd been expecting, but his house was exactly it the second I saw it.

The place was small. It looked funny on the large, tree-filled lot, almost like a shed that had been converted into a home. Probably a vacation cottage once, being that it was so close to the popular lake. Nice curb appeal. He had it all landscaped and pretty, with hostas and lilac bushes that were actually pruned and managed—not like mine.

We got out and walked around the yard first. He showed me the birdbath and the porch swing that faced the woods.

Then we circled back to the front and he opened the door to an excited Lieutenant Dan and a warm, sunny living room. It was an open floorplan with a newly remodeled, farm-style kitchen to the left and a small table with two chairs. He had two sophisticated tan leather recliners in front of the TV where a couch would normally be.

"This is cute," I said, petting the dog and looking around. "But you don't have a sofa."

"The chairs are comfortable."

"Yeah, but you can't Netflix and chill in these. How do you snuggle? And only two? What if more than one person comes over?"

"I don't want more than one person to come over."

"Clearly. The horror."

He gave me an amused look. "I just like people more when they're not around. Present company excluded."

I laughed.

Lieutenant Dan finished with me and hopped up onto one of the chairs, and I gave Jacob a look. "Oh my God. Is that *his* chair? You only have two chairs and one of them is for the *dog*?"

He gave me a shrug and a small smile.

I shook my head and wandered around looking at his stuff while he followed me silently. He had a big floor-to-ceiling book-shelf with framed photos tucked into it. Lots of plants. There was a prescription bottle for anxiety meds next to the coffeemaker in the kitchen.

He'd never mentioned being on medication for his anxiety, but I kind of figured. I liked that he managed his mental health. Better than punching holes in walls.

I picked up the bottle and shook it. "Does it help?"

He gave me a nod. "It does. A lot."

"Good."

I set the bottle down.

There was a remarkable amount of color in his house. Yellow walls, pops of blue, colorful backsplash in the kitchen, nice artwork. He had a pretty chandelier over the small table and stained glass hanging in a window.

He hovered just behind me, quiet. Like this inspection was a test and he was waiting for his grade.

"It's not like I thought it was going to be," I said, picking up a vanilla candle and sniffing it.

"How did you think it was going to be?" he asked from behind me.

I shrugged, setting the candle down. "I don't know. The way guys' places usually are. Cold and gray and serious. Or totally empty and you sleep on a mattress on the floor. I like it," I said, turning to him.

The corners of his lips twitched up.

"Did you decorate it yourself?" I asked.

"I did."

"You did a great job. You need a framed picture of us, though. In case your family comes over."

"I have one. It's next to the bed."

I put a hand on my chest. "Oh, sweetheart, you've thought of *everything*."

He grinned.

I nodded toward the hallway. "Do I get to see your bedroom?"

"Of course."

I followed him down a hall lined with framed family photos. We passed a small half-bathroom on the left. He opened a door at the end of the hallway and stood back to let me in.

His large room was clean and neat—hardwood floors with an Aztec rug under the bed. He had a wall-to-wall bookshelf, filled with more books. A forest green tufted chair with a throw pillow on it sat by the window. There was another bathroom at the other end of the room and a large dog bed for Lieutenant Dan in the corner. He had a small workout area with a rowing machine, and an organized weight rack with a rolled yoga mat leaning against it. There were a few plants, an abstract painting over the headboard— and the bed, with a white duvet and a mustard-colored throw folded down at the end.

The second I saw his bed, my heart did a small somersault. This was where he slept.

This is where he has sex…

The thought of that made me a little breathless. Because I would be lying if I said I hadn't thought about Jacob and sex over the last three weeks. A *lot*.

I found him *unbelievably* attractive. He was in great shape. But I was obsessed with his collarbone. It was the most random thing. I never knew a collarbone could be sexy until Jacob. Maybe because I saw so little of his body, I found the parts I could see so erotic? His forearms, his neck, his Adam's apple. The other day at the park he was playing with one of the twins and his shirt hiked up and I almost died looking at the two inches of stomach and the trail of hair I got to see.

And I *loved* the way he smelled. When we were in front of people we knew and we had to look like a couple, the first thing I did was get close enough to smell him. It was like clean laundry and soap. This room smelled like that. This whole place was Jacob, concentrated.

And I could picture us in this bed. I could imagine us coming back after a day of hanging out and maybe we'd be a little drunk and maybe he'd kiss me and maybe…

Maybe…

It was a dangerous word, maybe. And it was one I'd been thinking. A lot.

I couldn't deny how I was starting to feel.

It was like I was one of the abused animals he rescued. Like I was being coaxed out with food and soft words and gentle pats and I was starting to feel safe. And my hard NO to never being in a relationship again had begun to turn into a maybe…

But only with *him*.

Not that he was interested. Not that it was a good idea, even if he was. He was still in love with Amy. We worked together, he was Benny's kidney donor. If something between us went badly, I didn't want it to affect our working relationship or how he felt about what he was doing for my brother. It wasn't a good idea to muddy things or cross lines.

But I didn't want anyone else in this bed with him either.

The idea made me feel sort of panicked.

I didn't want anyone else to get handwritten letters. I didn't want him to smile at another woman or hang out with them. I felt oddly possessive of him and this little universe we'd built, which was equal parts ridiculous and scary, because how much of our universe was even real?

He was spending time with me so we could survive the scrutiny we'd be under once Amy was around. He was probably only coming over so much to take the pictures we needed and get to know each other enough to pull off our fake dating. If that wasn't a factor, would he be hanging out with me at all?

He spoke from behind me. "I told you I have a headboard."

I laughed a little too loudly. When I turned around, he was leaning in the doorway. He had his arms crossed and he was gazing at me with those soft brown eyes.

There is something so intimate about being in a man's bedroom. Probably because there's really only one reason why you would be...

I cleared my throat. "Don't you have a plant room?" I asked.

He nodded. "Yeah. Come on."

He pushed off the doorway and took me across the hall. When he opened the door, I sucked in a shock of air.

It was beautiful.

There must have been a hundred potted plants in there.

It was a sunroom with an antique desk pushed against a window overlooking the wooded yard. He had creeping vines, plump succulents, wide-leafed plants, and hanging baskets of ferns. A small fountain trickled in the corner. It was a little humid and it smelled earthy.

This place was a secret enchanted garden.

But then his whole life was, I realized.

This was his private world and almost nobody had access to it. It was by invite only, designed to be small and hidden away and only for him. I felt privileged to be here.

There was a large glass jar sitting on a wooden stand in the corner. It had several plants inside. The top was corked. "What's that?"

"It's a terrarium," he said from behind me.

"How do you water it?"

"You don't. It's a self-sustaining ecosystem. It waters itself."

"Huh. Cool. My kind of plant."

I turned to look at him. "You have a very beautiful life, Jacob."

Something that I couldn't read moved across his face. "Thank you," he said quietly.

I nodded at the desk. "Is this where you write to me?"

He slipped his hands in his pockets. "Yes."

I smiled. I liked the idea that his words were born here, in this magical room. It was so *him*.

Jacob knew who he was. He felt so fully formed. *Grown-up.*

His life was made up of hundreds of thousands of tiny choices, each thing in it selected by him and only him, so it was exactly what he wanted.

Imagine being the woman he picked to join him here. Having a gentle man like this one choose you to be a part of his private, insular world. To be as special as each thing he carefully surrounded himself with. How lucky that woman would be. And I wondered how Amy couldn't have felt that way. How she could have had the love of a man like this one and not wanted it.

I smiled softly around the room.

I liked that Jacob knew what he liked. He knew what he needed and he built a life around him that reflected that.

I'd done that once. I'd built a life.

Picked out furniture and framed photos and put vacation souvenirs on shelves. And then the man I'd done it with gave it to someone else. And now I lived in the shattered and fading remnants of my childhood instead. I lived with peeling linoleum and shag carpet and ugly furniture I hated.

I wanted to be this whole again. I would. As soon as Benny was healthy again, I'd move on. Move out. Find a place to make like this one. Be like Jacob.

Be like the old me.

I sniffed and turned to him. "This room reminds me of something my mom always used to say."

"What?"

"*Un hombre que puede mantener viva una planta tiene la paciencia de aguantar tus mierdas.* It means 'A man who can keep a plant alive has the patience to put up with your shit.'"

He smiled.

"I've never heard you speak Spanish," he said. "It's very beautiful."

I don't know why, but this made my cheeks heat a little. Maybe because the way he looked at me when he said it felt like he was telling me *I* was beautiful. And I liked that very much. Because, looking around this house, Jacob knew beautiful when he saw it.

He looked at his watch. "We should probably get going." But he didn't move from the door.

The fun part of the evening was over. We were moving on to stage two, the main event. Three solid hours of socializing.

And Amy.

He was nervous. And probably a little heartsick. Having to watch his ex celebrate her engagement to his brother while everyone looked on to see if he'd die of a broken heart wasn't going to be easy.

"Do you need a hug?" I asked.

He drew his brows down. "What?"

"You look like you need a hug. Can I hug you?"

We usually didn't touch unless it was part of the ruse, smoke and mirrors for an audience. But nobody was here to see this, and I honestly didn't know if he'd even let me.

He gave me one of his quiet pauses. And then he nodded. "Yes."

I closed the distance between us and wrapped my arms around him. "I am here for *you*," I whispered. "We'll get through this together and everything will be okay."

He responded by hugging me back. He tucked my head under his chin, and I felt his hands draw me closer. A warm, firm cage that I didn't want out of. And he must not have wanted out either because that tiny hourglass of appropriate hug time between family and friends ran out and we just...stayed.

And I let myself melt into it.

He was solid. Strong. But also soft somehow, like you could crash into him and not get hurt. The pulse of his neck beat against my cheek. The scent of his skin so near teased me and something warm tingled inside of me at the feel of his body held to mine.

All I could think about was how close his bedroom was. How all I had on under this dress was a thin G-string and an easily removed strapless bra.

I could feel his breath tickle my shoulder. His mouth was *right* there.

I wondered if he wanted to touch me. If he thought about it too. If he liked the way *I* smelled, and looked, and felt pressed against him.

Or maybe for him it was exactly what it was supposed to be. Nothing but a platonic arrangement.

Worse.

Maybe when I touched him, he wished I was *her*.

It was enough to snap me out of it, and I pulled away first.

When I let him go, his hands slid from my back down to my waist and we stood there like that for a fraction of a second. I cleared my throat and took another step. His hands fell away from me.

"Ready?" I asked, my voice a touch too high.

He peered at me, studying my face for a moment. Then he nodded. "Ready."

CHAPTER 23

JACOB

T hose motherfuckers are always up to something," Briana
said.

We were parked in front of my parents' house.

I shook my head at her. "No. Give me something else."

"Nope. That's it. 'Those motherfuckers are always up to something.' That's the get-out-of-jail catchphrase for the day."

"I can't say that," I said.

"Why not?"

"It's not how I talk."

"Jacob, this isn't supposed to be easy. You have to *earn* it."

She gave me a serious look and I couldn't help but smile. She
was so, *so* beautiful.

"I can't work the word *motherfucker*," I said, lowering my voice
on the last word, "into a casual conversation."

"Why? Jafar does it all the time."

I snorted.

"This is the phrase. It has to be hard or you'll just drop it the
second you get in there. You have to work for your alone-on-the-
stairs-with-the-dog time." She gave me a playful look.

"All right. But I'm telling you right now, I might not be able to do it."

"Of course you will. I believe in you, and how badly you want out of social commitments."

I laughed.

We'd just driven over from my house. She saw it for the first time today. She liked it.

I *wanted* her to like it.

I'd spent days making sure it was perfect. I'd bought a new duvet cover and a rug for the entryway. I dusted all my plants and bleached the sink. Weeded the garden and organized my books. I wanted her to be impressed.

"Give me a sec to touch up my lipstick," she said, pulling down the sun visor.

I let my eyes move down her body while she wasn't paying attention. Her dress was hiked up and I lingered on her thigh for a split second before I forced myself to look away.

When she was in my bedroom, my heart had thudded harder than it ever had in my *life*. Just her standing there turned me on. I'd had to adjust the front of my pants.

I couldn't stop thinking about her. All of her. All the time. And it got worse every day.

And the hug…

I knew the science behind what I'd felt. That the pressure of her contact was sending signals to my autonomic nervous system, quieting down my fight-or-flight response, oxytocin was being released, creating a feeling of calm and bonding.

But other things had happened too. Things that wouldn't happen if I'd hugged my sister.

I could still smell her perfume on my shirt. I could still feel where she'd been pressed into my body, and I couldn't ignore how much I liked it. How beautiful I thought she was today, how nice she smelled. How grateful I was that she was doing this, for whatever reason. And all this strengthened my desire to return the favor that was a favor to *my* favor. All I wanted to do these last few weeks was to show her how much I appreciated her and valued her friendship. My brain had broken off from worrying about the wedding and all that situation entailed, and it had moved on to how I could look after Briana. A quiet observation of her well-being had grown inside of me the way it did for all the people I cared about. Only not the same.

Not the same at all.

She closed the visor and smacked her lips. "Done."

"I guess we should get out," I said.

"Yeah. Are you ready?"

"I'm never ready for a party. I just come to terms with the fact that I have to go inside."

She laughed.

"Why are they doing it here?" she asked, gathering up her purse. "They couldn't rent a restaurant or a dining hall or something?"

"Everyone does everything here. Mom likes it. It's her way of always having us around."

"Huh. That's smart, I guess. They're not getting married here, are they?"

"No. I think some hotel on the North Shore."

Lieutenant Dan made an impatient whining noise from the back seat. He wanted to see Mom.

I sighed. "All right. Come on. Let's go."

When we got inside, the house was empty. The party was a luau-themed pig roast at the pool. Everyone was out back. We went through the living room to the sliding glass doors off the upper deck, and we could see everyone through the window. I let Lieutenant Dan out to go find Mom, but Briana and I stopped there to look.

My whole family was outside, along with Amy's parents and her sister. A few of my cousins milled around by the pool with Mom's best friend, Dorothy. Amy's best friend, Shannon, and her college roommate were over by the bar. A few coworkers and Amy and Jeremiah's friends sat at the tables. There were tiki torches lit and lights strung over the yard. Mom had hired a bartender, and drinks in pineapples and coconuts were floating about. The twins were running between tables and Grandpa was driving so fast in his wheelchair through the crowd people had to jump out of the way.

Amy stood in the middle of the throng with Jeremiah petting Lieutenant Dan. My brother was in a red Hawaiian shirt, telling some animated story, and Amy wore a white cocktail dress with a lei around her neck, laughing at whatever he was saying.

This was only the second time I'd ever seen them together as a couple. Once at the bar when they broke the wedding news, and now. But this time was different. It didn't sting the way it did last time. Actually it didn't feel like anything at all.

No. It felt like relief—because that could have been *me* down there, at my own engagement party with her. And that would have been the biggest mistake of my life.

I was glad it was over between us.

I think this was the first moment that I actually felt this way. I was *glad* it was over.

I didn't miss her. Seeing her with someone else didn't bother me. At all. Maybe because for the first time in my life I spent my days with someone who seemed to understand me, and the comparison just highlighted how wrong Amy and I had been together. And then I wondered why I'd let it drag on with her as long as I did.

How many years did I waste being that unhappy—that lonely? Why did I wait so long to do anything about it? To say something to her? To let her know how I felt? I'd just stayed, and I was miserable.

"Are you okay?" Briana whispered.

I shook my head, thinking about all the time I lost. "No."

And I wasn't done paying for it. Because I still had to get through today. This was Amy and Jeremiah's party, but *I* was the entertainment.

"Everyone's going to be looking at me," I said quietly.

"No. They're going to be looking at *me*. And I'm going to be looking at you. Like this."

She put her hands on my chest and peered up at me lovingly. Long lashes. Deep brown eyes.

Beautiful.

My heart started to pound, the same way it had when she'd been in my bedroom. It pounded the way it did when she called, or when I saw a letter from her, or when she came out of her house and jogged down the steps.

And she was looking at me now like she loved me.

I knew it wasn't true. But it felt true. Everyone else would think it was.

I stared back at her. She was holding my gaze and smiling softly and in that moment I wanted to lean down and kiss her, the same way I'd wanted to earlier at my house.

What would she do if I did?

I wanted to know if she ever thought of me like I thought of her. If she got excited to see me. If she had feelings for me beyond our friendship, or if she'd ever thought about it being more than this. I wanted to know if any of this was real. Because it was starting to feel real. At least for me.

I cleared my throat and looked away. "Come on. Let's get this over with," I said.

The Beach Boys were playing when we came outside. A blender

was running. There were probably at least a hundred people here and the party was loud, but it felt like everything hushed the second we started making our way down the stairs.

Everyone was looking at us.

Briana's hand slipped into mine and tightened, and I realized how absolutely unbearable this would have been without her. If I had to come here alone, I wouldn't have been able to do it.

"There they are!" Mom said, spotting us. She closed the distance between us with a coconut drink in one hand and a lei in the other, Lieutenant Dan hopping at her feet. "I waited to carve the pig until you two got here," she said, hugging Briana and slipping the fresh-flower necklace over her neck. She kissed me hello, and the party sounds resumed around us.

Gwen, Jewel, and Walter came over. Mom left to greet more guests and I stood quietly while Briana made small talk on my behalf, my anxiety at a low hum.

I had to go introduce Briana to Amy and Jeremiah and say hi. Soon.

It would never be as awkward as it would be right now. I knew we just had to get this initial introduction over with, let everyone stare at us, and the rest would only get easier. But I was dreading it. I was trying to rally my courage to go over there. But in the end, Amy and Jeremiah came to us.

"You made it!" Amy said, breezing in and parting the group.

"Thanks for coming." Jeremiah beamed, coming in for a hug in that confident way my little brother had. The easy rapport of a slightly drunk extrovert surrounded by his own people at his own party.

I felt frozen.

Shut off again, like that day in Benny's hospital room. Rendered mute by the complicated dynamic of this impossible situation and all the people watching me. Every single person at this party was holding their breath, wondering, How will Jacob deal with seeing Amy with his brother?

My dog pushed his head under my hand.

Amy's eyes went back and forth between me and Briana. "And this is...?" she asked when I didn't introduce them.

"Briana," Briana said, smiling at my ex. "Congratulations on the engagement."

I cleared my throat. "This is my girlfriend," I managed.

"I know!" Amy said, a little too brightly. "They told us you had one. We couldn't believe it."

I don't think she meant it to come out like that, but it did. I felt Briana tense next to me.

"I know what you mean," Briana said curtly. "When Jacob told me what this party was for, I couldn't believe that either."

Amy's mouth fell open. Walter buried his nose in his cup of beer, Gwen sucked air through her teeth, and Jewel whispered, "Damn. Double homicide," under her breath.

Jeremiah shifted his feet. "I was just telling Amy that the two of you work together?" he said, trying to change the subject.

"Yes," I said, regaining some of my composure. "Briana's an ER physician at Royaume."

"Do you like it?" Amy asked her with a forced smile, obviously trying to make conversation to salvage the bad start.

"Working with him? I *love* it," Briana said. She looked up at me with stars in her eyes. "You know what he said to me the other day? You guys will love this story. We had this patient with a degloving injury to the scalp. Half his face was peeled off, really gory. Anyway, we patched this guy up and Jacob grabs me and pulls me into a supply closet and looks me in the eye and says, 'Briana, I would love you even if you didn't have a face.'"

I almost choked on my laugh. Her story was so unexpected it completely threw me out of my anxiety spiral.

Amy looked back and forth between us like she was trying to tell whether Briana was joking.

I coughed into my fist, still smiling. "It's true. I said it."

Amy pressed her lips into a line. "That's so sweet," she said flatly.

Briana clutched my arm. "He's always saying stuff like that to me. He's *so* romantic." She grinned up at me for a second, then looked back at Amy. "We're moving in together."

My head whipped to stare at her.

Amy looked back and forth between us. "You're...moving *in* together." She said it slowly, like maybe she didn't understand.

"Yeah. He practically begged me," Briana said. "And then I was like, you're right, the walls at my place are *waaaay* too thin, we're keeping the neighbors up all night and this poor guy's always too dehydrated to drive home after...Anyway, it's been *so* nice to meet you," Briana said. "But I need a drink. Jacob? Want a drink?"

"Sure?"

Then she dragged me toward the bar and left them standing there.

Well. *That* was over.

"I *hate* her," Briana hiss-whispered as soon as we were out of hearing distance.

"Don't hate her," I said, still chuckling. "I'm sure this isn't easy for her either."

She muttered something in Spanish. Then she pulled me into a quiet spot next to the pool house. She closed her eyes and let out a long breath through pursed lips like she was trying to settle herself down. When she looked at me again, she shook her head. "I'm sorry," she said, softer now. "I get very protective over people I care about. And I did *not* like that."

"It's okay," I said, trying to hide how much I liked that she just said she cared about me.

She crossed her arms. "I mean, what is her problem? Was

that necessary? I cOuLdN't BeLieVe yOu HaVe a GiRlFriEnD," she said in a mock voice that was supposed to be Amy. "Why exactly is that so hard to believe? You're a *ten*. What is so fucking confusing??"

I arched an eyebrow. "You think I'm a ten?"

"You're an eleven."

I peered down at her, grinning. "So you'd still love me even if I didn't have a face?"

This drew a laugh, despite her annoyance.

"Where do you come up with this stuff?" I asked, smiling.

"I am *very* good at ad-libbing. Seriously, though. I really hope you don't let anything she says get to you."

"She's not a mean person. I don't think that came out the way she intended."

"Yeah, well, she'd better learn to be a little more intentional when it comes to you, because I'm not going to put up with it. I was two seconds away from taking my hoops out."

I looked at her, amused. "You know, you actually scare me a little bit..."

"You have *no idea* how scary I can be."

I crossed my arms. "You do realize that you're really going to have to live with me now, right?"

"Oh, ha-*ha*."

"I'm serious. My family comes over unannounced all the time. They'll know you lied."

She waved me off. "Put a pink toothbrush in your bathroom."

"That's not gonna do it."

The funny thing was, I *wanted* her to stay with me. I didn't like it when she went home at night. I didn't even like it when we both got off and we had to get into separate cars to meet later for dinner. I'd love it if she was staying at my house, even if I was only getting her on a technicality.

Even if I was only getting her for now.

An hour and a half later the caterer had carved the pig. A chocolate fountain with pineapple and strawberries had been rolled out and the flame throwers had just finished their act. Mom *did* know how to throw a party.

I was relaxed. We'd spent the time talking to Jill, Jewel, Walter, and Gwen at a long picnic table near the tiki torches.

I think Briana must have impressed Jewel earlier because my sister sidled up to her like she'd found a new member of her dog pack. Jewel responded to strong female leadership.

Briana was sitting so close to me her leg pressed into mine. I had a hand on her knee, and she kept leaning into my arm. I almost forgot I was at my ex's engagement party. Or that I was at a party at all.

Briana did that to me.

It was weird to say, but she made me feel alone—the way I felt when I was by myself. Calm and unaffected. Like it was just us here and not a hundred other people.

I liked being alone. With *her*.

The karaoke portion of the evening began. Briana leaned in to whisper so close to my ear I could have turned my head and kissed her.

"This party is brought to you on the backs of the Four Horsemen of the Apocalypse," she said quietly.

"You don't like karaoke?" I asked, turning slightly so that our lips were a fraction of an inch apart.

"I do. But today we're in your hell, not mine."

I was laughing at this when Mom and Dad came to the table with Amy and Jeremiah right behind them holding plates of chocolate-dipped fruit. They all sat down. Amy gave us a tight smile, and Briana returned it with one of her own.

Jeremiah nudged his fiancée. "I'm going up. What should I sing?"

Amy bit her lip like she was thinking. "'500 Miles' by the Proclaimers."

"*Awwwww*, cute!" Jill said.

My brother threw back the rest of his drink and ran up to the stage.

"So how is your brother?" Dad asked Briana. "I've been meaning to ask you. You said he was in the hospital? The day you two met?"

Briana and I made eye contact for a split second. We hadn't gotten around to telling my family about Benny. I guess now was as good a time as any. I gave her the smallest nod.

She looked back at everyone. "Well, actually, we have a little announcement about that. My brother Benny's in renal failure. He's on dialysis. He has a rare blood type, and it was looking like he might never get a kidney donor." She paused to hug my arm. "But Jacob is giving him one of his kidneys."

The whole table froze.

"Jacob…" Mom breathed.

Jewel's hands flew to her mouth.

Jill blinked at me. "That is such a *beautiful* gift."

Amy just stared.

Briana was tearing up. "He did all the testing without even telling me. He just did it." Then she looked at Mom. "He said he was doing it because of you. Because someone did it for you once."

Mom put a hand over her heart. "Such a good man," Mom said. "Oh, Jacob, I'm so proud of you."

I let a small, reluctant smile creep through. All my sisters were grinning. Walter was nodding. Dad was smiling at me, looking proud.

And Amy was leaning back in her seat with her arms crossed.

I peered over at Briana. She was beaming at me.

"It's like I always say," Mom said, wiping under her eyes. "Love shows up. That's how you know when it's real. And what a beautiful way to show up for someone, Jacob." Then she looked up over my head. "Oh, dear. Someone gave Grandpa a cigarette." She started to get up. "Probably your cousins."

"Those motherfuckers are always up to something," I said.

Briana barked out a laugh, and I leaned into her and snickered. I was having so much fun.

Briana smiled up at me, still giggling. "Jacob, can you get my purse? I think I left it in the taxidermy room."

She was giving me my out to go take a break.

I got up. "Sure."

I made eye contact with her before I left. She was going to follow me. I could tell. I couldn't wait to be alone with her. *That* was the reward. Not slipping out of the party or sitting on the stairs with the dog. It was getting her to myself.

I slipped into the taxidermy room and waited five minutes, and when the door creaked open, I turned and smiled. But it wasn't Briana.

It was *Amy.*

CHAPTER 24

JACOB

Amy shut the door behind her. "Do you have a second?" she asked.

I blinked at her. "Is everything okay?"

"I just need to talk to you."

I eyed her. "All right..."

I couldn't imagine what she wanted to talk about. We'd barely spoken since we broke up.

She paused for a moment. "What are you doing, Jacob?"

"What? What do you mean?"

"'I'd love you even if you didn't have a face'? Using the word *motherfucker*? Moving in together?" She shook her head. "What *is* this?"

I felt my heart rate pick up. "I don't know what you're talking about."

"I'm concerned about you," she said. "You're vulnerable right now. You just went through a difficult breakup and you meet this woman and she's moving in? Already?"

I crossed my arms. "You're marrying Jeremiah already."

She crossed her arms too. "I've known Jeremiah two years longer than I've known *you* and we work together every day—"

"Briana and I also work together."

"And in less than six months she's living with you?"

I shook my head at her. "Why do you care?"

"What if she has an ulterior motive."

"Like what?" I scoffed.

"Like getting you to donate a kidney to her brother?"

The words hit me like a smack.

"Did you start dating before or after she knew what you were doing?" she asked.

I went quiet. And my silence confirmed her accusation.

"I'm just saying that you should be careful," she said, going on. "It seems odd that she's so in love and you two just met."

I felt myself bristle. "Why is it so hard for you to believe that somebody might want me?" I snapped. "Just because *you* didn't?"

Her mouth fell open. "It was *never* that I didn't want you. You know that. It wasn't working. We were too broken to fix—"

"You didn't *want* to fix it."

"You wouldn't talk to me about anything! I felt like I was having a one-sided conversation for the last two and a half years—"

"You were! Thank you for finally noticing!"

She lowered her voice. "You are being *so* unfair. I was open to therapy. And we went into that session and you told me you didn't want to have kids with me. You didn't want to live with me, and you didn't want to get married. How could we work it out when you were that unhappy? You hated me so much—"

"I *never* hated you. I didn't want kids until we understood each other better. That's not unreasonable. And why are we even talking about this? It's over."

She nodded. "Right. It is. But I still care what happens to you. I care if someone takes advantage of you. Do you want to wake up six months from now and realize you've been conned into donating an organ for someone you don't even talk to anymore? I mean how do you know she's even who she says she is—"

"Stop. *Right* now." I stood there, breathing hard. I didn't want to hear another word of it.

I wasn't angry because of any of the old shit we were arguing about. I couldn't care less at this point what had gone wrong between us or what grudges she still held or how we could have salvaged it. I was upset because she was speaking my worst fear into the universe.

I didn't know how Briana felt—if she felt anything at all. Maybe she *was* just doing this for the kidney. I honestly didn't know. And now I worried maybe Amy was seeing something that I didn't. Maybe it was painfully obvious that Briana could never really want me, and everyone knew it but me. It made me panic and feel defensive and exposed and hopeless.

Because I was falling for her.

That was the truth of it. I was falling for her.

I was already afraid to look directly at what was happening between me and Briana for fear it would disappear. And I didn't like Amy questioning it or discrediting it—mostly because even *I* didn't know if it was anything for Briana other than the performance we'd agreed to put on.

Something clattered in the hallway. Jafar squawked. "Peekaboo, cocksucker! Bieber! Bieber!"

Amy stood there, hurt. She wasn't looking me in the eye. Her chin quivered and I instantly felt bad for being so short with her.

I dragged a hand through my hair. "Look. None of this even matters. It's done. And you know what? I'm glad it's done because you're with who you should be with." I paused. "And so am I."

"I know," she said quietly. "I just...I feel responsible for you. I don't want you to get hurt. I would hate that." She looked back at me. "I just want you to be okay. I want you to be happy. As happy as I am."

I gave her a small nod. "I know," I said, my voice low. "I believe that."

She paused for a moment. Then she seemed to decide something and she closed the space between us and gave me a hug.

"I'm sorry, Jacob," she whispered. "I'm so sorry I hurt you."

I let out a long breath. "I'm not hurt," I said, hugging her back. "Not anymore."

And it was the truth. Because I no longer cared.

I loved Amy. But I was not *in* love with her. I saw that now. I was completely and utterly over it. I wasn't angry. I wasn't resentful. This hug was as platonic as if I was hugging my sister—and I was.

It occurred to me that the universe had set something to rights when she chose Jeremiah. That maybe this was the way it was always supposed to be. Amy was always supposed to be a part of this family and a part of my life. She just wasn't for *me*. And it was obvious to me who was.

"You don't have to worry about me," I said, tucking her under my chin. "Because I'm happy. And everything between me and Briana is real."

Only I had no idea if that was the truth. But either way, today was the day I was going to muster the courage to find out.

CHAPTER 25

BRIANA

I waited five minutes and then I excused myself to follow Jacob into the taxidermy room.

Nobody noticed we'd left the table. The party was in full swing. Jeremiah was belting "500 Miles" on the stage and everyone was singing the chorus. I slipped into the house and made my way down the hall, and that's when I heard the voices. Jacob's and Amy's voices. They were arguing.

My heart *sank*.

I backed up against the bookshelf to listen, barely breathing.

"It was *never* that I didn't want you..." Amy said.

More muffled fighting.

"...one-sided conversation for the last two and a half years." Amy again.

"You were! Thank you for finally noticing!" he yelled.

I'd never heard Jacob angry. I'd never seen him upset. I didn't even know he was capable of it.

But of course he was capable of it. Because it was *her*.

This was just like all the times I'd stumbled onto Kelly and Nick arguing. Fighting because they couldn't be together.

Fighting because they were in love with each other and frustrated because it hurt. You don't argue with someone you don't give a shit about.

He was still in love with her.

Jacob was not over this.

But the worst part of all was that neither was she.

Amy must have followed him in here. Waited until she could get him alone to come corner him when Jeremiah wouldn't notice.

Or maybe she didn't. Maybe he'd cornered *her*.

And just like that, my Maybe I Could Date Him turned into a resounding No.

And I was so, *so* disappointed. Like a rug had been pulled out from under me.

I was instantly reminded that this arrangement was exactly what Jacob said it was—an arrangement.

He hadn't been falling for me. None of this was real. He was pining over someone else. And that someone else hadn't resolved her feelings for him, despite being engaged to his brother.

I wanted to cry. It was so fucked up.

Something in my gut told me they'd get back together. That I was witnessing the moment they both realized that seeing each other with someone else was just too hard.

She'd probably gotten jealous seeing us together. This was probably getting too real for her—the wedding was barreling toward her, Jacob had "moved on," and she was getting a reality check realizing that she and Jacob were truly over—and she couldn't handle it.

I already knew how *he* felt. He told me the day I agreed to our charade: *I love her.*

Unresolved love always circles back. It lingers. It festers. It builds inside of you until it has to come out, and it putrefies everything else. It makes you resent who you're with because they can't be the one you really love and never will be. It makes you compare and feel disappointed every time you realize no one is as good as *her*.

I knew this better than anyone. I'd already lived it once.

Something crashed behind me.

"Peekaboo, cocksucker! Bieber! Bieber!"

Jafar had knocked a frame off the shelf. I'd been so focused on listening I didn't even see the bird fly in.

I tore around the corner before the door opened and went back to the party.

Half an hour later Jacob and I drove home in silence. He'd come out of the house quiet and anxious. Amy came out a few minutes later, looking like she'd been crying.

He was so obviously bothered I didn't tell him I'd heard his fight with Amy or ask him what was wrong. Honestly, I was too upset to ask.

I wondered what I'd done to be cursed to relive the dynamics of my shitty marriage over and over and over again.

It wasn't Jacob's fault. He'd been clear with me right out of the gate that he still loved his ex. I'd known this going in. I couldn't even be mad. But it sucked. All I wanted to do was get home so I could dwell on it and feel sorry for myself in private.

He had lipstick on the collar of his shirt.

It was next to a red flower on the print, so it wasn't super obvious, but *I* saw it. Amy was wearing red lipstick.

I swear I could smell her perfume on him. It was probably just my imagination, but I kept getting the faintest whiff of peony when he moved. I wanted to throw up.

Had he kissed her? Had she kissed *him*? What had happened in that room? I stopped breathing through my nose and just stared out the window. What had happened was none of my business.

He pulled up to my house and I barely waited for the truck to come to a stop. "I'll see you tomorrow," I said flatly, getting out.

He didn't say bye.

When I got inside, Benny was in the living room with Justin.

"Hey," I said, going straight to my room.

I'd have to do his dialysis. But I wanted out of this stupid dress and the stupid flower I had in my hair. It felt tainted, like the whole night had been.

I'd felt pretty today. And now I felt invisible. Because the only one I'd wanted to see me didn't. He only saw her.

I yanked the flower out of my hair and tossed the dress onto a chair, then washed my face and flung my bra into the hamper. I put on the highest-waisted grandma underwear I could find and my fleece pajamas with a ratty *Vote for Pedro* shirt.

When I came out to hook up Benny, he nodded at me. "Hey, your boyfriend is pacing on the front porch."

"What?" I said, turning on the machine.

"He's been out there like twenty minutes. My Ring is blowing up."

I blinked at him. "He's just walking back and forth across the porch?"

"Sometimes he jogs down the steps and then comes back."

Justin snorted.

I pulled out my phone and opened the app. There he was. Pacing. Like a weirdo.

Technically he was only about fifteen feet away. I could open the front door to talk to him. But instead I turned on the app's speaker. "Jacob? Why are you out there?"

He stopped and looked at the Ring.

"I have a Ring Doorbell," I said. "I can see you. Doing whatever it is you're doing."

"Can you come outside?" he asked.

I let out a long breath. *Fine.* I tossed my phone on the couch.

"Don't spy on me," I muttered to my brother and his minion. Then I let myself out onto the porch and closed the door behind me. "What's up?" I said, crossing my arms.

He looked twitchy. His anxiety was high. Probably the Amy fight/makeout thing and he wanted to talk about it, which really was the least I could do considering we were friends and he was giving my brother an entire organ. But I had to emotionally brace for it anyway.

He didn't start.

"Jacob?"

He swallowed. "I uh . . . I wanted to ask you . . ." He paused to lick his lips. "I wanted to ask you if you would like to go on a date with me. A real one."

His words hit me like a ton of bricks. Knocked the wind right out of me. I felt instantly sad and defeated.

"Jacob, no."

His face fell. I had to close my eyes and let out a centering breath.

"Why?" I asked, looking at him. "*Why* do you want to date me? What is your reason for asking me. Here. Now. On this particular night."

He looked almost confused. "I . . . I like you. I like spending time with you. I—"

"Let me guess. You're ready to move on from Amy? Time to get back out there, put that relationship behind you?"

He blinked at me. "Well . . . yes."

I sighed. He wasn't asking because he actually wanted to date me. He was asking because he'd just had some messed-up, dick-punch interaction with his ex. He was frantic to get over her and wanted a distraction that would make him feel better. And *I* was here. A living, breathing consolation prize. Some desperate next-best-thing thing.

I didn't want to be Jacob's in-between solution. I didn't want to be what he did while he tried to work through this or figured his shit out.

I didn't want to be his second choice.

"Jacob, I know how hard this must have been for you to ask me this," I said, trying not to let him hear the fracture in my voice. "But I've done the 'Love the One You're With' thing. I'm never doing it again. Let's just get through the next few months. Do what we agreed to do. Be harmless to each other. And then the wedding will be over and you can date someone else for real. Okay?"

His expression went blank. Totally blank.

I knew the wheels were turning. Probably working overtime. And I felt terrible that he'd probably worked up the courage to ask me this and I rejected him, and he was probably regretting ever bringing it up. But I had to be clear. I was not going to be his rebound or his fuck buddy or his friend with benefits.

I'd only be his friend.

"I'm sorry," he said finally, his voice flat. "I didn't mean to make you uncomfortable. I'll never ask you this again."

I felt like crying.

The fact he didn't say anything else—anything about feelings— was almost an admission of guilt. Like he was acknowledging that his reasons for asking were exactly what I thought they were.

I looked away from him and nodded. "Thank you."

He paused another moment, peering at me. Like I might give him a different answer if he just stood there long enough and waited for it.

"Good night," he said.

Then he turned and walked to his truck.

I went inside and put my back to the door and buried my face in my hands. I wanted to claw my throat out. Throw something, scream into a fucking pillow.

I hated this so much. I *hated* it.

"Why's your boyfriend asking you on a date and you said no?" Benny asked.

I looked up and glared at him. "I told you not to spy on me."

"I didn't, you left the Ring app open on your phone. I turned it off when I realized."

I rolled my eyes and cleared the space to snatch my cell off the couch.

"Seriously, why'd he ask you that?"

"Just…don't bug me right now. Okay? It's complicated."

He studied me for a moment, but he let it go.

I guess I should be happy that my brother was enough of himself again that he gave a crap about what *I* was doing.

God.

I set up Benny's dialysis, doing my best not to cry in front of him or Justin, who was still sitting there with him watching TV. When I was done, I went to my room and called Alexis.

"Hey," she answered on the first ring.

I sniffed. "Can I come over?"

She was doing dishes. "Sure. When?"

"Tonight."

I could picture her looking at her watch. "You won't get here until midnight."

"One. Maybe one-thirty. I have to finish Benny's dialysis. You don't have to stay up. Just leave a blanket on the porch swing and let me in when you get up in the morning."

"What *happened*?"

I pulled the phone away from my mouth for a second while I choked down the lump in my throat. "I can't tell you now or I'm gonna cry. I can ask Benny to go to the dialysis center for a few days. I have two more days off work. I just need to get out of here and be somewhere else."

I heard her shut off the water. "Okay. But I'm waiting up."

"No, seriously. Don't. Just leave the door unlocked."

We hung up. I packed my bag, finished Benny's dialysis, and left.

Jacob didn't text or call me like he usually did at night. It made my stomach hurt. I felt like I'd just gone through a breakup.

Up until now I'd been able to pretend that maybe Jacob had spent so much time with me because he was actually a little interested in me.

And maybe he *was*. I believed that feelings could overlap. That he could be in love with Amy and maybe also have a crush on me.

But that wasn't enough.

I didn't want to share space with another woman inside of the man I loved. I'd done it one too many times. I was tired of making excuses for why it was okay to accept less than I deserved. At the very least I deserved to be with someone who had worked through their own shit. And Jacob hadn't. Clearly.

I got to the Grant House around one-fifteen in the morning— and Alexis opened the door before I got up the front steps.

"Ugh. I told you not to wait," I groaned.

She hugged me against her baby bump. "I'm a wartime consigliere. We don't sleep on the job."

Daniel greeted me with the dog when I got in the door. He'd waited up too. Now I felt even worse. He hugged me. Then he kissed his wife on the side of her head and went to bed.

I wanted her to go to sleep, but she hustled me into one of the guest rooms, lit a candle, settled onto the mattress next to me, and punched a pillow under her head. "Tell me."

And I did.

I told her everything. And I cried like a baby.

"I really liked him," I said, sniffling, wiping under my eyes.

"And now you don't?" she asked.

"I do. But I let myself get all twitterpated and I forgot what we were doing. I'm here to do a job, it's not real. You know I was actually thinking that maybe I could date him?" I let out an incredulous noise. "But he's not into me. He just wants me to help him get over *her*."

"Did he explain himself? Tell you about the fight with Amy?"

"No. And I didn't tell him I heard it. What would be the point? All he'd do is deny it. Try to convince me I didn't hear what I think I did—or he'd confirm everything, tell me that Amy would always be the love of his life, but that he's really ready to move on, which he's not." I shook my head. "You should have heard how upset he was. The way they were arguing. He doesn't get like that, Ali. He's all measured and reserved. Quiet."

"What's she like?"

I rolled my eyes. "Perfect. She looks like Rosamund Pike, but somehow prettier."

"You're pretty too," she said, closing her eyes.

"Ha."

What did it matter if I was pretty? Or smart? Or if he liked to spend time with me and confide in me and lean on me.

Because just like with Kelly, I still wasn't *her*.

CHAPTER 26

JACOB

I went back to my parents' house after I dropped off Briana.
I found Mom in the kitchen alone, wrestling the trash from the can.

"Jacob," she said when I walked in with Lieutenant Dan. "I thought you and Briana left hours ago."

"Mom, I got it." I took the trash bag from her and tied the top in a knot and set it next to the can to take out when I left.

I looked around. "Where's Dad?"

"He's dealing with the pool cleanup. It's not too bad, we're almost done."

I stood there, my hands in my pockets, looking at the floor. I didn't know why I came here. I just knew I couldn't go home. I'd never sleep.

"What's wrong, sweetie? You look upset."

Upset didn't begin to cover it. I was crushed. Embarrassed. Deflated. I was disappointed in a way I'd never felt before.

Mom waited, and when I didn't elaborate, she nodded to the sliding back door. "Come on. Let's go sit on the deck. We'll watch your dad fish Carter's swim trunks out of the pool."

"He got out naked?"

"As a jaybird. Streaked across the yard for five minutes before Gwen caught him. I swear between the twins and your grandfather, I've lost ten years off my life."

I cracked a small smile. We went to the deck and took a seat on the cushioned sofa. The luau was over. The tiki lamps were still lit, and leis and empty Solo cups were scattered all over the yard like a tropical Mardi Gras. Dad was down there with the pool net, scraping the bottom while the red cups rolled around in the breeze.

Lieutenant Dan jumped up and put his head in Mom's lap, and I looked at Mom's hands while she petted him. They were arthritic.

Her lupus didn't flare much anymore, but the damage had already been done to her body. She was tough. She worked through the pain and kept doing what she loved. And when she couldn't, we helped her.

Mom reminded me a lot of Briana, actually. They were both strong. And stubborn—and they knew themselves. Briana wouldn't have said no unless she meant no. She said it so quickly too. I cringed again at the memory.

"Did you and Briana have a fight?" Mom asked, breaking into my thoughts.

I didn't know how to explain this to her. That my girlfriend didn't actually like me, didn't want to go on a date with me, and intended to fulfill her promise to me like a contract that would be void upon completion of the work.

I couldn't believe she said that. That we just needed to get this over with and then I could just date someone else. Like she was interchangeable with some other random woman. Like girlfriend was a position I was trying to fill.

I didn't want anyone else.

She said she'd already done the "Love the One You're With" thing. Is that what she'd be doing with me if we dated? Settling?

The hurt crashed over me all over again. The humiliation.

I scrubbed my hands over my face. "I don't think Briana feels as strongly for me as I feel for her," I said. "And I don't know what to do about it."

Mom sat quietly next to me.

"Can I ask you a question?" She waited until I looked at her. "Why did you let it go on with Amy for so long? You were so unhappy. Everyone saw it."

I stared out at the pool for a long moment. "I was afraid of change," I said finally. "And I thought it was me. I thought any relationship I was in was going to be that hard because of who I was. *How* I was."

She shook her head. "Jacob. Have you ever heard the saying that if you're with someone who doesn't speak your language, you'll spend a lifetime having to translate your soul? Amy never spoke your language. That's all. Nothing wrong with either of you, just two different people. That's how I can tell Briana's different. She understands you, even when you don't say anything at all."

I looked at her. Mom had noticed that?

"You should see the way she looks at you," she said, going on. "When you're not watching. She looks at you like you're the best thing that's ever happened to her."

That wasn't love. That was gratitude for what I was doing for her brother. Relief.

Or it could just be acting. Not based on anything at all.

Mom looked at me gently. "Love shows up, Jacob. So show up."

I shook my head. "But *how*? What if she doesn't want me to?"

Mom laughed. "That woman is perfectly capable of telling you what she does and does not want. Ask her. If she sets a boundary, respect it. But if you ask her if you can show up, and she says yes? *Show up*. And don't give up on her. Because I haven't seen you this happy in a very long time."

I stared out over the pool. And I realized that I didn't even have a choice but to show up. That the urge to be around Briana was so strong it circumvented everything. Pride. Better judgment. Humility. Even my anxiety.

My anxiety...

For so long I let my life be dictated by my anxiety. Everything I did revolved around not getting uncomfortable, not leaving my safe space. I didn't have the tough conversations I should have had with Amy, and I didn't end it for fear of the unknown afterward. I stayed where I was because anything new was scary for me and I wasn't willing to risk it. I needed my life calm, easy, and static.

But I wouldn't do that with Briana. I'd leave my comfort zone. I had to. Because that's where she was. And for her I would go anywhere.

Even now, rejected and gutted, I still wanted to orbit around her, even if she never wanted me to land.

And it occurred to me that I only had a few more months when I *could* orbit her. When our arrangement made it okay. Expected, even. Because after that...

After that, the deal was off.

CHAPTER 27

BRIANA

My cell was vibrating.

The sun was cracking through the curtains. It took me a moment to realize where I was. Floral wallpaper. A four-poster bed. Alexis asleep next to me.

I'd come to Grant House.

I pulled out my phone and squinted at the screen. It was eight-thirty in the morning, and Jacob was calling.

I swiped to answer. "Hello?" I whispered.

"Hi. Good morning."

I rubbed my eyes. "Good morning."

Alexis started to stir.

"I was wondering if you'd like to go to breakfast," he said.

Huh?

That was a little unexpected. I thought he would feel all weird for a few days. Retreat into isolation like introverts do when they've had an unpleasant encounter and that I would have to make first contact.

"I'm not home," I said.

"Oh. Where are you?"

Alexis sat up and yawned into the back of her hand.

"I'm in Wakan," I said, making an exaggerated pointing motion to the phone and mouthing the word *JACOB* to let my best friend know who it was. "I'm here for the next few days."

"Oh," he said again. And then, "Can I come?"

I blinked. "You want to . . . come? *Here?*"

"Yeah. If it's okay."

Alexis started nodding vigorously.

"But . . . my friends are strangers," I said, like he'd forgotten who he was. "You only like meeting people you've already met."

"That's okay. I don't mind."

What in the world? "I . . . sure?"

"Okay. Can I bring my dog? If not, I'll leave him with Jewel."

I pulled the phone away from my mouth. "Can he bring his dog?" I whispered.

Alexis nodded.

"Yeah, that's fine, he can come," I said.

"Great. Text me the address. I'll leave in thirty minutes."

And then we hung up.

I turned and stared at Alexis. "He's coming," I said in disbelief. She grinned. "I know."

"*Why* is he coming? He doesn't like unfamiliar things. Or places. Or people. Or changes to his plans."

"No. But he definitely likes *you*." She beamed.

I just sat there, shaking my head. This whole thing was baffling, so out of character. Was he trying to show me there were no hard feelings for last night? He could have shown me he was over it with a text. He didn't have to drive all the way to Wakan.

Maybe he was so distraught over what happened with Amy that he needed a distraction and he didn't care what it was.

That was probably it. I might not be "the one" for him, but we definitely had a good time together.

No matter what the reason, this was an act of desperation. I felt a little deflated over the thought that him coming was just an extension of the same impulse that made him ask me out last night.

I sighed. "I have to go take a picture of the driveway," I mumbled, getting up.

"The driveway?" she asked.

"He needs to know where to park. It's a thing."

CHAPTER 28

JACOB

I was throwing everything into the duffel bag I used for my trips to the cabin when her texts came through. And when I saw them, I had to sit on the edge of the bed.

Briana: There's two people here, Alexis and her husband, Daniel. Daniel is a carpenter and likes to garden. He's also the mayor. Alexis was an ER physician but now she's the town doctor at the Royaume satellite clinic in Wakan. We usually just hang out, but we might ride bikes on the bike trail or walk into town and have drinks at the VFW. There might be some townspeople there, but I'll keep Doug off you. He's the only extrovert who'll bug you. Or maybe not, since you don't have boobs. 😆

Briana: When you get here you'll have your own room and bathroom. Here's a picture of your room and another one of where to park and one of Alexis and Daniel. The Grant House used to be a bed and breakfast and you can probably still Google it so you can see the property and get a feel for it before you get here. See you in a bit!

I set my phone down on my lap.

She'd known I needed the details. I didn't have to ask her, I didn't have to explain it to her—or not explain it and just deal with not having it.

She understands you, even when you don't say anything at all…

This is what Mom meant. *This* is what she saw.

Emotion swelled inside of me. And then I deflated all over again. Because even though she speaks my language, it didn't translate into her wanting me back.

CHAPTER 29

BRIANA

Alexis and I were sitting on the porch swing drinking coffee when Jacob pulled up.

My heart fluttered the second I saw him. I had to clutch my chest.

"What's wrong?" Alexis asked, watching me watch Jacob put the truck in park.

I shook my head. "I don't know." But really I did know.

I was stupid for this man.

He had me all turned over and inside out. Just looking at him made me happy. I wanted to run down the steps and jump on him and kiss his face like an excited puppy.

I stayed where I was.

He got out of the truck with a duffel bag over his arm and Lieutenant Dan hopping behind him. Jacob had a plant in his hand. Lieutenant Dan spotted me and bounced up the steps to see me. I was petting him when Daniel opened the front door and Hunter ran out. Hunter took two seconds to sniff Lieutenant Dan's butt, then bounded down the steps and did the jumping-all-over-Jacob, sloppy-kiss thing that I wished *I* could do.

Jacob put down his bag and crouched to pet the dog. This was probably going to be the best part of the day for him. He'd hate the rest of it. The strangers and the socializing and the new place. I still didn't understand why he'd come.

He looked up at me, laughing while Hunter made a long, excited *roooooooooo!* noise, and I swear to God, all my resolve not to be Jacob's rebound side-chick almost dissolved into thin air. I couldn't even look away from him. That's how messed up he had me.

Sometimes it felt like Jacob and I were two magnets being flipped over and over and pressed together. Pulling us in, pushing us out, pulling us in.

Pulling *me* in . . .

Alexis leaned over and whispered, "He's handsome."

"I know," I grumbled. "Of course he is. Anything to make this harder."

I went down the steps to meet him. "Hey," I said, stopping in front of him.

He straightened and slung his duffel bag over his shoulder. "Hey."

Then we just stood there, both of us gazing into each other's eyes, for some reason. Why did it feel like we should be making out right now?

Ugh. Someone needed to turn the hose on me.

Daniel came down the steps with Alexis to save me from myself, thank God, and I introduced them.

Jacob handed Daniel the little plant he had. "Briana tells me you garden," Jacob said. "I brought you this."

Daniel's eyes went wide. "A variegated Elephant Ear."

Jacob smiled, like he'd just gotten out of a birthday party at a bar. "I propagated it myself."

"Wow, seriously? Thanks," Daniel said, turning it around in awe. "I know exactly where to put it. This is awesome."

Jacob looked relieved that his gift had hit the mark and turned back to me with the puppy-dog, hat-in-hand smile that always made my face go soft.

"I'll show you to your room," I said, nodding over my shoulder.

He left Lieutenant Dan hopping around the yard with Hunter and followed me up the stairs. We stopped on the landing to look at the big stained-glass window.

"This is beautiful," he said, studying it.

It was a black bear in a clearing in the woods. The sides of the window were thick green forest with trees with tall brown trunks.

"I bet this is original to the house," he said. "Weird it wasn't on the website, it's so unique."

"They built Grant House in 1897," I said, starting up the stairs again.

"I know," he said, following me. "I read all about it. I love places like this."

I brought him into the second guest room. He dropped his bag on the hope chest at the end of his bed and peered around.

"This is nice."

"Yeah."

When his eyes came back around to mine, I was standing there in front of the fireplace with my hands in my back pockets, and again I got the urge to hug him. I was simultaneously glad that he was here while also wishing that we were at his parents' house instead so we'd have a reason to touch.

Two days that I couldn't even hug him. My body screamed to reach for him. I wanted to feel his warm hand in mine or his body pressed against me. I wanted to smell his skin, if only to erase the memory of Amy's perfume from last night.

And then I felt so, so sad all over again.

Not mine.

Here with me, but his heart's somewhere else.

Remember that.

"Hey, maybe we should post a selfie," he said.

I cleared my throat. "Yeah. Good idea. We can tell everyone we're at a romantic bed-and-breakfast."

He nodded behind him. "Maybe we should be sitting on the bed?"

"Totally. Definitely. Let everyone think that's where we're spending the whole weekend."

That's where I *wish* we were spending the whole weekend...

He got onto the mattress and I climbed on the other side. It was a twin, so we really had to squeeze in. He lay back against the headboard and opened his arm to let me snuggle up next to him and my whole body melted at the contact.

This.

This was what I needed. I could have stayed here forever.

He settled into the pillows, and I got adjusted against his chest. He smelled warm and familiar, and I could see why he could convert dogs who hate men and lure timid cats out from under sofas.

Jacob made me feel safe. He was like a living lullaby. A softly spoken word. The smell of coffee and toast in the morning or a cozy fleece blanket. The rain pattering on the roof on a day where you don't have to go anywhere or do anything.

I wondered if sex with him would feel like slipping into warm water. All enveloping and just right. I bet kissing him would feel that way too. He was so gentle and careful. I bet he'd kiss me softly. And then hard. I'd put a hand on his jaw to feel his five-o'clock shadow and then move it to the back of his neck to pull him closer. I could picture the feel of his lips and his tongue and his teeth. His breath on my mouth and his chest rising and falling against mine the way it was right now...

I was so in my head I had to remind myself what I was *supposed* to be doing. I cleared my throat again and angled the camera, taking longer than I needed to, just to have a second more in his arms.

He didn't look at the lens, though. He tilted his head so his nose was in my hair and closed his eyes. It looked great for the picture. Like this was a private moment with a man who was in love with me and we were catching this in a candid photo.

I had the strongest urge to set down the phone and tip my head up to his and see what would happen.

Instead I took the picture and hopped off the bed.

I had to pretend to be busy putting the picture on Instagram so I wouldn't have to look at him while my heart rate went back down.

It really was a good picture. Tender. Intimate.

Then I realized that Amy would see this and all it would do is make the situation between them more tense. It might even be the thing that tipped the scales.

Jacob's family seemed pretty chill. If Amy did switch brothers again, I knew they'd get over it. They'd have their moment. Jewel would probably be the most vocal. She seemed like she didn't have a lot of time for drama and bullshit and she'd definitely give her two cents. But then they'd all probably just shrug and accept it and move on.

I honestly didn't see her wedding to Jeremiah happening.

I mean, I'd do what I'd said I was going to do, which was to be his girlfriend in the meantime. But then I'd get dumped. Again.

I was glad he'd come today. Because we only had so long to keep pretending.

CHAPTER 30

JACOB

Would you punch me in the face for one billion dollars?"
Briana asked.

We were at the VFW in Wakan. It was nine p.m., and we'd
been here for a few hours after dinner at Jane's, the little diner
on Main Street. We'd spent the day wandering the town, going
to antique stores, getting ice cream, checking out the farmers'
market. We were sitting in a booth at the back of the bar with
Alexis and Daniel.

Briana waited for my answer like this was a serious question.

"If we were married," she said again, "and someone offered you
a billion dollars to punch me in the face, as hard as you could,
with my permission, would you do it?"

"No," I said. "I would not punch you in the face."

Her eyes got wide. "You'd *better* punch me in the face, Maddox.
I'd punch you in the face."

"For a billion dollars I'd actually be okay with that," I said.

She gasped. "Oh, so you can get punched in the face, but I
can't? That is so sexist."

"It is not the same thing," I said. "I'm stronger than you. I
could shatter your jaw."

"And I couldn't shatter *your* jaw? This is one billion dollars we're talking about. Xfinity needs to go to college."

I barked out a laugh.

"Who's Xfinity?" Daniel asked over his beer, looking back and forth between us.

"Our fictional, traumatized daughter whose name was chosen so we could get free internet." She looked back at me. "Tell me you'd punch me in the face, Jacob."

I looked at her, amused. "I thought we were supposed to be harmless to each other."

"You being the only reason why I'm not a billionaire is not being harmless to me. That harms me greatly."

I shook my head. "I can't hurt you. I'd pay one billion dollars *not* to hurt you."

She gave me a small, reluctant smile.

Doug made his way over to the table with a guitar in his hand.

Briana rolled her eyes. "Doug, do you know what the definition of insanity is?" she asked, raising her voice so he could hear her before he got to the table.

He looked indignant. "This isn't for you," he said, holding up his guitar. "You had your chance."

Briana snorted.

"There's fresh meat over at the bar." He nodded to a pair of women drinking beers.

Briana craned her neck to look at them. "Oh. Well, make sure you call them meat to their faces. Women like that."

Doug seemed to think this over. "That's a good idea. I'll do that. Thanks."

Everyone laughed.

Doug nodded to Daniel. "Hey, spot me twenty bucks, yeah?"

Daniel dug in his wallet and pulled out a bill.

"Thanks," Doug said, taking it and shoving it into his shirt pocket. "Wish me luck." And he left.

"He's gonna need a lot more than luck," Briana said.

"You're never getting that twenty back—you know that, right?" Alexis said to her husband.

"I do," Daniel said into his beer. "But at least those poor women will get free drinks."

Briana shook her head. "That guy has more red flags than a matador."

Alexis laughed.

Briana turned to me. "Want to walk back? I am here to relax and make fun of Doug, and I am all out of Doug."

"We'll probably stay for a bit," Alexis said, rubbing her belly. "The house is unlocked, you can just go in."

I put money on the table, and we slid out of the booth and started for the door. I wanted to leave, but not because I wanted to go. I wanted to be alone with Briana.

I was having a good time. Briana had said if I got overwhelmed at any point today, we could go, which helped a lot.

When I was a kid, Mom would always try to gently coax me into new activities. She'd never force me. But she'd tell me that if I went to the birthday party or the field trip, or the day camp, she'd wait in the car outside, and if I wanted to leave before it was over, I could. Most of the time I'd have fun and I'd end up staying. And then after a while she didn't need to wait at all. It was knowing that leaving was an option that gave me the courage to try.

Briana was the same kind of safety net. And I bet she didn't even realize how much it changed the outcome for me.

Amy had always thrown me into things with both hands, and then couldn't understand why I was anxious and withdrawn and wanted to leave the second whatever it was began. But with Briana I felt slowly submerged. Gently set down. And then once I was in,

I was comfortable. I felt like everyone else probably felt. Calm and easy and normal. It protected the shelf life of my internal battery. And I don't even think this was a conscious thing for her most of the time. I think she just inherently knew to do it.

It was just one of the many amazing things about her.

We came out into the warm early June air and started for the house. I had to fight the urge to take her hand.

Touching her in public was second nature to me now. But that's because most of the time we were in public, one of my family members was there, and touching was necessary to hold up our façade. We didn't have that here. Daniel and Alexis knew about our arrangement, so I didn't have an excuse to put a hand on her back, or brush her hair off her face, or sit close enough that my leg pressed into hers. It was the only thing I hated about being in Wakan.

I'd suggested taking a picture for Instagram earlier for the sole reason of getting the hug that I couldn't get when I arrived. And then I didn't want that hug to end. I wished we could have shut the door and stayed in that bed. I wanted to hibernate with her. Forget the rest of the world existed.

I squinted at something large standing under a light post across the street. "Is that . . . a *pig*?"

"Oh, yeah," she said. "That's Kevin Bacon. He's Doug's. He's like the town mascot or something. He just runs around and takes selfies with tourists."

He was huge. At least three hundred pounds, and wearing a reflective vest.

"Can we pet it?" I asked.

"Yeah, let's go."

We crossed the street and the pig grunted at us as we came up. He was enormous and pink. I crouched and ran a hand over his head and he snuffled around us, looking for food. He found the mints I had in my pocket and I pulled them out and unwrapped them and let him eat them from my hand.

His vest had a Kevin Bacon hashtag and a Venmo on it.

"I have to give it to Doug, he *is* a hustler," Briana said, eyeing the Venmo. "*Doug* would punch me in the face for a billion dollars."

"Then I'd have to punch Doug in the face for free."

She gawked at me trying to look serious, but she was fighting a laugh. "You're punching the wrong person. *I'm* the billion-dollar punch—though I do understand the impulse to punch Doug for nothing. But still."

I chuckled, petting Kevin's wiry fur.

"No, but seriously," she said. "We need to get on the same page with this."

I shook my head. "I'm not doing it. I'm not punching my wife."

"Nick would do it."

"Well, it sounds like there's a lot of things that Nick was okay doing to you that I would never do."

She bobbed her head. "Okay, good point."

"And why is the money that important?" I said, standing. "You make a good living. You don't need a billion dollars."

She looked up at me. "Jacob, I grew up poor. Extremely, *extremely* poor. Like, food-instability poor. No matter how much I have, I will never turn down the means to never live like that again."

"Oh," I said. "I didn't realize your childhood was that tough."

She shrugged, looking at the pig. "It was. I mean, it was good. But it was hard. I had to start working at a pretty young age to help my mom. She used to clean houses, back before she got her nursing degree, and I'd go and help her."

"How old were you?"

"Ten? Eleven?"

God. I couldn't imagine working that young.

"It was better for Benny," she said. "By the time he was ten, Mom had a good-paying job and I was working at Starbucks and waiting on tables. I'm glad he had it easier."

I was glad he did too. But I hated that she'd struggled.

I would do anything to keep her from struggling.

We made our way onto the bike path that led back to the house. The moon was out. We were walking under some trees along the river, and I slowed a bit so it would take longer. When we got home, she'd probably go to bed, and then I wouldn't see her until tomorrow.

"So where was your dad in all this?" I asked.

She breathed in through her nose. "Gone. My parents divorced when my mom was pregnant with Benny. I haven't seen my dad in almost thirty years."

"Where is he?"

She shrugged. "Back in El Salvador? I don't really know. I don't care. I think he has like, a whole other family. Anyway, Mom always had more than one job until she started nursing. Then she got hired by these rich white people when their grandma got too old to live alone. They trusted her. Mom took care of that lady for six years. She was really good at it. When the lady died, she left my mom some money. Mom used it to help put me through school and buy the house we'd been renting. The one I'm in now." She looked at me as we walked. "Anyone who says money isn't everything has never had to live without it."

We walked for a moment in silence.

"Well, I still wouldn't punch you in the face," I said. "But I would work hard enough so you'd always have everything you need. I'd go hungry so you could eat."

She gave me an amused look. "I wouldn't let you go hungry for me," she said.

"I know. That's why I'd never tell you."

"You wouldn't *tell* me?"

"The truest sacrifices are the ones no one knows anything about."

She paused. "Jacob, you are too pure for this earth."

I laughed a little.

She glanced over at me with a small smile. "You know, I actually believe that you'd do that, and most of the time when men say valiant things, I don't."

I looked down at the paved path. She had no idea the things I would do for her.

"Given this backstory, I'm a little surprised that it was me and not you naming our kid Xfinity to save money," I said.

"I would gladly sacrifice myself, but I'd never sacrifice my kid," she said. "The whole point is to give them a better life than the one you had."

"She could have a good life named Xfinity."

"Yeah, but maybe she'd have a great life named something normal, like Ava."

I smiled. "Okay," I said, glancing at her. "We'll name her Ava."

She twisted her lips into a smile. "Good. Ava Xfinity—*Ortiz*. I'm not taking a man's last name, and I'm not letting my kids do it either."

"You didn't take Nick's last name?" I asked, glancing at her.

"I did. And then I had to change it back. When Mom got married, she took my dad's last name too, and then she had to change it when he left, which meant she changed my last name also, which was of course *her* dad's last name. I've had three different last names in my lifetime and it's all been to carry on some stupid patriarchal tradition. I will never do it again."

I shrugged. "Okay. I'll take your last name, then."

She laughed, but I wasn't kidding. I glanced at her. "You know, if you really wanted to show Amy, we *could* drag this on a little longer. Maybe say we're engaged. Get married. Have a few kids."

Live happily ever after...

"Ha. Don't tempt me. I'm petty and I love a long con."

I chuckled. My phone vibrated in my pocket and I pulled it out and checked the screen. Jill.

"Hold on, I have to take this. Jill?" I said, answering the phone.

"Where are you?"

"Wakan. With Briana. Why?"

"I'm at your house."

I grinned. "Hold on." I put the phone on speaker. "Okay. Can you repeat that?"

"Uh, I'm at your house?"

I looked at Briana. "So what you're saying is, you've come to my home unannounced and uninvited to see me at a very late hour."

"Uh, yeah. Why? I do it all the time. I need to borrow your bread maker."

I gave Briana an I-told-you-so look.

"I'll be home tomorrow," I said.

"Ugh. Fine. Also, Jane left a bag of coffee on your porch. Tell Briana I said hi."

I hung up with her and smirked at Briana. "Jill says hi."

"You bake your own bread?" she asked.

"Really? That's what you took from that phone call?"

"Okay, I get it," she said. "They come over a lot and you're worried they'll find out I'm not living there. I'll just come over a lot too."

"And if they poke around?"

"Why would they poke around?"

"Because they're nosy and bored and they lack boundaries."

"So I'll leave stuff there. I'll put a box of tampons under the sink. Leave a bra draped over a chair."

I shook my head. "Not good enough."

"Jaaacob," she whined. "I can't stay at your house. I'd feel horrible."

"Why?"

"Because you like your alone time."

"No I don't," I said quickly—too quickly. I cleared my throat. "I roomed with Zander for almost six years. I don't mind living with someone." *The right someone...* "I think letting my family see us living together is a good idea," I said.

She glanced at me. "You do?"

"Yeah. It means we're serious. I never lived with Amy."

She pulled her face back. "You didn't? Why not?"

"Because being around her that much wore me out," I said.

"And being with *me* that much wouldn't wear you out?" She gave me a look that called bullshit. "We work the same shift. We'd literally be together twenty-four/seven."

I know. "If I'm being completely honest, it would not wear me out to have you with me that much," I said.

"You're just saying that so I don't feel bad that I've pigeonholed you into either living with me or explaining to your family why the living-together thing didn't work out."

"I'm saying that to you because it's true."

She went quiet for a moment. "Have you talked to Amy recently?" she asked.

That was an odd question. "I talked to her for a bit yesterday at the luau."

"Oh yeah? When?"

"When I went inside," I said.

She nodded at the trail. "What'd you guys talk about?"

I let a long breath out through my nose. "It was an argument, actually."

"About what?"

I paused. "Old stuff." *You.* "It was nothing."

I didn't want to talk about it. I didn't want to tell Briana that Amy didn't believe Briana wanted me—because she didn't. I didn't want to bring up the irony of Amy's accusation.

When I didn't go on, Briana did. "She was probably jealous."

I scoffed. "She wasn't."

"Trust me, she was. She probably thought you were gonna pine over her for the rest of your life and now you've got some new girlfriend who's obsessed with you and she can't handle it."

I had to look away from her. Because Briana being obsessed with me was so far from the truth it hurt to think about it.

"I think she's still in love with you," she said.

I let out an incredulous noise. "She's not."

"Yeah, she is. I *deeply* dislike her," she said.

"Don't dislike her."

She went quiet next to me.

"How did it make you feel?" she asked after a moment. "The fight?"

I thought about how I wanted to reply. I decided on the truth. "Like shit."

She didn't respond. But she *did* reach over and thread her fingers in mine. My heart leapt at the unexpected touch. The heat of it radiated through my entire body.

She squeezed my hand and leaned into my arm until I looked down at her.

"I'm sorry someone made you feel like it's hard to love you," she said.

My chest got tight. She peered at me with so much earnestness I wanted to stop right then and there and kiss her.

But this wasn't love in her eyes. This was pity. Or comradery. Or friendship. It was like the hug she gave me the other day. It was meant to comfort me. That's all.

I knew this, and it didn't change a thing. I still wanted to kiss her.

I was my own greatest enemy now. Because I knew how this ended and wouldn't lift a finger to save myself. I couldn't.

I didn't have to come here today. I could have put up walls between us and stayed home. We didn't need to keep spending so much time together outside work or family events. But how could I give away even a moment of seeing her and talking to her? I couldn't justify it.

I would have come no matter where she was, or what she was doing. I would have met her at a party. Or a busy bar or a nightclub. My desire to see her overrode my own self-preservation instincts—in more ways than one.

We got to the house and she let go of my arm. I opened the front door to let Lieutenant Dan and Hunter out to go to the bathroom and we stood on the porch waiting for them.

"Hey," I said as we watched the dogs sniffing the lawn. "You left your sweater in my truck last night. I brought it."

"Oh, thanks. Can I get it now? I was actually looking for that."

"Sure."

We left the dogs outside. Lieutenant Dan wouldn't run away. He was too treat-motivated to do anything other than come back in once he did what he had to do.

We came up to my room and I dug in my duffel bag for the sweater while she waited by the hope chest.

I'd kept the sweater next to me on the seat on the drive over so I could hold it to my nose. It smelled like her. I wished I could keep it.

If she lived with me, things like this would be everywhere, all the time. Her shampoo would be in my shower. She'd use my coffee mugs. Her toothbrush would be next to mine on the sink.

I wanted these mundane things so badly I couldn't even stand it. I'd never wanted this much of Amy. Amy was right when she'd pointed it out. I spent so much time pushing her away, keeping her at arm's length. But I *chased* Briana. I wanted to make my life desirable to her so she'd want to be a part of it. I was buying a sofa for the living room because that day she came over she said you couldn't Netflix and chill in the recliners. I knew there was less than a one percent chance Briana would ever cuddle with me on a couch—but I wanted to have the couch just in case.

If I was being honest, what I really wanted to do with her wasn't in the living room at all.

I wanted to push her down on my bed in that red dress from the luau and play out every scenario I'd imagined over the last few weeks. Wanted to pull off her underwear, slide her dress up over her hips, bury my face between her legs...

I had to shake it off.

It felt disrespectful. Like I was violating her just by thinking about it. And I'd been thinking about it a *lot*. I couldn't help it.

A heavy gust of wind rolled through the drapes, and the door to my room slammed shut.

Briana jumped. "Oh my God, that scared me," she said with a hand on her chest.

It must have been a back draft. Maybe Alexis and Daniel just came in the front door?

I pulled out the sweater and handed it to her.

"Thanks," she said.

Then we just stood there. The door was closed. The lights were dim.

It was just us and a bed.

It felt like the end of a date. An amazing one where the chemistry was off the charts and you wanted to invite them in to stay the night because their leaving felt premature and wrong.

This was the kind of date that never ended. It turned into breakfast the next morning and then dinner the following night and then finally after so many sleepovers you just move in with each other because being together is so organic that doing anything else would be ridiculous.

Her leaving this room felt ridiculous.

I had to remind myself that she wasn't feeling what I was. *She* didn't feel the chemistry. *She* didn't feel any attraction to me or attachment to me.

She was doing a job.

If she'd said yes to that date, I would have poured everything into it. I would have treated that opportunity like a once-in-a-lifetime gift. It would have been precious to me, the chance. I never would have worked harder for anything in my life than I would the tiny possibility of convincing her to consider me an option.

But I'd made my interest known, and she'd made her disinterest clear.

And that was that.

She cleared her throat. "I'll see you tomorrow. Good night."

I slipped my hands into my pockets. "Good night."

I watched her walk to the door like I was watching the wrong ending of a movie I loved and knew by heart.

But when she went to let herself out, the door was stuck shut.

CHAPTER 31

BRIANA

What do you mean it's stuck?" I said.

Jacob was rubbing the back of his neck. "It's stuck. I can't get it open."

I stared at him. Then I went back to the door and started tugging desperately on the handle. It was like trying to open a bank vault.

"No..." I breathed. "No, no, no, no, no..."

"Are you claustrophobic?" he asked, looking worried.

No. I was not. "Yes," I lied.

"But we eat lunch in a supply closet—"

"That door isn't locked!"

I pulled out my phone and called Alexis, pacing in front of the fireplace while Jacob threw open the windows and the bathroom door to help me with my fictional fear of enclosed spaces.

She answered on the second ring. "Hey—"

"Ali? We're locked in Jacob's room."

"What?"

"There was some freaky breeze, the door slammed shut, and now it won't open."

I heard the sound of her coming in the front door while she

relayed this to Daniel. "We just got home, we'll be up there in a second."

Forty-five minutes later, we were still trapped.

Jacob had been trying to troubleshoot from our side, but the issue wasn't the lock. The door had swollen itself into the doorway. Like a broken finger swelling around a wedding ring.

"I'm just going to cut it," Daniel said resignedly through the speaker on my phone.

"No, don't cut it," Jacob said quickly.

I gawked at him. "What do you mean don't cut it?"

He nodded at it. "That's an antique door. It's probably original to the house. It's irreplaceable."

"We are trapped here!"

He peered at me calmly. "Look, my cabin does stuff like this. The foundation settles and the house shifts. Humidity makes the doors stick. It just rained yesterday, that's probably what's going on."

Jacob raised his voice. "Daniel, do you have a dehumidifier?"

"In the basement, yeah."

"Okay. Set that up in the hallway. Let's run it overnight. See if we can't dry out the wood a little. If we can't get it open in the morning, we can reevaluate."

"Good idea," Daniel said from the other side.

I looked at Jacob bleakly. "All night? We have to stay here all night?"

"We were going to bed anyway," Jacob said. "We have a bathroom, water, we just ate. We don't need anything—"

"I do! I need...my *retainer*!" I said desperately. "I can't live without it!"

He gave me the amused look of a parent entertaining the wild story of a three-year-old.

I couldn't stay the night in this room with Jacob. I couldn't share a bed with him. I looked over at it in a half panic. I'd never actually seen a bed that small—wasn't this a bed-and-breakfast once? Didn't they specialize in beds meant for couples? Was this a child's room???

"I could always get a ladder up there," Daniel called through the speakerphone. "But you'd have to climb out onto the roof—"

"Yes. Absolutely." I nodded enthusiastically. "Let's do it."

"You are *not* climbing out onto a roof," Jacob said.

"Why?"

"Because you could fall. And look at the windows. They only open four inches wide. You'd have to birth-canal yourself out of it, you'll get stuck."

"I agree, Bri," Alexis said through the phone. "It's too dangerous. I think the plan is good, just stay where you are."

I looked at Jacob in despair.

"Excuse me," I said, and I took my phone to the bathroom and shut the door.

"Alexis, take me off speaker and go to your room," I whispered.

There was a pause and the sound of a door closing. "Okay, you're off speaker."

"I cannot sleep in here tonight."

"Why?"

"Because I will have sex with him."

She snorted.

"It's not funny," I hiss-whispered. "Your house has locked me in a thirst trap and I'm so sex starved and into him I'm not going to be able to say no. My legs will probably shoot straight out like one of those fainting goats the second he so much as breathes on me. This is a crisis!"

I could tell she'd moved the phone away from her mouth so I wouldn't hear her laugh—which I totally did.

"Ali, the man literally propositioned me last night."

"He asked you on a date," she said, still snickering. "He didn't ask you for sex."

"Yes, he *did*. We already go on dates. Every day. He wasn't asking me to get emotionally involved with him, because he's not emotionally available and he's seen my dating profile and he knows I'm not either, so what he was *actually* asking was if I'd be interested in maybe having sex with him."

"That is a very dizzying argument..."

"So now I'm locked in a room with a man that I'm half in love with and *extremely* attracted to, who wants to have sex with me, and I'm sorry, but I have about as much willpower as a piece of broccoli."

She lost it. It took her a solid minute to stop laughing long enough to reply.

"Look, there are extra toothbrushes in the drawer under the sink," she said, still wheezing. "I can slip your retainer under the door and we'll take care of Lieutenant Dan. Also, you should know the walls are *very* thick..."

I groaned, sitting heavily on the closed lid of the toilet. "I can*not* believe this is happening..."

"I can."

"What is that supposed to mean?" I grumbled.

"Let's just say that sometimes things happen here that I can't explain."

I put my forehead into my hand. "God. And why is the bed so fucking small?"

"Daniel's re-staining the old frame. He put that one in the room until he's done."

"It might as well be a hammock."

She was laughing again. "Bri? I think you've just made it to the Only One Bed scene."

"Ha-*ha*."

When I hung up with her and came back out into the room, Jacob was crouched in front of the fireplace, poking it with a metal rod.

"What are you doing?"

"Starting a fire," he said, standing. "It'll help dry the room out on our side."

Of course. We're sharing a tiny bed, *and* there's going to be a romantic fire. Perfect.

He stood there giving me that earnest, hat-in-hand, puppy-dog look again. He knew I didn't want to be here. I sighed and resolved to try and be less visibly miserable. This wasn't his fault.

He looked over his shoulder at the bed and came back to me. "So...what side do you want?" he asked.

Sides? We were going to have to sleep stacked on top of each other.

I sighed. "What side do you normally sleep on?"

"The right."

"Okay. I'll sleep on the left."

I looked at what I was wearing. I was in a tank top and jeans. My boobs would be everywhere the second I lay down.

"You can borrow a shirt," he said, reading my mind.

"Thanks."

"It's just sleeping," he said.

Ha. Right.

I changed into the shirt he gave me. It smelled like him and made the whole situation a million times worse. Alexis slipped my retainer under the door, which I actually didn't want to wear in bed with Jacob, but I'd made such a big deal about it I had to. It made me lisp.

His shirt was long enough to cover me. Barely. I debated sleeping in my jeans, but that idea actually *did* make me feel claustrophobic, so I just got under the covers as quickly as I could to keep from accidentally flashing him.

When Jacob got in, his entire left side was pressed into my body. After some awkward, apologetic shifting that seemed to be mutually geared at keeping his penis as far away from me as possible, we agreed to sleep back to back. It would have been easier to let him spoon me, or for him to lie on his back with me sleeping curled up next to him in the crook of his arm, but there was no way I was doing either. It was *waaaaay* too slippery a slope.

My knees were halfway off the bed. I'm sure *his* knees were halfway off the bed.

He cleared his throat. "You know, we'd fit better if we—"

"No," I said, cutting him off.

He spoke over his shoulder. "We hug all the time. It's not sexual."

I had to hold back a maniacal laugh. "It's not that. I'm just... *really* claustrophobic," I lied. "I can't have someone hugging me right now or it'll make it worse."

He was quiet for a beat. "Okay." He went back to facing his side of the room. And then over his shoulder again, "Do you want to stay up and talk for a little while? It might be hard for you to sleep if you're anxious."

I let out a long breath. Then I rolled onto my back and he rolled onto his.

"What do you want to talk about?" I asked.

"You could ask me one of your weird questions."

"My questions are not weird," I said, lisping through my stupid retainer.

He propped himself up on his elbow. "'Would you rather drink toilet water or eat dirty kitty litter?' That's not weird?"

"That was an excellent ice breaker, meant to get to the core of who you are as a person."

"Uh-huh." His eyes were creased at the corners.

"Well, what about your questions? They suck too."

"My questions are great. You just don't take them seriously."

I gasped. "I have taken *every* question you've asked me seriously." Major lisp on *seriously*.

He looked amused. "Really? Your near-death experience was when your thighs were rubbing together at Disney World on your twenty-fifth birthday—"

"I WAS FIGHTING FOR MY LIFE, JACOB."

He laughed and his chest rumbled against my arm. It rumbled everywhere. He was so close.

We were alone...

I swear his eyes flickered to my mouth for a second and I had the brief realization that if he kissed me right now, I wouldn't say no. I couldn't. It was like I was under some spell. I had just enough strength to hold my ground, but not enough to save me if he advanced. I *prayed* that Jacob would be Jacob tonight and be respectful. He always was. But what if he wasn't?

A very specific part of me was *hoping* he wasn't. My traitorous vagina was putting on war paint and blowing a Viking horn like it was about to go ransack Jacob's village.

I cleared my throat. "These get-to-know-you questions are very important for our fake relationship."

"And what exactly did you learn by asking me what kind of mullet I'd be?"

"I learned your hair grows out curly and you have a great laugh?"

He cracked up again. He was still smiling when he went on. "You should ask me real things. Things with substance."

"You're not ready for my substance questions. Believe me. They're extremely invasive."

He adjusted himself on his elbow. "Try me."

I sat up on my elbow and looked at him. "You can't handle it."

"I *can*."

I narrowed my eyes. "No."

I lay back down.

"What? What do you mean, no?"

"No. I don't have a kiddie pool, Jacob. I go right from Would You Rather to the deep end. It's Truth or Dare on steroids. We're not there. We might never be there."

"Just so I'm understanding what your hesitation is, you think I won't be willing to answer the heavy questions you might ask me."

"That's what I'm saying."

"I will."

I lolled my head to look at him.

He peered at me steadily. "I mean it. Ask me whatever you want. What do you want to know?"

I sat up against the headboard. "I want to know what's in your search history."

"What?" He laughed.

I shrugged. "That's what I want to know. It's worth a thousand questions."

This was when he was going to bail. No way was this man letting me see what weird porn he liked to watch.

"Okay." He sat up, reached for his phone on the nightstand, and handed it to me.

I stared at it in shock. "Uh . . ."

"My password is 7438."

I was literally rendered speechless.

"Why would you agree to this? I was just calling your bluff."

He looked me in the eye. "There's nothing about me that I'm afraid for you to know."

I just stared back at him.

My heart felt tight and I couldn't even explain why—but then I knew why. Because for so many years my own husband made himself a stranger to me. He had a whole double life I knew nothing about. And here was this man who *wanted* me to see him.

All of him. He didn't want any secrets between us. He just gave me his damn PIN.

I grabbed my phone off the nightstand and handed it to him. "Then you get to see mine too. My password is 9008."

"Okay. And just so you know, I don't ever change my password," he said.

"Okay."

"That means that you'll always have access to my phone. And my debit card."

I gawked at him. "Jacob! You just gave me your debit card PIN? You cannot give that out."

He gave me an amused look. "Why? I can't trust you?"

"Of course you can trust me." I lisped hard on the word *trust* and he smiled.

"Well, if I can trust you, then what's the problem?"

I let a breath out through my nose. "Your bank PIN shouldn't be the same PIN as your phone. It should be two separate PINs."

"Okay." He took his phone from me and did a few swipes. He thumbed something in, then he handed it back to me. "There. I changed my password. Now it's the same one as yours."

"Jacob!"

"What?" He was laughing. "Now you won't forget it."

"Why would I need to know your password?"

"To check a text for me while I'm driving, to open my phone to take a picture, to look at my calendar to see if we're available on the same day—"

I gave him a look.

"What? We're spending a lot of time together. There's going to be a situation when you'll need to get into my phone. If you don't want to use it, don't ever use it, but at least you'll have it if you need it."

I peered down at the cell in my hand and I felt my face contort the tiniest bit and I realized a lump was rising in the back of my throat. I stared at the black screen so long he noticed.

"Are you okay?" he asked, dipping his head to look at me.

No? Not even a little?

I guess this was going to be the first heavy truth I volunteered as part of this exercise.

"I didn't know my husband's PIN," I admitted quietly. "Because he gaslighted me into thinking I was paranoid and controlling for asking for it."

I raised my gaze to his and watched understanding move across his face.

"You and me?" he said gently. "We're different. We agree to be harmless to each other."

The words broke my heart. Jacob's promise to be harmless to me felt more earnest than my own wedding vows had at the end.

I believed that he wanted to be harmless to me. But mostly because Jacob was harmless to everyone.

He watched me for a long moment. Probably to make sure I was okay. But it felt like I was trapped in some hypnotic trance and I couldn't look away. I could see the flecks in his eyes. Feel his breath just tickle my face. He was one small lean from being able to kiss me.

I couldn't imagine how Amy'd had his love and devotion and didn't do everything to keep him. Didn't want it, or see it for the precious thing that it was.

I looked away and broke the spell. "Are you sure you want to do this?" I sniffed. "It's super invasive."

"I'm sure. I don't care."

I swallowed hard and took a deep breath. Okay. Here we go.

I picked up his phone and went to his search history. Most of the first page was Googling Wakan. I smiled when I saw that he'd Googled every single place I told him to before coming.

Before the Wakan searches he had a long history of searches for...sofas?

I looked up at him. "You're shopping for a sofa?"

"Yeah," he said, sitting against the headboard. "I actually wanted to show you. See what you thought."

He peered over at his search history and tapped on one. A navy-blue sofa came up. "That one. What do you think?"

"Why are you getting a sofa?"

"To replace the recliners like you said."

"You're replacing your chairs because I came over one time and casually said you should have a sofa?"

"I want to have the kind of living room you like."

My face went soft.

He was making plans for me?

Permanent, furniture-type plans—and we were just friends. Nick wouldn't even commit to having dinner with my mom when she came to town. Probably because he'd had one foot out the door for the last half of our marriage. I wasn't on his long-term agenda. And Jacob was over here like, "I've known you for two months, you might come over again, which sofa do you want?" It made me laugh a little.

"I like it," I said. "But you don't want to go sit on it first? What if it's all hard?"

"If I go, will you come?"

"You want me to come?"

"Yes."

"Okay." I nodded. "We'll go sit on sofas."

He smiled and I went back to his phone while he looked at mine.

He was being awfully quiet.

I couldn't honestly remember what I'd Googled in the last week. Nothing scandalous. I think there was a long jaunt where I was researching menstrual cups. But I refused to be embarrassed by period products and Jacob couldn't care less. I don't know a doctor who would. And even if there was something humiliating in there, I kind of wanted him to see it. I wanted him to see all my ugly parts and my dirty secrets. Like, here's all my neurotic shit. Here's me on a two a.m. rabbit hole, Googling psychic mediums after I saw a TikTok that said one solved an unsolved murder in Alabama. And look! Instead of going to bed after, I searched for some little plastic dicks I wanted to put on the light switches in Benny's room as a prank. What do you think of that? Is it weird enough for you?

It's like I wanted to see if he still wanted me around after he knew me. The unscripted me. The real me. The messy me.

Maybe because at some point Nick knew me like this, and he decided he preferred someone else.

I remembered when I'd looked at Nick's search history, when I'd hacked his laptop and finally saw what he'd been doing after the lid was blown off of his double life. It was like a timeline of deception, a detailed account of every lie he'd told.

Here he was Googling to figure out which five-star hotel was closest to his office so he could fuck Kelly on thousand-thread-count sheets on his lunch break. Here's him searching for flower shops to send bouquets that weren't for me. Oh, and here's Nick searching for first-class flights to Cancún while I was asleep next to him in bed. He was getting them for a romantic vacation with his girlfriend that he was planning to tell me was a work trip.

When *we* flew places, he flew us coach.

You know what I didn't see in Nick's search results? Not a single search result for pregnancy. Or parenthood. Or cribs or car seats or baby names...

Anyway.

Jacob's phone was a *very* different search history experience.

I liked seeing what Jacob did when no one was watching because it was exactly what he *said* he did. Down to the Google search for the nursery he said he was going to check for rosebushes for his yard and the IMDB for actors on *Schitt's Creek* and the Chuck & Don's website for treats for Lieutenant Dan.

Jacob was who he said he was. All the time. And to me, men were never who they said they were. But this one, by all accounts, sort of *was*.

And it scared the absolute shit out of me.

I think I would have felt better if his search history was just Andrew Tate quotes and six hours a day of Pornhub because then I wouldn't feel like I had to keep looking for the catch-22. I wouldn't have to continue to be braced for the big letdown when Jacob Maddox showed me his true colors. I could just go, "Ah. There it is." And then my heart would start making the building blocks again for the wall I liked to keep around it.

I think, subconsciously, that was what I was hoping for. I wanted him to disappoint me. I wanted to get past the façade that everyone shows the rest of the world and see who he really was unscripted.

But the plan had backfired. Because I was in love with Jacob unscripted.

I loved that every time we'd gone out to eat over the last week, he'd Googled the menu so he'd know what to order when we got there. I loved that he'd Googled El Salvador and then the little town I'd told him my mom was from. I loved that the day we took the twins to the park and Carter said he wanted him to wear raccoon socks, Jacob had gone on a multi-site crusade for them. I loved that he Googled plants. I loved it. It made me want to climb him for having this wholesome hobby that wasn't boning someone else.

I loved it.

I loved *him*.

And then I froze where I sat.

Oh my God...I *loved* him.

But how could I not? He was the most lovable man alive. I think you'd be hard-pressed to find anyone in Jacob's life who *didn't* love him.

But I *loved*, loved him. Not in a friendship way. Not in an admiration way. In an if-you-weren't-in-love-with-someone-else, I'd-take-a-chance-on-you way. An I'd-give-you-everything way.

But he *was* in love with someone else. And just yesterday they'd been whisper-fighting in a room full of taxidermy animals, and she'd left her lipstick on his collar and her perfume on his shirt. She'd sent him home shaken and sad because she still had the power over him to do that.

So I should just stop thinking about it. Because me loving him didn't matter as long as he loved her.

I handed him his phone back. "Here."

He gave me my phone back too. "I have to know, did you go with the DivaCup?"

"Ha. Do you wish we would have stuck with the mullet questions?"

He shook his head. "No. I like your super invasive, completely inappropriate get-to-know-you activities."

I laughed a little.

He held my gaze. "Anything you want to know about me, you just ask me."

Will you go back to Amy when the time comes?

Do you have any sort of feelings for me at all?

If you could love me back, would you never hurt me or leave me?

If we were pregnant, would you Google it?

I smiled at him for a long moment and his eyes flickered again to my lips.

"Hey," he said, talking to my mouth.

"Yeah?" I said, talking to his.

"Do you want some bourbon?"

I looked up. "You have *bourbon*?"

"Yeah. I brought it for Daniel and Alexis, but then I saw she was pregnant and I started second-guessing if it was inconsiderate to give it to her, so I kept it. We could open it."

"You don't drink, though."

"I drink. I just don't drink when my anxiety is high."

"We're in a house-hostage situation—it's not high now?"

He shook his head. "No."

A grin spread across my face. Then we both hopped out of the bed at the same time.

CHAPTER 32

JACOB

We were sitting on the floor in front of the fire with our backs against the hope chest at the end of the bed. It had been an hour since I'd procured the bourbon from my duffel bag, and Briana was very, *very* drunk.

We were playing a drinking game with a deck of cards we found in the nightstand. We had to fling one into the fireplace, and if we missed, we had to take a drink. The score was one to four, not in her favor.

She was leaning into my shoulder and I pried the bottle out of her hands. "I think we're done with this," I said, putting on the top and setting it next to me.

"I wish we had Cheez-Its." Her retainer made her lisp.

I chuckled a little and she lolled her head to look up at me. "Don't laugh at me. With your...your perfectly symmetrical face and your nice teeth and the puppy-dog thing."

I smiled. I didn't know what she meant about the puppy-dog thing, but I'd take the teeth and symmetrical face any day.

I had never been so happy to be trapped in a room.

She was wearing my shirt. It would smell like her when I got it back. I couldn't wait. It was a little short, though, and I kept getting glimpses of things I probably shouldn't be seeing. I was happy about this too, but also knew she was too buzzed for modesty, so I'd pulled the blanket off the bed and wrapped her in it.

She hiccupped.

"Do you need to throw up?" I asked.

She shook her head. "I never throw up. Ever."

"Ever?"

"Nope. Not even norovirus can take me down. I have a cat—a cat iron—a *cast*-iron stomach—have you ever heard of the two beers and a puppy litmus test?"

I shook my head, smiling at her. "No."

She rubbed her nose. "You ask yourself would you have two beers with this person and let them watch your puppy for a weekend? Some people are a yes/yes. Some are a no/no. My ex was a yes/no. He was fun to be around, but I couldn't rely on him."

"Amy was a no/yes. She was reliable but she wore me out."

"I've been thinking that for me you're a yes/yes," she said. It came out "yeth/yeth."

I smiled at her gently. "You're a yes/yes for me too."

"Good. Because I want to tell you something. Because I think you should know what kind of person I am, you know? Like, what I'm capable of?"

"Okay…"

"You might not like me after."

I gave her an amused look. "I'm sure I will like you."

She shook her head. "No. This is really bad. Like, it's *so* bad. It's about what I did to Nick. When I found out."

I peered down at her. She looked so serious I pivoted to face her. "Tell me."

She looked at me a moment like maybe she was reconsidering.

Then she leaned over my lap and grabbed the bourbon, pulled the top off, took a swig, and set it back down.

"Wow, that bad, huh?"

She came back to her side and looked up at me with a sniff. "So when I was in college, I used to work at Starbucks, right? And when I'd get a rude customer, I'd make their drink extra good. Like, I'd use cold-pressed coffee in their Frappuccino instead of the coffee concentrate, that kind of thing? And I wouldn't tell them what I did so they could never re-create it. That way for the rest of their life their drink would never be as good again and they'd always be chasing that one time and they'd never enjoy it the way they did that day."

"*Okaaaaay . . .*"

"This isn't the part," she said. "This is so you can get it, okay? So you can see how diabolical I am."

I chuckled. "All right . . ."

She looked at me bleakly.

I arched an eyebrow. "What'd you *do*?"

She drew in a long breath. Then she mumbled something too low for me to hear.

I dipped my head. "What? I couldn't hear you."

"I said I poured glitter all over the house."

I choked on my laugh. *"What?"*

"Five gallons of it. I put it on the blades of the ceiling fans too. For later. I got a ladder and I took so much of it and I poured it up there so when they turned on the fan—"

I descended into a fit of laughter.

"It's not funny, Jacob! I'm not proud of this, this isn't how rational people behave!"

"No, you're right," I said, wiping at my eyes. "You should be in jail. I'm calling the police."

"Jacob!"

I had to put a hand over my mouth so I wouldn't wake up Alexis and Daniel, I was cracking up so hard.

Part of this was the bourbon making me loopy, part of it was the story, but most of it was the morose, serious way she was telling it. Like she was confessing to a murder.

"That's not all." She swallowed hard. "I stole the microwave plate. And the lightbulb out of the fridge. I took the lid for the blender and the oven mitts and the garage door opener and I untuned his guitar and I tore out the last five pages of the book he was reading. I put red Kool-Aid in the shower head and peeled the labels off all the canned food and I put raw shrimp into the curtain rod on the window next to the bed—*stop laughing!*"

I was practically crying.

"They call it Pulling a Briana Ortiz at work," she said miserably. "It's so embarrassing. I think the nurses tell it to their boyfriends to scare them straight or—"

I had to pull her in and kiss the top of her head. I couldn't help it. She looked so despondent.

"They had to replace the carpet," she whispered. "They couldn't get the sparkles out."

"Well, in your defense, I think he deserved it," I said, chuckling into her hair.

She nodded into my chest. "He did. He really did."

"Where do you get five gallons of glitter?"

"Amazon." Sniff. "Prime."

"Of course. Do you regret it?"

"No."

I let a laugh out through my nose.

She stayed there for a second, sniffling against my shirt. Then she sat up and wiped her hair off her face. "Tell me something nobody knows about you."

"What?"

"I told you this. It's my most embarrassing thing. So you tell me something now."

I sat back against the hope chest and gave it some thought.

"Okay," I looked back at her. "When I came into Benny's hospital room, I froze up because you were so beautiful."

Her jaw dropped. "What?"

"I couldn't even talk."

She giggled. "Stop!" She pushed my knee. "You're just saying that to make me feel better about the glitter."

I looked at her steadily. "I'm serious."

She gawked and I smiled.

"Well, I can't stop staring at your collarbone," she said.

I looked at her amused. "My collarbone?"

"I think it's so sexy." She lisped on *sexy*. "And your forearms. I love them."

Well. *I* was never wearing long sleeves again. Winter was going to be rough.

"When I was sitting at the restaurant talking to you that day, it rained," I said. "I was on the patio. I got drenched."

Her mouth fell open. "You sat in the rain just to talk to me?"

I looked at my lap for a long moment before looking back up at her. "I'd do a lot more than that for you."

She raised her eyes to mine and we peered at each other in the silence.

The fire crackled and warmed the side of my face and the flames danced across her irises and I wanted to kiss her so badly every inch of my body screamed.

And that was the moment.

The first time my brain consciously registered what my heart had been telling me for the last few weeks.

I wasn't falling in love with her.

I already *was*.

It's funny how similar longing feels to grief. Even though she was right here, all I could think about was the part that was missing. The part I'd never get.

I was destined to love her up close and then eventually from a distance, and she'd never know it or love me back.

It stole the air from my lungs. It stole the strength in my arms and legs. It made me weak with disappointment and hopelessness, and I knew I would always carry the ache I felt in this moment.

Briana was a catastrophic life event. A thing that changed everything. And I wouldn't be the same after this. All the women I'd ever met and all the women I ever would fell away beneath her.

She had me.

And it wasn't because I was slightly buzzed, or feeling sentimental, or because of the way the fire lit her face, or how my shirt clung to her body. She *had* me. And I suspected she always would. No matter how this ended.

Nothing could have prepared me for *her*.

I reached out and put a hand to her cheek. A rule, broken. A boundary crossed. I had no reason to touch her like this. Nobody was watching.

But she didn't move away. She just closed her eyes and leaned into it and I tried to pour all the love I felt into this tiny contact. Like maybe it would help me reach her. Maybe she could feel it and it would change something that likely wasn't ever going to change.

"What does this one mean?" she whispered.

"This one what?" I said softly.

She opened her beautiful eyes and looked at me. "This quiet," she said dreamily. "I know all of your quiets. I know when you're alone with me and you're quiet, it's because your brain is still. And when you're in public and you're quiet, it's because your brain is loud. But I don't know this one. What's this one?"

I held her gaze. "This one's you."

She smiled and then scooted over and curled up against me and I got to put an arm around her. She snuggled into me and it was everything. My entire universe condensed to a single place and time.

"Jacob?" she whispered.

I put my nose to her hair. "What?"

A long pause.

"I love you."

I breathed out into her hair and closed my eyes.

She was drunk. Everyone loves everyone when they're drunk. But even though she didn't mean it the way I did, I almost said it back. But her breath had gone steady and I knew she was asleep.

It didn't matter.

Nothing we talked about tonight would feel real tomorrow anyway. At least not for her. But I got to hold her. That was real. That was at least something.

The fire burned down to embers and I stayed there until my back hurt from leaning on a hope chest. Then I picked her up and carried her to bed. And while she was cradled in my arms, she muttered something about teleporting.

CHAPTER 33

BRIANA

The door was open.

I woke up sprawled half on top of Jacob with a headache, the driest mouth I'd ever had, and a rock-hard boner under my thigh.

Oh my *God*. I bolted up and scrambled out of the bed.

Jacob sat up, only half awake. "What happened?"

"Nothing. The door's open. Plan worked," I said, grabbing my clothes without looking at him. Then I realized that every time I bent down, my ass peeked out from the shirt he'd loaned me. I tugged the back down with one hand and fled the room clutching my clothes and what was left of my dignity with the other.

I couldn't remember half of last night. My memory got foggy somewhere after shot number three. I think I told him about the glitter. Ugh.

I took the longest shower of my life, chugged some water and Motrin, and came down to face the firing squad. Alexis immediately cornered me in the kitchen, but I had no gossip for her other than I got blackout drunk and woke up with a hard-on under my leg.

Jacob kept looking at me over the table at breakfast.

I'd glance up and he'd be sort of silently gazing at me. I usually knew what he was thinking when he was quiet, but I couldn't read him this time, which made me *certain* I told him about the glitter and now he was probably wrestling with the fact that his fake girlfriend was also likely a serial killer.

He must have carried me to bed. No way I'd gotten myself there. I'd been passed out and flat on the floor and he'd probably had to dead-lift me.

Jacob was so soft and gentle I never really gave him credit for how physically strong he was. He reminded me of those sweet, docile draft horses they use for riding lessons for children. You forget that they weigh a couple thousand pounds and could pull a loaded wagon.

I wished I'd been coherent enough to remember him carrying me. The whole thing was probably very sexy.

After breakfast, Jacob and I drove home in our separate cars.

On the way home I thought about the penis. I thought about the penis a *lot*.

I knew there was going to be a peen encounter. I just knew it.

I knew clinically that his erection didn't mean anything. He'd been sleeping. It was just a sign of a properly functioning blood and nervous system, nothing to get excited about. Only I also knew that the next time I picked up my vibrator, that was one hundred percent what I'd be thinking about. Jacob, warm and sleepy in the bed with me. Me, waking up to him hard. Only in my fantasy scenario I didn't run from the room. I slipped a hand under the waistband of his underwear to wake him up instead...

What if we just did it?

Hooked up for the duration of this arrangement. Two grown adults with needs and an understanding, that's it. Friends with benefits.

As if that's all he'd be...

And that was the biggest reason of all why I couldn't cross this line. Because I didn't think I could separate the sex from the feelings I was having.

No. I *knew* I couldn't.

And I couldn't let myself fall more in love with a man who was in love with someone else. I couldn't be his second choice. I couldn't be his fall-back plan.

But God, I wished I could.

I'd let this man turn me inside out. Grind me into dust. Flip me like a pancake. I wanted him to do things to me that I hadn't done with *anyone*. He had me worked up in a way that was making me creative. I'd eat a Pop-Tart naked off his bare chest.

I didn't know how it was possible to love someone this much and be just as attracted to them at the same time. How you could absolutely adore someone and want to take care of them and put Band-Aids on their boo-boos and simultaneously want them to pile-drive you into a headboard. I wanted him to whisper sweet things to me after bending me like a pretzel in every sexual way possible, and then I wanted to watch him sleep and stare at his face with heart-eye emojis.

These two things had never existed for me side by side before. Not like this.

I'd been attracted to my husband. I'd been in *love* with my husband. But not the way it was with Jacob. Not even close. And I had to wonder if this is how Nick had felt about Kelly.

I *hated* it.

Because if it was? I got it. I really did.

Nick should have left me first. He should have never cheated on me. But if I'd felt this way about Jacob when I was married to Nick... it would have been torture. It would have made me question if who I was with was the right one.

It would have been enough to end a marriage.

It was two o'clock when I finally pulled up to my house. I dragged myself out of the car and up the front walk, planning on going to bed to sleep off the rest of my hangover, but when I opened the front door, I immediately knew something was wrong. Very, *very* wrong.

The air smelled like chicharron.

Mom was here.

I mouthed a silent cuss word and Benny poked his head out of the kitchen. "Hi, BRIANA. Nice to have you back, BRIANA."

I gave him a death glare and a second later Mom came out behind him. She had on her old apron, and her wild salt-and-pepper curls were tied up on top of her head. *"Hola, mija!"*

"Hola, Mamá," I said, hugging her.

Benny was glaring at me over her shoulder. He was in an apron and I just knew he'd been Mom's prep cook for however long she'd been here.

She held me out from her and shook her head at me in disapproval. "So skinny. You aren't eating? Where is your boyfriend? He doesn't feed you?"

"He feeds me, Mamá."

She pursed her lips. "He's probably too skinny too. You doctors never eat. I'm making pupusas, come help me with the masa." She went back to the kitchen without waiting for me.

I slumped. Benny shot me a vindicated look. Now it was *my* turn to suffer.

I loved my mom. She was an incredible woman. Strong, capable, a survivor in a hundred different ways—but she was a lot.

Mom lived to care for others. And when the people she loved were in crisis, this instinct went into overdrive. She'd come home to her newly divorced and apparently emaciated daughter and her ailing son in kidney failure. She was going to scrub down every surface of this house and feed us until we begged for mercy.

Benny looked over his shoulder toward the kitchen and then closed the space between us.

"I can't *believe* you called her," he whispered. "We had a deal."

"She called *me* last week. Was I supposed to send her to voicemail?" I whispered back. "I told her you had a donor and you were fine. I didn't tell her to come!"

"I've been making curtido since eight a.m. Apparently I'm sick enough to need her to fly across the United States, but not sick enough to not chop cabbage."

I snorted at this, which earned me a more pointed glare. "How long is she staying?" I asked quietly.

He held up ten fingers. Then he started pulsing them. Twenty, thirty, forty, fifty—two *months*???

I groaned quietly. *"Whhhhy?"*

"To be here to nurse me back to health." He jabbed a finger at me. "This is *your* fault—"

"*My* fault?" I whispered. "How is that?"

"You made me give up my apartment," he whispered. "I'm trapped here."

I crossed my arms. "Well, if it makes you feel better, I'm trapped here too."

"It doesn't. It does not make me feel better, Briana. You suck."

"Gil didn't come?" I asked.

"Nope."

Ugh. Gil buffered her. It was always better when Gil came. He *liked* being mothered and bossed around. It was sort of their thing.

"Maybe it'll be fun?" I said hopefully.

Benny gave me a look like No, It Will NOT Be Fun. "The kitchen's a mess. It looks like the whole mercado blew up in there."

He took off his apron and smacked it into my hands. *"Mamá, me siento un poco cansado,"* he called around the corner. "Gonna go lie down."

"Okay, *mijo*. Briana will help me," she called back from the kitchen.

He smirked and I rolled my eyes at him. I was way too hungover for this.

I spent the next four hours helping to make enough pupusas for a small army. We also stripped and washed all the beds and reorganized every cabinet in the kitchen. Mom announced that she was going to give the cat a bath once he came out of hiding, and I knew we'd never see Cooter out from under the sofa ever again.

I knew why she was like this. Cooking and cleaning were her stress response. When we were growing up, there was so little she could give us, but even if there wasn't money, she could always give us a clean home. And she wanted to feed us now for all the times she couldn't before—and she did. In amounts that attempted to compensate for the lean years, times a million.

This extreme nesting would settle down once Mom had the house the way she wanted it. The cooking would never end, but she'd stop cleaning the ceiling fans once she felt we were being adequately cared for.

Mom would be great when there were grandchildren. She'd be a wonderful Mamá Rosa—she was a wonderful mom. It's just that Benny and I didn't need this level of mothering. But when there were infants around? She'd be a dream come true.

I felt bad I'd never been able to give her any grandkids. I'd always feel bad about that.

We got caught up while we cooked and cleaned. I told her about my "boyfriend." She wanted to meet Jacob. *And* his family.

His family was no problem, but I worried about Jacob. He'd be the center of her attention and he'd probably get overwhelmed.

I couldn't decide if it would be better to introduce them at his parents' house, where she'd have more distractions and the focus wouldn't be so squarely on him? Or alone, when the stress of Amy and Jeremiah wouldn't be a factor, because they'd probably be there.

And then I had a moment of wondering if I should even introduce them at all. Because in a few months Jacob and I would break up anyway. But then I realized if I didn't, Mom would think I didn't want him to know her or that he didn't want to meet his girlfriend's mom.

I'd have to make her believe we were real, the way I had to make everyone believe it. I had to set up these foundations that I'd eventually have to tear down.

The lie just kept getting deeper and deeper. And I hated it. Not because I had to tell it, but because I wished it weren't a lie.

I showed Mom how to set up Benny on dialysis. I had to admit, that was a major bonus of her being here. Mom was a nurse, and she was very capable of sharing this load. Having two of us who could do this would give Benny the flexibility of doing his dialysis pretty much whenever he wanted to, even when I was at work. He wouldn't have to wait for me to get home.

When I finally went up to bed, it was eleven and I had four missed texts from Jacob. One making sure I got home okay. Another one thanking me for letting him come to Wakan, and two more with some selfies we took yesterday. I smiled at the selfies.

I'd loved the last two days so much. I loved just being with him. Talking to him, doing things with him. When I was with Jacob, it didn't matter where we were, I didn't want to be anywhere else. He was like that terrarium in his plant room. A self-sustaining ecosystem. Everything I needed or wanted was wrapped up into one human being. It didn't even seem possible.

It occurred to me that this is what true compatibility must feel like. Easy. Being with Jacob was easy in a way that I never knew existed. And it made me realize how much of my marriage had been forced. How we never had anything to talk about. How he didn't seem to like my family or make any effort to get to know them or Alexis. Even things like vacations. I'd want to explore and he'd want to relax. These things seemed insignificant at the time, just small differences of opinion or minute preferences. But they glared now. Like proof that something was off and always had been. That maybe I'd married a six out of ten on the compatibility scale—which can work with effort. But Jacob was a ten out of ten. A yes/yes. Jacob didn't take work.

Jacob was perfect.

I made one of the pictures of us my screensaver and moved all the icons away from his face so he wasn't covered. I liked seeing his smile looking back from my phone.

I'd have to take this down when we broke up. Wouldn't be appropriate then. But I could have it for now.

When I called him, he answered right away.

"Hey. You're not sleeping, are you?" I asked.

"No. Just journaling. You got home okay?"

I climbed onto my bed. "Yeah. My mom is here."

"From Arizona?"

"Yup." I punched a pillow under my head. "She's here for Benny's transplant."

"Oh. Can I meet her?"

I laughed a little. "You want to meet *more* of my people? You haven't had enough?"

"Well, I didn't enjoy Doug very much, but I liked Alexis and Daniel."

"Okay, Doug is not my people. I do not claim him."

He chuckled.

"My mom actually does want to meet you," I said. "*And* your family."

"Great. Let's set it up."

Again with the enthusiastic meeting of my inner circle. This man was really putting in the work for this charade.

"What if your family slips?" I said, lowering my voice. "About the kidney. Benny and my mom don't know you're his donor."

"We could just tell them."

I wrinkled my forehead. "Tell them? I thought you didn't want a bunch of people knowing."

"I can handle two more."

I twisted my lips. "I don't know..."

"What?"

"These two people are going to be a lot. There's probably going to be crying and hugging."

"It's okay."

It was a little weird that he was so willing to do this. All of this. I mean *I* had to know his family for the thing, but he didn't necessarily need to know mine. It seemed like extra work for him.

"You're so social lately," I said.

"I want to know your friends and your family."

I don't know why, but his words gripped me right in the heart. I guess because that's what a real boyfriend would do. Want to meet the people I loved. He was probably doing this because introducing my family to his made this fake relationship feel more authentic. I couldn't really think of another reason why he'd want our families to meet, especially because meeting people he didn't know was his least favorite thing in the universe.

"Okay," I said. "How do you want to do it? Do you want me to tell them you're Benny's kidney donor before you see them? I feel like if I do it in front of you, it'll be awkward."

"Sure."

"When do you want to do the family meet-and-greet thing?"

"Let me call Mom and see what day works for her."

"All right." I yawned.

Then we just stayed on the phone for a moment, not saying anything.

This time last night I was in bed with him in Wakan. I wished I were in bed with him now too. I'd see him at work tomorrow, but it wasn't the same.

"Jill came back over today," he said.

It was weird, because I felt like he said it to remind me that we were supposed to be living together. Like he was thinking about me being there with him too.

"When your mom meets my family, she's going to tell them you're living at home," he said.

Oh, *crap*. I hadn't thought about that.

"We could always tell her the truth," I said. "Like, the actual truth. That we're not dating."

"No," he said quickly. "I don't like that. It's going to get out."

I sighed. "Okay. Let me think on this. I'll figure something out." I rubbed my eyes. "I have to go to sleep. I'll see you tomorrow, okay?"

"All right. I'll see you tomorrow. Good night."

But then we didn't hang up.

I waited for the moment of disconnect. I wanted him to do it. It couldn't be me, at least not tonight. But it never happened.

We stayed on the phone in silence. Thirty seconds. A minute. Two.

He'd probably just forgotten to hang up. His phone was probably sitting on his desk and he was back to scribbling in his journal and he didn't even notice the call hadn't ended. Only I didn't hear scribbling. I could only hear the soft trickling of the fountain in his plant room.

Maybe he'd set the phone down and left? But for a moment, I allowed myself to believe that he was doing what *I* was doing. He was keeping me for a few extra precious moments.

I let myself reach across the silence. I was looking at him now in my mind. His soft, tender eyes, the curve of his lips. The tic in his jaw when he was giving me one of his quiets. The one I didn't know.

I could feel him through the line. I could smell him. He was becoming 3-D, shaped by my memory of the constant study of his face and his movements and his moods. He floated in front of me like a ghost, coming through the thin connection of our phones.

I wanted to run to him. To walk out of this place and get in my car and go straight to his house. Burst into his plant room while he sat at that desk and throw myself at him and take whatever he was willing to give me, no matter how small, or temporary, or insignificant. I could feel my body and my heart and my mind wrestling with one another. One screaming for him, the other one too afraid to act, and the last one arguing rationally that this would be a terrible, terrible idea.

And he probably wasn't even there. Just a phone, abandoned on a desk. And me, making things up.

I pulled the cell away from my ear and looked at the screen. Then I pressed the End Call button.

Hanging up with him and going to bed alone felt like the saddest thing I'd ever done in my life.

I waited until dinner after work the next day to talk to Mom and Benny. Mom had made pollo encebollado, chicken thighs in a tomato onion base. It was my favorite dish. Of course she'd made ten times more than we could ever eat and it was all going into the quickly filling deep freezer in the garage. Oh well. At least I wouldn't keep wasting money on DoorDash.

I'd given this situation with Jacob a lot of thought. I'd decided to move in with him, just for a few months.

He was right. My mom would definitely blow our cover to his family if I was still living here. Moving in with him was the only way to make sure his family didn't catch us in this lie I'd told. It was so stupid. I should never have done it. Amy just made me so mad and I wanted to rub it in her stupid face.

Anyway.

I'd promised Jacob that I would make this fake relationship believable. And I was the one who'd made the claim we were living together. He was obviously stressed about it or he wouldn't be insisting on it so much. Plus, this house was officially crowded with Mom and Benny in it. Mom could do Benny's dialysis; I didn't have to be here. So I was going to Jacob's after dinner.

We were finishing up eating and I wiped my mouth with a napkin.

"So I have something I need to tell you guys," I said.

Mom paused with her fork halfway to her mouth. "Are you pregnant?"

"No, I am not pregnant."

I couldn't help but note that she looked disappointed.

Mom was extremely traditional. If I were pregnant and unmarried, she would not be happy. But apparently me being childless and unmarried at my age was even worse.

I let out a long breath. Then I looked at my brother. "Benny, Jacob is your kidney donor."

I heard Mom's fork hit the plate.

"He didn't want anyone to know," I said. "But he's given me permission to tell you. Also, he's asked me to move in with him and I've agreed. I'm leaving. Tonight."

My brother looked stunned. Mom had her hands over her mouth. Then she got up and headed straight to the fridge.

I twisted in my chair. "What are you doing?"

"Packing food for him. Briana, make him a plate."

"Mom, I'm not going yet—"

"*Si, claro que se lo vas a llevar!*" She was pulling Tupperware out of the fridge. "If you do not go and feed that man right now, I will go there and feed him myself."

I groaned. Jacob didn't know it yet, but his freezer was about to be full of Salvadorian food. Forever.

I looked back at Benny. He was just blinking at me.

"You don't have to make a big deal about it," I said to my brother. "He's introverted too. He won't like a big show of gratitude or anything."

Mom pulled an insulated bag from the pantry and went for the deep freezer in the garage. When the door to the garage closed, Benny licked his lips. "You're not doing anything stupid for me, are you?"

I wrinkled my forehead. "What?"

"You're not like, hooking up with him for this. Right?"

I shook my head. "No."

I could tell by the look on his face that he didn't believe me. "Why'd he ask you on that date?" he said. "The other day?"

I leaned forward. "Benny, I need you to believe me when I tell you that Jacob would never do anything to take advantage of me. I am *deeply* in love with this man. And only five percent of that is because of what he's doing for you."

I realized in that moment that it was true.

It was amazing that Jacob had so many endearing qualities that donating an organ to my brother only represented the smallest reason why I loved him.

Benny peered at me for a second. Then he looked away from me and nodded.

"I'm sorry I'm leaving you here with Mom," I said quietly.

He sniffed. "It's okay. I get it. Tell him thanks."

"I will."

I put a hand over his. "I want you to know, though, that I would have done anything I needed to do to make this happen for you."

He nodded again.

And I guess I sort of already was. Because in making this arrangement with Jacob, I'd signed up to break my own heart.

CHAPTER 34

JACOB

Someone knocked on my door. Lieutenant Dan jumped up and started barking.

I was in my plant room journaling. It was almost nine p.m. Probably Jewel. My other two sisters had already been here in the last twenty-four hours.

I sighed, set my pen into the pages, and shut the notebook. I got up and opened the door to ... Briana?

She had two suitcases, a cooler, a duffel, and an insulated shoulder bag.

"Hey—"

"I'm moving in," she said. "But just for a few months."

My grin ripped across my face. *Instant* happiness.

She came in carrying the duffel and the cooler, an excited Lieutenant Dan hopping around her feet.

"What's in the cooler?" I asked.

"More Salvadorian food than you and I could ever eat. And it's going to keep coming."

I beamed as I took her luggage straight to my bedroom closet. I cleared out a space for her on the rack and consolidated a few drawers so she could have them.

I couldn't even describe how happy I was to have her here. She would be the last person I saw before I went to bed and the first person I saw when I woke up.

I pictured my bathroom, steamy after her shower, smelling like her perfume and her shampoo. Her things scattered through my house. A sweater on the back of a chair. Her shoes by the door. Her lipstick on my cups. These little insignificant things that felt so huge and meaningful.

I came back down the hallway as she came out of the kitchen. "I managed to get it all to fit in the freezer," she said.

She looked around the living room with hands on her hips. "I think it'll fit here."

"What will fit here?"

"The air mattress."

She began pulling a crumpled rubber wad and a black pump out of her duffel bag. My smile faded. I thought she would sleep in my room. In my bed. With me.

"You don't have to sleep on the floor," I said. "We can share my bed. It's big enough."

"No. I think it's more appropriate if we don't share a room."

"But we've done it before. And that bed was way smaller—"

"It's just better, Jacob."

There was something final in her tone. She plugged in the pump and started blowing up the mattress while I watched, deflated.

Even when I was getting more, it was still not enough. It still wasn't real.

I stood there hoping the mattress wouldn't fit. It did.

When she was done, she sat on the bed and gave it a little bounce.

I frowned at her. "Well, what are we going to do if someone knocks on the door?"

She shrugged. "I'll just shove it in the plant room."

"And you think you can do this fast enough?"

"Sure."

Then, almost on cue, someone knocked on the door. She looked at me and her eyes got wide. Then she bolted to her feet and grabbed the mattress.

She lifted it sideways. "Help me!" she whispered.

I crossed my arms. "Don't you think you should be prepared to execute this plan on your own? I might not always be available. What if I was in the shower?"

"You're not in the shower!" She was shuffling sideways, holding the clunky mattress against her legs.

"Well, we have to plan for the worst-case scenario, don't we?"

She knocked over a lamp. "Jacob!"

I was grinning. "Nope."

She made a guttural shrieking noise and tipped over a planter. It fell sideways and dirt spilled onto the hardwood.

I started cracking up.

She squeezed down the hallway, knocking picture frames onto the floor the whole way to the plant room. It was so funny I didn't even care she was leaving a path of destruction in her wake.

A moment later a door slammed, and she came back looking flustered. She stopped in front of me breathing hard, her ponytail crooked, and she jabbed a finger at my chest. "You and me? We are about to have our first fight."

It was all I could do to try and keep my face straight.

Someone knocked again.

She gave me a narrow-eyed glare and stomped to the door and opened it.

It was Jewel.

"Hey! What a nice surprise!" Briana said, a little too brightly. "Come in!"

My sister stepped inside and paused to take in the scene. A

lamp on the floor, frames all over the hallway, plant on its side, Briana's hair a mess. I came up behind her and slipped an arm around her waist.

Jewel looked back at us. "Uh…what the hell are you guys doing in here? Your house is trashed."

Briana smoothed her hair down. "We were having sex. Things got a little wild."

"You should see what she did to the bed," I said.

Briana snorted.

Jewel nodded slowly. "*Okaaaay.* Well, good. Gwen says you guys look sexually frustrated."

Briana and I blanched in unison.

"Here's the melon baller I borrowed. I'm gonna go now." And she left.

I turned to Briana after the door clicked closed.

I cleared my throat. "I'm not sexually frustrated," I lied.

"Well, *I* am," she scoffed.

I felt heat rising up my neck. There was such an easy solution…

She crossed her arms. "I'm not talking to you for five minutes. I am very mad at you."

"Am I getting the glitter?"

She sucked in air. "Thin ice, Maddox."

My lip twitched and she tried not to smile, but she couldn't help it.

She went to my room, presumably to unpack her bags into my closet. I grinned after her.

An hour later I was at the kitchen table with her, eating a plate of the food she brought. It was the best meal I'd had in as long as I could remember. Chicken thighs in a brothy sauce. Her mom was an excellent cook. "You said there's going to be more of this?"

She pulled her knee up under her chin. "Jacob, double down on your deep-freezer space."

I poked at my food a little. "I'm sorry you have to be here while your mom's in town."

"I don't mind being here."

I raised my eyes to her. "You don't?"

"No. I totally don't. It'll be so fun. And we can carpool to work."

"We can finish watching *Schitt's Creek*," I said.

"And we can walk Lieutenant Dan together and do the sofa-shopping thing—this will be so good for Instagram. Also, I want you to know that I'm going to give you your space. If you need to disappear into the plant room or whatever, I totally understand."

I doubted there would be much of that. I didn't want to disappear when she was around. I wanted to be wherever she was.

I gave her a key, sheets, and a blanket and pillows for her bed. I set up the coffeepot like I always did for the next morning— only I made twice what I normally did, and even this small thing made me smile.

We'd be together all the time, in the same place. The idea of it made me feel elated.

I never thought I'd want that. I could never imagine wanting someone all the time. And even this wasn't enough, because she was in the other room at night and not with me.

From this point on, and for the first time in my life, I slept with the door open.

For the next week we fell into a routine, and I was the happiest I'd ever been.

We bought a sofa. It wouldn't be delivered for another week, but we drove the old armchairs up to the cabin anyway and spent the night. We went swimming off the dock and she made me practice the lift from *Dirty Dancing* with her, which meant I got to touch her, even though nobody was there to see it. Made my whole day. Then we dried off and walked to the restaurant and had dinner.

She didn't bring up the story I told her about me talking to her in the rain there. So she didn't remember. It was just as well.

We came back after eating and sat in the armchairs in front of the fire talking until we couldn't keep our eyes open.

Amy always said the cabin was boring because there weren't any bars within walking distance or enough rooms for friends to stay with us. When I told Briana that, she'd looked at me confused and said, "How could it be boring when *you're* here?"

I loved every minute we spent together. Every single minute.

Briana and I were back at work today. We had dinner with her mom and brother at my parents' house tonight after we got off.

I stood across the ER, by the door of a patient room, watching Briana at the nurses' station. She was sitting with Jocelyn, charting. Zander came over and stood next to me. "What are you doing?"

"Watching Briana. I sent her flowers. I'm waiting for them to get here."

"What'd you send her flowers for?"

I smiled. "She's mad at me."

"For what?"

"She asked if I'd eat her if she were a gummy bear. I said yes."

He guffawed and Briana looked up from her computer and narrowed her eyes at me. She gave me a thumbs-down and I laughed.

Zander eyed me. "This thing is still fake, right?" he said, his voice low.

My smile fell the smallest bit. "Yes. It's still fake."

"Are you sure?"

I blew out a breath. "I asked her out a few weeks ago. She said no."

"She said *no*?" He looked back at her. She glanced at me and shook her head, trying not to smile. "Well, are you gonna ask her again?"

"No. It's not like my offer expired. If she changed her mind, she'd tell me. She doesn't like me like that."

He peered over at me. "Do you like her like that?"

I was quiet for a beat. "Yeah. I do."

I saw the flowers drifting down the hall and backed up a little into the doorway. The moment Briana looked over and realized they were for her was my shot of serotonin for the day. Her beautiful face lit up and she took the card from the stick and opened the envelope. I watched her read it and laugh. The card said,

Dearest Briana,

My deepest apologies. I clearly did not understand the assignment.

—)

She looked up and searched the room for me and she beamed at me when she saw me, and my heart was full.

I would give her this every day. I'd spend the rest of my life looking for ways to make her smile at me like that. I lived for it.

When she came over, everyone was watching us, as usual. I knew she'd put on a show. We couldn't touch too much at work. PDA wasn't permitted. So what we did here was act like we wanted to touch, but the rules wouldn't allow it. She'd stand extra close to me, looking up at me like if we just weren't at work, she'd kiss me. I loved that the best. When she did that, it felt like she loved me back. I let myself pretend.

She stopped an inch shy from being able to hug me. "Zander," she said, nodding at him. Then she crossed her arms and turned to me. "Thank you for the flowers, Dr. Maddox."

"So you forgive me, then?" I grinned.

She shrugged playfully and looked away from me.

"How about if I buy you dinner Saturday?" I asked.

Her eyes slid back to mine. "I want Chinese food."

"Okay."

"I get to place the order and you have to go get it."

"Sounds fair."

She arched an eyebrow. "I'm going to order half the menu."

"Of course."

We were leaning into each other, smiling.

"*Dios mío*, get a room," Hector said, walking up.

We laughed a little and moved apart, but we didn't break eye contact. We were so good at this.

It was hard to believe one of us was in love and the other one was just good at pretending.

"Hey, you got a patient asking for you in room three," Hector said to Briana.

Briana gave me one last flirty look. "Duty calls," she said, jogging backward. "I'll see you at lunch."

I watched her, grinning like an idiot, until she disappeared beyond the sliding glass doors of room three.

"And you're *sure* it's fake..." Zander said.

My smile fell.

"I'm sure." *For her, anyway.*

We were just friends. This would all end in a few weeks after the wedding. And my heart broke every single day thinking about it.

The wedding was in four weeks. Benny's kidney transplant was in five. I figured we'd probably keep up appearances for a few weeks after that. Then that would be it.

That would be all.

I went back to work.

Hector came back over ten minutes later while I was reading a chart. "Hey, some *pendejo*'s making a move on your girl."

I looked up. "What?"

"Yeah, he's all over there like, 'Give me your number, let's catch up.'"

I stared at him. "Did she give him her number?"

"Yeah. Guess she knows him or something? I'm tellin' you, you better get over there. That guy's all over her and she's into it. And he's hot too. I mean, not as hot as you, but, like, pretty damn close."

For a long moment, I looked at the door of the room she was in. Then I set down the chart and forced myself not to run.

CHAPTER 35

BRIANA

Jacob sent me flowers.

I know it was just for Instagram, but still. Even though he didn't send them for the reason I wished he sent them, he'd probably spent all day picking them out. That's how he was. I could picture him worrying about it, checking reviews for the florist before committing to using them. Maybe even calling the flower shop to request a different-color rose or vase from the picture on the website.

Stuff like this made me wish harder than usual that things were real. Maybe if Jacob were slightly less thoughtful, or sweet in the evenings, or kind to his patients, I wouldn't be so far gone.

Who was I kidding? Even if he was half the man he was, I'd be gone.

He did this thing in the morning where he'd lean in the doorway of the hallway, holding a cup of coffee and talking to me while I sat on my air mattress. His hair would be messy and he'd be in his rumpled pajamas and a T-shirt that probably smelled like him. And he just looked so...lovable. It was one of the times that made it the hardest to not be able to hug him unless someone else was around to see it. I bet he'd be warm and sleepy. I bet his lips would be soft and he'd taste like coffee and I could run my fingers through his hair.

But instead I'd just sit on my stupid inflatable bed, pretending I was happy to be out in the living room on the floor instead of cuddling in his room with him.

I loved living with him. I *loved* it.

I liked that he always had classical music playing on the lowest volume. He used scent beads in his laundry, and his towels always smelled like lavender. I liked that he burned candles when it rained. I liked it when he talked softly to his dog, who was every bit as in love with Jacob as I was. I liked hearing his footsteps coming down the hallway, or his bed creaking when he got up in the morning. I liked when he'd come quietly into the kitchen without waking me up to start the coffeemaker, or when I'd be almost asleep while watching TV with him on his bed and he'd drape a throw blanket over me and turn off the light.

Jacob was thoughtful and gentle. He was patient and kind. And his home was like being invited into a beautiful bird's nest, where I felt insulated and safe. But I think I knew in the back of my mind that the thing I liked about Jacob's house was Jacob. He was the key element in the self-sustaining ecosystem that was this life. Nothing worked without him.

I slid open the sliding glass door of room three to see the patient who'd asked for me.

"Levi!" I immediately broke into a grin.

The man sitting on the gurney with the bloody gauze wrapped around his hand smiled. "I thought this was your hospital."

"What are you doing in Minnesota?" I said, closing the door.

He held up his hand. "Slicing my palm open with a paring knife."

I sucked air through my teeth.

"I can finish this," I told the resident prepping him. They let themselves out, and I slipped on gloves and took a look at his laceration.

"Oh, yeah," I said, peeling off the gauze. "You really did a number on yourself." I gave him a mock-serious look. "Are you gonna be brave while I stitch this? No crying."

"Really? You want me to lean on toxic masculinity? You? If it hurts, I *will* cry."

I shook my head with a laugh. God, Levi. Handsome and charming as always.

I closed his hand back around the gauze. "So how's your wife?" I asked.

"Good. We're divorced."

I pulled back. "Really? You guys looked all happy on Instagram."

"Yeah, well. It didn't work out. We're still friends, though. I saw you got divorced too. I was sorry to hear that."

I shrugged, peeling off my gloves. "Shit happens. What are you gonna do."

"So remember Cindy?" he asked.

I tossed my gloves in the trash. "Cindy Baker? Your neighbor? Totally. We used to play *Guitar Hero* with her in your living room after school."

"She's why I moved back."

I raised my eyebrows. "Seriously?"

"Yup. She friended me on Facebook last year in the middle of my divorce stuff. We moved in two weeks ago."

I shook my head. "Imagine that. Your soul mate was the girl next door."

"I know. It's wild."

The sliding door opened, and Hector came back in.

Levi grinned. "Both of us divorced. Who would have thought? I hope it's okay if I say your husband was an idiot."

"You have no idea."

He looked at me approvingly. "You look good, though. Scrubs suit you."

I beamed, leaning back on the counter. "Thank you. You should see me covered in blood and vomit."

He laughed.

"Hey, we should go for drinks sometime," he said. "Catch up."

"Yeah, sure," I said.

Levi nodded at me. "Give me your number."

I pulled out my phone and turned to Hector. "Can I get you to clean this up and get some lidocaine on it? And I need a suture tray."

"You got it, *boss*." There was a touch of attitude there on the word *boss*. He gave me a weird pursed-lip look and left.

Levi watched him go. "What was that about?"

I rolled my eyes. "Who knows? If he's not dramatic, he dies."

Levi gave me his number and I texted him Hi so he could save mine in his phone when his hand was free. "There," I said, putting my cell away.

He studied me for a second. "You know I got tested for Benny."

I smiled. "You did? Thank you."

"Did he get a donor?"

I nodded. "He did, actually. He gets the transplant next month. A perfect match."

He smiled. "Good." Then he paused. "Hey. It's really good to see you."

I nodded. "Yeah, you too."

"I'm not saying that I stabbed myself on purpose just to have an excuse to come track you down, but it's definitely been the highlight of my day. I bet Cindy would like to hang out too. Get the band back together."

I was cracking up at this when the door slid open again. It wasn't Hector, though—it was Jacob. "Hey, I was wondering if I could get a consult," he said, leaning into the room.

"Sure." I looked at Levi. "I'll be right back."

I came out into the hallway. "What's up, whatcha got?"

He nodded over his shoulder. "I'm about to drain an abscess the size of an orange in room six. I thought you might want to watch."

I grinned. "*Awwww*, you come bearing gifts? I can't, though. I'm going to do these stitches." I nodded over my shoulder.

"Just have a resident do it."

"Nah, I'm gonna do this one."

He nodded slowly. "Do you know him or..."

"Yeah, remember I told you about the family my mom worked for when I was growing up? The one that hired her as a nurse for their grandma? This is their youngest son. We sort of grew up together."

"Oh. Can I meet him?"

I laughed. "You want to *meet* him?"

He crossed his arms. "Yeah, why not. I want to meet someone you grew up with."

"He's a stranger. You are aware of that."

"I think I can handle it."

I shrugged. "Okay. Come on."

We went back into the room and Levi sat up straighter as we came in. "Levi, this is my friend Jacob. Jacob, this is my childhood friend Levi Olsen."

"I'd shake your hand but..." Levi said, holding up his injury.

"Levi had a run-in with a paring knife," I explained.

Jacob nodded and slipped his fists into his pockets. "Well. You're in good hands."

And then he just...stood there.

"Well," Jacob said again after a moment. "Nice to meet you." Then he looked at me. "Eight for dinner tonight at my parents'."

"Yup..." I gave him a slightly confused look, since the dinner was for *my* mom and *my* brother, so of course I knew what time it was.

He stood there just long enough for it to be weird. Then he left.

I looked back at Levi.

"Is that your boyfriend?" he asked.

I laughed a little. "Yes. It's a long story."

He nodded. "He seemed kinda jealous."

Now I *really* laughed. "He's not, trust me."

God, I wish he were.

CHAPTER 36

JACOB

She introduced me as her friend. Her *friend*.

Even eight hours later, I couldn't stop thinking about it as I waited for Briana and her family at my parents' house.

Briana had wanted to pick up her mom and her brother and meet me here. We hadn't been able to do lunch together like we planned, so I didn't get a chance to ask about Levi—I winced when I thought of him. Levi. What kind of a name was that? It sounded like a garden tool.

They'd seemed comfortable with each other. She'd taken *way* too long to stitch him up. I'd stared at the door of room three until I actually did have to go drain that abscess, and when I was done, she was still in there.

What had they been talking about?

I was chewing on my thumbnail. My anxiety was humming again. It had been quiet for weeks and now it was back. I couldn't tell if it was the dinner tonight or *Levi*.

Her friend.

I was probably overthinking this. I was *sure* I was overthinking it. Maybe she introduced her boyfriend as a friend to everyone? I mean a boyfriend is a type of friend. Right? It wasn't technically wrong.

But the problem was that I wasn't her boyfriend. Not really. And maybe she'd wanted him to know that.

I paced in the foyer, waiting for her to pull into the driveway so I could meet her at the door. It would only be my parents, Jane, and Grandpa today. Everyone else had to work. I was grateful for the smaller crowd because I was already feeling drained. By *Levi*.

When Briana and her family finally pulled up outside, they were ten minutes late. As they came up the walkway, I took a deep breath and opened the door with my best smile. "Hey, there you are."

"Sorry, we had a little detour," Briana said, coming in and kissing me on the cheek. My heart skipped. I didn't normally get kisses of any kind.

At least she wanted her mom and brother to know I wasn't a friend.

She stepped aside to introduce me to her mom. "This is my mom, Rosa."

"Hi—"

The woman threw herself at me. "Our hero!" she said with a faint accent. "We prayed for you, and God brought you to us. Thank you."

While she hugged me, Briana shrugged at me over her shoulder with a smile.

"You're welcome," I croaked.

Rosa peeled herself off me and held me by the arms. "I told Briana, that's a special man you have. You take care of him. You give him all the good sex—"

I blanched.

"MOM!" Briana looked horrified.

Rosa looked nonplussed. "What? You're living with him, it's not like I don't know."

Well, Rosa was going to *love* Joy.

Benny came up behind his sister, who was still shaking her head. I nodded at him. "Nice to see you again."

"Yeah," he said awkwardly. "Thanks. For the thing."

"You're welcome."

Briana slipped an arm around my waist and hugged me from the side, and I looked down at her and got lost for a moment the way I always did when I got hugs from her.

"You smell good," she said, smiling up at me.

I wished I could lean down and kiss her. That's what a real boyfriend would do here. Just a quick peck and a smile.

Instead I said, "You too."

Instead. Everything I wanted to do with her, I did something else instead.

Grandpa came blazing down the hall at warp speed and snapped me out of it. He rolled so close to Briana she had to jump out of the way.

"You got my cigarettes?" He glared at her.

"No, I still do not have your cigarettes," Briana said, crossing her arms.

"Were you supposed to bring them?" Rosa asked.

Briana shook her head. "He's not allowed to have them, Mom."

"The hell I'm not!" he bellowed. "This place is a prison!"

"Grandpa..." I said.

Then Mom and Dad came down the hall with Jane to save me. I introduced my parents. Benny introduced himself to my sister as Ben, for some reason. Then my parents swept Rosa and Benny off for a tour of the house with Grandpa and Jane, and Briana and I were alone for a moment.

She slumped the second they were around the corner.

"I'm sorry about that," I said. "I locked up Jafar, but there's nothing I can do about Grandpa."

She snorted.

"Are you okay?" I asked. "You were late."

"Yeah, check out what *I* did on the way over. I saw a dead possum, so I stopped to get it for your dad—and it wasn't dead."

I barked out a laugh.

"When I picked it up, it hissed at me and I fell backward. My mom thinks I've officially lost it. I landed in a bush and she had to pick leaves out of my hair. I bumped my elbow." She lifted it up and frowned at it.

I grinned. "Want me to look at it?"

She rubbed it. "No, it's fine."

I gave her an amused look. "You don't have to bring my dad dead things."

"But I want to be his favorite," she whined.

I chuckled. And then I just gazed at her. I'd missed her, even in just the hour since I'd seen her at work.

It didn't feel normal for us to be apart now. And when we were together, I still wasn't getting as much of her as I wanted.

I was always starved when it came to her. I lived off crumbs, never getting full. Even now, standing in this hallway in a place where we could touch, I couldn't, because nobody was standing right here to see it. All of it, everything I got, was performative, and the deprivation was getting to me a little more every day. Even to just tell her that I loved her would be something. It seemed a waste to love her as much as I did without her ever knowing it. To be unaware that her very existence was my reason for smiling, for being happy to wake up in the morning.

Her phone chirped. She dug in her purse and looked at it. Then she turned off the sound and put it away.

"Alexis?" I asked.

"No." She didn't elaborate.

Benny and her mom were here. *I* was here. If it wasn't Alexis, who was it? But then I knew.

I cleared my throat. "So, I was thinking, it's probably best if we tell everyone we're dating. Just in case."

She tilted her head. "Huh?"

"You introduced me to Levi as your friend."

She wrinkled her forehead. "Did I?"

"Yeah. It was just something I noticed. I just think we should be consistent, you know?"

"Sorry. Freudian slip," she said. "Hey, what do you think about me telling him the truth?" she said, her voice low.

My pulse quickened. "Why would you do that?"

"He doesn't talk to literally anyone we know. I don't like lying if I don't have to."

She wanted to tell him she was single. *Why* did she want to tell him she was single? I felt panic rising in me like acid. I didn't even know what to say.

She changed the subject and nodded in the direction my family had gone. "We should go find them, before my mom thinks I've abandoned her." She looked back up at me. "Also, I'm going to have to serve you your food tonight, or my mom is going to think I'm mistreating you."

I gave her a look. "But it's *my* parents' house..."

"Just let it happen, Jacob. I'm to treat you like the prince you are. My mom already left flowers to the Virgin Mary to thank her for sending you. You've been elevated to saint status."

Well, at least her mom was pulling for me. I'd take what I could get.

CHAPTER 37

BRIANA

I was driving Mom and Benny home from Jacob's. Dinner had gone well. Benny got to talk to Joy about her transplant. I think it made him feel better. He'd never actually met anyone who'd been through the surgery.

"Why was the parrot screaming about Bieber?" Benny asked from the back seat.

"He wakes up every day choosing demonic possession," I said.

"And what's up with the weird room with all the dead things?"

"I did not like that room," Mom said. "So many eyes."

"His dad's a taxidermist. I think they're funny," I said, turning onto the freeway. "You didn't like the raccoon on the skateboard?" I asked my brother.

Benny shrugged in the rearview. "Yeah, I guess."

"Briana, why don't you give that old man a cigarette?" Mom asked.

"He's on oxygen, Mamá. It could make him hypoxic."

"So? Does he have dementia? He can't decide if he wants to smoke himself to death?"

"No, he doesn't have dementia."

"Then why no cigarette? You tell him, 'Look, I give you this, and maybe you can't breathe. You still want it?' And if he says yes, then it's yes. I'd give him one. *You* should give him one."

"Joy doesn't want him to have them."

She waved me off. "*Uno no lo va a matar.* He's a grown man, you give him what he wants. He's going to die, you let him die happy. And that goes for me too. Don't you tell me I can't have what I want because you're trying to make me live forever. I want to die doing the things I love. I want to be happy until the very end."

"Okay, Mamá."

"You want to be happy?" she said, going on. "Marry an ugly rich man who loves you more than you love him." She nodded at the windshield. "This one's not ugly, but he's got the rest of it. *Enculado.*"

I snorted. "Jacob is *not* whipped."

She pulled her face back to stare at me. "*Estás ciega!* Are you blind? I like this one. I *never* liked Nick."

"Ha," I said, changing lanes. "Now you tell me." I let a slow breath out through my nose. "Jacob definitely does not love me more than I love him, Mamá."

She scoffed. "You *are* blind. You're worrying in the wrong direction. Worry the other way."

"Why doesn't he ever kiss you?" Benny asked.

"He kisses me," I said defensively.

"No, he doesn't. He always looks like he wants to, but he never does."

I shifted in my seat. "He doesn't like PDA."

"But he's always holding your hand and touching you and stuff."

"Kissing is different."

"It's not *that* different..." he mumbled.

"If he asks you to marry him, say yes," Mom said. "You're not getting any younger."

"Okay, Mamá? I just went through a horrible divorce and we've only been dating for five seconds."

"And he's already giving your brother an organ. *Dios mío*, what more do you want? I like him. Good job, good-looking. He's very polite."

"He is polite." And generous, and kind. "But just so you know, I probably won't ever remarry."

She pivoted to look at me like I was speaking in tongues. "Why?"

"Because it didn't end well for me?"

She waved me off again. "You just be smart about it. You make him give you an expensive ring. You put your name on everything, all his property. Then if he leaves you, you take his house."

"Mamá!"

"What? That's what I did with Gil. It's how I know he's not going to leave me. He can't afford it."

"Gil is obsessed with you and couldn't live without you," I said.

"And if he did, he'd do it without his house." She shrugged.

I laughed. Then I looked in the rearview. "So what'd you think of Jacob's family?" I gave my brother a twisted-lip smile. "BEN."

"Shut up," he muttered.

"Jane's pretty, huh?" I said, looking back at the road. "She's single," I sang.

"I know. She told me."

I gasped. "You asked her?"

"No. She asked *me*. And then she said, 'Me too.'"

"So? What are you gonna do about it?" I asked, looking at him through the mirror.

"Nothing. Not like this," he mumbled, gesturing to the catheter under his shirt.

My face went soft. "One more month, Benny."

"I liked his family," Mom said. "Good people."

"Speaking of good families," I said. "Levi Olsen came in today."

"Levi? Little Levi?"

"Yeah, he moved back. He wants to have drinks."

Mom eyed me. "Jacob's letting you go?"

"Okay, first of all, no man tells me what I am *allowed* to do."

She crossed her arms. "Why not? You don't tell *him* what to do?"

"Uh, no. I don't."

"You should not be going there when you have a boyfriend," she said.

"Levi is not trying to make a move on me. He's dating Cindy Baker. She will be there."

"Take Jacob with you," Mom said.

"Why?"

"So he won't get jealous."

I rolled my eyes. "Mamá, he is not going to be jealous. And Jacob is not a let's-go-have-drinks-with-my-random-friends kind of guy. He doesn't like stuff like that."

She *tsk*ed. "Men get jealous, *mija*. At least tell him to go so he knows he can. It's like you've never met a man before."

I couldn't explain to Mom that this man wasn't going to get jealous. That he wasn't going to care one bit who I had drinks with.

Because this man wasn't really mine.

CHAPTER 38

JACOB

When Briana got home from dropping off her family, I came down the hallway to meet her.

"Hey," she said, letting herself in. "It's late. I thought you'd be asleep."

"I wanted to make sure you got home okay," I said, leaning in the doorway.

She smiled. "I think my brother likes your sister," she said, taking off her shoes by the door.

"I think my sister likes your brother."

She set her purse down on the credenza and padded up to me in her bare feet. "Do you want to watch TV in your bed?"

"Yes," I said, too quickly.

With the armchairs gone and the sofa not getting delivered for a few more days, the only place to watch TV was on my bed. I liked this so much I was hoping the universe would intervene on my behalf and my new sofa would fall off the back of a truck.

The last time we watched TV in there, she'd fallen asleep. When I woke up in the morning, she'd already gone back to her air mattress, but still.

We brushed our teeth next to each other in my bathroom. Then she shut the door to change into an old T-shirt and some shorts I liked, and came out and climbed under my comforter.

It was moments like these that made my heart ache more than usual, because it was so easy to picture us together. Just another night in the casual life of a happy relationship. We were a couple in love, getting ready for bed, watching TV.

Only we weren't.

We were friends. Maybe even less than friends, since I didn't have any way to know if she'd even be here if it wasn't for what I was doing for Benny.

"You look tired," she said. "You okay?"

No, I spent the whole day concocting scenarios about you and Levi in my head?

"It's just been a long day."

She turned onto her side and propped herself up on her elbow. "Are you going to be okay for tomorrow? That's a lot of socializing two days in a row."

Tomorrow was the bachelor party. The guys were all going bar hopping in a limo, and Amy was having a girls' thing at my parents' house.

"I'll be okay."

"You sure? A limo? Bars? Extroverts spawn at night, it could be really bad."

I snorted.

"The Evite Amy sent me said we're making candles," Briana said, grimacing. "She didn't want to go ride a mechanical bull in a wedding veil? Do something fun?"

"I guess not," I said. "Maybe she really wants to make candles?"

Briana nodded at me. "I'll make you one. What essential oil do you want?"

I rubbed my forehead. "Something for stress."

It was nice that Amy invited her. She was trying to include Briana, and I appreciated it.

I, on the other hand, wished I hadn't been invited to the bachelor party. Spending a night in a limo going to loud bars with a group of my brother's drunk friends made me preemptively exhausted. I almost didn't RSVP. But then Briana made a good point, that if I didn't, it would look like I wasn't okay. I was Jeremiah's only brother. I had to be there. And I especially had to be there if I was attempting to look supportive.

And also, if I didn't go, Briana wouldn't go to Amy's party.

My sisters and mom would be there. It mattered to me that Briana was a part of the things that my family did. That they embraced her.

Even though none of that would matter in two months—not that we'd talked about the ending or when exactly it would take place. But two months from now the wedding would be over and I'd be over a month post-op. The agreement would be fulfilled.

How much longer could I expect her to stay?

I went quiet at this and stared at the show on the TV, looking right at it and not seeing a thing.

Her cell phone pinged in the silence. She picked it up and laughed.

"Who's that?" I asked.

"Oh, it's just Levi." She bit her lip while she typed in her reply. *Levi.*

"You've been talking to him a lot today," I said, trying to sound nonchalant.

"Yeah. It's been nice catching up."

I cleared my throat. "Did you two ever date?" I asked.

"Me and Levi? Nah." Then she smiled. "My mom used to always joke that I'd marry him one day."

"Why?"

"She thought he had a crush on me. I don't know."

My mouth went dry. "You never wanted to date him?"

She looked over at me. "This is going to sound a little eighteen-hundreds Victorian England, but his family wouldn't have really approved of that."

"Why not?"

She looked at me pointedly. "We were the help, Jacob."

"But you're not the help now." I regretted it the second I said it out loud. I was wingmanning him, for God's sake.

She made an amused noise. "No, I have definitely leveled up since high school." She looked back at her phone. "I'm having drinks next weekend at his house. I was thinking the day you were going to take Lieutenant Dan to the vet? I'd be back by the time you got home."

My stomach dropped. She was going to his *house*? Was this a date?

I was afraid to ask. Because I was afraid of the answer.

I knew at some point this would happen. She didn't want me, so she'd date eventually and I had no control over it. I just thought I'd be spared this for now, safe, tucked away in the rules of our arrangement.

But she was single. And she wanted him to *know* she was single. Maybe he already did. If it never got back to anyone we knew, what was the harm in her doing whatever the hell she wanted?

She could sleep with him that day. The thought made panic rise in my chest.

I had no right to tell her not to go. I didn't even have a right to be upset. All this, me and her—this was a *favor*. This wasn't real. We weren't fucking REAL.

Her phone pinged again. Then again. And again.

It wasn't loud, but my reaction to it was physical. Every time a text came through, my shoulders creeped higher, my pulse went up. The sound was so triggering, it felt like gunfire.

Ping.

Ping ping.

Ping ping ping.

"You know, I'm actually pretty tired," I said, picking up the remote and turning off the TV. "I think I'm going to go to sleep."

Her face fell. "Oh."

She sounded disappointed. I don't know why. She wasn't even watching the show, and she could text in the living room.

She got up. "Okay. Good night." And then she went back to the air mattress.

I was disappointed because she wouldn't accidentally fall asleep in my bed and the rest of the night was ruined, but I couldn't keep watching her check her phone.

I turned off the light, but I couldn't sleep. My mind went on a merciless tangent instead. What was he saying that made her laugh? Was he funnier than me? Did she get butterflies when a text came through? Would I have to watch her date him? Right in the middle of our deal?

I was ruminating and it wasn't healthy and it wasn't getting me anywhere. So I used the skills I'd learned in therapy. Redirected my thoughts. Tried to ground myself by focusing on what I knew to be positive and true.

Briana sought out *my* friendship in the beginning, so she must like me. She said she feels protective over me. She laughs when I joke with her. She compliments me. Tells me I smell good, that I have a nice smile.

And it *was* possible I was reading too much into her texts with Levi. She'd just reconnected with him today, and they probably just had a lot of catching up to do.

This helped a little—but not enough.

I fell asleep for an hour and woke up after having a restless dream about a bear attacking me on a hiking trail. Then I lay in bed worrying a plane was going to hit the house, or that one of the twins would get into an accident, or that I'd lost my birth certificate.

Had I lost my birth certificate?

I got up and looked for it, digging through the safe in my closet. When I found it, it was two in the morning, and I was wired. I wanted to go for a run. To tear through the streets at full speed and outpace this feeling, or wear myself out to the point of exhaustion so I'd be too tired to think. But I couldn't leave without going out the front door, and I didn't want to wake Briana. So I used my rower instead.

After forty-five minutes, I was dripping with sweat and no closer to sleeping than I had been before I started. I took a shower and figured I might as well journal to work through some of what I was feeling. So I tiptoed to the plant room and wrote. After two hours of that, I finally felt de-escalated enough to fall asleep around six, but I was up again at eight, right on schedule.

And then she texted him the whole day.

In the kitchen when I was making her breakfast. In the living room on her air mattress. In the bathroom while she was doing her makeup. Then the whole way to my parents' house for the bachelor and bachelorette parties.

She never stopped.

Her phone was on silent now, so I didn't hear the pings. And I didn't ask if she was talking to him, but I knew that she was, and I filled in every awful scenario in my mind: He was flirting with her, and she was flirting back. She couldn't wait until our arrangement was over so she could date him openly. Her mom would be happy about it because she always thought they'd get married and now maybe they finally would.

My nerves were frayed. By the time we pulled up to my parents' house, the gnawing in the pit of my stomach was starting to make me feel sick. I was getting overheated and sweaty. I kept wiping my palms on my pants. I had to check three times that I'd put the truck in park. I couldn't remember.

"Okay," she said, finally putting down her phone, pivoting in her seat to face me. "So here's your catchphrase of the day. Ready?"

I wasn't ready. I couldn't concentrate. "Yeah."

"'In this economy?'" She smiled. "That's it. That's the phrase."

I just stared at her. "Okay."

She eyed me. "It's a good phrase, Jacob."

"Yeah."

She tilted her head. "Are you okay?"

"I'm fine."

I wasn't. I was feeling dizzy. I felt like my brain was detaching from my body. I couldn't breathe right.

I wanted to tell her she couldn't go to Levi's next week. I wanted her to stop texting him. I wanted the phone to stop silently going off.

More than that, I wanted her to want me back. I wanted us to be real. I wanted this to be different and it wasn't going to be different and I felt like I was collapsing from the outside in.

It was hard enough to deal with the reality of Briana's non-feelings for me. But at least I had these few months. At least I got to be close to her, even if it was just going to be for a little while. But that safe space had been breached now, and water was spilling in, and I was drowning.

"Jacob?"

I blinked at her.

She was looking at me weird. "You don't have to go to this."

"What?"

"The bachelor party. You can just say you don't feel well or something. We can go home."

"I'm... I'm fine."

She studied me. "You look nervous."

"I'm not."

She narrowed her eyes at me, but I got out before she could press me. My legs felt like Jell-O. It was all I could do to pretend to be normal. Walk normal. Breathe normal.

Lieutenant Dan was walking next to me, pushing his head under my hand.

When we got in the house, I couldn't focus. The twins jumped on me. Jafar was strutting through the hallway squawking obscenities, Grandpa was harassing Briana, who was harassing him back, and the whole thing felt like it was happening underwater. Time felt elastic. I couldn't tell how long we'd been here. A minute? An hour? Did the limo get here yet? No. I would have remembered. *Would* I have remembered?

Then I was in the living room, sitting on the sofa with everyone.

Amy and Jeremiah were there and about twenty other people for the parties.

Briana was holding my hand, but I swear I could hear her phone going off, even though I knew the sound was down. My heart rate was up and my mouth was dry and Lieutenant Dan was shoving his head under my arm, and I had the realization that I was having a panic attack.

Amy and Jeremiah were making some sort of announcement. I was in a fish tank.

I could see Amy's mouth moving. "We're having a baby."

And then I was conscious of everyone's eyes darting to me and I said the only thing I could think of saying because I had to get the hell out of there. "In this economy?"

Then I fled from the room while I could still make my legs carry me.

CHAPTER 39

BRIANA

As soon as Amy made the announcement, Jacob disintegrated. The shift was palpable. The tipping of a teetering glass on the edge of a table. Shattered.

His anxiety had been high all day. Probably because he knew he had this bachelor party and was already worn out from dinner with my family last night. He'd been sort of moody and detached from the minute he woke up. I'd been trying to give him space since he was people'd out, so I'd spent the day watching TikTok videos and texting Alexis so I stayed out of his hair. But now I wished I'd gotten him to stay home instead. He wasn't in a good place to hear this news on his best day.

He used his escape phrase and practically ran to the steps leading to the basement. By the time I got down there, he was sitting on the little futon sofa in the room with the pool table, crying and breathing into his hands.

He was having a panic attack. Like, an actual panic attack. Because Amy was pregnant.

My heart *broke*.

I stood in front of him, watching him have a breakdown on

this futon, and I couldn't begin to describe the way it felt seeing him like this. Watching him live the moment he realized that it was really over because there was going to be a baby now and they might have figured it out before that, but now it was real.

She wasn't leaving Jeremiah for him.

Amy and Jeremiah were going to be a family.

It was over.

All his hopes were over. He was heartbroken, and so was I.

I was right here. I was *right here* and I was in love with him and he didn't care because he couldn't even see me past her. I had fallen completely and utterly in love with him and he had stayed completely and utterly in love with someone else.

I started to cry too.

I just stood there in front of him, my shoulders slumped, tears starting to roll down my face.

Lieutenant Dan was almost frantic, trying to crawl into the space between Jacob's stomach and the hands he had cupped over his mouth. And I wanted to crawl into that space too.

Screw it. I did.

I moved the dog over and climbed into Jacob's lap. I straddled him in my blue summer dress and wrapped my arms around his neck and put my lips to his ear and just kept whispering the same thing over and over and over again. "I love you. I love you. I love you."

He responded immediately. Like I'd reached him in the fog and he was clinging to me before he lost me again. His arms wrapped around me and he buried his face in my hair and it felt like the magnets that had been flipped and turned and flipped and turned had finally snapped together and spun to a halt.

"I love you," I whispered. "I love you so much."

Even if you don't love me back. Even if it never matters to you or means anything or goes anywhere. I love you.

His breathing was labored.

I put my hands on his wet cheeks and looked him in the eye and started reciting the grounding exercises I used for panicking patients in the ER.

"Look for five things you can see," I whispered. "Four things you can touch. Three things you can hear. Two things you can smell. One thing you can taste."

But he didn't look for any of them. He just looked in my eyes. It must have worked, because after a few moments, I felt him calming down. His breathing steadied, his heart rate settled. When it was clear he was coming out of it, I put my forehead to his and closed my eyes.

Love me. Just love me instead. I'd take care of you. I'd protect you and shield you and be anything you needed. I'd be harmless to you…

He shook his head gently against mine like he could hear my thoughts. "I can't fucking do this anymore…" he breathed.

Neither could I. But then I couldn't even bring myself to get off his lap. The power this man had over me terrified me because there was so little I *wouldn't* do. I was glad he never asked more of me after he asked me on that date, because I wasn't capable of saying no to him. Even if it was against my own best interest. *Especially* if it was against my own best interest.

Why was I spending all my time pretending that I wasn't in love with a man in love with someone else? Why was I doing this? Why was I torturing myself? *Again.*

It was so unfair.

I squeezed my eyes shut tighter, trying to hold it back, but a sob choked me. He pulled away to look at me, worried. I turned, but he tipped my chin back to him. "What's wrong?"

I just shook my head.

"Briana, *look* at me."

I opened my eyes. His face was so close I could see the tears on his lashes, the red rims of his eyelids. We breathed into each other's space and he stared back at me, one of his quiets, the one I couldn't ever read.

He was so perfect.

His face was like art to me. The slope of his nose. The angle of his jaw. The black flecks in his eyes, the fullness of his bottom lip. I studied him unapologetically. Canvassed him up close with so much longing I felt like my heart would give out under the strain of loving him this much.

I was aware of everything. Every point of contact. My hands on his warm, firm shoulders. My dress hiked up, my bare thighs against his thighs. The tickle of his breath on my face, his belt buckle pressing low into my stomach.

He was looking at me too. His face looked tortured and pained, and I hated that she did this to him. That she could.

We just peered at each other. Me loving him, and him loving her. He raised a tentative hand and wiped a tear off my cheek. "Briana..." he whispered.

The sound of my name caressed my ears.

There was something so intimate hanging in the space between us. I was hypnotized by it. By the proximity to him and the hand on my skin and the way his sad eyes were roaming my face.

His gaze moved to my mouth.

He pressed a thumb to my bottom lip and pulled it down the slightest bit. And then he did the worst possible thing. The absolute worst thing he could *ever* do. He drew my face to his and kissed me.

Just a light brushing of his lips to mine. A little test.

I failed. I kissed him back.

It all unraveled after that.

Any boundaries, any semblance of proprietary or politeness that we'd maintained all these months, were instantly gone. Hands raked into my hair and I wrapped my arms around his neck and the kissing became a desperate, starving, frantic extension of everything we'd already been doing—only there was nobody here to see and no reason for it other than I couldn't deny him anything he wanted and both of us were out of our fucking minds.

This man was hurting. He was looking for some kind of distraction or escape from what he was feeling and I knew this.

I devoured him anyway. And he matched my energy a thousand percent.

His tongue plunged against mine, he nipped at my bottom lip, parted for me and started again. Opened and tasted, pulled back and nibbled, and kissing him was everything I'd imagined it would be and more. We already knew how to do this. We already had a rhythm, like we'd already kissed a thousand different ways over a hundred different lifetimes. I knew his mouth. I knew his whole body. I knew all of him with my eyes closed after months of watching and wanting, and he knew me too. I could feel it in every touch.

I drew in closer and his hands started to wander. He ran a palm up my calf, under my thigh, and pulled me into his growing erection with a grip on my ass. I lifted his shirt and pressed my fingers along his bare chest, rocking against the hard edge in his lap. When he slid fingers into my underwear and circled, kissing roughly down my neck, I knew without a shadow of a doubt that I was about to fuck him on this futon. I had zero control over any of it and I didn't even care. I literally couldn't stop.

I didn't even want to.

I tugged at his belt until he took over and unzipped himself. He raised his hips to get his pants far enough off for me to pull him out.

And then he was in my hand. And he was so hard.

This was for me.

Maybe nothing else he felt was mine, but *this* was. It turned me on to think I could turn him on. That if nothing else, at least I could do this to his body. I slid my hand up and down, stroking him between us. He put his hand firmly over mine and made me go faster.

I was coming undone. It was all too much and not enough.

I wanted to get on my knees and put my mouth on it and taste him, but when I started to climb off, he grabbed my hips and pulled me back. He crushed his mouth to mine, yanked my underwear sideways, and eased me down on top of him. The noise he made in the back of his throat as he slid inside me almost finished me right there.

It was fireworks. Explosions. Nothing else existed outside of this moment.

My brain was screaming *yes*.

Yes to *everything*.

YESSSSS.

All of our clothes were on. I didn't care.

The door was probably unlocked. I didn't care.

Everyone upstairs was going to take one look at my wrinkled dress and kiss-bruised mouth and know what we did down here—I didn't care.

I didn't *care*.

I'd fantasized about this moment so many times. Jacob had made me orgasm a hundred ways in the last few months, only he'd never actually been there for it. And I must have said this out loud in my delirium because he breathed, "Me too" into my ear. And then in a gravelly voice, "You in the red dress at the luau. You in my shirt. You in your scrubs. Always you..."

Our breath was shallow. My hair fell around him like a curtain, and his hands lifted my bare thighs and guided me up and down. The momentum built in my core and it was so good I was going to scream his name if I didn't bite my lips closed when it happened and then he was groaning and I was gasping, and I felt him tensing and pulsing into me and I had an orgasm that made me forget my own fucking name.

I loved him so much.

I wanted to die, I loved him so much. I wanted to crawl inside of him and live there. I wanted to spend the rest of my life just being with him. Adoring him. Protecting him. Living in all his quiets. Letting him touch me any way he wanted to, as often as he wanted to.

A head on his shoulder in a movie theater. A kiss before bed. A cuddle in the dark. Growing old and holding his hand.

Anything he wanted. Anything he needed. I wanted to be his anything.

But I *wasn't*.

The reality came down slow and then all at once. The heated moment passed, and my head started to clear and I realized what I'd just done.

This man was in love with someone else.

I'd promised myself that I would never let a man love me with only half of himself ever again. I wasn't even sure I'd just gotten half of Jacob. I wasn't sure I'd gotten any of him at all.

I don't even think Jacob was there.

"Oh my God, you guys are *always* making out."

We turned to Jewel standing in the doorway.

"He's in the basement!" she called over her shoulder. "He's just sucking face with Briana. As usual." She looked back at us. "The limo's here."

She rolled her eyes, turned, and left.

We looked back at each other, out of breath. My dress was covering his lap, but he was still inside me. My face stung from the shadow of his beard, my hair was tangled and sticking to my wet cheeks.

His eyes dropped to my mouth and he slid a hand into the back of my hair, but before he leaned in to kiss me again, I scrambled off him. "No," I said, tugging my dress down.

I was so disgusted with what I'd done I couldn't even look him in the eye. I'd just had sex with him, he was dripping into my underwear, and suddenly watching him do his belt buckle felt too personal.

I started to shake. I couldn't tell if it was from the orgasm or the adrenaline or the soul-crushing disappointment in myself.

"We can never do that again," I said, finally mustering the courage to look at him.

He blinked at me, rumpled from the sofa. *"What?"*

"I should have never done this…" I breathed. "It was a mistake. I'm sorry."

The silence between us was like a vacuum. It wasn't the cessation of sound, it was a world where sound didn't exist. I couldn't stand the way he was looking at me.

I was trying *so* hard not to cry. I didn't want him to have to deal with Amy and my feelings too.

"You're going to miss the limo," I said, my voice cracking.

He shook his head at me. "I don't *care* about the limo." He started to get up. "Briana—"

I backed up. "No! Don't touch me."

It was amazing how clear his eyes looked now as he stared at me. Sharp and focused. Like a storm had passed and the sun was out and he was seeing every single flaw on my face. Every flaw in my personality.

Maybe he was finally seeing the thing that made Nick want someone else.

I couldn't stand the scrutiny. I couldn't stand the reality.

I ran to the bathroom and locked the door.

CHAPTER 40

JACOB

I was whiplashed. I felt like I'd been in an emotional car wreck and I'd been ejected. What the *hell* had just happened between us?

I stood outside the bathroom door not knowing what to do.

Briana said she loved me. She'd said it over and over. And then we were kissing and pulling at each other's clothes and then I was inside her and it was the most amazing thing I'd ever felt—and then it was over, she was embarrassed, and it was a *mistake*? What *happened*?

I didn't want to go in the damn limo. I wanted her to come out and talk to me. I couldn't process this without more information. I couldn't settle on how to feel until I knew what was going on with her.

How could it be a mistake? How could anything that felt like that be something she regretted? And it wasn't just the sex. She had feelings for me. It was there. I felt it, I didn't imagine it, I know I didn't. She said she loved me. She *did* say it.

A long horn blared from the front yard.

I put a hand on the door. "Briana, please let me in."

"Jacob, just *go*."

She was crying.

What had I done? Had I done something wrong? I rested my forehead on the frame and squeezed my eyes shut.

My brain was misfiring. It was chaotic and foggy. I was somewhere between the tail end of a panic attack and an earth-shattering development with the woman I loved, and I couldn't think straight. I was overstimulated and upset, and I needed to level myself.

I stayed with a hand pressed to the door for another long moment. Then I pulled out my truck keys and reluctantly set them in the middle of the coffee table so she could go if she wanted to. And I took my dog and left.

I didn't get in the limo. I told Jeremiah the truth—I was having problems with Briana and I'd had a panic attack. I couldn't care less at this point if he believed it. Maybe Jeremiah thought my issue was about the baby. I didn't care about that either. I was beyond giving a shit what anyone thought anymore.

I called an Uber.

I calmed down a bit on the ride home. By the time I got there, I'd stopped shaking.

I texted Briana when I got into the house.

Me: I went home. I left the keys to the truck for you.

She didn't reply.

Her air mattress was popped. It sat flat and limp in the living room. I stood there and stared at it. It felt ominous. A sign that things were ending. That her time here was done.

My anxiety pitched and rolled.

I kept going over everything in my head. Trying to pinpoint the moment things went wrong or the reason why she'd have sex with me if she didn't want to.

Her perfume still clung to my shirt.

She'd been so wet. I could still feel the rocking of her body on top of mine, hear the moan when she came. She'd wanted it as much as I did. She'd practically climbed me. She *did* climb me.

She'd said she loved me.

Or had she?

Maybe she hadn't meant it like that. Maybe she said it the way my sisters said it. To make me feel better. To let me know they cared. Maybe she didn't mean it the way *I* meant it.

Maybe I'd heard what I'd wanted to hear.

I was on a loop of the limited information I had. There was nothing I could do to sort it out. I couldn't know what was going on until she talked to me. All I could do was try to center myself and be ready when she came home. So I did the only thing I could do. I sat down and journaled.

CHAPTER 41

BRIANA

I cleaned up and came out to join the bachelorette party fifteen minutes after Jacob left. I debated leaving too, but I didn't want Amy to think her announcement had sent Jacob on a death spiral that I had to leave to nurse him through. I mean, it *had* sent him on a spiral, but my staying at least made it seem less of a big deal.

When I got upstairs, everyone was in the kitchen melting wax and listening to Michael Bublé. It was Jane, Jill, Jewel, Gwen, Joy, and then half a dozen women I didn't know but vaguely recognized from the engagement party.

It felt like I'd walked onto the set of a comedy. I stood there with just-fucked hair at the bachelorette party of the woman my fake boyfriend was in love with, while Jafar weaved through feet under the table squawking, "Alexa! Order garlic bread!" and the Amazon Echo was replying that garlic bread was already on the shopping list. It was all I could do to not maniacally laugh.

Someone shoved a cocktail at me that I tasted and then held until the ice melted because it was pure tequila with a drop of guava syrup. Then I made a stupid candle.

I had to move out of Jacob's house. I couldn't stay with him after this. I didn't even know how we'd continue to do this fake relationship for the couple of weeks we had left. It was going to be so awkward and so physically painful to even hold his hand, now that I'd crossed this colossal line.

I was trying not to think too hard about how good the sex had been.

It wasn't really working.

He was such a good kisser. It wasn't even funny how good he was. If he'd kissed me before this, I would have been a goner weeks ago. I started to get worked up even thinking about it.

All I could think about was touching him, the way his tongue had tasted and how he smelled and the sounds he'd made.

I thought about how he'd made me touch him. The way he'd yanked my underwear to the side. Rougher than I would have expected from him. Unapologetic. He was not shy with me *at all*. I had a feeling I'd only scratched the surface today, that Jacob would be full of surprises in bed. I could almost picture him pinning me with that quiet, reflective gaze he has before pushing me up against a wall, pulling my underwear down, telling me what to do...

Oh my God, see, *this* was my problem. I couldn't even focus.

I looked down at my candle. The wick was crooked. I'd been making this thing with the only two brain cells that hadn't been dedicated to the sex tape I was rewatching in my head.

I was a mess. How could I be harmless to him when I couldn't even be harmless to *myself*?

Some little part of me said that maybe if we started a sexual relationship, it would lead to more. Maybe he would eventually get over Amy and fall in love with me. We were already friends, we had physical chemistry. A *lot* of chemistry. Like, a disproportionate amount. We didn't have love, but that was still two out of three, right?

Pathetic.

Imagine trying to talk yourself into a friends-with-benefits situation in which you were head-over-heels in love and you knew *he* was actively wishing you were someone else.

I *hated* myself.

My sulking was disrupted when some drunk woman named Shannon who'd been talking too loudly and wearing a maid of honor hat stood up and clinked her fork to the side of her glass. Everyone looked up from their project.

"A toast!" she bellowed.

She was barely able to stand. This oughta be good.

Amy smiled and everyone lifted their cocktails.

Shannon swayed for another moment. "To Amy," she slurred, holding up her martini. "A woman who would have been married years ago if Jacob hadn't strung her along! Huzzah!"

The party fell into an instant hush.

Amy set her mocktail down. "Shannon, that's not true—"

Shannon scoffed. "What do you mean??? It *so* is?! He lost the best thing that ever happened to him because he's too anxious to function." She laughed at her own joke.

All my jumbled, discombobulated emotions suddenly jerked to attention and honed in on her like a laser.

"He functions just fucking fine," I snapped.

The room collectively gasped. Shannon blinked at me like she'd just realized that I was here. She peered around red-eyed, looking for allies. She didn't see any.

"What?" she said, throwing up a hand. "He didn't even go in the *limo*. What man can't handle a bachelor party?"

I set my untouched drink down with a clink and glared at her. "He has social anxiety. You expect him to come to some loud-ass limo party with your verbal-diarrhea husbands, and you wonder why he didn't suddenly turn into some social butterfly? He should get credit for even trying. You have no idea how hard he has to work to just fucking show up. And he does it because that's what love does—*it shows up*. He's shown up for Amy *and* his brother since the second this started. He has been a goddamn saint through *all* of this. *He* is not the asshole. *You're* the asshole."

Jafar squawked, "ASSHOLE!" from somewhere under the kitchen table.

Every mouth in the room was open. Amy was wide-eyed, Jane was red, Jill was nodding, Jewel looked like I had her vote for president, and Joy was stifling a grin.

I stared down Shannon until she looked away first. Then I pulled the keys out of my purse, got up, and left.

I drove to the gas station down the street, bought seven different kinds of candy bars, a pack of cigarettes, and a lighter. Then I drove back to the house, snuck in through the garage door, and went straight for the sunroom, where Grandpa watched TV.

"What the hell do you want?" he muttered when I came in.

"Give me any crap and I'll change my mind."

I wheeled him out the sliding glass doors and into the screened-in gazebo in the wooded part of the yard.

I took off his oxygen, moved his tank, opened the pack of cigarettes, and held one out in front of him just out of reach.

"I know you're of sound mind, so I know you understand when I say that if you choose to take this, it may worsen your lung condition. You would be smoking against my medical advice and probably to your detriment."

He narrowed his eyes. "Shut up and give it to me."

I rolled my eyes, lit the cigarette, and handed it to him. Then I dropped into a chair and started eating a Snickers like it was a burrito.

The old man eyed me. "Tough night?"

"You have no idea."

He took a long draw on his cigarette and blew the smoke

in rings. "You having trouble with my grandson? Want me to straighten him out?"

I snorted. "Can you make him love me?"

"Doesn't he already?"

"No," I said. "No, he doesn't."

He took another puff. "And here I was thinkin' he was the smart one."

He finished his cigarette and I gave him another one. I opened a Milky Way and sat there eating it while I stared through the screen into the dark abyss of the yard, contemplating all my questionable life choices.

Jacob never said he loved me back.

I said it to him so many times and not once did he say "You too." But he *did* let me know he thinks of me when he jerks off. I'd be absolutely thrilled about this if he also happened to be in love with me as well.

If I had any question about what this was for him, that was my answer.

I had to bury my face in my hands.

This was my fault. All of it.

He'd been crystal clear with me since the beginning, that he was in love with someone else. This was completely on me.

Maybe if I hadn't gone off and told Amy that Jacob and I were living together, I wouldn't have moved in there and wouldn't be so worn down from seeing him in gray sweatpants every day.

Maybe if I'd tried to calm him down in a way that didn't involve straddling his *lap*, I would have had the fortitude not to have sex with him on a futon in his mom's basement.

I groaned. I had sex with him. On a futon. In his mom's *basement*.

I was like a parody of myself.

Even though this was just sex for him, now that I wasn't going to be doing it again, he was going to feel rejected and like he did something wrong, because that's just how Jacob was. And I was going to feel embarrassed and like I couldn't count on myself to make the right decisions, especially when it came to him. The only way I could be sure it wouldn't happen again was to stay away from him.

I'd still keep my promise. I'd attend his family functions through the wedding. But I couldn't ever be with him alone and I couldn't spend time with him outside of the agreement.

I'd messed this up. I'd ruined the time we had left.

I still had my face in my hands when I heard footsteps. A second later someone opened the gazebo door. I looked up. *Amy* stood there.

We stared at each other in surprise. Then she looked over at Grandpa smoking and her mouth fell open.

My jaw set. Fuck it. "Go ahead," I said, sitting back in my seat. "Tell Joy. I don't even care."

Amy blinked at me. Then she held something up. A pack of Marlboros.

"We all give them to him," she said sheepishly. "Well, the girls do. It's sort of how you know you're in the family? When you start sneaking Grandpa cigarettes. He smokes a pack a week."

"Two," he said proudly.

I turned and gawked at him. *"What?"*

He didn't reply, but he looked pleased with himself.

I looked back at Amy. "How does Joy not know?"

Amy shrugged. "She does. She told Greg as long as she's not enabling it, she can't feel guilty about it. And she said he likes the chase? That it keeps him sharp?"

Grandpa looked at the glowing end of his cigarette. "I always could make the ladies do whatever I wanted. Haven't lost my touch."

I shook my head at him. *Unbelievable.* "You almost ran me down with your wheelchair. Several times."

"You got out of the way, didn't you?"

He managed to get a laugh out of me.

Amy stood there for a minute, looking self-conscious. "Can I sit?"

I blew a breath out through my nose. Then I nodded at the chair across from me. She sat down on the edge of the seat like I might change my mind and make her leave.

She licked her lips. "I'm sorry about Shannon," she said. "She was out of line. She was very drunk, and I sent her home."

I didn't reply.

"Jacob never strung me along," she said, going on. "He didn't do anything wrong. And you were right. I never really appreciated how hard it is for him to show up—*I* didn't do enough to take his anxiety seriously. I deserved what you said. Probably more than anyone."

She peered back at me.

I looked away from her. "Do you want a Twix?" I mumbled.

"Oh God, yes."

I dug into the plastic gas-station bag and handed her the candy bar, and she unwrapped it and took a bite. She closed her eyes while she chewed. "Thank you," she breathed. "I am starving, all the time."

I studied her for a moment. "How many weeks are you?" I asked.

"Eight." She took a deep breath and glanced at me. "Honestly, I've been so sick and exhausted I didn't even want to do this party."

"Is that why we made candles instead of pole dancing somewhere?"

She laughed a little. "The candles came out pretty awful, didn't they?"

"Mine has a hair in it."

She cracked up and I couldn't help but smile. She finished the candy bar and rested her head on the back of her chair.

I lit another cigarette for Grandpa. "Don't you need to go back in?" I asked her.

"Nah. I told everyone I was feeling sick and needed to go lie down. Joy moved everyone into the living room and she's showing them vibrators she likes."

I looked over my shoulder toward the house. "Oh, man. I'm missing that?"

"Like you need it?" she said in an amused We-both-know-what-kind-of-earth-shattering-sex-Jacob-is-giving-you kind of way.

I bobbed my head at the comment that I would have had to pretend to understand just an hour ago. God.

"Is it true he didn't get in the limo?" she asked. "Is every-thing okay?"

I don't know what it was. Maybe that she looked sort of vulner-able sitting there. Or maybe it was the genuinely concerned way she was looking at me. But I didn't want to lie about it.

"We had a fight."

She peered at me. "I'm sorry."

She didn't press for more information. But I decided to give it to her anyway.

"I think I'm a little more in love with him than he is with me."

Amy blinked. "I *seriously* doubt that."

I scoffed.

"No, I mean it," she said. "I have *never* seen him the way he is with you." She shook her head. "He never wanted to live with me or spend time with me. He didn't look at me like he looks at you."

She was wrong, of course. Jacob didn't feel any sort of way about me. I wasn't really living with him. I wasn't even really dating him. If anything, this just showed what a good job we'd done making everyone believe. But I did appreciate her saying it, trying to make me feel better.

She tucked her hair behind her ear. "You know, I thought—at first—that maybe you were only with him for the kidney," she said, sounding a little guilty. "But I was wrong. I can see that you really love him and how good you two are together." She smiled a little. "It makes me really happy that he's found that. He *deserves* that."

I studied her face. She meant it. She really did want him to be happy.

This was the moment that I decided to like her.

She was a lot less evil than I had imagined. She wasn't really evil at all. I could sort of see why all the Maddox boys were in love with her.

It sucks when you actually like the other woman.

It sucks more when it happens twice.

An hour later the party wrapped up and I drove to Jacob's house.

When I walked in the front door, I set my purse down on the credenza and I heard the door to Jacob's plant room open and him coming down the hallway.

Lieutenant Dan met me first, and Jacob came in after him and stopped and stood in the doorway with his hands slipped into the pockets of his pajama bottoms. He searched my face, giving me one of his quiet looks. The ones where the wheels were turning.

My air mattress was deflated on the floor between us. It had started to sag last night and now it was officially dead. I stared at this, while Jacob stared at me.

I could smell the flowers he'd sent me. He'd put them on the coffee table so I could see them when I woke up. Seeing them made me want to sob. This part was over now. I couldn't believe how badly I'd ruined this. Nothing would ever be the same. I hadn't just ruined the quality of the time I had left, I'd also ruined our friendship. Muddied it. Made it weird.

It wasn't weird for *him*. He'd wanted this, to add benefits to the arrangement. He'd probably just been happy for the distraction.

It was me who couldn't deal now.

"You can sleep in my room," he said. "I'll sleep on the floor."

But I shook my head. "No. I'm going home." I raised my eyes to his.

He paused for a long moment. "Why?"

"I just can't be here."

He dragged a hand down his mouth and looked away from me. When he came back, he held me with his tired brown eyes. "Briana. Just...come to bed."

My stomach flipped. I felt the power of his summons like a whisper into my soul. *Come to me, Briana. Come...*

I felt my heart reach for him.

It made my eyes dart to his mouth. It made my fast-twitch muscles ping with the urge to fling myself at him and let him carry me to his room and do whatever the hell he wanted to me. Roll on top of me and pull my underwear down and kiss me until my lips hurt again.

But I shook my head. "No."

He peered at me. "Why?"

"Jacob, I need you to help me, okay? Don't try to kiss me again. Don't even touch me when we're not in front of your family. Let's just get through the wedding and be done with this. Okay?"

"That's what you want?"

"I just said."

"Sometimes people say things they don't actually mean."

I threw up my hands. "What do you want from me, Jacob?"

He paused. "Everything. I want *everything*. I want us to be real."

I laughed almost manically. "What are you even talking about? You are in love with someone else!"

He stared at me. *"What?"*

I shook my head at him. "Look, I know that this thing with us would be convenient for you. And I appreciate that you find me attractive, I really do. But I'm not going to be your consolation prize because it didn't work out with Amy."

"You think I'm—"

"Jacob, don't bother denying it. I heard you fighting with her the day of the luau. You came out with lipstick and perfume on your shirt and then you asked *me* out so you didn't have to dwell on it. Then today you had a panic attack because she's pregnant—"

"I had a panic attack because you're texting *Levi.*"

I blinked at him.

"That day at the luau? I was fighting with Amy because she was worried you were using me for my kidney. That you didn't actually want me. And so I asked you out because I didn't want to believe her. I wanted it to be real between us, I wanted to *make* it real. And she was right. It wasn't."

He shook his head. "I don't *care* about Amy, Briana. I don't love her. I don't think I ever did. I'm *glad* she's pregnant, I *like* being an uncle. And you know what? If you're only with me for the kidney, I don't care about that either. Because I am so fucking in love with you, I'll settle for anything. Even that." His voice broke on the last word.

I just stared at him. For the first time ever, I was totally mute.

"Use me," he said, his eyes resigned. "Use me for whatever you want. Just *stay.*"

The words froze me in place. I had to learn how to breathe again before I could speak. "You don't love her?" I whispered.

He shook his head slowly. "No."

We stood there in a thick moment of silence. My heart pounded into the quiet.

"Jacob, I am so in love with you I can't even stand it."

I watched this information transform his entire face. "What?" he breathed.

"I'm in love with you too. I thought you wanted her. I thought—"

"Say it again." He swallowed.

"I'm . . . I'm in love with you."

I watched the words hit him like a physical thing, pushing the air from his lungs and filling his eyes with hope.

He closed the space between us in three long strides and gathered me to him.

"Say it again," he whispered.

"I'm in love with you," I gasped.

"Again."

"I'm in love with you."

He laughed, blinking at me through tears.

"This is real?" I asked.

He nodded. "It's *always* been real."

I let out a happy sob.

I could feel it in everything suddenly. The way he touched me, the energy coming off him, the look in his eyes. And then I realized that I had always felt it. *This* was his quiet. The silence that I couldn't decipher. It was me.

I was hit with a meteor shower of realizations. I could touch him. I could sleep in his bed and cuddle him on a couch and hold his hand for no fucking reason other than I wanted to. I could kiss him . . .

He must have been thinking the same thing, because his eyes dropped to my lips.

He put an exploratory hand out to touch me, like he wanted

to test that he could. It hovered for a second and then he slipped it gently into my hair at the nape of my neck and put his forehead to mine and closed his eyes. His breath tickled my lips an excruciatingly long moment before he let his warm, soft mouth connect with mine. Every *inch* of my body came alive.

He kissed me like everything he had was being poured into this beautiful, tender, gentle thing. He folded around me, warm and strong, and I knew I would always remember this living room. The dim lights and the smell of vanilla candles and the limp air mattress by our feet. "Clair de Lune" playing softly from a speaker on a bookshelf, the simple white T-shirt and sweatpants he was wearing that smelled like his body and his soap and *Jacob*.

I wanted to feel him. I wanted to explore his body like it belonged to me. I wanted to know him with all my senses, with my hands and my eyes and my mouth. I wanted to hear his heartbeat and smell the warmth that clung to his skin.

And he wanted that too.

I couldn't believe it. It was real.

I started to tear up.

Jacob pulled away and looked down at me. "What's wrong?"

I couldn't even speak, I just shook my head.

He brushed the hair off my forehead with a soft thumb. "What? Tell me."

"This is what it feels like to be truly loved. I've never felt it before. And I didn't even realize it until just now."

He smiled at me gently. "Yes. This is what it feels like."

And we stayed there holding each other, inseparable, immovable, tangled like a tree that had grown into a chain-link fence.

CHAPTER 42

JACOB

No fair, you're leaning," she said, smiling up at me, biting her lip.

I was leaning. She was right.

Briana had her back to the wall in the hallway of the hotel, and we were playing the game where we stood as close as possible like we wanted to kiss. Lieutenant Dan sat at our feet. We were waiting for Jewel and Gwen to come out so we could walk down to the ceremony. It was the wedding day.

I stood about an inch from Briana in my suit. She had on a green cocktail dress and heels.

"You can't kiss me," she teased. "I have my lipstick on."

"Can I do this?" I asked, my voice low, leaning down to press my lips to her bare shoulder. "Or how about this?" I moved to her collarbone. "Or this?" Her neck.

She was already out of breath. "You better stop," she whispered.

"Or what?" I said, my lips so close to her skin I could practically feel her pulse.

"Or you're going to have to take me back to the room," she breathed.

"Then let's go back to the room…"

"Oh my God, knock it off," Jewel called, coming out of her room with Gwen and the twins.

Briana and I laughed, and I backed away from her.

Carter and Katrina ran to me, and I crouched in my suit to pick them up. Carter was the ring bearer, so he was in a little tux with a pink boutonniere. Katrina was the flower girl, so she had on a poofy white dress and a crown of fresh pink flowers.

"What socks?" Carter asked.

"Alligators. And look what Briana has." I nodded at her.

Briana pulled her hair off her shoulder to show him her green smiling-alligator earrings.

The twins giggled and squirmed away from me to run toward the elevator.

Jewel looked exasperated. "I have to deliver these two to Mom in the bridal suite. You guys should go sit. Jill and Walter are already down there."

"Where's Jane?" I asked.

"Meeting her date in the lobby," Gwen said, still putting in an earring.

"Jane has a *date*?"

My sister was shy and didn't usually bring boyfriends around until they'd been together for a while.

"That's what she said," Gwen replied. "She was very hush-hush about it."

I raised my eyebrows at Briana. "A date."

She gave me a wow face.

I loved that Briana knew my sisters. That our worlds were blending. I loved that we got to hold hands even when no one was around to see it. I got to touch her when I felt like touching her—which, frankly, was all the time. We had sex like we were trying to make up for every day we wanted to and couldn't. Over the last month all my cardio was in bed.

We texted I Love You to each other from across the ER at work. Left it in little notes. Whispered it in the dark. Said it right in the middle of a conversation, just because we could.

My life was a fairy tale.

I didn't take one second with her for granted. I swore to myself I never would. Being able to hold her while we watched a movie or come up behind her to hug her while she drank her coffee or put a hand on her thigh under a table—it was all a gift. A privilege. And I vowed always to honor that. I wrote about it in my journal—when I had time to journal. I was too busy living the dream that was my life to sit down and document it. But I was so happy.

We got to the courtyard where the ceremony would be taking place and took our seats. There was a trellis dripping with flowers where Amy and Jeremiah would say their vows. The weather was perfect, and the smell of roses ensconced us.

"The wedding coordinator did a good job," Briana said, looking around. "I love weddings."

I peered at her. "Would you ever want to get remarried?" I asked.

She gave me a look. "You don't have to be married to spend the rest of your life with someone."

"You don't want to marry me?"

She gave me an amused look. "Are you asking?"

"And what would you say if I did?"

"I'd say you cannot marry a man you just started dating. No matter how good the sex is."

I paused to grin. "How long, then?"

She laughed. "I don't know."

I pivoted to look at her straight on. "Six months? A year?"

"Are you putting a reminder in your phone?"

"I'm serious. I think we should talk about it."

Her face went soft. She looked like she was about to reply, but then she peered over my shoulder. "Oh my God..."

I turned to see Jane and her date walking down the aisle to take their seats. Her date was *Benny*.

Briana beamed. "Hey, BEN."

He ignored her and followed Jane to the front row.

I turned to her. "Did you know they were talking?" I asked.

She shook her head, still smiling. "No. He probably thought I'd tease him. Which I totally would."

I looked back at Benny. "He looks good."

She nodded. "He's putting weight back on, he's exercising."

"He's going on dates."

She gazed at me. "He looks good because of you. Because of what you're doing."

I put a hand to her cheek. "Will you still love me when I don't have any more organs to give?" I asked.

"I'd love you even if you were a talking head in a jar," she said, speaking to my lips.

"I'd love you even if you didn't like dogs."

She gasped. "I'd love you even if I was a gummy bear and you ate me," she breathed.

"I'd eat you even if you weren't a gummy bear..."

"Guys, it's getting fucking gross," Jewel said, sitting down next to us with Gwen. "Like, we get it, you're obsessed with each other. Quit it already."

We both laughed. I was just about to get back to my wedding question, but the bridal march started. Everyone shushed and shifted to watch as the wedding party began to make their way down the aisle.

First Amy's mom. Then Jeremiah, looking like a kid on Christmas morning. His best man, then the two groomsmen and bridesmaids side by side. Katrina tossing flower petals, then Carter with the ring pillow.

When Amy finally came down the aisle with her dad to join Jeremiah under the trellis, we all stood.

I felt complete tranquility. I was happy for them. Genuinely happy. The universe had righted itself, and everything was as it should be. Nobody was looking at me to see if I was going to implode, and if they did, they quickly realized I was busy living my own love story and they didn't look again.

I'd actually been looking forward to this night for weeks. I couldn't wait to slow-dance with Briana, eat the wedding cake, and then go up to our hotel room after. I was happy about the family photos we would take today because she would be in them, and I'd get to look back and remember that this day was part of the beginning of our lives together.

I was excited about all our firsts.

I peered over at her. "I wish the me of today could send a message to the me of three months ago," I whispered.

She smiled. "Oh, yeah? And what would you have told yourself?"

"I would have said that when this day came, I wouldn't care about the wedding because I'd be madly in love with someone else."

She laughed quietly. "Would you have believed it?"

I shook my head with a grin. "No. Probably not."

It was too good to be true...

CHAPTER 43

BRIANA

This was hands down one of the best weddings I'd *ever* been to—not like the last couple I went to. Nobody followed me around with a guitar. My date didn't drink too much because he was in love with the bride, like Nick had at Kelly's wedding. Tonight my date couldn't keep his hands *or* his eyes off me.

Jacob was relaxed and happy. *I* was happy.

Jacob slow-danced with Katrina. It was seriously cute. I couldn't stop smiling at the image of him looking over at me, his eyes creased at the corners and a little girl in a tulle dress standing on the tops of his shoes.

In addition to the many cigarettes I'm sure Grandpa got, Joy wheeled him out herself and gave him a cigar after dinner.

And Jane's date was *Benny*.

When I finally cornered him, all he did was shrug and say, "I didn't tell you 'cause you just would have made a big deal about it." Yup.

Benny was smiling the entire wedding. He was smiling like someone who had a whole life ahead of him. Because he did. In a week he'd have a new kidney. A new start. He was seeing someone he was excited about. He was looking forward. I had to call him Ben the whole night.

Jacob let me have his cake. It was from Nadia Cakes and it was red velvet—and then I caught the bouquet. Everyone was cheering and I was laughing so hard. Amy came over and gave me a hug. Jacob was beaming.

It felt like one of the best nights of my life—like the first day of all the rest of my days, for some reason. And it made me start to think about what Jacob said about me marrying him.

It was way, *way* early for that. I'd never wanted to get remarried. At least I thought I didn't. But as Jacob had a tendency to do, he made my No turn into a Maybe.

I didn't hate the idea of his family being my family. Of Joy being my mother-in-law, and Jewel and Jane and Jill being my sisters.

And I *adored* the thought of being his wife. Of him introducing himself as my husband. It made me feel proud. Like maybe wife *was* a title I wanted again all of a sudden.

So maybe. Just... *maybe.*

We stayed until the very last song.

When the lights came on and everyone started trickling out, Jacob took my hand and I grabbed my bouquet and we headed through the hotel lobby with Lieutenant Dan to the elevators.

I was holding my shoes. Jacob's tie was draped around his neck and the top two buttons of his shirt were undone. He had his sleeves rolled up and he'd put his jacket around my shoulders.

When the elevator doors closed behind us, he drew me in and kissed me. His mouth tasted like the champagne send-off toast. He ran a hand under my ass and pulled me into him. "When we get back to the room, I want you to sit on my face," he said, his voice husky.

I was breathing hard. "Like, *sit* on it, sit on it?"

"Sit on it, sit on it."

"Okay. If you die, you die."

He laughed and devoured me again.

I was going to let this man snap me in half like a glow stick when we got up to the room. I wanted to break the bed.

I'd had more sex in the last month than the entire last two years of my marriage. On our days off we didn't leave the room except to grab the DoorDash delivery off the front porch and let out Lieutenant Dan. We ran out of condoms so many times that Jacob finally went to Costco to get the bulk box.

The elevator pinged two floors down from ours. We stopped making out, and he moved his hands to my waist as a courtesy for whoever got on, but we were still panting and looking at each other's lips when the doors opened.

"What do you think about room service?" he asked quietly, rubbing his nose to mine.

"*Yeeeesss.* I'm starving." My stomach had been gnawing at me for the last two hours. "If we order now, it'll show up right when we're done," I whispered.

He laughed a little. Then we both noticed that the door was still open but nobody had gotten on.

Jacob glanced over first. Then I turned too. And my blood ran cold.

It was the Tower of Terror at Disney World on my twenty-fifth birthday. The elevator doors opening to show you something awful and confusing before plummeting you to your death.

It was Nick and Kelly.

They stood frozen, like deer in headlights. Nobody moved.

They were dressed up. She had her arm hooked in his. Nick's brown hair was shorter. He looked fitter than before. He was tan. He had a band on his wedding finger. Kelly's blond hair was down around her shoulders. Pink lipstick. Dangly gold earrings that looked like leaves. She was wearing an enormous diamond wedding ring. She was glowing.

And she was pregnant.

I felt instantly nauseous. Lieutenant Dan made a crying noise in the silence. Time stood still.

Nick cleared his throat. "Uh, we'll take the next one."

I stood there for another painful, paralyzed moment. And then the doors closed in slow motion.

The whole thing had taken less than fifteen seconds. And the bomb was nuclear.

"Briana?" Jacob said, staring at the side of my face.

I couldn't hear him. My ears were ringing. My knees were weak, my vision was getting dark around the edges.

And then I threw up all over his shoes.

CHAPTER 44

JACOB

re you okay?" I asked.

Briana had her forehead against the truck window. We were almost home. She hadn't talked for most of the ride. Or in the hotel room while we packed up this morning. Or anytime, really, since the encounter in the elevator last night.

It was a long moment before she answered me. "I'm sorry I threw up on you," she said again.

"That's never happened to me before—in my office job as an accountant."

She laughed a little, but there was no mirth in it.

Lieutenant Dan was sitting with his head on her lap. He'd been whining and crying to get to her from the back seat so badly I finally pulled over and let him sit with her. Same thing last night. I had to let him sleep on the bed.

"Was that the first time you've seen them together?" I asked.

She didn't reply. I reached over and grabbed her hand. She didn't squeeze it back.

Something was off.

I understood why she was upset. Running into her ex-husband

and the woman he'd left her for and seeing that they were married and pregnant had to be jarring.

But there was something else going on too. She hadn't looked me in the eye since the elevator incident. And it made a knot form in the pit of my stomach and my anxiety fire to life.

Maybe I was worried about something that wasn't anything to be concerned about? She was just in shock and not feeling well and needed some time to process.

But she didn't take the bouquet this morning. She'd been so happy to catch it last night. She'd said she wanted to dry it. And then she just left it on the hotel dresser. When I went to pick it up, she said she didn't want it. It felt like some kind of omen that I didn't want to think about too closely.

We drove the rest of the way home in silence. When we pulled into the garage, she got out. I grabbed her luggage out of the trunk, but she wouldn't let me take it up the steps to the house for her. She just mumbled that she had it and started walking, dragging it without waiting for me. When I came in after her, she was standing in the living room staring at the couch.

"I'll make you some soup," I said, setting down my duffel bag. "Maybe we can watch a movie? Or *Schitt's Creek*?"

I came up behind her and hugged her. She tensed. My stomach dropped.

"What's wrong?" I asked.

She wriggled slowly away from me, like she was shrugging out of a dirty jacket and didn't want to touch more of it than she had to.

She turned to look at me with bloodshot eyes. "I'm going home."

I swallowed. "Okay…" I said. "I'll go with you."

"No."

My heart was picking up. "All right. When will you be back?"

"I'm never going to live with you, Jacob."

It was like a dagger that came out of nowhere.

"I'm never going to live with you, and I'm never going to marry you. If you want that, find someone else."

"I...I don't want someone else—"

"Well, maybe you should." She stared at me red-eyed and defiant. Like it was me against her all of a sudden.

I shook my head. "Why are you fighting with me?"

"I'm not," she said, her voice clipped. "I'm just telling you the way it is."

I licked my lips. "Look. What happened last night was traumatic. Let's talk about it—"

"No."

I studied her face.

"Briana," I said carefully. "I'm not going to do to you what he did. If you're worried about that—"

She burst into laughter. Deep, guttural laughs like I'd never heard from her.

"You don't know what you'll never do," she said. "Maybe you'll get sick of me. Maybe you'll meet someone else you can't live without. And then I'll come home early and my Bluetooth will connect to your phone when I pull into the garage and I'll get to hear my friend telling my husband of ten years how much she enjoyed fucking him on my new duvet." She cracked up, like this was hilarious.

"Oh," she said like she just remembered. "And then he leaves me for her, and while they're in my house, eating off my plates and sleeping in my bed, I miscarry our baby. Alone. In my shitty childhood bedroom with my shitty *Smallville* posters on the walls. Which worked out great for him because he didn't want *my* baby anyway."

I blinked at her. "I...I had no idea that happened to you—"

"Well, it *did*. And no, you won't do that to me, Jacob. Because

I won't let you." She grabbed the handle of her luggage and started for the door. "I don't live here. I want to go home. I want my mom."

I grabbed her wrist. "Briana, I'm not him—"

She yanked her arm away from me. "*Every* man is him! You are *all* the fucking same!" Her voice cracked on the last word. "You aren't until you *are*." Her breath was coming out shaky. "You won't like me once you really know me, or you'll find someone else or you'll want something different and *then* you'll leave. So just do it now. Save me the trouble."

My chest was rising and falling, sheer panic pulsing inside me. I didn't know what to say. Everything I said was making it worse, and I didn't know what to do.

Her face changed a dozen times in the long seconds we looked at each other. Anger. Hurt. Sadness. Fear. And then finally something softer and resigned and broken.

"I need to be alone right now, Jacob," she whispered. "Just… leave me alone."

And she left.

CHAPTER 45

BRIANA

Mom handed me a hot tea and put a hand to my forehead. "No fever. Maybe just a stomach bug." She sat on the bed next to me.

I held the mug in my hands and stared bleary-eyed into the amber liquid. I felt hollow. I *was* hollow.

I'd faced Nick completely defenseless. The anger that had shielded me all this time had disintegrated without me noticing, and then when I'd needed it, I'd had nothing to protect me.

They were married now. She was pregnant. They'd gotten their little happily-ever-after.

If I'd had the baby, where would I have been in all this? The single mother to a newborn? Like Mom? A child Nick hadn't cared one ounce about and was probably relieved that I'd lost?

The fallout from our divorce still wasn't over. It had just evolved. It wasn't even about Nick anymore. Now it was a cautionary tale for the relationship I was in, because what had I learned? What was different this time around? I was head-over-heels in love— again. I was living in a house that wasn't mine and could be taken from me—again. I was vulnerable and exposed and blindly trusting someone.

And I was pregnant. Again.

I hadn't known it until that moment in the elevator. I'd felt that tiny wave of nausea, and it was like a lightbulb went on and my brain and body realized it at the same exact time. And it happened while face-to-face with Nick and Kelly and the reminder of how it turned out whenever I thought I was safe with someone. I was staring at exactly what happens when I give all of myself with complete abandon, while simultaneously realizing that I'd just fucking done it again.

I'd learned nothing from Nick. Not a thing.

Jacob and I were so new. Of course he loved me now. But what about when I wasn't fun? When I was sick, or moody, or the sex tapered off, or if I lost the baby because maybe I couldn't carry one to term in the first place. Would he want me if I couldn't give him kids?

The tears came.

We'd been careless. Not every time, but enough. It had taken so long to get pregnant with Nick I didn't think it would happen this easily. It was like my poor, abandoned eggs realized this was their last chance and they stormed the gates.

I put the mug on the nightstand and pulled my legs up and tucked my face into my knees.

Mom put a hand on my shoulder. "What's wrong, *mija*?"

I breathed into the fleece of my pajamas. It smelled like Jacob's lavender laundry beads and the orange-scented lotion I'd put on my legs after the bath Mom made me take when I came home. I knew I'd never be able to smell either ever again without it summoning this moment.

Mom started to rub my back and it made me cry harder.

"I'm pregnant, Mamá." The words eked out of me. It was the first

time I'd spoken them into the universe since the time it happened
with Nick. Only this time I wasn't excited. I was terrified.

"Are you sure?" she whispered.

I nodded into my knees. "I took two tests when I got home.
I'm sure."

"How many weeks?" she asked.

I raised my head, wiping at my cheeks. "Your pregnancy starts
on the first day of your last period. So five, probably."

"He doesn't want it?"

I shook my head. "He doesn't even know yet."

"You didn't use protection? Two doctors, you don't know how
babies are made?"

I laughed dryly and put my forehead into my hand.

She let out a long breath and we sat quietly for a moment. Then
she peered over at me. "He's a good man."

My chin started to quiver.

"He'd make a good papá," she said. "A good husband. And I
don't say that about very many men, *mija*."

"I'm not marrying him."

She looked at me perplexed. "Why not? You might be having
his baby." She gestured to my belly. "You don't want to be a
family?"

Of course I wanted to be a family. But when did that actually
work out? It had never worked out for me—not in the family I
grew up in or the one I thought I was making for myself when I
married Nick. Why would this time be different?

Only it *was* different. It was *worse*.

Loving Jacob felt like falling up. Like there was nothing to stop
me so I'd just keep going forever. And if I hadn't seen Nick and
Kelly last night, maybe I would have. I would have just continued
in this fugue state I was in, blissfully ignorant—because Jacob
had made me forget what he was. But now I remembered.

Jacob was a *man*.

And men do what men do.

I suddenly viewed my sweet, docile boyfriend like a wild animal raised in captivity. Tame and domesticated—but might still bite one day, just because the instinct was bred into his genes.

There wasn't enough rage in the universe to get me through it if Jacob hurt me. It would kill me. I would never come back from it.

"I'm never getting married again." I sniffed. "I'm not doing any of it. I don't even know if I should stay with him."

She pulled her face back. "What? What do you mean you're not going to stay with him? *Oye, estás siendo ridícula!*"

"Mamá, just stop."

"Pregnant, with a perfectly good man who loves you—do you think being a single parent is fun? You don't remember how it was?"

"I can't, Mamá."

"Why?"

"Because it will hurt too much when he leaves!" I snapped.

She went silent.

"I can't do it again," I said, my voice wavering. "I *can't*. Especially now. You don't think I want to? That I don't wish the idea of being pregnant and shacked up with a man I'm in love with didn't scare the absolute shit out of me? I don't even know what to feel right now. I don't. I don't even know if there's going to *be* a baby in a week. And if there is, I don't know that I can give her the childhood I had. It's better this way, so when he leaves, it doesn't break her—" I cracked on the last word and I buried my face in my hands.

I felt like a short-circuiting toy. Sparks popping and wires frayed. I'd been fine. A fully functional, happy human being. And then all at once I wasn't.

I just sat there and cried. My sobbing was so loud I was glad Benny had a life now and he wasn't home to hear it.

A hand squeezed my shoulder, and after a few minutes, I started to settle down.

Mom handed me a wad of tissues. "I'm sorry," she said, softer now. "I never knew it affected you like that. I always thought it was me and you, and we did okay."

I took a few deep, steadying breaths. "We did. We did do okay. That's the only way I know *how* to be okay. On my own. Where I don't have to trust anyone to be there."

Mom paused for a long beat. "Briana...I know your dad wasn't a good man and Nick wasn't a good man. And maybe I taught you that none of them are and that's my fault. I just wanted you to protect yourself, not to be afraid of loving again. I did. I found Gil. I'm happy. It's the greatest revenge to be happy. To have a good life. So have one. With *him*."

I took a deep breath. Then another. I looked up at my mother with wet eyes. "I love the quiet gentle life of that quiet gentle man," I said. "I *want* to be brave enough to love him with my eyes closed. I just don't think I can."

I wished I could. Or I wished I loved him less. Because then the stakes wouldn't be so high. There wouldn't be as far to fall if he let me down—*when* he let me down. And I was already so far gone.

Jacob had managed to slip me into his life, so gently, so seamlessly, that I didn't even realize how much of myself I'd already surrendered until I stood in his house this morning, suddenly fully awake.

When I was looking around his living room, it was like I'd blacked out three months ago and woke up pregnant and a common-law wife to a man I'd just met. That was the reality of this. I'd *just* met him. We hadn't even gone through a full season yet together, and I was *living* with him and expecting his damn baby.

If I didn't know Nick after twelve years, how could I possibly know Jacob after just a few months? And no matter how well you know someone, or for how long, you can never be in their head. You can never know what they're really thinking. Even if it feels perfect, even if *they* feel perfect—perfect isn't actually perfect.

There's always the chance of rejection.

My heart wanted to believe that maybe Jacob *was* different. Maybe we were soul mates, and that's why it had all happened so fast and so easily. But my brain screamed that I was just stupid—making impulsive, irresponsible decisions with a stranger. And it was one thing to do this when only my heart was on the line. But it was something else to do this to a child.

I had no doubt Jacob would be a wonderful daddy. He'd always want our baby. But he probably wouldn't always want *me*. And I didn't want my kid to have to see me crumble into a million pieces when that time came. Watch us separate one day, him packing his bags and moving out the way I'd watched my daddy do once.

I had to make choices now to protect her later.

I blinked into the room, staring through tears at the dark spots on the walls where posters used to be.

I couldn't explain the intense, panicked flight response I was feeling. The need to *run*. Push him away before he hurt me, like all the other important men in my life had. Get myself to safety before it was too late, insulate myself before history repeated itself.

I put my face to my knees again.

I was desperate for him to tell me I hadn't made a horrible mistake. I wanted Jacob to make me all the promises and tell me it was going to be okay, that I was safe and loved and he wanted this and he wanted me. I wanted him to tell me we were different, and I wished to God that I was the kind of undamaged person who could believe something like that.

But I wasn't. And I probably never would be.

CHAPTER 46

JACOB

Briana called out of work on Monday and the day after. Those were the last two shifts we had until the time off for the surgery.

She had called me the night she left. She'd apologized in tears for snapping at me and told me she just needed some space. She'd asked if I could come over on Wednesday to talk. And so I waited for Wednesday. That was all I could do.

This change in her felt deeper than just the shock of seeing her ex with his new wife. There was something else going on, and I couldn't figure out what it was.

I missed her so much. I didn't know what to do. I was living somewhere between anxiety and a dull panic attack, constantly. My heart felt like it was grasping around in the dark, searching for hers because it used to be there and now it wasn't.

I couldn't sleep without her. I lay in bed at night, my mind racing. I'd poured myself into my journal because my feelings had nowhere else to go.

Nothing was okay. Nothing.

When Wednesday mercifully rolled around, I had to get blood-work done before going to see her. The transplant was the day after tomorrow. I'd be driving down to the Mayo Clinic at five a.m. on Friday to be checked in for pre-op at seven.

I picked up some pita bread and soup she liked and headed over to her house. Rosa let in Lieutenant Dan and me. She hugged me and looked about as worried as I felt.

"I'm glad she's seeing you," she said, her voice low.

"Rosa, what's wrong?" I asked quietly. "She's not talking to me. I don't know what I did."

She looked sorry for me. "You didn't do anything. Just tell her you love her. Okay? Make sure she knows."

I studied her face like I might be able to glean more information from it. But the older woman just patted me on the shoulder and sent me down the hallway.

When I came up to the room and saw Briana, I wanted to run to her the way my dog did. The urge was so strong I had to put a hand on the door frame to keep from sprinting the distance between us.

She was sitting up in bed, wearing a baggy T-shirt. Her long hair was in a braid. She was pale, and even though she was smiling and petting Lieutenant Dan, she looked sad. I set the food I brought on the dresser and came around the bed, sat down, and gathered her into me. She surrendered like she was just as relieved as I was to have her in my arms.

"I missed you," I breathed into her hair.

It was a long moment, but she said it back. I had to squeeze my eyes shut to keep myself from crying from the relief.

I climbed into the bed and pulled her down onto my chest and just hugged her. She started weeping softly and I kissed the top of her head and smoothed her hair. "What is it?" I whispered. "Tell me what's wrong."

When she finally did, she did it with her cheek pressed to my heart. "I'm pregnant, Jacob."

I froze. "You're *pregnant*?"

I pulled away to look at her. "Briana, that's...that's wonderful," I said, beaming. "That's..."

But *she* wasn't smiling. Her chin quivered. "I don't know if I can carry it. I couldn't carry the last one."

I nodded and took her hands into mine. "Okay. That's okay. That's not your fault if that happens. We'll deal with that if it does. Come home. Come home and I'll take care of you."

She let out a shaky breath. "Jacob, I can't live with you. I meant that. I meant everything I said that day. I shouldn't have said it the way that I did, but I *did* mean it."

I shook my head. "I don't...I don't understand."

She pressed her lips together like she was trying not to cry. "I'm not sure I'm in any place to be in a relationship."

My stomach bottomed out. "What are you talking about?"

She didn't answer me.

I licked my lips. "Look, I know you had a hard time in your last marriage. It won't be like that with us. I love you. Please. Come home. Or let me be here—"

"No. I can't. I've thought about this a lot over the last two days." She looked away from me. "Jacob, I don't know how to be all-in anymore." Her eyes came back to mine. "I don't think I'm capable of it. Or any of the things that entails. Especially now. I can't be the carefree, throw-caution-to-the-wind person I was before Nick. I can't pretend like I don't know how these things end—"

"It's not going to end. Why would it end?"

Her eyes looked so sad.

"You are perfect, Jacob. But I am not. You won't always want me and I'll always be braced for it. I'll never relax. I'll be waiting for the shoe to drop. I'll never feel secure. I'll never really trust you. I'll just push you away and I'll be miserable and I'll make *you* miserable."

"I'm miserable without you," I said. "*That's* what makes me miserable." I swallowed. "Look, I understand what you've been through. I do. And we didn't plan all this to happen this fast. It's unexpected and it's scary for you. I get that. We can slow down. We can take a little break if you need it. I can give you space, but I will *never* leave you, Briana. Do you hear me? *Never.* Every single thing that matters to me in this world is in this bed. I love you."

I squeezed her hands as she sat there, looking at them between us. Her chin started to shake.

Please... believe me.

"Jacob... it's just best—"

"Don't do anything. Please. Just wait. Don't make any big decisions right now."

"Wait for what, Jacob?" she said quietly. She raised her eyes to mine. "What will change?" The way she said it made my heart crack right down the middle.

"Maybe *you* will," I said. "Maybe your mind will catch up with your heart."

"I don't trust my heart. That's the problem."

Lieutenant Dan nudged his nose under her arm and she started crying softly again. I wanted to carry her off and put her where I could keep her safe, pack love around her and insulate her from whatever was eroding her.

But I couldn't do that, so I just held her instead. I folded my arms around her, and she clutched my shirt like she was afraid I would vanish. But *she* was the one who was going to vanish, not me.

I felt panicked. I didn't know how to love her better than I already did. How to show her I wasn't like her ex or her father. She had all of me—there was nothing else I could give her—and if that wasn't enough to convince her, what else could I do?

We stayed holding each other for a few minutes. When she finally stopped crying, she spoke against my chest.

"I'm sorry, Jacob." She sniffed.

"Sorry for what?" I said gently.

She went silent for a long moment. "I'm broken." The hopeless way she said it made tears pinch from my eyes.

"We're all a little broken, Briana. We are a mosaic. We're made up of all those we've met and all the things we've been through. There are parts of us that are colorful and dark and jagged and beautiful. And I love every piece of you. Even the ones you wish didn't exist."

I pulled away to look her in the eye. "What do you need? Tell me what to do. What can I do to fix this?"

She was quiet. "You can't give me what I need."

"Try me."

She searched my face. "I need to be able to see into your soul."

I shook my head. "I love you. You know that."

But I could see in her eyes that she didn't believe me.

She didn't look at me again after that. But she let me hold her and she let me stay. That was at least something.

A half an hour later I brought the soup to her in bed. She didn't eat much of it. She was distant and withdrawn, and my anxiety pulsed and clawed around.

The surgery was the day after tomorrow, and knowing I was about to be helpless when she might need me made me feel panicked. I didn't want to be laid up in a hospital for a week and not able to get to her. If she lost the baby, I wouldn't be able to be there. I didn't want not to be able to carry her to bed, or drive to her house if she decided she wanted to see me, or not to be able to take care of her for the next two weeks because I'd be post-op.

But there was nothing I could do about any of it.

When she fell asleep curled into me, I fell asleep too. For the first time in days I could close my eyes without my brain racing because it was wondering why she wasn't with me. I didn't even know how exhausted I was until the moment that my body finally let go.

There's a special peace in sleeping next to someone you love. When you slip into the dark holding them and wake up and they're still there and you know that everything that matters is just opening your eyes away.

When I felt her hands wandering my body, the light was no longer coming in through the curtains. I didn't know what time it was. I don't think she was really awake and neither was I, but I slipped a hand under her shirt and she slid one down the front of my pants and it was dreamlike and somewhere between awake and asleep and it felt good to touch her and for her to touch me. To have some proof that she still wanted me, even if it was just this.

We didn't talk. Talking would have ended it. We just kissed and took off each other's clothes and made love in the dark. But she felt like a ghost, going through the motions of the things she used to do while she was alive.

When I woke up again, it was morning. And then she asked me to leave.

I didn't want to go. But forcing my company on a woman who wasn't sure she even wanted me around would only make things worse. So I left.

Rosa said good-bye to me on the way out like it was an apology. Then she handed me a casamiento and egg sandwich wrapped in a paper towel and told me I needed to eat. I left holding that and feeling more despondent than when I got here.

I did what I could to stay centered for the rest of the day. I journaled. Watered my plants and packed my hospital bag. Forced myself to eat. Got the house ready for me to be gone for two weeks since I'd be recovering at my parents'. I could see that Briana wasn't in any place to take care of me while I recovered, and I didn't want to burden her with it. I went to drop off Lieutenant Dan with Mom. When I came into the house, I found her in the living room, reading, a moment after Lieutenant Dan found her.

She smiled up at me over my excited dog. "Jacob. Are you ready? It's the big day tomorrow." She closed her book. "Are you sure you don't want me to come?"

I dropped on the couch next to her. "Don't come. I'll be home in a week and you'll be spending plenty of time with me then. I need to stay here after the surgery."

She looked confused. "You're recovering here? Is Briana taking care of Benny? I thought Rosa was doing it."

"She is."

"Is everything okay?" she asked.

I rubbed my forehead. "No," I said.

She set her book down on the coffee table and waited. And I told her about everything except the fake dating—how Briana changed after she saw Kelly and Nick, what Nick did to her, that she'd lost a baby last year. That she said she'd never marry me or live with me, that she was distant and despondent.

And pregnant.

Mom sat and she listened. When I was done, she let out a long exhale. "How do you feel about the pregnancy?"

I leaned forward with my elbows on my knees, staring into the cold fireplace. "Happy. Excited. Wishing she was excited too. But she's not." I looked at her. "What do I do, Mom? I think she's going to leave me."

"Jacob, she's traumatized."

I stared at her.

"She's in the first serious relationship since her divorce, she has an unplanned pregnancy, and her last pregnancy ended in a traumatic miscarriage that she went through alone. She comes from a broken family where she was abandoned by her own father while her mother was expecting. She's terrified and she's trying to protect herself—and she might be so scared that she's willing to sabotage the relationship so that it ends."

I shook my head at her. *"Why?"*

"She'd rather things end on her terms than have the rug pulled out from under her again. It's the only way she can feel in control of the outcome. It is a very common trauma response, Jacob."

"But...but I would never do that to her," I said. *"Never."*

She looked at me gently. "I know, sweetheart. But sometimes the hardest thing isn't trusting the next person. It's trusting *yourself.* She doesn't trust herself to choose well. Given her history with important men in her life, she may even feel that severing her relationship with her child's father is in the best interest of the child. None of the fathers in her life have ever stayed, Jacob. Seeing Nick moved on with his new pregnant wife must have been incredibly difficult, given the circumstances. Had Briana not lost that pregnancy, that man would have been the father of her baby. And it was clear he didn't want Briana or the baby he almost made with her. Why would you be different? Why would *you* be the one who sticks around?"

She dipped her head to look at me. "Has she had any therapy? Talked with anyone?"

I sat back against the sofa and dragged a hand down my mouth. "I don't know. She doesn't have a therapist now, I know that. I don't know what she did back then."

Mom nodded. "Well, if I had to guess, knowing what I know of Briana, she probably didn't. She's tough. Self-reliant. She'd try to muscle through it. But if you don't deal with trauma, it just circles back around. She's probably depressed. And depression lies, Jacob. Nothing it's telling her is true, but she can't know that in her state without help."

I looked her in the eye. "So what do I do?"

"You *know* what to do. It's what you did with him." She nodded at the dog sleeping at my feet. "You move slowly. Be consistent. Give her reassurance. Make her feel loved and safe. *Show up*. Don't give up on her and make sure she knows you never will. And try to get her into therapy."

I blew a breath through my nose and nodded. "Okay."

"She must love you very much," she said.

"Not as much as I love her. I don't even think it's possible that she could," I said quietly. "She's it, Mom." I looked at her. "I think I knew it the moment I laid eyes on her." I laughed a little. "Even though she was telling me off."

She smiled gently at me and put a hand on mine. "I want you to know that watching two complete strangers fall in love has been one of the greatest gifts of my life."

I stilled. "What do you mean?"

She grinned ruefully. "Come on, Jacob. It's my job to know when it isn't real. And also when it *is*."

CHAPTER 47

BRIANA

It was surgery day. Mom and I came down last night and got Benny admitted. Jacob was driving down with Zander.

I ate a dry bagel from the hotel's breakfast buffet, had a decaf coffee, and managed to keep both things down. I realized if I never let my stomach get empty I was less nauseous, so I took a box of Cheerios with me and ate a few at a time every couple of minutes like I was feeding a fire.

I tried not to think of adapting to this pregnancy. I didn't know whether it was a long-term situation. I didn't know if I'd be carrying around boxes of Cheerios in a week. I was just dealing and not allowing myself to think beyond one day at a time. One minute. One second.

When we got to the hospital, Mom ran down to the cafeteria to get me some tea. I headed to the surgical waiting room and found Alexis sitting in one of the gray chairs. I practically fell into my best friend's arms. "Thank you for coming."

I'd told her everything last night on the phone, sitting alone in the hotel parking lot in the car while Mom was sleeping. Alexis was planning on coming and visiting after Benny and Jacob were in recovery, but after we talked, she'd changed her plans and drove down this morning instead.

"Zander was just here," she said over my shoulder. "He went to go talk to the surgeon. Jacob's already checked in."

Just hearing that Jacob was close made the floodgates open again. I dropped into a chair and buried my face in my hands.

I felt like a sponge. I couldn't stop crying. And every little thing just wrung me out. I knew I wasn't in my right mind. I was barely hanging on, and nothing was making it better.

I didn't care that Benny was getting his transplant today. I didn't care that I was still pregnant and holding, almost six weeks in, or that Jacob seemed to still love me—for now. No matter how many good things were happening around me, this fear just swallowed me and held me in its dark belly. Everything felt hopeless. And I didn't know how *not* to feel like that.

I felt Alexis sit next to me. "Are you still thinking about breaking up with him?" she asked softly.

I sniffed and nodded into my hands.

"Oh, Briana."

"I know."

It was all I could say.

"It's normal to be scared," she said gently. "You've been hurt, it's hard to feel safe again. This is just the flinch."

I wiped under my eyes with the top of my shirt. "Maybe the flinch is the only thing that keeps you from getting hurt again."

"Maybe the flinch is the only thing that keeps you from being *happy*."

I looked at her and she held my gaze steadily. "Bri, you are the bravest woman I know. So be brave."

My chin quivered.

She reached over and pulled some tissues from a box and put them in my hands. "He really loves you. I could tell before I even met him. I could tell by the way you talked about him that he did. Even Daniel saw it."

I clutched the Kleenex in my lap for a long moment, just staring at the translucent spots my tears made on the tissues as they fell.

"I have to go," I said, my voice weak. "I have to go see him before they take him in."

I rallied what little of my strength I had left and stood.

Alexis looked up at me from her seat. "Bri? When he tells you he loves you, believe it. Be brave and believe it."

I took a deep breath and gave her a nod, even though I knew I wouldn't.

I wandered the halls until I found his room. Jacob's face lit up the second he saw me. It made me feel guilty and horrible and exhausted.

He was in a hospital gown with a blanket over his lap. His handsome face was tired and maybe a little anxious. But mostly it was searching. Like he was hoping to see something on my face that I know he didn't see.

I sat on the chair next to his bed while they finished putting in his IV. It was one of those quiet moments where I used to think we were agreeing to be harmless to each other. Only I wasn't being harmless to him. And I didn't trust he wouldn't be harmless to me.

When the nurse finished up and finally left us alone, he held out his palm. I scooted as close to his bed as I could. I took his warm hand, and he threaded his fingers in mine and squeezed. He leaned over and kissed the top of my head and I had to pinch my eyes shut.

"How are you?" he whispered.

"Better," I lied.

I looked up at him. His gentle brown eyes. The face that once made me forget to be cautious and afraid.

I wanted to go back to that time. Be blissfully oblivious.

I couldn't go back.

"How are you feeling?" I asked, forcing conversation. "Are you nervous?"

He held my gaze. "I'm not scared of what's going to happen in there. I'm scared you won't be there when I come out."

My chin trembled and I had to look away from him.

"I love you," he said.

Tears welled in the corners of my eyes.

"You know, love shows up, Briana. And even if you keep me away from you, my heart will still be where you are. So just let me *be* where you are."

I was crying again. "I love you too," I said. "I really do."

I put my head on his bed and he put a hand on my hair and we just sat there in silence. And I got the feeling he was happy he was even getting this.

A nurse pulled back the curtain. "All right, it's time to go. Are we ready?"

Jacob nodded, but he never took his eyes from me. They began to wheel him out, and I got up to walk next to the bed. I held his hand until we got to the double doors of the staff-only area. I leaned down and kissed him with tight lips, trying not to cry.

Maybe Jacob and I would end, right on schedule. Just like we'd always planned. Only now it wasn't fake. Now it was too real.

"I have something for you," he said. He gave me a flat package wrapped in brown paper that he had stashed under the blanket.

I wiped under my eyes. "What is this?"

"It's something I want you to have. I marked where you should start, but you can read anything you want."

"You got me a book?"

"It's a story, yes."

I sniffed. "Okay." I tucked it under my arm.

"If you start now, you'll be done by the time I get out." He put a hand on top of mine, which was clutching the rail of his gurney. "I love you," he said. "I'm always going to love you. No matter what."

Then they wheeled him through the doors, and he was gone.

I didn't want to go sit with my mom and Zander and Alexis in the waiting room. I needed a minute alone. So I followed signs for the hospital chapel and took a seat in a pew.

It was serene and quiet. There was a large blue stained-glass window over a small altar. Flowers. Nobody else was in the room, which was good because I was probably going to cry here since I couldn't seem to stop.

I set the package Jacob gave me on my lap and stared at it blankly.

It had a brown hemp string around it. I took the end in two fingers and pulled and pried the paper off. It was a notebook.

It was a journal.

His journal.

"Oh my God…" I whispered, picking it up.

It was his diary. Why?

I ran a finger over the brown leather. It had his initials pressed into the cover. The leather was soft from handling and the whole thing felt almost warm in my hand, like the hours he spent with it absorbed him.

I opened it to the page with a green Post-it sticking out. It said, *This is the day I met you. Start here.*

He wanted me to read his diary.

I was breathless.

I couldn't read this. It felt like a violation. These were his most private thoughts in here, this was more invasive than looking at his search history, I couldn't.

But he wanted me to. I couldn't give him much right now. I couldn't make him promises or even promise that one day I could. But at least *this* I could do. So I opened it to the page he marked, steadied myself, and started to read.

It was a love story. *Our* love story.

The day he met me and the first time he laid eyes on me.

...She was so beautiful it caught me by surprise. I just stood there, I forgot what I was even doing...

He wrote about how shocked he was when I told him to bring cupcakes and how grateful he felt. The way his mood lifted when I replied to his first letter. Then a recap of every letter I wrote him and how they made him feel. How he cherished every single one and he had them saved in a special drawer in his desk.

The time I DM'd him on Instagram and then talking to me on a patio in the rain—He sat in the rain? Just to talk to me? He'd been eaten alive by mosquitoes. I remembered that, seeing all the bites on his arms. He didn't tell me.

I laughed when he talked about how he'd obsessed for hours about what to eat in the supply closet with me. Then it was the moment he decided to donate his kidney to Benny, and how he did it for me. Not Joy. Not Benny. For *me*.

...Seeing her so happy when she heard the news made everything I'll go through worth it for that one moment alone...

He wrote about how his heart raced every time he saw me across the ER or every time I touched him, how hard it was to pretend he wasn't falling in love with me.

...I feel my heart twisting around her in a way that is completely out of my control and can never be undone. I can't put it away and I can't unknow it and I can't slow it down. I don't even want to...

Then asking me out and me saying no and how crushed he was, but he didn't want to give up, so he followed me to Wakan.

...I had to go. I didn't care that it was outside of my comfort zone or that even asking if I could be there with her was inappropriate, because any day I'm not with her is just wasted time. And I'll already never get all the time I want...

Then the moment he realized he was in love with me. I was passed out drunk and he was holding me in front of the fireplace at Grant House. He said his back hurt for a week from leaning on that hope chest, but he got to hold me so it was worth it.

...It's funny to think that even sitting there on the floor with her, uncomfortable and tired, was better than sitting anywhere else in the world without her. I didn't even want to go to sleep because I'd rather be awake and with the woman I love than risk being alone in my dreams...

Then the next day we were on the phone with the silence stretching between us. He'd stayed on the line because he couldn't stand to be the one to disconnect. I thought *he'd* been the one who'd forgotten to hang up. But he hadn't. He just didn't want to let me go.

...I stayed, just listening. I sat there thinking that I was lucky to still be with her in the silence. And I realized that this is what true love feels like. Clinging even to the stolen moments you're not supposed to have...

He wrote about loving when my perfume was on his clothes, some random time that I kissed him on the cheek and it was everything. How hard it was to not be able to touch me. How much he liked making me smile. How he'd search for little things to get or to do for me.

...I sent Briana flowers today. I always bring her things just because. But nothing with her is just because. There are a thousand reasons in every second of every day...

Hating every time I texted Levi. There was a long entry from the morning of the bachelor party when he couldn't sleep because he was so worried I wanted someone else. Then another long entry from later that night after the futon in the basement. His confusion and fear and hurt. It was like being there with him, seeing it through his eyes, feeling everything he felt.

And then we were together.

And he was so, *so* happy. He had less time to write because he was spending so much time with me.

...I thought I'd been in love before. I'd called it love, I'd believed it was love. But Briana is the lesson. She's the one who taught me what it really feels like to live for someone else...

Then I saw Nick and Kelly.

Jacob wrote pages and pages about how he felt when I wouldn't talk to him. How afraid he was that he was losing me. How he would do anything to bring me back and his heart was breaking because I was so sad and he missed me so much and he felt helpless.

...When she ghosts me, she haunts me. I can still feel her all around me only I can't see her or touch her and I know, without a shadow of a doubt, that I can't go the rest of my life like this. This isn't living. Nothing is anything without her...

This part was hard to read. I put the journal facedown on my thigh. It took me a minute to regain my composure. When I did, I picked up the diary, wiping under my eyes.

And now he was at my house and I was telling him about the baby. He was happy.

I smiled through tears.

He was worried about me and the pregnancy, but he said he'd love me and be with me no matter what. He'd Googled cribs and strollers and a body pillow for me, and he'd ordered lollipops on Amazon that were supposed to help with nausea. It made me laugh-cry. He was excited. He wanted to take care of me.

He wasn't like Nick. He didn't wish the baby would go away. He wanted me. He wanted *us*.

By the time I got to his last entry, hours had passed and tears were streaming down my face. I found an envelope there and opened it with shaking hands.

Dearest Briana,

I know you're scared. You have every right to be. But someday, decades from now, when our grandchildren are grown and our hair is gray, and we've spent a lifetime being harmless to each other, you're going to find this letter yellowed and wrinkled, forgotten in a shoebox. You'll read it and you'll remember how frightened and unsure you were once. How afraid you were to give yourself to someone, how hard it was to trust again—and you'll smile. Because I'll still be there. And we will still be in love.

Yours truly,
Jacob

I completely lost it. I set down the letter and sobbed into my hands.

He let me look into his soul. And the only thing in there was *us*.

I knew right then and there that I was going to fall up.

I had to let go of any grasp on my old life, on my old insecurities or fears or scars, or I was going to miss out on the best thing that's ever happened to me.

Him.

Maybe I wasn't ready. I might never truly be ready. But I was going to do it anyway.

I was going to be brave.

CHAPTER 48

JACOB

I came out of the anesthesia like I was coming out of a dream I couldn't remember. Awake and then out again. Beeping machines in the fog. The feeling of a bed being rolled from one room to another. Muffled talking. Lights in a hallway. A voice I knew, one I didn't. The one I knew I couldn't place, but I felt calm hearing it, and I knew someone who loved me was in the room. Then I drifted out again. Then I was awake and a little more awake, and she was there, holding my hand. I looked at her until my eyes focused.

"*Heeeeeeey.* It's you..."

She smiled. It was different now. Brighter.

She leaned down and pressed a long kiss to my face and I couldn't really remember why this was a big deal, but I knew it was.

"You're so pretty..." I said. Or that's what I thought I said. It felt like it came out jumbled.

She grinned. "Always hitting on me. Don't try to talk yet. You just got out."

I closed my eyes. Asleep again.

It felt like time had passed when I woke up. I was in a different room. I was still out of it, but not as much. A nurse was taking my vitals. Briana was still holding my hand.

The nurse finished, and I tried to sit up.

"No no no. Lie down." Briana put a gentle hand on my shoulder.

I winced. "Why do I feel like I've been hit by a truck?" My voice sounded raspy, and I remembered that I'd been intubated.

"We harvested your organ. You said I could have it, remember?"

"You just took the one, right?" I shifted a little and grimaced, sore.

"I'll get the nurse to give you some morphine."

"I'm going to be sixteen again?" I said tiredly. "Passed out on Jäger in a cornfield?"

She laughed and put her chin on top of my hand on the bed. "You know, they almost didn't let me in here. They said I had to wait until you were awake and you could ask for me. They only let me in because you had me listed on your intake paperwork as your *wife*."

I gave her a small, tired smile. "I'm trying to manifest the things I want by speaking them into the universe."

"And you want a wife?"

"Only if it's you."

She peered gently at me. "I'm open to discussion."

My heart rate picked up. We both knew it, because the heart rate monitor started beeping out of control.

She scooted closer to me. "I'm going to move in, if that's okay," she said. "Maybe we can start there? Take it slow?"

I smiled quietly at her. "Yeah. I'd like that. But why don't we get a new place. That way you'll feel like it's yours too."

Her eyes went soft. "Jacob, you don't like change. Moving is stressful."

"I don't care. I'll do it for you. We'll put both our names on it—or just yours if that makes you feel better."

She bit her lip and nodded. "Okay. Thank you."

I squeezed her hand. She squeezed it back.

"I'll go get Lieutenant Dan from Joy and watch him until you get home," she said.

"Thanks."

"And I'll take care of your plants."

I let out a long *"Nooooooo,"* and she laughed.

My eyes felt heavy. I closed them for a second and then opened them again.

"How is Benny?" I asked.

"The surgery went well. No complications. His new kidney's already producing urine."

I arched an eyebrow. "Really? So fast?"

She shrugged. "It's a perfect match."

"Someone told me once that even a perfect match isn't perfect."

She held my eyes. "This one is."

We gazed at each other for a long moment. Then she got up and put her forehead to mine and closed her eyes. I closed mine too. I was still a little loopy and the darkness behind my lids made everything feel like a dream.

"Did you read it?" I whispered.

She nodded. "Yes. I did."

"I like Ava for a girl," I said, opening my eyes to look at her.

"Ava Xfinity?"

"Ava Xfinity *Ortiz*."

She laughed, then sat back down. I raised my hand to touch her face. She turned in to it and kissed my palm, and I knew my nightmare was over. She'd returned to me.

"I'm so sorry, Jacob," she whispered. "I was really scared."

"I know." I rubbed a thumb on her cheek. "I know you were. But you know how social situations are hard for me? And you help me with that?" I said softly.

She sniffed and nodded.

"I know trust is hard for you. So that's what I'm going to help *you* with."

Then I just lay there, looking at her. Feeling the peace and calm that I only felt alone—with her.

"What?" she asked.

"I'm afraid I'm just drugged and none of this is really happening."

"It's really happening, Jacob."

I closed my eyes. "How do I know?"

"Because love shows up. And here I am."

JACOB

Two Years Later

"Your catchphrase of the day is 'Slow and steady wins the race.'"

I smiled at Briana. "Really? You think I'm going to need one? *Today?*"

I had Ava on my hip. She was in a little yellow tulle dress with a matching yellow bow around her head. She was trying to put my boutonniere in her mouth, so I switched sides.

Briana gave me a look. "I think you *especially* need one today. There are like twenty people out there." She nodded to the backyard.

"My immediate family, your immediate family. Jessica, Gibson, Zander and his husband, Alexis and Daniel. I think I can handle that."

She shrugged. "If you say so. But feel free to use it if you need to." She reached back behind her wedding dress and fanned the train.

The wedding was up at our cabin. We'd finished the remodel last year and decided to do the ceremony and reception in the yard in front of the lake. We hired a wedding planner, and there was an elegant tent set up for the reception. Besides that, not much about this wedding was traditional.

We were standing inside by the back door while everyone finished taking their seats outside, because I was walking Briana down the aisle myself. She didn't like the idea of someone bringing her to me like she was "property changing hands"—her exact words. She wanted us to walk as equals. And it was less anxiety for me than standing there in front of everyone waiting for her to come to me.

There wouldn't be a sweetheart or head table for everyone to stare at all night. We'd be sitting with our best friends and their spouses at a table mixed in with everybody else. No first dance—we'd dance when everyone else did. Nothing that put too much focus directly on us—me—other than the ceremony itself. We just wanted to celebrate with our friends and family, and Briana knew what I needed to be comfortable—which is why I was pretty sure I wasn't going to need her get-out-of-jail-free phrase. It was also one of the many reasons I loved her so much.

I smiled at her, standing there in her white dress, holding her flowers. "Are you sure you want to marry me?" I asked. "I don't have any organs left to donate."

"I thought about that and I almost bailed. But then you went and changed your last name to Ortiz and made it weird. It'd be kind of a dick move if I didn't marry you now." She twisted her lips.

I laughed. I'd done a lot of things over the last two years to make sure she knew this relationship was nothing like her last one.

I still had the same PIN on my phone—hers. And we went to couple's counseling once a month, just to make sure we maintained our communication skills, and I never lost sight of what she needed in this relationship to feel safe. She'd gone to counseling without me too, to work through some of the lingering feelings about her last marriage and her childhood.

It was good that we had that foundation, because she'd had a short bout of postpartum depression after Ava was born. We got her through it. Then I started having panic attacks at work when Briana's maternity leave was up and Rosa had to go back to Arizona to be with her husband. Leaving Ava with a stranger when she was still so small made me feel anxious.

Briana liked going to work and didn't want to give up the security of having a salary. So we talked it over and decided I would quit my job at Royaume to stay home with Ava until she started school. So I was a stay-at-home dad. I loved it. My mental health had never been better.

They started playing the wedding song we wanted to walk down the aisle to. "Falling Up" by Will Heggadon. It was time to go.

The wedding planner came out of nowhere, talking into a headpiece. "Ready?"

Briana looked at me, holding her bouquet.

I smiled. "Ready."

Briana hooked her arm in mine and I adjusted Ava on my hip. The coordinator opened the front door of the cabin and Briana and I came out onto the porch. Everyone stood.

I didn't like this part, where everyone was going to stare at us. But I very much liked the marrying-the-love-of-my-life part, so it was worth it.

We walked the aisle, smiling at our handful of guests. Daniel sat holding his daughter, Victoria Montgomery Grant, next to Zander's husband.

Alexis and Zander, our matron of honor and best man, waited for us under the trellis with Lieutenant Dan, who hopped on one foot at the sight of us coming.

Rosa and Gil were beaming as we passed. Gibson and his wife were in the same row. Gibson *still* hadn't retired.

Jill and Walter were with Jewel and Gwen, who sat with the

twins between them. I raised my pant leg discreetly to show them the squirrel socks I had on. They were eight now, but they still loved it.

Ben sat with my sister Jane. They'd moved in together last year. They rented my old house from us after Briana and I got our own place. Our new place had lots of room for the baby and an extra guest room for when Rosa visited. We had *two* deep freezers completely full of Salvadorian food.

Benny's kidney transplant held, and he was doing great. He was running marathons, was back to work, and had become as much a part of my family as Briana. There were rumblings that he and Jane were next. Briana said she was going to personally hand my sister the bouquet.

We passed Grandpa, and Briana snorted quietly. He was openly smoking. Mom shrugged like she'd given up. Dad winked at me.

When we got to Amy and Jeremiah seated on the corner of the first row, I stopped and handed Ava to her aunt. My little brother was holding my niece, who was only a few months older than my own daughter. They'd be good friends one day, just like Briana and Amy were.

Briana handed her bouquet to Alexis and took my hands.

We'd written our own vows.

I looked in my beautiful wife-to-be's eyes and couldn't believe how lucky I was. She took my breath away, every day, just like the first time I saw her.

The officiant said a few words about marriage, and loving and supporting each other. He read a poem about two very different people being the perfect match because they filled the parts the other one was missing. And then it was time for the vows.

I'd thought long and hard about what I wanted to say. And what I'd come up with felt exactly right.

I looked her in the eye. "Briana, I agree to be harmless to you."

She smiled, because she knew that was all of it. It was the only promise she needed to hear.

It was her turn. She gave me a wry grin. "Jacob, I agree to be harmless to *you*."

The smile ripped across my face, followed by the sting of tears. And then I really couldn't feel everyone's eyes on me at all. It was just the two of us, alone together, showing up. Because that's what love does. It shows up. And I'd never stop doing it.

I kissed my bride.

ACKNOWLEDGMENTS

Thank you to nephrologist Dr. Jared Fialkow for your expertise and ER nurse Terri Saenz Martinez and Kristyn Packard, LPN, for answering a million DMs about life in the ER. Thank you, Liesl Burnes, RN, for the random and frequent late-night messages asking weird hospital questions. Beta readers Kim Kao, Jeanette Theisen Jett, Kristin Curran, Terri Puffer Burrell, Amy Edwards Norman, Dawn Cooper, and sensitivity reader Leigh Kramer— I couldn't do it without you. Thank you to Sue Lammert, a licensed clinical counselor specializing in trauma, Dr. Karen Flood, and Dr. Julie Patten, licensed psychologist, for helping me to depict the mental health aspects of this book with sensitivity and accuracy. As always, my disclaimer that any errors in this book are my own and are no fault of the people who advised me.

A big thank-you to the Forever team for all they do: my editor, Leah Hultenschmidt; publicist, Estelle Hallick; cover designer, Sarah Congdon; production editor, Stacey Reid; Michelle Figueroa, Tom Mis, and Nita Basu from the audio team; and the countless other people who worked so hard to get this book into your hands.

Thank you, Valentina García-Guzio, for help with the Spanish. Thank you to Stephanie Arndt for the title suggestion when we had to rename the book at the last minute, and a nod to Sara Reda for chatting with me via DMs for days about what narrators I should check out for the audiobook.

Stacey Graham, I can't believe we're five books in! OMG! Thank you for taking me here, I'm loving the ride!

READING GROUP GUIDE

DISCUSSION QUESTIONS

1. At the beginning of the book, Briana feels so much despair about her life situation, how nothing has worked out like she planned. Have you had thoughts like that in your life? Were you able to turn things around or find a different kind of outlook?

2. Compare and contrast Briana's bleak outlook with Benny's. What role does hope play in combatting depression?

3. How did Jacob's social anxiety shape his daily life? Did you recognize some of those qualities in yourself or in others you know? How might Jacob's story change your perception of meeting someone who seems shy or aloof at first?

4. How did writing letters, instead of texting or emailing, influence Briana and Jacob's relationship at the beginning? When was the last time you've written a letter and who did you send it to?

5. Jacob uses journaling and exercise as his forms of self-care when his anxiety flares. What kinds of self-care help relieve your stress?

6. At one point, Joy tells Jacob: *If you're with someone who doesn't speak your language, you'll spend a lifetime having to translate your soul.* Do you think Amy was selfish for not understanding Jacob better, or were they just incompatible

from the start? How much of a strong relationship comes down to innate compatibility and how much is empathy and understanding?

7. Briana destroyed Nick's house after she caught him cheating and later felt embarrassed for being so petty. Have you ever done anything in the heat of the moment and regretted it after?

8. Jacob has such a colorful family full of distinctive personalities. Who was your favorite and why? Who did you relate to most? How are the Maddoxes similar or different from your family?

9. How has Briana's view of men been shaped by her mother and her own life experiences? Could you understand why Briana was afraid to love Jacob?

10. Have you ever considered donating blood or an organ? Why or why not?

AUTHOR'S NOTE

When my editor asked me to write a little something about my reason for the themes in this book, at first I thought maybe I'd talk about my experience with anxiety, or my desire to write my first divorced heroine. But when I sat down to start, I realized that the story I wanted to tell was a lot more personal. So personal, in fact, that it's only just now that I can even bring myself to talk about it.

Here's me taking a big breath.

In 2020, in the midst of everything horrible that was going on in the world, I started to notice that I was losing my hair.

It wasn't super obvious. It was so minor I thought maybe I was imagining it. It just seemed a tiny bit thinner than usual. Maybe it was the stress of the pandemic and the election year, or perhaps I was a little bit anemic. My periods were awful, so it could have been that. I felt totally fine. I started taking iron and told myself if it didn't improve in a few months, I'd go see my doctor just in case.

When I finally did see my doctor, my entire world was turned upside down.

I had chronic kidney disease.

Within the span of one week, I was diagnosed with that and a lifelong, progressive autoimmune disease, the cause of my condition. And the prognosis wasn't good. I was given a thirty-three percent chance of my kidney disease going into remission, a thirty-three percent chance of it staying the same, and a thirty-three percent chance of going into full renal failure within five years. I was forty years old.

I went from being a perfectly healthy woman who didn't even take a multivitamin to someone who saw a different specialist every week. I slipped into a world of painful procedures and treatments. I had a kidney biopsy. I was placed on a slew of medications. I got a second opinion. Then a third. I absolutely hate needles and now I was getting blood drawn two, sometimes three times a month.

The doctors wanted to place me on chemo drugs to suppress my immune system to try to stop the onslaught, and I was terrified about what those would do to my body. I was terrified to have a depressed immune system during a pandemic before a vaccine was available. I Googled my autoimmune disease and tumbled down Facebook-group rabbit holes, where I read stories about people getting ulcers on their eyes and losing all their teeth. I sat in a Starbucks parking lot sobbing after realizing that my favorite drink didn't taste the same because of what my autoimmune disease was doing to my salivary glands.

I slid into a depression. My best friend was so worried about me she slid into a depression too. I cried every single day. I was put on a restricted renal diet and couldn't eat the foods I loved. I was no longer allowed to take NSAIDs, so my painful periods became excruciating and unbearable. The quality of my life plummeted.

This diagnosis broke me.

And the whole time nobody outside of my inner circle knew a thing. I was posting on social media, promoting my books, and acting outwardly normal. I wrote *Part of Your World* in the midst of all this, somehow managing to churn out my most successful book to date. Everything looked amazing from the outside, but really I was living the worst year of my life.

Your kidneys don't like to tell you when they're sick. In fact, most people don't show any signs of sickness until they're in stage-three kidney disease. I was extremely lucky that I noticed my hair thinning and I didn't wait longer than I did to get checked out. There wasn't scarring on my kidneys yet, so my doctors agreed to a wait-and-see approach to give the less-toxic medications a chance to start working before they put me on something harsher.

But every month for half a year the labs were the same. I wasn't improving. I would get anxiety the days leading up to and after my bloodwork. The emails with my results would give me panic attacks when I'd get the notification, because it was never good news. My world revolved around my health issues. I was Benny. And then all of a sudden and out of nowhere, my labs came back a little better.

I tried not to get my hopes up, but the next month my numbers dropped even farther. Every time my bloodwork came in, it was an improvement on the month before. My hair started to grow back and my autoimmune disease got quiet and my coffee started to taste good again—and then *POOF.* A year after my diagnosis, I went into full remission. I got my life back. Just like that. I'll be on medications for the rest of my life, I'll always have my autoimmune disease, and it could always flare up again, but a full remission gives you a wonderful prognosis. I don't think even my own doctor expected what happened. I was very, very lucky.

I've always been a vocal supporter of organ donation. In fact, I mention it in most of my books. But now I truly understood the other side of it and the impact that needing a transplant makes on the life of the person who receives it. I know what it's like to live the hundreds of what-ifs. To be worried you won't get an organ if you need one. To watch your world get smaller and smaller as your declining health closes in on you—and I funneled all of that into *Yours Truly.* I knew I wanted our hero to be the kind of hero

I almost needed, so I made Jacob a kidney donor. I wrote the psychological impact of a life-altering, chronic health condition into the book, not just in Benny but through Briana, a helpless witness to his suffering—because when you have people who love you, they hurt along with you.

All of my books are made up of fragments of my life. Some you might recognize from my social media. Some you will never know. As Jacob says, we are a mosaic. We're made up of all those we've met and all the things we've been through. There are parts of us that are colorful and dark and jagged and beautiful. All my books are mosaics of me and my life experiences pieced together with touches of fiction. To entertain you. To help you escape. To educate and hopefully change the way you see the world and what you put into it. My hope is that through this book, and through sharing my own story, you may one day consider the gift of organ donation. It changes lives.

ABOUT THE AUTHOR

Abby Jimenez is a Food Network winner, *USA Today* and *New York Times* bestselling author, and recipient of the 2022 Minnesota Book Award for her novel *Life's Too Short*. Abby founded Nadia Cakes out of her home kitchen back in 2007. The bakery has since gone on to win numerous Food Network competitions and has amassed an international following.

Abby loves a good romance, coffee, doglets, and not leaving the house.